THE FOSSIL DOOR

CELIA LAKE

He wants to know why. She wants to belong.

Gabe was born into privilege - money, a loving family, and encouragement to follow wherever his curiosity leads. Assigned to help investigate a failed magical portal in the Scottish Highlands in 1922, he's more than up for the challenge. He won't let an old injury - or the rumours of a lethal magical beast - get in the way of solving the problem.

Rathna, the Portal Keeper he's been assigned to assist, is not at all what he expected. From their first meeting, it's clear that she's skilled, with a rare talent for magical energy. Her brown skin, the way she doesn't talk about her family, and her prickly insistence on proper form leave Gabe wondering, but she refuses to talk about anything other than their work.

As Gabe and Rathna begin to investigate, mystery piles on mystery. The portal is on the side of a steep mountain for no good reason. There's an unknown man asking questions about Rathna's family. Even getting a drink in the pub has risks. As they begin to trust each other and share their secrets, Rathna becomes sure Gabe will disappear as soon as their work together is done.

The Fossil Door features a ferocious desire to learn why things are as they are, a London-born Bengali heroine, awe-inspiring geology, life-changing secrets, and chosen family. Set in the magical community of the British Isles in 1920s, the Mysterious Powers series can be read in any order, and each book ends with a happily-ever-after (no cliffhangers.)

ONE

Rathna knew the bell would ring a moment before she heard it. She always knew that kind of thing. She had since she was a child, but she'd learned not to talk about it. Other people thought it uncanny. It gave her enough time to set down whatever she was doing, take a breath, and go see what Morah Avigail needed. This time, she had been sitting at her desk in the downstairs office. She grabbed the book she'd planned to bring upstairs and prepared to go up.

Of course, she'd been expecting this. Someone had come from the Ministry just after lunch, asking for her mistress. Whatever else his business had involved, it had included one of the formal letters with the seals that indicated some official communication. She didn't think it was an assignment, as Morah Avigail was unlikely to leave the house again for any length of time. It could have been something about a pension, perhaps.

Whatever it was, Sarah, their maid, had shown the man out twenty minutes later, and it had been quiet for the two hours since. Rathna suspected her mistress had had a nap, and would refuse to admit it.

That was no bother, as Rathna had plenty to keep her busy. She was a fully trained portal keeper, but there was always more to read. The second stone on the Southwark portal had a resonance that had bothered her when she ran the usual checks this week. A year ago, she'd have asked Morah Avigail to come have a listen and a look. She supposed she'd have to see about getting someone else out, it would take two to set up the harmonies properly.

They were spread thin, these days, the Portal Keepers. It wasn't just the War, though that hadn't helped. A number of their company had been elderly even before the War, a generation older than Morah Avigail, who was now past ninety. While tending the portals wasn't a physically strenuous job, it was magically quite challenging. It needed a knack for the stones and the waters and the plants, depending on the portal itself, but it also took rather a lot of ability to direct the magic properly. Or coax it, depending on your theory and preference in doing the work.

Rathna stopped at the mirror in the entry hall, checking to see that she was presentable. Her dark hair was properly pinned back into a tidy bun. The forest green dress was not the brighter shade some part of her yearned for. If it didn't highlight her brown skin, it didn't fight with it either, and it was a shade Morah Avigail thought was professional and appropriate.

She had another flash of wistfulness as she looked in the mirror, wishing she saw something more like her mother's bright dresses before she died, and set it aside. Those flashes had been happening more frequently, the past few months, for reasons she didn't understand. She had to discard it, as she always did. The time for that was in her room at night, alone, not when she had things to be doing, and especially not when she was expected elsewhere.

She then trotted up the stairs. Morah Avigail would certainly send her down again, on at least one errand, so she'd learned it wasn't worth the bother of bringing up a fresh drink. She got it wrong at least one time out of three, and neither she nor Morah Avigail could abide the waste. At the main bedroom, she knocked, precisely, twice.

"Come, come." The voice inside was as clear as it had been when Rathna began her apprenticeship, but as Rathna opened the door, she was reminded again that the mind and voice were still sharp, but the body was not what it had been. Where Morah Avigail had been hearty and hale until six months ago, she was faded now, into herself. She was wearing a too-pale green bed jacket that did not suit her. It had been made by one of the daughters-in-law out of yarn sensibly unwound from someone else's discarded sweater.

One should not complain about the kindnesses shown by others. Or so she'd been taught. Even if they had a very strange idea of colours that flattered.

"Morah Avigail." She preferred the term, for all it wasn't one she'd been familiar with before her apprenticeship. It meant teacher, and she'd much preferred that, once it was offered, to the formal Magistra or Mistress of Avigail's rank.

Technically, being a full member of the Portal Keeper's Guild, Rathna didn't need to use either anymore. She wasn't supposed to, even. She would do the proper thing in public, pretend they were all equals, that she didn't need to defer. But she'd known since she was eight that claiming equal rights would raise people's hackles.

Morah Avigail knew that lesson too, though for somewhat different reasons. It was why they'd got on so well from the start.

"Tsk. Come here, do, sit on the bed." The pale hand patted the bed. "You won't jostle me. I'm sure you're curious, aren't you?" Her voice had the light accent of her original Yiddish, more in the twists of the words than anything more.

Of course Rathna sat, carefully. "I noticed the letter."

Morah Avigail shifted to pat her hand. "You have an assignment, if you will accept it. And I think you should." She lifted a hand, pointing with the pencil she'd been holding. "You will listen to it, and then you will fetch me a pot of tea. We will discuss it thoroughly, and you will agree with me."

Rathna laughed, she couldn't help it. "And I will be sent to do your bidding, as always."

"No." The word was sharp this time. "It is time things change. I will not be here so much longer. You must learn to put your own feet on the road, not just carry along as we have."

Rathna wanted to argue. She also knew how futile it was. That didn't change the wanting. Instead, she took a breath, damping down the little flare of her magic that happened at such times. She'd wondered if other people had that, but she'd always been afraid to ask, worried it was one more way she was different. She took another breath for good measure, and she nodded. "As you wish, Morah."

"I am never going to break you of that, am I?" This time, Morah Avigail's voice was affectionate, and her hand reached to pat again.

"Not in private, no."

Someone else might have argued. The matrons in the orphanage of her late childhood would have suspected something was wrong, and she should be punished for her wrongness. Her teachers at Schola would have been largely unsure what to do with her but they would have left her alone. Morah Avigail, though, she laughed. "As you wish."

Rathna glanced at the letter, face down, on the bed tray. "The letter, Morah?"

"There is a portal in Scotland causing some difficulty. Someone must go to see to it."

"A city?" She didn't mind cities. It was not the only reason she was in London, near the Spitalfields portals, but she liked the bustle. The people calling out, the markets she could walk through, the way she heard a dozen different languages walking down some streets near the docks, in a block or two. It wasn't quite like the memories of her childhood. But it was close enough to touch and be real, and remind her she hadn't made it all up.

"No," This time, Morah Avigail sounded sorry. "Quite remote. The western coast, the countryside."

"That's quite a new portal." Rathna had not particularly studied it, she'd never had the need to. But she knew the map as well as any of them did.

"A few years. It has been temperamental for several months, and now it has failed."

"Failed." It came out a bit flat. That was an interesting challenge, but it promised a tediously long trip.

"Failed. You'll have to take the train, I'm afraid."

Rathna permitted herself to make a face at that, grimacing. She hated trains. They were loud and noisy and dirty and metal. Metals were not her strong suit, she did much better with stone and with trees and earth. Worse, trains involved rather a lot of people who would probably not be kind to her. "What kind of portal?"

"Stone. Now, you go away and make me tea, and bring

me the proper books when you come back, and we will talk these things through."

Rathna stood, brushing out her skirts, and went. Again, she knew there was no point in arguing. Morah Avigail had never punished her. She had been a kind and patient mistress in the arts of keeping a portal humming happily along. Her disappointment was a far harsher thing to bear, and it only took a look and perhaps half a sigh. That did not make things easier, just simpler to manage.

Making the tea properly was as soothing as it always was. There were the little rituals of tea leaves, and water, and setting the tray just so. She had fetched the books they'd need, set on the other half of the tray, unbalancing it a bit. She'd also let Sarah know they'd likely be wanting supper upstairs together. By the time she returned, Morah Avigail was dozing. Rathna set the tray down as silently as she could, before settling into the easy chair by the window with one of the books, this one about the most recent additions to the portal tree.

Half an hour later, there was a slight cough from the bed. "Tea, please."

The pot had kept itself properly warm. For all Morah Avigail was cautious with her money, she didn't skimp on the tools they used all the time, and that definitely included the teapot. Their work paid respectably. It was more than enough to keep Sarah and have enough food on their table and proper clothes and the various needs for their work that weren't provided by the Ministry, as well as an extensive private library.

But Morah Avigail took her charity seriously. And of course she wanted to make sure she had enough put aside so she could help her grown children and grandchildren when one of them had a bad spell. That meant that things were used to the edge of their usefulness, and perhaps a bit further. They'd had three weeks of tepid tea in January, before Rathna had convinced Morah Avigail that they really should replace the teapot now.

Rathna set the tea cup up, and the plate of biscuits, and then put herself firmly on the bed, facing her teacher. "I will go. As you said." Morah Avigail laughed, and Rathna was quite glad to do anything that brought that light to her more times. Every amusement mattered more. "How long do you think I'll need to be there?"

It wasn't just that she disliked the countryside. Or was baffled by it, that might be a better way to put it. Most certainly, she didn't want to be away if Morah Avigail took a turn for the worse. She knew she'd be shouldered out by Morah Avigail's proper family. Rathna couldn't argue with that. But she wanted to be there to be shouldered aside.

"A month or more, I suspect. And I am fairly sure that is rather less time than I have left. You worry, my dear, rather openly. My condition for accepting, to that nice and somewhat uncertain man from the Ministry, was that there be a quick way to get you home if needed. They are making proper arrangements."

Rathna had never been able to hide either her worry or her relief, and she didn't bother to try to hide the latter now. "Thank you." She didn't say more, she didn't need to. They both knew, for all they rarely talked about it.

"What have they told you about what happened to it? What do we know?"

Morah Avigail snorted. "The report is there. Read it out to me, and we will begin our proper plan." The systematic approach to reviewing the nature of the portal and how it had rooted was part of the training. Then, working through whether there were gaps or breaks in the energy, if something nearby had disturbed it, all of their methods. Then, before Rathna could read, further Morah Avigail coughed. "You will have company in the work. One of the Penelopes from the Guard. The Ministry man said it was Gabrielle Edgarton. I don't know more than that, yet."

Rathna nodded once. She didn't like the idea much, someone fussing and jostling her, but she was not the one being consulted here. If the Ministry were being like this, it must be important to someone with power. She picked up the report and began to read.

TWO

Rathna found the trip to Glencoe exhausting. It wasn't just the length of the trip, but the expectations. The train itself was more or less straightforward. There was a sleeper train that left London after ten at night and arrived in Fort William about twelve hours later. Someone was supposed to meet her there with a carriage and bring her to the ferry that would take her across the river to where she was staying.

But this was an ordinary non-magical train, with all the complications that meant. She'd known before she left that people would be judging her. Assuming things. Whatever it was they decided, it was exhausting to hold up the weight of their regard, and dangerous if she ignored them.

This trip had been better than some she'd taken. Two older women treated her like a personal maid, demanding things, while they were waiting to board, despite the fact her travelling clothes carefully looked nothing like a uniform. She was wearing a travelling dress and sweater of rich burgundy, not at all a colour a British servant would be likely to wear. She was aiming, all told, for the sort of thing a bookish spinster might prefer. It was near enough the truth, and when it worked, it got her treated politely but left alone.

She had looked over her glasses - she had a pair with plain glass on for show - and said, "Beg pardon?" in the plummiest tone she could muster. She'd learned that one far before coming into Morah Avigail's care, from one of her teachers at school. Mistress Olwood had taken her in hand and taught her all the ways she didn't fit in, and all the ways she could fool people into thinking she did. She never felt at ease, but at least now she rarely ran into more than tedious sorts of trouble.

Thankfully, once they were on the train, she'd been left alone except for the more than adequate service. She'd made a request for a simple breakfast and tea. She had resigned herself long ago to having to make compromises about what she ate. She didn't know all the proper rules, she hadn't learned them before her mother died. Since then, she'd spent far too long with other people making the decisions about what got cooked.

However, she could not face the full English breakfast, or whatever the Scottish version might involve. Toast and jam and an egg would do nicely. And tea. She believed firmly in the power of tea.

That had left her alone with her thoughts, and the beginning of the journey was uneven, with more frequent stops. She hadn't expected to sleep much, between the metal all around her and the movement. She was a light sleeper, alert for small changes. She always had been, and even more since she'd gone to the orphanage. Since she wasn't sleeping, she was thinking. She found herself not much pleased with several things.

The first was how long it had taken her to realise that there was something insulting about the way this had been proposed. She was a full member of the Guild in her own right. The request should have come to her, directly, not to Morah Avigail. It should have been her choice about who she consulted with, before taking it on. She'd brought that up the next day, before the man from the Ministry came back to get his necessary forms and documents signed.

Morah Avigail had waved her hand. "They are forgetful, you know that. They think you are still an apprentice." It fell flat, even though Rathna appreciated the effort.

The second issue was the list of things she had been told to prepare for. Her working case, of course, she expected that. It had not left her hand, not while she was going to the train, not while she waited. And now it was tucked away right by her bed, so she could grab it if anything happened. That was the other reason for not eating in the lounge. If someone tried to steal it, even to interfere with it, they'd get an unpleasant surprise. But she would have to deal with the effects of the charms, and that was always awkward and time-consuming.

Her larger case, however, held a number of items. She had been told to bring clothing she could ride in, for an extended time, not something normally in her wardrobe. She'd had to have several sets of split skirts made up quickly. She'd also spent time digging her two pairs of riding breeches out of the trunk in the attic, mothballed since her apprenticeship. Those wouldn't do in many settings, however.

All of that had left rather less space for books than she'd liked. She'd been working late at night to write up the notes from the volumes she hadn't had room for. She'd even had to carry her wool cloak with her, separately.

Rathna could ride, of course. Adequately, at least. She'd been trained in it, because sometimes the only way to get to a portal was on horseback, if it were not working. She'd learned that the same way she'd learned how to tell if a small boat were seaworthy, or if a canal boat were too sluggish, or when a carriage was being driven poorly. Automobiles she'd had to sort out for herself, but she had a sense of them now.

But horses were large, and not very predictable. She did not fancy traipsing around Scotland, probably in the rain, on one. And apparently this portal was some distance from where they would need to stay.

Third, there was only one small magical community, a tiny village of fifty or so, near two non-magical villages, on the southern shore of a river. There were slate quarries, her orders had said, so she assumed the villages were full of hard-working men and their families. Rathna suspected that might come with a fair bit of noisy drinking and suspicion of people who weren't like them.

The former meant she'd not be getting much sleep, even with some charms to baffle the sound. She didn't blame them too much for the latter, but it meant she'd have to be careful not to be caught alone. She was instantly identified as different, even in many parts of London, and difference could be dangerous.

Fourth, she hadn't been provided with any additional information about this Penelope who'd be joining them. She'd not had time to go to Trellech to find out more, even if there had been more to find out. There often wasn't. Morah Avigail had needed some help sorting things while Rathna was gone, making sure the books she wanted were upstairs or easy for Sarah to find downstairs.

She hoped this Gabrielle Edgarton, whoever she was, was at least moderately competent, and could handle herself. The Penelopes she'd worked with before had been fifty or sixty. They rarely complained, but a room above a rural pub wasn't likely to be much to their taste any more than it was to Rathna's. Never mind, they'd have to make do.

Chances were good that Edgarton would be professional, at least. The Penelopes as a whole tended to care a lot more about competence than birth or origin. If you could do the work, and well - and Rathna could - then you got their respect. Perhaps grudgingly at first, but Rathna took pride in the fact that each time she and Morah Avigail had worked with one, the Penelope had settled into the work smoothly.

Which brought her to the last problem, and the one she could do nothing about. Portals, properly alive portals, shouldn't just stop working. Certainly not without some complaint first. She had no idea why there was one in Glencoe in the first place, or what had gone wrong. It would be an interesting problem, but she wished she had more information, beyond the records in the original establishment file. They were annoyingly basic, and the man who'd done the work had died since.

That particular problem occupied her late into the night, and from when she woke up promptly at six until the train pulled into the Fort William station. There was indeed someone to meet her, though he said nothing beyond her last name, and grunted at the back of a cart.

She loaded herself and her two cases in, without any assistance, and settled in for a bumpy ride. The scenery, at least, was distractingly stunning, winding down the side of the loch until the cart turned down a river inlet.

The ferry was noisy and smelly - there were cattle and sheep, and other smells she wasn't sure she wanted to think about closely. On the other side, she followed the directions she'd been given. She was to follow a particular road up along the river valley, and take a right at the appropriate sign, about where the road turned into what the enclosed map labelled as an "indifferent road". Given the state of the "good road" from Fort William, she was rather dubious about what that meant.

Well after two in the afternoon, she turned up at the appointed inn, pleased to see the little signs of a magical establishment. She felt the warding first, and then the brush of the keep-away magics. Most people barely noticed them. Since her job depended on feeling the subtle influences of a place, she found it reassuring to notice what other people were supposed to ignore. From the outside, the place seemed better than a few she'd stayed in. That little tickle of magic that she heard backed that up. It was a subtle song, but pleasant. There was reasonably fresh paint on the shutters, and the whitewash looked about the same age.

She made her way through the front door, such as it was, and looked around to get her bearings. There was a man behind the bar, and a woman bustling around picking up the lunch dishes. Rathna cleared her throat. "Afternoon. Someone arranged a room?"

"Ah." Rathna couldn't make sense of whether that was disgust, dismissal, or simple fatigue. "Earlier than t'other."

"I'm here first?" The accent was strong, but not so much so Rathna couldn't make some sense of it, though she knew she'd be lost if they switched into Scots around her. She had a fair bit of Welsh, among her other languages, but not that.

"Aye. Sent a note, back here tonight. Will you be coming down to eat?" She looked Rathna up and down, and Rathna suddenly couldn't face it.

"Sandwiches, in my room?" she suggested. "Or if you've a chicken pie, something like it?" She'd prefer not beef, but around here it was more likely to be mutton, anyway. Probably.

The woman gave her a sharp nod. "Up here." She led the way upstairs. "Facilities there." Rathna was grateful she was now back on magical ground, as it were. Even here, in the back of beyond, there would be hot running water and a proper bath. Also a respectable sort of lavatory, if the cleaning standards kept up with the rest of what she'd seen so far.

"I gather we have horses?" It wasn't so much that she wanted to make conversation, as that the silence was increasingly awkward.

"Aye." Then the woman relented. "I'm Gormlaith Macdonald, himself is Eoin. Been here thirty years, never had anyone from the Ministry say boo before this portal."

Rathna didn't know how that felt, but she could imagine it had been a bit startling. "I'm sorry if they were difficult. They forget what it's like for people, I think."

That sympathy got her a sudden look, then a slight nod. "Didn't listen, them." Gormlaith shook her head, then opened the door at the end of the hallway. "T'other is there." Across the way. "We're down by the kitchen, back of the house. If there's trouble. Other room's empty right now, unless someone's flat drunk. Probably not tonight." It was a Thursday.

The room itself was not large, and the ceiling suddenly made Rathna glad she was not taller. It had all her requirements, though, with a reasonably sized bed and a desk of adequate size for most people, if small for her needs. The bed would make up for it. And a wardrobe, she'd have space to put things away properly. She glanced around and nodded. "Thank you, this will do very well. Would it be a problem if I had a wash up?" She pitched word choice quite precisely. English, she couldn't help that, she fundamentally was, whatever else she also was, but educated, not too posh.

"Water's good until supper. Sandwiches at half five, before we get busy, then. Tea, beer, whiskey?"

"Tea, please. With cream, if you have it to spare."

That got her a nod, a slow one, evaluating, and it made Rathna not at all sure where she'd mis-stepped. But Gormlaith said nothing and disappeared back down the hallway.

Rathna had time for a wash, a short nap, and a lengthy slow supper of hearty sandwiches over her books, before there was a knock on her door, around eight that night. When she opened it, there was a tall young man, slenderly built with sandy blond hair down past his shoulders, tied back in a tail. He wore the sort of informal country tweeds that looked like he lived in them, and he had a cane leaning against his leg.

"Good evening. I'm Gabriel Edgarton. Sorry to be late, I got a bit caught up, missed the ferry I meant to take."

THREE

The woman who answered the door was quite a bit younger than Gabe had expected. Her skin, eyes, and hair - brown, rather darker brown, and black - made it clear her background was Indian.

She was perhaps six inches shorter than he was, and dressed in sensible working clothing, all sturdy cotton or linen, and ankle boots. She hadn't made herself terribly comfortable when it came to the clothing, even this late in the evening. She had a few smudges of ink on her right hand that suggested she'd been writing a fair bit.

She was certainly older than he was, but nearly everyone was, given he was barely twenty-two. He'd assumed whoever they assigned would be on the younger side for a portal keeper, since this was rather remote, but he was expecting forties, at best. She must be within a decade of his age. Probably half that. There was no silver in her hair, and the Portal Keepers tended to show silver early.

Gabe waited. This was always a tricky bit. He assumed this Rathna Stone had been given his name in advance, as he'd been given hers. It was probably not the family name that was causing a problem here.

Besides, for all his father was well known in the Guard, and was a Lord of the land, a magistrate, and half a dozen other positions and honours of various sorts, he wasn't widely talked about outside the Guard or those elite social circles. Papa was pleasant and kind and did his work well, and that didn't cause much general gossip of the sort that made it to papers and tea shoppes.

The Portal Keepers tended to only go in for gossip as a personal hobby, not as a matter of professional necessity, like the Penelopes did. So, it was probably the usual thing, that she'd assumed the name was Gabrielle, emphasis on the double-l and e.

"Gabriel Edgarton, the Penelope assigned to this case," he repeated, holding out his hand. "You must be Mistress Rathna Stone. May I come in, or would you rather come across to mine? We ought to sort things out, at least a bit, tonight, make the start of a plan."

She blinked at him, then snapped her mouth shut, without offering her own hand in turn. "You're late." Her voice was clear, clipped, precise. He knew that tone, that it was probably covering half a dozen other emotions.

"I'm sorry. I came up two days ago, went across to Skye to see about some reagents for the office. You tell people you're going to be somewhere, everyone presents you with the nearest thing to a shopping list." It seemed like she might respond to Gabe putting on his ordinary-person voice, grounding things in the everyday and rather quotidian. Not that Gabe actually did his own grocery shopping very often.

It worked. She said, rather automatically, the way people tended to, when you lead them down a well-worn conversational path, "Oh, did you find what you were looking for?"

"Five puffin eggshells, a golden eagle feather, three red deer antlers, and some bones from a mountain hare." He was gleeful about the last one, and he couldn't help letting it show. Her expression quickly made him remember that other people did not usually find bits of flora and fauna nearly as desirable. Especially the bones.

Quickly, he added, "That's for Aunt Mason. She does a lot of research these days." Which didn't really explain anything, but Aunt Mason was inexplicable, even to people who knew her well. "Look, shall I get us something to eat or drink, and we can sort things out?"

Mistress Stone nodded once, "Tea." It was a bare word. At least Gabe knew what to do with that. He took a step back, let her back away from the door, and went downstairs to see about some tea, leaning on the cane as he went. It was hard to tell from such brief comments, but he was fairly sure that was a London accent. He exhaled, navigating carefully down the stairs. His ankle was aching more than he liked, he'd had a rough climb yesterday for the puffin eggs.

Once in the pub, he had a bit of a wait, a chance to look around the place. It was a relatively busy evening, he suspected. Most of the tables were three-quarters full. Finally, he caught the pub keeper's eye, and said, "Tray for upstairs, if I can. Tea for her, pint for me, and if there were a scone or two, that would be a fine thing." He kept his voice light. He couldn't hide being English, not here, but he could make himself as inoffensive as possible, and avoid bringing out the posh.

There was a bit of a bustle, and Gabe settled in to let people examine him. If this went the way he expected, the brief appearance would get the gossip going, and sometime tomorrow evening, someone would come and demand Gabe explain himself. It would be a long day. Whatever else they did they'd have to have a good look at the portal, and he hoped it wouldn't be one of the more energetically aggressive demands.

For now, he pretended the room wasn't examining him, idly looking along the pictures behind the bar, as if he were completely fascinated by whatever sporting activities those were. At least he assumed that was what it was, from the large logs involved. There were photos of a boy on a pony, and a young man. Gabe realised he'd have to tread carefully there. There had been no signs of a young man a little older than he was about the place.

A minute later, the tray was set down in front of him. "Need it brought up?"

Gabe considered. If he were sensible, he'd say yes. He wasn't inclined to be sensible. He couldn't handle the cane and the tray both, but he'd manage, he always did. "Ta, no, I'll manage. She say anything about breakfast?"

"Nah. Seven."

That was decidedly earlier than Gabe would prefer, but the offer wasn't exactly a question. "Seven," he agreed. "And if you could make up a lunch to take with us, we're likely to be out all day."

That just got a grunt and a nod, and the man went back to cleaning the bar, leaving Gabe to rearrange himself. He slipped the cane into what would have been a sword belt in another time, so it hung at an angle behind him. He could still foul himself on chairs or tight corners, but he'd be a lot less likely to trip over it.

No one commented. He laid bets in his head that someone would ask him tomorrow. Maybe breakfast, maybe supper. No longer than that. There was that sort of antici-patory question in the room.

Getting back up the stairs was a slower process, one he tried to approach with dignity, but he made it without drop-ping anything, or spilling any of the drinks. He was about to knock on the door - it was ajar, not fully closed, when she opened it. "Come in." Again, her voice was brisk and sharp.

Gabe nodded, and found she had rearranged things a bit. A stack of books were set along the window ledge, which was deep plaster, sturdy enough as long as the windows didn't leak. There was a space on the top of her desk for the tray. "I gather breakfast is at seven." Once the tray was set down, he straightened. "Where would you prefer I sit?"

She gestured at a wooden bench, probably mostly meant for sitting on while lacing up sturdy boots, and took the desk chair. "So." She looked him up and down. "You're the Penelope assigned here?" She watched him, closely, as if she was fully taking his measure.

"I am. Pardon about the name, I gather it confuses everyone." He managed to repress the comment he often made here, that his parents hadn't expected he'd become a Penelope. Near any other profession, it wouldn't be so awkward.

Her eyes narrowed, and he decided that lightness of speech was not the way to go here. "Rathna Stone. You're not an apprentice, are you?"

Gabe shook his head. "Finished eight months ago." He lifted his chin and added, "Shortest apprenticeship in three centuries. I really am competent." He reached into his shirt and tugged out his medallion, the unique one the Penelopes wore, of a central Guard coin ringed with amber. The amber in his was a deep honey colour. She had the good manners not to reach out and touch it, but she leaned over to peer at it, before she settled back.

"Specialities?" She didn't say much, rather using her words precisely. In other circumstances, Gabe would have appreciated that. He liked people who said what they meant, without all the fluttering. In this case, it was becoming a bit unsettling.

"Well, I'm here because I'm one of the few people available to be away for an extended period who is also up for clambering around the mountains and riding at length. But they thought my memory for unusual cases might be handy here. I'm aiming at becoming the resident expert on structural magics in the Penelopes, though of course I'm not actually an expert yet. I'm up for whatever diagnostics you might want."

"Even with..." She hesitated, then wordlessly gestured at the cane.

"It aches, but it still works." He kept his tone light. "Before you ask, not the War." Because she had been about to ask. People always did. Then he ventured a question of his own. "May I ask about your own recent projects?"

"Tending the London portals. I live with Magistra Avigail Levy, in Spitalfields, we see to all of them."

Gabe inclined his head, and then reached to take his beer, tasting it. He'd tried the local when he first arrived, and it was refreshingly bracing, if a bit more malty than he preferred. "Have you had a case like this before? And, pardon. How formal would you prefer to be? I defer to your preferences, you are both senior and also, this is all about the portal."

Her chin went up, as if that surprised her. "First names in private. Appropriate formality in public?" she offered after a moment's thought. "Also, honestly, saying Penelope

Edgarton all the time would be time-consuming. And confusing."

"Terribly inefficient, yes." He gestured, hoping she'd circle back to the question of the case.

"I've read the report of the problems, and the write-up of the establishment for the portal Unfortunately, the man who did that has since died. I've not had an assignment like this, exactly, but I know my work."

Gabe spread his hand. "I am sure you do. I am assuming we start by going and looking at the thing tomorrow, bar something like torrential rain, but I don't know how you would like to proceed."

Rathna frowned at him again. He suspected he was going to see a lot of that expression, a pursed-lip disapproval of something. Then she straightened her shoulders. "I will have to see it. Tomorrow." Despite that being Saturday.

Gabe nodded, but that didn't help any. "What should I bring, then?"

She stood and said, "Your usual case. Whatever you'd normally bring."

That was not much help, not really. Gabe took a breath and then tried again. "It would be easier if we knew a bit more about each other. You went to Schola, I'm assuming?"

A series of emotions flickered across her face, just as quickly repressed into that disapproving expression. "Don't do that." Her voice was crisp. "I will see you in the morning."

Gabe blinked several times. He didn't think he'd pushed too far, but that was a sudden shift. On the other hand, both politeness and sense meant that the only thing to do was to make as orderly a retreat as he could. "Can I take the tray down for you?"

"No."

Gabe swallowed and stood. "Breakfast, then." He almost added the "Sleep well" he'd have added to any colleague. Any other. Then he took himself, his rather bruised pride, and his beer out the door. Before he was at the stairs, he heard her latch the door.

The pub had thinned out a bit in the interim, and he settled at an empty table, after asking for a sandwich. Everyone left him alone, which was good on one hand. He was neither in the mood to parry questions, nor was he sure what he wanted to say if someone asked. He devoured the sandwich he'd ordered and then did his best to go up to bed without letting his mood show.

FOUR

SATURDAY MORNING, THE INN

The next morning, Gabe made certain he was downstairs at five to seven. He was not a morning person, he had not been since he was a small child, but he knew how to approximate it. He had dressed for a day out, in riding breeches and jumper.

He already had the tall leather boots on, which had the advantage of fully supporting his ankle, even without the additional reinforcing charms. The wax jacket for outdoors was slung over the chair next to him, long enough to keep his thighs warm even if the wind picked up. The outfit would be utterly unremarkable for anyone who spotted them, which was very much the point.

Precisely at seven, Rathna came down, wearing a split skirt and vest of green tweed, a white blouse, and boots, looking very proper. "Good morning." She sounded very proper, too.

Gabe had considered this carefully, how to handle this. "Good morning. Our host said he'd be by to ask about breakfast once you were here, there is strong tea on the way." Then the delicate pause, of precisely the right length to show seriousness and due deference. "I apologise, for giving offence last night."

She raised one eyebrow. "How do you think you did that?" Bother. She wasn't going to leave it at the apology. His mother would approve, and Gabe wasn't sure what he thought about that.

"A too-personal question. I promise I will not do it again and let you decide what you feel I should know."

Her chin went up, a little sharp jerk. "And how long do you expect to be able to keep your word? You seem an inquisitive sort."

"That is my job." Gabe spread his hands, apologetically. "And my nature. I am endlessly curious about nearly everything. It is sometimes a virtue, but there is an awful lot out there to lure me. I will confine my interests somewhere other than you." Another man of his background would have been badly offended, to the point of a duel, by someone questioning his word. Gabe didn't have that luxury.

She gave another of those pointed nods. "We'll see." She wasn't giving an inch. They were interrupted then by the tea, and the brief list of the breakfast available. Gabe asked for something sturdy, a full Scottish, while Rathna ordered porridge and an egg. She let out a breath, looking at him steadily. "You were right we should discuss our plans. I looked at the map, but are you familiar with the area?"

"I had a ride around when I first got here, up to where the stone is, but did not examine it closely. A modest distance on horseback, three miles. It's up near what they call Ossian's Cave. Not the cave itself, but set into the rock a bit below, a little gap. There'll be a short hike to get up there, but it's not far from where we can leave the horses."

Rathna nodded, considering. "And horses?"

"In the barn. I'm an excellent rider, they have a perfectly reasonable mare for you. Highland ponies, so small and sturdy, but used to the ground."

There was another nod, and she seemed a bit distracted. Gabriel wanted to ask more, but he'd learned that was not going to work well. Instead, he said. "My kit will fit in saddlebags with room to spare, at least for today's work. Can I help you bring things up?"

That made her rock back and think a little. "Saddlebags?"

"Provided." Gabe was prompt with that. "I asked for the usual general kit for this, with some of the extras for remote locations. If you have a hard-sided case, you may need to repack things, but the bags can carry quite a bit. I - pardon, saw your cloak, you'll likely want that. As we get up higher, the wind picks up."

"Have you done much in Scotland?"

Gabe wriggled a hand. "I grew up in Kent, but I've been all over, since. A fair bit up near Snowdonia, I was there for three months working on a series of investigations. Not much in Scotland, just a week or so, and that wasn't the Highlands." Again, he rather wanted to add the quite reasonable question, something like 'and you?', and he had to refrain.

"I'll ask you to see to what we need, then." Her voice was clear, decisive. She'd decided to trust his competency that much, then. Or perhaps, if she had spent most of her time in London, it was more that she distrusted her own skills.

"Easily done." He smiled, trying to keep things light. "I already asked for packed lunches, and said we'll likely want a hearty supper, when we get back. I find mountains to be hungry work, on the whole, even before the rest of it. But if you'd prefer something else..." He let that trail off.

Rathna considered. Precisely, she said, "We will likely be working together for a bit. I don't eat beef or pork if there is an option otherwise. Mutton, lamb, poultry, or fish are all fine. If you end up arranging meals, please take that into consideration as possible." She said it as if she expected Gabe to argue with her, or be annoyed.

Instead, he nodded. "Shellfish? Not that I expect it to come up here, in particular."

She shook her head. "No shellfish. I don't have the taste for it."

Gabe nodded, making the appropriate mental notes. "Anything else you prefer not to eat? I gather lunch is cheese or egg mayonnaise sandwiches, today, so that won't be a problem."

Rathna shook her head. "I prefer things simple, rather than fussy, but again, not a difficulty here, I suspect. Food that looks like what it is." That, now, that was interesting and perhaps just a tad revealing. Gabe considered asking her if there were things she particularly liked. They might well end up with a trip somewhere with more options. But that would be prying, and he'd said he wouldn't.

At that point, the food came out. Once it was delivered, Gabe decided to risk one more question. "You don't mind if I eat something you don't? I know some people find that distasteful. I could take my plate elsewhere, if you did."

Rathna looked at him for a long moment, peering down her nose, as if he were some form of wildlife she had never seen before, and was entirely dubious about. Then she shook her head side to side, once, deliberately, before she looked down and began to eat in silence.

He did the same, glancing up, every so often, to see how

her pace was, and matching it as nearly as he could. Given he had a fair bit more food than she did, it took a bit of doing. But he was a young man who ate even more heartily than most his age because of the demands of the magics of his profession. At least the way he usually went at them, wholeheartedly and fiercely.

There were Penelopes who excelled based on logic and examination. That was not him. He'd long since thrown his lot in with the Penelopes who followed the threads of magic in all the subtle ways. He'd wanted to trace those threads back to their origins, from the first time he'd known that was a thing you could do with your life. He'd been eight. He wasn't brilliant at it, yet, a lot of what that needed was experience. But he was going to be.

And this trip was a chance to get that, by himself, not under someone else's shadow. No one he'd talked to had an idea why a portal would just cease to function. Certainly, some did, but usually there was an obvious cause. Damage, from an earthquake, for example, something that broke the connections of the alignment. You didn't need to be a portal keeper to know that was part of how they worked.

As Rathna began to slow down, almost done with her porridge, she looked up, examining him carefully. "How careful do you think we need to be, of showing our magic?"

"It's fairly remote." Gabe had already considered this. "There may be a few people out, but it's a bit early for pleasure hikers. I gather most of the people around here won't be too startled by seeing a flicker or two out of the corner of their eye. Nothing that breaks the Pact, of course, directly, but the occasional flash shouldn't be a problem. Both the stones themselves, and I gather a fair number near here have the Second Sight, or something akin."

Rathna pursed her lips. "I do not require flashes of light for my work. I gather you do?"

"Occasionally. They're indicative of different circumstances, especially some of the diagnostics. They're brief, though, and generally one can angle them to avoid any problems."

"See that you do." That was crisp and sharp, and Gabe tried not to feel offended. Again. It wasn't that she was assuming he was useless, that was something, but she kept exerting her control over the situation. He didn't blame her, precisely, he'd had enough conversations with Aunt Mason about that particular dynamic, a younger woman being the one in charge. He didn't understand it all, but he didn't have to, he just had to make proper allowances in his plans.

"Perhaps I could bring the saddle bags to you, and we could pack?" Gabe offered this as they finished their food, and were draining the last of the tea. "Then we can set off. They're in my room."

There was the tiniest hesitation, then she nodded. "Yes. Do that." It was as clear an order as he'd ever heard. He took a breath. Perhaps she'd relax a bit once they'd seen the thing. He hoped. Otherwise, this was going to be a long trip, penned up in a rural inn where they were rightly suspicious of a posh Englishman, and with no other outlet.

He stood, waiting for her to lead the way up the stairs, then ducked into his room to grab the saddle bags. His tools were in one side, with space for a modest packed lunch at the top. The other side was empty bar the usual compact first aid kit, with a few more additions to suit the remote area. He'd included a small survival kit, with firestarters and warmers, and a small tin for heating water. He had his pocket knife, and for that matter his wand.

She had put a hard-sided case on the bed, the clasps

clicking open as he brought the packs in. "This one's mine, the other side is empty. And this one's yours. We'll want to leave space for the food. Future days, we might want a bit of grain for the ponies, if we intend to have a longer ride."

Rathna made a small sound that in someone else he'd have called a grunt, but that wasn't quite a sniff. She was sorting through things in the case, then folding them into a length of padded fabric, placing things quickly and precisely into pockets of the fabric. She stopped with her hand over two of the things in the case. "Can you ensure no one touches these?"

Gabe nodded. "Your preference in precautions? Is there anything that would interfere?"

She waved a hand. "Nothing that affects the vials directly. Lock the case, fix it to the ground so it can't be moved. Something like that." Not her area of expertise, then.

Gabe glanced around and considered. It was no good fixing something to a piece of wood that could be cut out given a bit of time and determination. And while the inn had been their only choice near enough the portal, two of the Guard he'd talked to had said the Maclains were in fact decent folk. He'd also been told to ignore the historical gossip, the local families were much less prone to cattle raids these days.

"Here, can I take the case?" He had a brilliant idea, somewhere no one would be terribly likely to look at it. He got down on his knees and peered under the bed. Judging by the dust, it was moved occasionally, but recently enough that it wasn't likely to happen while they were here. He hummed a charm, feeling his hands warm with it, then pressed the case up against the underside of the bed.

"Put your hands flat under there, and say 'Solvitur' and

twist your hands, pivoting on the heel, so they spread open, about twenty degrees." He kept his voice even.

"The passive, not the active?" Rathna waited for him to move, then took his place.

"If you'd prefer to loosen the various attachments on the bed accidentally...." He let his voice trail off, seeing what she did with that. He was rewarded with her looking up, blinking at him, and the quickest glimpse of something that might be a distant cousin of a smile.

"I'd rather not." she agreed, then she tried it for herself, clearly telling the container "Solvitur." He could see it settle in her hands, the way the weight dipped them down.

"To put it back, now it's set, just press it up."

She nodded once, putting it back in place, and then brushing off her hands and standing up. "Thank you." She glanced at the saddlebags. "I'm ready. I suppose the horses are next."

Gabe nodded. She did not sound at all pleased by the prospect, but he wouldn't dare bring that up. The horses were inevitable, given their task. He at least appreciated she didn't whinge about it. "The horses. Picking up our lunch on the way by." He then pushed himself upright and waited for her to lock up before following her downstairs.

FIVE

Rathna was not at all sure about this. It had all seemed manageable in the assignment, but the reality had hit her, rather hard, last night. Here she was, in rural Scotland, with the assistance of someone she did not know, never mind the fact he was barely out of apprenticeship.

The bed had, in all fairness, not been as lumpy as that time she and Morah Avigail had been stuck in Devon for three weeks. But it was not at all as comfortable as her own room, set up just the way she liked it. The desk was barely adequate for one book, never mind the three or four she preferred to have spread out with proper book snakes to hold them open. She would manage, of course. She just wished the managing did not also involve horses.

Or, for that matter, having someone else so close. She'd realised last night how uncomfortable it felt for there to be a man she didn't know in her room. It wasn't that she couldn't work with men, she'd certainly done so before. But it had been some time since she'd been close to a man anywhere near her own age who wasn't related to Morah Avigail or her extended family.

Morah Avigail had encouraged her to walk out with a few young men during her apprenticeship, to see what she thought about making a match. In the end, Rathna had found all of them more of a bother than a pleasure, one way or another. There were the assumptions common to most women, that she would spend her time organising what they needed to remember, or running the household. Worse, there were the things that had seemed more particularly her burden.

Two had made it clear she was a temporary pleasure, that they'd never make an ongoing commitment to someone of her dubious background. Two others had been more subtle, but equally dismissive. None of them, in the end, had even tried to hold up their own weight in the relationship or even behaved as that might be worth considering.

On that note, she had to give this Gabriel a modicum of credit. He had made a decent apology, once prodded. He had been generous with his assistance this morning without overstepping, especially finding a safe place for her case. Several of the vials needed extra protection. They could be dangerous in the wrong hands, or if spilled accidentally. No one needed that. And he'd seen to what they needed today, while giving her input if she wanted it.

All of this almost distracted her from the imminent need to mount up. She could feel her skirts around her ankles, uncomfortably long, and the ankle boots below that. It seemed unfair she was in clothing that was less practical than Gabriel's, but that was the lot of women. At least she wasn't being put in a sidesaddle.

He had led her along to the stables, around the side of the inn, where two sturdy horses were waiting. Ponies, she supposed. One was a sort of dappled white, and the other a sandy brown, with a darker mane and tail and legs.

"This is Verity, who you'll be riding." He patted the sandy one on the shoulder. At least Rathna was pretty sure it was still a shoulder when it was a horse. "This is Livet." He patted the white one. "She's a bit more of a handful. Here, for a moment, can you put your fingers there, and let me see about your stirrups?" Rathna did as he asked, though she wasn't sure why. He made a small adjustment to the straps, lengthening it a hole, then going around to the other side.

"She's... what do you call that colour?" Rathna frowned. "And that's a people name. Is that normal?"

"For horses? Sometimes. Depends on the custom. Verity is what's called dun, and Livet is a dapple grey. These are the dapples, these little shaded spots here."

Rathna nodded, then looked Gabriel up and down. "You ride, you said."

"Since I was five and on a leading rein. I'm glad to see to what they need." He turned, apparently checking things one more time before lifting one of the saddlebags into place on the dun one. Verity. Rathna would have to remember that.

"Even with..." Rathna hesitated. "Even with your ankle? I notice you don't have the stick."

Gabriel turned, and there was a sharp flash of something Rathna couldn't begin to name in his expression. It fled as quickly as it arrived, and instead he said, his voice even, "The boots are a wonder. And I've got a stick, shrinks up small, for the mountain bits."

He waved a hand, and the mare turned to peer at him for a moment, as if considering what to do about that. He immediately went back to soothing her with a pat on the shoulder. He paid attention, then, Rathna knew enough to spot that, to the little signs. "You needn't worry about that. Quite fit for work."

Rathna almost wanted to ask more, about what his limits were, but there was something a tad forbidding in his manner, somehow, even though he turned back, smiling. "So, there's a mounting block here. Let me get Livet ready, and I'll help you get sorted."

She couldn't do anything but nod and stand back. When he handed her the reins, she held them. Verity blinked at her, sedately, and then did something odd with her hind foot, resting the edge of the toe on the ground, half-closing her eyes. Sedate might not be a full enough description, but as long as the horse kept up as needed, taking a rest when she could probably wasn't a bad thing. "Is she all right?" Rathna was sure this wasn't normal.

Gabriel glanced at the mare, and grinned. "That's cocking her foot. Usually, it means she's relaxed. But if you notice anything odd, please ask. Sometimes that sort of thing is a sign of a problem." He went back to efficiently getting his own horse ready, leaving Rathna uncertain what to feel. How was she supposed to know what was odd, when all of it was odd?

Within a couple of minutes, he nodded. "Right. Bring her over here, to the block? You go up on that, and you can swing over." He set her up neatly, and Rathna found it surprisingly easy to sort herself out.

"What do we do on the other end, when there's no convenient block?" The thought occurred to her as she was settling in the saddle. This horse was very wide, it was more like straddling a barrel than the sleeker sharp-boned horses she'd been on before. Her thighs were going to ache tonight. Probably by noon.

"If we can't find a suitable rock or a log, I can give you a boost." He said it easily, before turning to check his own mare. She'd been trying to nibble on his pocket and he tsked at her, before checking something on the saddle again, and snorting. "So you're one of those, Livet, aren't you? Blow yourself up to see what I'd do."

His voice, talking to the mare, was relaxed, chatty, entirely at ease. Then he went round the other side of the horse, and was obviously about to mount. She frowned, she'd been told you always mounted on the left. It was one of the rules. He swung up smoothly, with one small hop. His leg breezed a good foot over the mare's back before he settled into what even she recognised as an excellent riding seat.

She was still staring at him when he looked back at her. "Easier with the bad ankle. And it's not as if I carry a sword, that's the reason for mounting on the left." No one had ever explained that to her. Granted, people generally didn't explain the reasons for things, even when they told you the proper, expected way to do them.

"Not a knight, then, or a lord?"

Rathna could have sworn he went still for a moment, but then he was patting his mare, and saying, "Have a feel for your stirrups. Your knees should be comfortably bent, that looks about right. Let me know if they feel uncomfortable, right?" He stretched a little in his own, as if he were getting a feel for things. "Are you ready, do you think?"

Sitting around here would not make her more ready. "Ready enough. She's shorter than other horses I've ridden. And wider. But I suppose that's how they're made?" She sounded more dubious than she wanted to.

Gabriel grinned, suddenly, another of those flashing expressions. "It suits them, you'll see." Then he shifted his weight and did something invisible. Livet took two neat steps backwards, before pivoting slightly, so he could move into the lead. "The road down is pretty smooth going, and so is the first bit along the river. It'll give us a chance to get used to each other." Livet made a little stomping kick, and he immediately did something that made her calm down.

Perhaps he was as good a rider as he'd implied. If that was also true about his other skills, he'd been giving her a fair analysis. They might just manage this in a reasonable amount of time.

The initial stretch down the road wasn't too bad. Gabriel kept his horse at a sedate walk, which was good. Rathna remembered the trot as being highly uncomfortable, and the canter as being far too fast. Once they'd got going, she found Verity had a rolling smooth walk, like being rocked side to side in a rowboat, almost.

She watched Gabriel, in front of her, who was needing to do rather more work. She couldn't figure out what he was doing, but Livet kept wanting to break into a jog or react to things. Once, she'd clearly decided that a bit of taller brush held something terrifying, and took several startlingly large hops sideways. Verity ignored whatever it was entirely, but within a couple of moments, Gabriel had Livet back in hand. He didn't seem upset or annoyed.

It made Rathna feel a bit more kindly toward him. He was still deeply inexplicable, and more than a little startling, but she had to admit he'd already been useful. There was no way she could have managed this herself, and without his skills she'd be relying on one of the locals. Most people would certainly have made her feel more wrong-footed, for not being good at horses, when she'd put her time into learning other things.

She also had to admit the scenery was gorgeous. They

were coming down into a river valley, and Gabriel gestured to the right. "We're going that way, and up to that." Which was, as far as she could tell, a rather large bit of hillside rising up from the valley. Close enough she could see the height clearly.

"We're going up there?" Rathna was not at all sure what she thought about this at all, but it was far too late to turn down the assignment. She'd have to at least make an attempt. And hope she wasn't entirely out of her depth. Or her height, if that were the proper way to put it.

Gabriel turned in his saddle and nodded. "Not too far up, at least not today. It's better than it looks, I promise."

Rathna was sure he had a different set of standards than she did about such things. She nodded once, and focused on enjoying the river. Rivers made sense to her. She'd grown up on her parents telling stories about the naga who lived in the rivers, about the way a river blessed a place, and all the things that came from it.

SIX

Gabe felt the day was going well enough, considering. Rathna had at least been willing to look past the initial awkwardness, and she hadn't been offended about his help with the ponies. Which was good, because horseback riding was clearly not one of her better skills. He supposed it wouldn't be, if she'd grown up in London, she'd just have learned what she needed to to get by.

To be fair, she was actually managing fairly well, though Verity was making it easy for her. The dun mare had a nice easy gait - he'd been up on her when he checked the ponies out when he first arrived. He'd had too many assignments - three was plenty - where the horses assigned weren't up for the work, and it would be unkind to ask them to do it.

These were good working mares, and he'd felt better about the inn in general after seeing them. They'd been well fed, their hooves tended to properly, and the tack in good working order, with the unmistakable smell of saddle soap and linseed oil. And they'd been treated well, they didn't expect abuse or harsh correction.

The ride went smoothly, and they barely saw anyone, even in the distance. He turned up the path he'd discovered, pausing to call over his shoulder "There, that little gap. There's a notice-me-not."

Rathna nodded once, but didn't say anything, as he continued up to the little flat spot. There were a couple of trees, suitable for hitching the horses to. Once they'd dismounted, Gabe went around to loosen the girths, and take the saddlebags. Rathna took hers comfortably - stronger than she looked, he thought.

That gave Gabe more time to remove the bridles, swapping them out for halters and long leads. "They should be fine here, there's a fair bit of brush." He then went and rummaged in his bag, and brought out the expanding bucket he'd packed, before holding his hands over it and summoning water. He'd got good at that one early on, especially since it came in handy so often. It meant he didn't have to go down to the river and haul water up, or water both horses there.

When he looked up, Rathna was watching him, the saddlebags over her shoulder, as if she weren't sure what to make of him. What she actually said wasn't about that at all, though. "They'll be all right for the day?"

He nodded. "We can spend our time up there, looking at the portal. I'm at your disposal. I don't know an awful lot about how they work."

"You're not supposed to." Rathna's voice was crisp, but he was fairly sure there was a little amusement there too. "We'll see how much you pick up. Ready, then?"

Gabe nodded, leaving the bucket where both mares could get at it, and tying it to a branch so it should stay upright. "I'll need to check on them, around lunch." Then he rummaged in the saddle bag and drew out the stick he'd brought. It was baton length at the moment, about the length of his forearm.

He took ten or so steps away from the mares. Then he murmured the word that expanded it to a proper walking stick, at full length, rather than the half-length he sometimes used for better leverage. He preferred his inside cane with the handle when he could; it spread the weight a bit better along his hand, but this did nicely.

Then he nodded. "Up this way." Gabe set off at an easy pace, and again, he was pleased to see that she kept up quite well. She was better on rough ground than many people he'd worked with were. They made their way along a narrow path, barely worn into the scrub grass. Gabe found it harder going than he wanted to admit, but he managed to keep a respectable pace. He stopped about fifteen feet from the two standing stones that made up the portal here, the arch forming over them.

"How can I be of help?" He leaned a little on the stick.

She looked him up and down, before she turned back to the portal, distracted. "Let me have a look, first. Stay back, you - you make noise." It sounded as if she were listening to something else, then. There were a few birds, the small sounds of any outdoor space, a bit of wind. No imminent sheep or cattle or whatever the local sort of domesticated wildlife might be. Or the less domesticated, for that matter, though he wasn't terribly worried about that.

So he stayed. She went up, cautiously, step by step, waiting to see if the ground shifted, and also with her head cocked, as if she were listening for something intently. It was clear, just watching her, that she had a system, an ingrained caution built on observation and patience. Different than how he preferred to go at things, but sensible. He couldn't hear whatever she was listening to, but he could feel something, like a faint vibration, a hum of magic that was more impression than sensation. Which was odd, if the portal was not working.

Rathna spent a good twenty minutes circling it slowly. He could tell she was being systematic, like Lucy and Aunt Witt were, but he couldn't tell if that were her natural preference, like it was for them. He checked his watch twice, and after that, settled into making careful observations about the landscape. He noted everything he could see, before shifting so he could see how much traffic there was along the river road, such as it was. It was only when he heard "Come up, please, carefully, don't touch anything." that he turned and moved up the slope.

The stones didn't look unusual, precisely. He'd had plenty of opportunities to look at the portal at Veritas, over the years, his family home. But that was quite an old portal, established in the first years after the Pact. This one, in contrast, was the one of the newest ones added, from what the assignment information had said, though there was another in progress.

"Yes?" He kept his voice even. From the way she was grimacing, this was not going to be an easy solution. He'd largely expected that, honestly. This had seemed unlikely to be a simple problem from the first.

"How much do you know about portals?" Her voice was still even, rather distant. Gabe recognised it immediately as the way he sounded when he was not at all happy with what he was finding, and needing not to scatter his thoughts or focus.

"I'm familiar with the one near my family's home," he said, and gave the coordinates, rather than the name.

She nodded, absently. "Quite old, that one. We've come

to use different techniques." She gestured at the stone. "Tell me what you can sort out, please."

Gabe couldn't tell if she was testing him, or if she was wanting to confirm something without biassing his commentary. "May I touch the stone, or would you prefer not?" Something in him wanted to touch it, to understand what he was feeling, to work through it from first principles, up close.

"Not just yet. Tell me what you know about a portal, first, before that. And what you - what you perceive."

He nodded again, clasping his hands behind his back to reduce the tempation to reach out, his walking stick leaning against his collar bone.He turned his attention to explaining what he knew, concisely. "Portals are, fundamentally, grown rather than built or made, though of course there's a structure to the growth. That process is kept quite private, without written records available to those outside your guild. Though from the sources I could consult, I gather that the oral sharing of information is somewhat more common."

He glanced up to see a flicker of a smile, or something, anyway. Good enough reason to continue. "From the notes I could find, I gather they fall into broad categories - stone, plant, and water. Which frankly didn't make much sense to me, because one of those things is not like the others. But the Trellech portals are water-anchored? And this one is stone."

Rathna nodded, then considered. "That was more than I expected." It wasn't grudging, he could tell that, but her tone was otherwise difficult to read. "You are correct this is a stone portal. Recently established, three years ago, and until a couple of months ago, acting entirely normally."

Gabe nodded. "The report said that there were a few

odd events, but when someone came to check it, it had gone dark."

Rathna nodded, reaching to touch the stone. "This. It should have been glowing. It's not a bright glow, it's more like being able to see it breathe? A small thing, that you only notice when it's gone."

Gabe blinked. "Oh. Wait. You mean that they're like the Glaedwine approach, only with more of the solar cycle effect? Diurnal, at least?"

Rathna raised one eyebrow. "You are rather better read than I expected."

There were at least three ways Gabe could go with that one. He wasn't insulted. Most people didn't deal directly with the Penelopes, and didn't know how far their range of knowledge extended. Or their ability to research at the drop of a hat for a new case.

The reality, of course, was that he'd picked it up over the course of the summer between his third and fourth years at Schola. He'd been certain then that his mother and Uncle Gil had staged that series of discussions that had ebbed and flowed around everything over those holidays. Uncle Gil had finally confirmed it last year after Gabe had brought out his journal to prove he'd thought about them staging the conversation at the time. Explaining that, though, was not on.

Instead, he shrugged. "I pick up all sorts of things. Don't assume I know something, but I'm quick to catch on." He then sketched a bow. "So, when establishing a portal, I am assuming you do something, details unspecified, to gather the energies of the area. Then you anchor them into something that can breathe with the flows of magic, neither hardening up nor flooding the area."

It earned him another of those arched eyebrows.

"People do not normally think about that aspect. How hardening the flow causes problems."

Gabe shrugged. "I did say I'm aiming at being the resident expert on buildings and related magics. One of my uncles has a particular specialty in it on the academic side, which gives me a head start." He then looked the stone up and down. "May I touch it now, or would that cause problems?" It was starting to make his fingers itch, wanting to.

Rathna shook her head. "Touch away. It's, well. Think of it a bit like the Sleeping Beauty tales. So deeply asleep it won't wake without the proper kiss."

It was his turn to raise his eyebrow. "That's a very specific sort of metaphor." He then stepped forward, resting first his left hand on the stone, then after a couple of breaths, the right one. He could feel the magic there, a barely perceptible sensation, between his hands. But it was so quiet it was indeed like an enchanted sleep, or the deepest of lakes. Lochs, he supposed, around here, where there was no sign of what was going on deep below the surface.

When he looked up, after a minute, Rathna had stepped back, her arms crossed, watching him.

"So, where do we start?"

SEVEN

SATURDAY, AT THE PORTAL

Rathna took a breath. On the collaborative front, this was at least somewhat promising. Gabriel was asking her advice, and giving her space, rather than muscling in. Though the way he was built, muscling wasn't the right word for it. He still wasn't dictating what to do.

On the other hand, she had no idea how to proceed. She'd never seen a stone quite like this, or heard one like it, since she tended to hear the flow of energy rather than feel it, like Morah Avigail. They'd had long arguments about which way provided better diagnostic detail.

Morah Avigail's community had an entire culture around that sort of argument. Rathna admitted that applying it to the keeping of portals was perhaps a bit unusual. Normally it would be food or celebrations or which actions were more laudable or which translations were more correct.

The problem was, she wasn't sure Morah Avigail had ever seen anything like this, either. Rathna half wanted to call a pause, retreat by train to Trellech, and do research in the library there. And yet, she was fairly sure that wouldn't actually help. She put her hand on the stone again, frowning.

It was as if everything were quiet, hushed. Whatever song there might be there was so muffled that she could barely hear it. Just the hint that it should be there, something other than total silence. Whatever was wrong, she wanted to fix it. It tugged on her, the wrongness, the out-of-tune silence where silence shouldn't be.

When Rathna looked up, still trying to form an answer. Gabriel had taken a couple of steps back and was looking at the overall space. "May I sit?" he asked.

"Your ankle?" She bit off the comment a moment too late.

He just shook his head, as if he were amused by something. "I want to sketch the layout, and do some measurements, if they won't bother you."

That made Rathna step back and peer at him. "Is that how you start all problems?"

His shoulder twitched, and he shifted to settle on a low flat rock about five feet from the portal stone. "One of the ways. Each problem is unique, but they all exist in the same world, the same possibilities. Seeing how they're the same and different from other things I know about, that often gives me a place to start."

Rathna nodded. "I want to do some more investigation. How - would it be a problem to have an hour or so working quietly, no conversation?" In her experience, people tended to want to chatter. She wanted to go the slow path of her training, laying out each aspect, every detail, piece by piece to map the ground. The way this was wrong, she'd been trained to be cautious, to examine first, well before doing anything.

Gabriel immediately brightened. "That would be grand. I'll let you decide when we're done, but that would be a help to me too."

Not what she'd expected at all. She watched as he settled himself more comfortably on the stone, drawing a small pencil case of rolled leather out of his jacket pocket. He then settled in to make various small marks she recognised as sketching out the proper perspective points. He didn't look at her, just off into the distance, as if making sure of the proper alignment of the mountains in their line of sight.

She, in turn, backed up. Setting her own bag down, she took out the small case of working stones. Different materials, different resonances. She ran her thumb over the stones, trying to decide where to start, and then shook her head. She would be orderly about it. It was how she'd been trained, and it was also just a sensible approach, to avoid missing anything. She had her working set with her, and more back in her room at the inn. Rathna took a breath, then unwrapped the small wooden case that held each stone in its own padded container, and found her working tool to lift them out.

It looked to anyone else like a queer sort of tea-strainer, a wide carved lattice work of finely polished oak that encased the stones. It wouldn't do for the most sensitive work, but it made it much easier to avoid dropping a small stone on the hillside. She would start with the basics, before working along to the gemstones. Going through the igneous and metamorphic stones took her a good twenty minutes.

She glanced up then. Gabriel had stood, now measuring a set of things with an extendable ruler that didn't require him to touch the stone. She appreciated that, it would have upset her readings. Or at least it might have if they'd been any use. Instead, what she had were a series of tests telling her that the bulk of the nearby rock was igneous and metamorphic. That much, any idiot trained in geology could tell by looking around on the ground. Even if they hadn't read some of the various academic articles from earlier in the century, about this having been a volcano, which of course she had.

She hesitated, then tried the sedimentary stones as well. It was proper to be systematic, after all. A strong result seemed less likely, from what she could see around her, but there was in fact a resonance there. Limestone, more than anything else, which suggested some long-dry ancient sea, now raised up by the mountains. She would need to do more research on that, if it turned out to be relevant.

The gemstones were, perhaps, a little more informative. The obsidian reacted, as she'd expected, but her spinel had a slight pull she hadn't anticipated. Few of the other stones reacted, though the amber suggested some form of extensive natural magic at play. Her amber tended to be more reactive than the jet, especially to recent magic. Most of them were roughly what she would have expected, but she could not explain the spinel at all.

That stone had often been a little finicky. Her kit wasn't gem quality, of course, which also could make a difference. But she certainly didn't have the money for that, not like some of the seniors in the guild who had beautifully faceted stones set in more neutral ivory, which set off the way the gems would glitter. The spinel, though, had that slight twitch of sound, a little burr that might turn into a grace note or a harmonic but never quite did.

Rathna set it aside carefully in the tray, touching the edge for a moment to confirm the charmwork that would keep the stone in place was active, then stretched. It had been more than an hour, she was sure. Without disturbing her, Gabriel had prepared a snack, elevenses, or something of the kind. It was laid out on a blanket on the grass. He was still seated on a stone, making further notes in his little notebook. She took her time putting her stones away, each in their proper segment, and then stood, bringing the case with her, and her notebook.

"Thank you." She wasn't sure what else to say, then before her wits caught up with her. "Do you usually make sure people are fed?"

Gabriel grinned at her, and pushed one of the sandwiches over toward her. "There's another set for later, although I admit I'm a bit stumped and want to retreat to my books."

"You too?" Rathna took the sandwich, suddenly ravenous. It was indeed a perfectly reasonable cheese sandwich. A moment later, he handed over a hard boiled egg, as well.

Gabriel nodded. "I'm not seeing any obvious reason the thing should have failed. No magic in the area that seems out of place, though I admit I haven't gone far afield. If you have more to do here, I might take Livet and make a broader circuit, as far as we can reach."

"Not up the mountain?"

Gabriel grimaced. "I'd rather check the easier spots first. That's not the easiest of climbs. I did go a bit further up, when I came out here before, but didn't see anything out of place." He considered. "Or feel it, either."

"I don't hear anything. It's as if the stone is muffled."

When she looked up, Gabriel had tilted his head, as if that had revealed something important to him. "What should it sound like then?"

She wriggled her fingers. "It would be easier if I'd had a

more in-depth musical education from when I was little. I did the full five years at Schola, of music, but I don't have names for much of it, we didn't go nearly as far into that as I wanted."

"No focus - no, you'd have been doing your specialisation by then. Ritual of course. Time and Place?"

"And Materia. And there are only so many hours in the day." She shrugged, then risked something else. "Also, Professor Hallerton didn't think much of my voice."

She watched Gabriel, out of the corner of her eye, more obviously busying herself with her sandwich. "Mezzo-soprano?" he asked after a moment.

It was not a particularly personal question, and she supposed she had invited it. Most people assumed she was an alto. She nodded. "He complained about my accent, in choir. Too common. And he didn't like my compositions."

"Well, I can certainly see why you wouldn't specialise there, then. Better to be somewhere that appreciated you." He said it as if there would be plenty of places that would. That had not been her experience, but she had no idea how to explain that to him. Instead, she said, "You? Did you do music?"

"Tenor. He kept trying to jam me into playing the hero in whatever production we were doing. Not quite suitably blonde, I'm a bit dark, but there are charms to solve that. But then I went and broke my ankle the last spring, and he was utterly infuriated at me, as if I'd done it solely to upset him." Gabriel shrugged. "I knew I was going to the Penelopes well before my fifth year, so they set up special tutoring for me, I didn't do the usual projects. I liked the singing, but not so much that I'd put up with someone being awful for it."

Rathna was even less sure what to do with that, so she

focused on the sandwich again. "This isn't bad, by the by. For future requests. What did your study get you?"

"As I said, not as much as I hoped." He leaned back on one hand, utterly relaxed, and she wondered how he could do that, be so confident. "I'd like to talk through the portal with you more, but perhaps when we can sit down with books and notes and reference material?"

They were both rather startled to hear a cough from someone nearby. "What're you lot doing here?" Their interrogator was perhaps in his fifties, and his picture might well have graced the definition of 'grizzled'. He was wearing rough tweeds and an old jumper, a cap pulled down on his head, and scuffed boots.

Gabriel glanced at her and then stood. She let him. She might be senior, but he was the sort of person who would be taken more seriously here, being male, white, and posh. Though admittedly, the posh might not actually be a help in these parts.

"We've the proper permissions from the Ministry. We're boarding with the Maclains." He didn't mention the first names.

The man looked him up and down. "Gormlaith's folk." He jerked his chin at the portal. "I can see that, aye."

Gabriel nodded. That answered one of the questions, then. She'd thought the protections extended a bit further. "We're looking to see what the matter is with it."

"Don't need the thing. Did perfectly fine without it." The man looked Gabriel up and down, as if trying to size him up, and not quite managing the maths. "You ask Gormlaith about it. Tell her Geordie told you to."

With that, he turned sharply, and went stomping off, back down the hill. Gabriel watched him go, not relaxing until he was well down the path, his hands crossed in front of him, wrist over wrist. He was somehow intent, like the the stories she'd read in the orphanage about hunting hounds. "I'll be setting wards of my own in future."

Rathna nodded, not at all sure what to make of that, or of the sudden feeling of being utterly out of her depth in the face of an unexpected threat. Portals, she knew. There were too many ways a person might be dangerous, and she knew she didn't know them all.

When she looked back at Gabriel, he nodded once. "If you ask me, I think we should take that advice, and go ask our hostess what's up."

Rathna couldn't argue with that, even if Gabriel was taking the lead. "Take our time packing up, so we don't seem to be fleeing?" she suggested, a bit cautiously.

She was rewarded with a broad smile. "Keep them guessing, yes. Let me know when you're ready."

It took her a good twenty minutes to add her final notes so she could work on them in the inn. By the time she was ready, Gabriel had everything from their meal packed up, as well as his own records.

EIGHT

The ride back to the inn had gone smoothly enough. Livet had been more restless than he'd expected, a kind of skittishness that suggested something scary lurking, like a sheep in the bushes. When they got back, Gabe saw to both mares, while Rathna went up to get first crack at the bathing room.

After Gabe had his turn, he changed into more casual clothing. Comfortable trousers and short boots, a shirt and long vest, before he brushed his hair back and knotted it with a bit of leather cording. He knocked on her door, carefully. He didn't want to impose, but they did need to talk.

Rathna opened the door after a short pause with a sharp nod. "Talk here, before we go down and see if we can get Gormlaith's attention?" She offered it cautiously, as if she knew that was the sensible thing, but perhaps wasn't sure how that would play out.

"I can't think of a better solution." He gestured at the door. "We should probably close that and do some privacy charms. Yours or mine?"

Rathna looked him up and down. "Yours, and I might add something." Testing him, then. Fair enough.

He considered, for just a moment, the best strategy here. If it were just the sort of academic sparring he would normally have expected, her getting a sense of his magic, he'd do this without the wand. However, they'd already had one worrisome encounter, never mind whatever it was that had affected the portal in the first place, and that made him want to be more cautious.

Gabe gave the little twitch of movement that would release his wand from the holster on his left forearm, covered and obscured by his long sleeves. Then he did the gesture he'd practised painstakingly in the mirror every day for months after his parents had presented him with the wand. All that practice made it look like he was actually withdrawing it from a long pocket along his thigh, angling his body slightly to make the sleight-of-hand smoother.

Her eyes widened slightly at the wand. They were expensive and known to be highly personal, and he'd been fairly sure such a thing was not one of her routine tools. Mind, in his case, the holster was worth near as much as the wand itself. He politely ignored her expression, and began the series of soft incantations that ensured privacy for them, covering not only the door, but the walls, ceiling, and floor.

Then he did a second pass, this one more visible and trailing a pale golden light. This was to check for any magical telltales that would suggest someone had meddled here, or left something that might break that privacy. Then one more pass, for any other magic present. Her case glowed, and his pocket, where he had his immediate working tools, and a few minor charms on the suitcases, but nothing unexpected. Not even anything on the bed, for comfort. Though having slept in his own bed, he wasn't surprised by that lack.

"You don't trust our hosts?" Her actual question was soft.

"I'm not sure, honestly." Gabe gestured and then slipped the wand back into his pocket for the moment. He found the thigh pocket both uncomfortable and hard to draw from quickly, but you couldn't have everything. "Better to be cautious and not need it."

"And a wand?" He'd given it even odds she wouldn't ask, at least not right now, but he was pleased she admitted her curiosity.

"You deserve my best work." Gabe was clear on this. "As does this puzzle. I'm lucky enough to have a wand, and it's..." He found himself wanting to explain this more than he'd expected. "It's a sort of blasphemy not to use it." He gestured at her case of stones. "Like pearls losing their lustre when they're not worn, my mother says." He inclined his head at the notes. "You'd expected something different up there, hadn't you?"

He could see her almost continuing her initial line of questions, but as he'd hoped, the more pressing question of their work distracted her nicely. Not that he wasn't starting to be nearly equally intrigued by and frustrated with how sharp her curiosity could be when something caught her eye.

"I did." Her voice was quieter now, and she gestured at the chair, moving to perch on the bed this time. That was good, she was relaxing at least a little with him. He'd been worried there would be that painful offended stiffness for far longer. He was sure she hadn't even realised she was doing it. "It looked for all the world like something drained the connection. It wasn't dead, I've seen that before, once. It's unmistakable."

"Like it was deeply asleep, you said. An enchanted sleep." That she'd picked the Sleeping Beauty story as the metaphor was telling. He tilted his head, thinking. "Can you tell me more about how this was established? More to the point, why here?"

Rathna shrugged. "The Naples Scourge," she said. "There was no way to get supplies here without the train to Fort William, and then the cart journey. Anyone deeper into the highlands, it's even further."

That made sense, at least. "And there are other health-related reasons. Are there other portals established around the same time, then?"

"There were eight on the schedule, but only this one and one other actually happened - that's up in the north, Thurso."

Gabe tapped his fingers on his knee, crossing his leg to get more comfortable. "And they have to be set up some-where with a physical connection to Great Britain, I have that right?"

Rathna flushed, that was interesting. Though it was a bit hard to spot on her skin, it was more the way her eyes crinkled. "It depends on the type. We've worked out how to do a stone portal, over water, but it takes the right kinds of stones, and not everywhere has them. Granite's best, for that kind of work. But we've only set up a few that cross water, since we figured that out. And not places with heavy traffic, they can't take the load. Otherwise it's ferries and ships and whatever." She flicked her fingers, distracted. "Most people aren't so precise about the geography. They don't realise the islands make a difference."

Gabe shrugged. "It makes a difference for some of our

reagents, where they come from. I had that drilled into me quite early. The precision."

Rathna glanced up, giving him a long slow look up and down. Her cleverness seemed more like the Penelopes he worked with, rather than otherwise. He couldn't decide if he should be even more cautious, or if he should see where this took them. She could be a quite useful connection for his work if she were willing to talk to him. Not just this case, but future ones.

It would be very much to his future benefit to have someone familiar with portals who could help with the occasional question. She was young, not so much older than he was in the grand scheme of things. They could be working together, professionally, for a long time to come.

"Your training." It came out clipped, precise. "What exactly has it been thus far?"

He'd expected something like that, honestly. And about now, though he had not had to explain it often. Up until recently, either people knew his background, or Aunt Mason or someone else had explained. Or Lucy Doyle, his terrifying and wonderful apprentice mistress, who had given him no ground.

"I was in Salmon House, at school." To the surprise of many, including both his parents. "I've had some experience of the Penelopes since I was small. My mother has worked with them for some consultations, two of my aunts by courtesy are senior Penelopes now. I grew up with it."

"And apprenticed promptly, then? Did you have trouble getting them to take you on?"

He shook his head. "I made my case after my third year at school. The War was on, of course, they weren't sure they'd have someone for me to apprentice to, or that I'd be able to, right away." He gestured at his ankle. "The ankle meant I wouldn't get called up until it healed and they sorted out someone to keep an eye on me. When the War ended, I got assigned properly, to Penelope Doyle." It sounded like a proper name, of course. "If it's confusing, I also call her Analyst Doyle."

Rathna's lips twitched. "I always thought it must be a trifle confusing. Has any Penelope ever been named Penelope?"

"Five times. in the last two centuries. They usually go by their middle names." He glanced up, and smiled a little. "Anyway. I managed to talk them into letting me do all five specialisations, and enough of herbology and protection magics to be getting on with. Incantation, ritual, alchemy, materia, and sympathetic magic."

Rathna raised her eyes. "Like Lugh, then, isn't it? The salmon? Being skilled at so many things? How did you find the time?"

"For one thing, I'm not much of a bohort player." He shrugged. "I don't have the competitive streak for it, not the right way. Nor pavo, before you ask about the horses. I gather I'm too independent-minded, too. It's not that I want to do it all myself, but I want to make sure it's done right."

"And yet..." Rathna looked him up and down again. "You let me do what I needed today, without interfering."

Gabe shrugged. "You know your work better than I do. It's the first time I've done much with investigating a portal. Using them, certainly, but that's entirely different." Then he grinned. "Besides, better to see if you're competent - you clearly are - and then fuss, rather than start out with the fussing. You are senior here." He had his own standards, for how he handled questions of hierarchy.

Rathna opened her mouth, closed it, and then tilted her

head, looking at him. "You're a quite interesting puzzle, you are."

Gabe felt as if she were wishing to apply her diagnostic stones to him. As he'd had something of the same impulse, watching her steady manner of working, he couldn't blame her. He just blinked, looking hopeful.

She waved a hand. "They spotted my skill with portals early on. My second year. Found me Morah, pardon, Mistress Avigail Levy. I stayed with her during my holidays."

Gabe managed to repress his urge to ask, just barely. He'd not been able to get a profile on her, like he would have with any of the Guards.

Something must have tipped her off, though, because she added, her tone repressing any desire to pry, "I was orphaned by the age of eight."

That seemed utterly unfair to Gabe, and before he could think whether he should say it, he promptly said, "I'm sorry for your losses." Then, searching his memory, he added, "Their memories a blessing. Isn't that right, for Mistress Levy's people?"

Rathna inclined her head, just once. "That is not my... not my people," she admitted. "But kindly meant." She looked a bit startled that he knew it. His parents had a wide circle of acquaintance, and his mother had a very thorough sense of what etiquette he should master, quite early on. Of course, that didn't inform him about what her own practices or lack thereof might be. Then she changed the subject, rather abruptly. "What do we do downstairs?"

"I was thinking bluntness would go well here. We find a reasonably quiet table, let it be known we'd like a word when she's got a chance, and go from there. We're still early enough it shouldn't be too busy." Gabe could go along with her redirection, simply enough.

"Our mysterious visitor, and, is there something else?"

"Local legends, I'm thinking. I did a little research before coming up here, but I'm beginning to think it wasn't nearly enough."

Rathna peered at him, but instead of asking him to expand, she pushed herself off the bed. "Better now than later, then. I'd rather be up here for the night before it gets too busy."

Gabe couldn't argue with that, though he wasn't sure how to weight her likely reasons. She was English, darker-skinned, a woman, a portal keeper. Any of them might make for a less than easy evening, never mind the more personal things like a dislike for noisy crowds. Or the fact it was Saturday, and a good drinking day for at least some of the nearby folk.

NINE

Rathna was less and less sure what to make of this Gabriel Edgarton. There were ways in which he was exactly what he had seemed at first glance: well-off in all the ways that mattered, money and family and education. He had a sense of stability that she found herself deeply envying, for all she knew rationally that he was not making a particular point of his blessings at her.

She herself had had none of that. Not until she came within Morah Avigail's enveloping compass. That second year at school, she had come to see if any of the students had a knack for portals. When she called Rathna in for a baffling and intimidating private interview, there had come the now-predictable question, "Have your parents promised you elsewhere already?"

At least half of Rathna's yearmates had been. It was as common to arrange apprenticeships as marriages, or at least align things so they might be the logical choice.

She had shaken her head. "No, mistress. I'm an orphan. I stay at the orphanage in London during the holidays."

Morah Avigail's eyes had lit up. There was a brief lift of her chin, and a "Not, I think, this year. I will be in touch."

It had been Deputy Headmistress Acharya who had explained it to her. The Mathematics professor was Indian - her mother had been born in Bombay. The differences in caste, in traditions, in language had all been vast. Far too huge for most anyone except the other students of Indian families to understand. And the other students were also very different.

They didn't exclude her from the festivals celebrated during term time, but no one had gone out of their way to explain things to her. They assumed she knew, the way they knew. It had been kindness, of a particular sort, and she had been far too shy to ask, to bridge the gap between a child's understanding and a young woman's.

But when it came to the portals, the Deputy Head-mistress had laid it out for her. Apparently, the portals were not a thing anyone was expected to know about unless it was their particular responsibility. That it would be a respected profession. One where she would advance based on her skill, have steady work. That she could learn all she wanted.

At the end of term, Rathna had been found herself whisked away and then tucked into a spare bedroom in the Spitalfields row house. Morah Avigail had explained that her people considered it a particular blessing to help widows and orphans, but wasn't it convenient that Rathna had a gift with skills Morah Avigail wanted to share.

She'd never regretted it. She'd never felt entirely at home with Morah Avigail, there were customs and rituals and yearly cycles that always felt wrong to her, for all she was included as much as could be. There were limits to that, seeing as she was not one of their people, and not inclined to convert. But she had been fed, clothed, given a warm and dry place to sleep, her own room, even. They'd even apparently enjoyed explaining their rules, the reasons for them, where they came from, in a way Rathna had never been offered at school.

She'd been treated first with kindness, and then with fondness. And more than that, access to all the books she might want, and as much ink and paper as she needed. Rathna rather thought that Gabriel Edgarton had never had to measure out the length of his thoughts against the remaining sheets of paper. Or the last drops of ink in the bottle.

On the other hand, he did not seem to have the flaws she would have expected. He did not try to take over, or talk over her. Once she had set her line in the rock, he had not pushed across it, waiting for her to offer relevant details of knowledge or background as she saw fit. He did not fit any of the patterns she was familiar with. He might be as eager as a puppy, sunnily sure that the world existed for his pleasure and edification. But there was something just a tad compelling about his bright curiosity.

Before she could get too caught up in her thoughts, he led the way downstairs. Without seeming to go to any effort, he found them a table in a nook near enough the door they could leave promptly when it got noisier. He let her sit. "Let me see about a bit of supper and if Gormlaith can spare us a few."

Whatever he said, it had prompt results. He went over to the bar, and had a word with Gormlaith. She'd kept him waiting for a couple of minutes, preparing a tray. He'd spent them saying inaudible things that made the men at the bar laugh and clap him on the shoulder. She'd caught a glimpse, as he'd turned back, an expression of a peculiar sort of satis-faction, as if he'd expected that.

"Mistress Stone, Gormlaith says she has fifteen minutes, perhaps a bit more."

Rathna did her best to look serious and slightly impos-ing, which was not one of her better skills. "We had a visi-tor, out by the portal, who said we should talk to you."

From the way Gabriel's chin went up, she was sure that wasn't how he'd have handled it, but she always felt honesty was the better route. It wasn't solely whatever ethics she'd picked up from different sources, but a ruthless practicality, she was a horrible dissembler. She could avoid a topic with the best of them, or divert a conversation she didn't want to have, but actually dancing around something, that was beyond her.

"Aye, mistress? What about?"

Rathna settled her shoulders. "He said to say Geordie told us to ask. And that there shouldn't be a portal there."

Gormlaith threw back her head and laughed. "Oh, Geordie, was it? He's well known for being sheep-mad, seeing things. Up on the hills by his own self far too long. Not a dangerous man, mistress, but opinions, he's got plenty of those."

Gabriel settled himself down, tucking his feet in under the table. "Your people here are known for your opinions, Gormlaith, so I'm told."

It made her laugh again, more comfortably this time, Rathna thought, as if the teasing flattery had done some-thing important.

"True, true. Well, there are some legends. Nothing modern folk would put stock in, never mind Sassenach from the south. Barely worth mentioning."

Gabriel leaned forward. "Oh, we're curious about everything about that bit of rock. Seeing as we're going to be spending a fair bit of time on it."

Gormlaith looked from one to the other. "Supposing neither of you has heard of a beithir. Being...." She waved a hand to encompass the whole of England as southern city folk, no matter how a fair number of the border counties would object.

Rathna glanced at Gabriel, but she saw the same curiosity on his face she felt herself. "Animal? Vegetable? Mineral?" She tried to make it a little bit of a joke, Gormlaith seemed to be responding well to Gabriel's easier manner. She thought her tone came out a bit flat, but Gormlaith laughed.

"Animal. Well, snakelike, more or less. You ken dragons, yes?" She settled back in her chair a bit, looking from one of them to the other.

Gabriel nodded. "Never met one to say hello to, but I'll allow they're a thing people sometimes come across." Rathna just nodded, though it sounded like he might have a bit more direct conversation about them than she had.

"A beithir's a bit like a wingless dragon. Lives high on the mountain in caves, or in the corries. They've a powerful venom in them, and if you're stung, you must rush to the nearest loch or river, before the beithir gets there. They're the lightning bolt, the sudden danger."

Gabriel took this in, remarkably calmly, Rathna thought. "And there are tales of them, right around here?"

"Oh, aye. Do you have a map on you?"

Gabriel rummaged in his pockets and pulled out his notebook, unfolding a map. He turned it around for her, with all the little gestures of politeness.

Gormlaith peered at it, as if looking at a map, at least one that detailed, was not a thing she did often, then she put one finger down. "This is us. This valley here, leading down to the Coe. And that's the portal." Rathna nodded, following it.

"And here's where the beithir was, the one the mountain's named for. Beinn a' Bheithir. Story goes she made her lair up there, until she was so much a terror that the people lured her out, onto the loch. Only, she left a whelp, and when it grew, it had a brood. There's a tale about a farmer discovering them in his hay, burning it all around them, to clear them. Mortal danger on the land, a beithir."

Gabriel blinked. "And you think there is one?"

"Geordie thinks yon portal might lure one back here. That it'll bring the lightning and the thunder down. Can't say he's wrong, can you?" She peered, fiercely now, at Rathna, before fixing on Gabriel again.

There was a long silence, as if none of them knew what to say next. Rathna certainly wasn't sure. She was used to London, where there was all sorts of lore about buried rivers and severed heads thrown into them. Sometimes even a ghostly polar bear fishing in the Thames by the Tower. That was entirely different than venomous dragons, surely a dragon was bad enough without poison.

Gabriel managed a comment after a longer pause than Rathna thought he liked, "Well, since we're just hearing about the beithir, I can't say what I expect of them. Is there anyone around here who might know more about them?" He gestured slightly. "We'd pay for their time, proper."

Gormlaith raised an eyebrow. "Tithe coin or proper coin?" The tithe coins were a sort of scrip that took money off what was owed for taxes and tithes. Useful, Rathna knew, to some people, but not to people who'd not be paying much tithe anyway.

"Either." Gabriel was prompt about that. "We'd likely need only an hour or so."

"I'll think about it." She pushed away from the table. "I should be seeing to the drinks."

Gabriel nodded. "Thank you," he said and then added a coin from his hand to the table. Rathna hadn't even seen him take it out, and she was sure Gormlaith hadn't either. It earned him a sharp nod, but a more approving one, before Gormlaith stood and swept off back to the bar.

Rathna waited until she was well across the room. "You took over that conversation." It came out more edged than she'd meant it to.

Gabriel blinked at her, then he nodded. "Pardon."

"I didn't say it was a problem." Rathna still couldn't keep that note out of her voice. She felt rushed now, to explain herself.

Instead of justifying himself, or explaining things she already knew, Gabriel looked at her, evenly. "You can tell me, if you want to lead. I didn't think you wanted to. Perhaps we should come up with a cue? In case I don't read you correctly."

Rathna had the disconcerting sense he read her quite well indeed, for all they had a very short acquaintance. The Penelopes, as a group, were supposed to be sharp-eyed about items and magics, but not nearly so good at people. He was not what she had expected in any way. "That might help." She nodded once. "I'm not upset. She was responding well to you, and that's what matters."

"You helped. That animal, vegetable, mineral line. I wasn't sure what it was either."

Him confessing that did make her feel better. "I'm coming to the conclusion there's rather a lot about this portal that was never written up." Rathna didn't like the implications. "What do you think about the beithir? Is that a real thing, or is she pulling our legs?"

"Well, the mountain's called the same thing, or near enough. There might be a reason for it. But that's why I wanted to talk to someone else. I'm hoping there's some old granny or granda who'd be delighted to tell us the gossip a few hundred years back."

Rathna snorted. "Well. And you knew how to handle that."

Gabriel nodded. "That's a discussion for later, too. Here, we should eat. We can talk upstairs, but it's going to start to get crowded down here." It seemed like he liked that idea as little as she did, but she wasn't sure why.

Rathna nodded, and peered at the tray. There was a quite manageable chicken pie, thick with a pale gravy, and beer to go with it. They ate silently and quickly, before she slipped upstairs when a crowd of middle-aged men came in, already a fair bit rowdy.

Gabe had expected to follow Rathna upstairs fairly promptly, but he was not quite done with his meal when she slipped upstairs. "Come up when you're ready."

He couldn't tell if he was meant to take his time, or meant to hurry, and so he'd planned to split the difference, a reasonable five or ten-minute pause. Enough time for her to use the lavatory or wash up or look at her notes, not so long she'd be kept waiting.

He was still not at all sure what to make of her. She still hadn't shared overmuch about herself, just those few fragments. Orphan at eight, taken up by Mistress Levy rather later than that. Five years, maybe six.

Gabe had no idea what that was like. They'd had fears about his father, once or twice, when the work he did for the Guard had become dangerous. During the War, as well. But everyone had that. He'd always known that his mother, his sister, his aunts and Uncle Gil and Uncle Magni, would be around. Aunts and uncles by choice rather than blood, but still, they counted.

Rathna hadn't had anyone, it sounded like. He didn't know how that worked. So much of who he was was tied into his family, both good and bad. Mostly good, to be fair to them. He'd known plenty of other young men - and young women - of the appropriate families who had been kept in tight limits, only permitted certain things.

His parents, to their great credit, had encouraged him to follow what he was good at, even though he knew it made things awkward for them, if not worse. He'd never escorted the same woman to a big party more than once, partnered spinster aunts at the smaller gatherings without comment. He knew they'd fended off more than one person wanting to arrange a marriage to his excellent prospects.

As Mama had quipped, just because her arranged marriage worked out wonderfully, that didn't mean it was a good idea for anyone else. Especially these days. Mind, he'd rather thought she also hadn't considered any of the young women proposed as a candidate nearly good enough for him. Mama had standards, and they included the ability to make intelligent conversation, ride, and some particular personal expertise or passion.

Not that Gabriel had minded. He'd been spoiled by his parents. Most of all by the dance they did with each other mentally - and he was quite sure still physically - much as he preferred not to think about the details.

He'd have to marry eventually, but the few people near his age he'd found at all intriguing at school were promised elsewhere or already married now. He lived in hope of meeting someone who'd challenge his mind and give him the same sort of certain love his parents had. These days, he was fairly sure he'd need to do a trip elsewhere, to France or Germany, or even America, and hope for a stroke of luck in the meeting.

That woolgathering meant he'd finished his meal. Gormlaith swept by, taking the dishes away, and he considered. Another beer, for upstairs, would go well. Being drunk had never appealed to him. Right now, though, a bit more would ease the aches from his ankle and the annoyances of coping with his leg.

He made his way over the bar, nodding politely to the knot of men leaning on it. They were all weathered, in their forties or fifties, at least.

"You here about the door?" One of them jerked his chin, precisely in the direction of the portal, out across the crags of the hillside. His voice had the rough burr of the local dialect, but it was English, not Gaelic.

Gabe nodded, not sure what form of address to use here. "I am."

"And she with you?" That was a jerk of the chin up toward the stairs.

"She's senior in this." He smiled as easily as he could manage. "Mind, most people are senior to me."

As he'd hoped, it got an easy chuckle. "Pup, you are." The first man stuck his hand out. "Duncan." Then he jerked his chin at the other two. "That's Alasdair, and that's Stuart. All Maclains."

Gabe spread his hands and sketched a small bow. A bit of self-deprecation didn't hurt in this case. Better people think him harmless than anything else. "I gather that's common around here." Gabriel gestured. "Gabriel Edgarton. English, pardon that."

That got him another amiable round of nods and chuckles. Stuart gestured back toward the town. "We work the quarry."

Gabe considered that. "With the rest?" He wasn't sure what term would be considered polite here.

"Sure. They're clan, aren't they? And family."

That was curious, though the oaths everyone made to the Silence at eleven meant these men weren't telling things they shouldn't. "But this is your pub, and they have one in the village."

Alasdair eyed him as if he were somewhat dense. "Of course, lad." He then gestured broadly, almost hitting Duncan on the arm. "Down in the town, you went by it, coming in." He then looked Gabe up and down. "You came, went, came back."

Gabe nodded. "Took a trip to Skye, before Mistress Stone got here. An errand for people back south."

"Funny sort of errand. You looking for birds, then?"

Gabe shrugged slightly. "Feathers, some stones. Nothing rare." It wouldn't do any good to make anyone know they had things that might be worth taking. He was young, he wasn't foolish. They were on other people's land, in their inn, and research only went so far in teaching you the local customs that actually counted. Just like no one had mentioned a large venomous serpent in his briefing. He was trying not to think too much about that just yet.

Alasdair considered his answer. "What do you do, then?"

Also tricky to answer. This far out, if you said you worked with the Guard, everyone would shut up like a clam, and saying he was a Penelope didn't help either. "I investigate magical oddities for the Ministry." Entirely true as far as it went, and anyone who knew what that meant out here would also have a good idea why he'd put it that way. "My colleague's a specialist in portals."

"Specialist, is it. Not one of us, though?"

"Oh, born in London, she said." Gabe blithely ignored the layers of implication in that sentence. "We're interested in lore about the mountain. Where Oisin's cave is, that one. Um, up on Aonach Dubh?" He was fairly sure he didn't mangle the name too badly.

That got him another round of snorts, and a "We're quarry folk, not mountain folk. You ask around, though. Might find someone."

Gabe nodded. "Anyone you might suggest to start with?"

There was a brief conference, this time, clearly shifting into Gaelic, because Gabe promptly only understood about one word in twenty, mostly names. Finally, Stuart gestured. "Ask Gormlaith to tell you if Jamie comes by, point him out to you. She'll know which one."

That was generous enough. From the way the three were watching him, he suspected there was a bit of a catch somewhere, but probably not a dangerous one. He smiled, warmly. "Ta, for the tip. Let me buy a round for you, yeah?"

It got him a more approving round of nods, and Stuart clapping him on the shoulder, enough to rattle him a bit.

"Oisin's Cave, then? You been up there?" Alasdair was looking at him.

"It's a bit of a climb, haven't tried it yet. Should I?"

"You know mountains, lad?" Clearly, he was going to be lad for them until the end of time. He'd been called much worse, honestly, and it wasn't like it was wrong.

"In Wales, Snowdonia." Which got some approving nods of respect. Even here, they had a sense of that remote and hefty sort of mountain. "Not a thing to take on without understanding the place."

That got another nod. "Haven't been so many up, the last few years. War did a lot of folks in."

Gabe nodded as they swerved onto more risky ground.

He didn't comment, but that didn't stop anyone from asking.

"You serve?" There was a flick of a nod at the cane, which he had with him. That was the question he'd been expecting, that no one had quite worked around to earlier. It was right on time.

He'd given a lot of thought over the years to his possible answers to this question. He had a dozen that were all true enough, but didn't give too much away. Like his thoughts about that whole horrible mess. "I was still recovering at the Armistice." Leaving it opaque where the injury occurred. "Knew plenty who served with honour, though." Including two of his better friends, a year older, who'd never come home, and Del, who'd come back changed.

There was a silence. There was always a silence at such moments, and Gabe had long since learned not to rush it.

Alasdair nodded at the photographs. "Go gentle with Gormlaith, then. Her son, the Somme. Donal was a fine young man."

"Ta." Gabe took a breath. "I wouldn't want to hurt her. She's been a kind hostess." Then he glanced around and deliberately called out, "Mistress Gormlaith? A round for my friends here, another for me. I'll take mine upstairs, by your leave?"

It brought Gormlaith, in a moment of quiet, back toward them. The bit of flattery made her smile at him, and of course it forced a change of subject quite rapidly.

Alasdair looked him up and down and snorted as she went to pull the pints. "Not such a pup."

Gabe shrugged and grinned. "Plenty I don't know. Yet. Thank you, all."

There was a rolling burr of Scots that Gabe couldn't begin to understand again. Gormlaith brought his pint by, and he nodded to her, pushing coin across to pay the tab, and then went upstairs.

He was certain that they started talking about him as soon as he reached the door. But he knew better than to turn around and give them the satisfaction of knowing he was curious. They were friendly at the moment. That didn't make them safe. He knew that entirely too well.

ELEVEN

SATURDAY EVENING

I t was rather longer than Rathna had expected before she heard the knock on the door. She had time to wash up, brush her hair out and braid it for the night, in a long tail down her back. A tad informal, but her neck was aching a bit.

Then she had somewhat fretfully taken to working through her stones, doing the simple charms to clear away the day's work. She held each in her hand, the smaller ones cupped in the wooden scoop to keep them safe. It felt soothing, useful, and regardless of how it felt, it needed to be done.

She had got all the way through, which meant it had been at least fifteen minutes or so, when she heard the knock at the door. Rathna had not managed to pick up her book, other than setting her notes out on the desk. She closed the lid of her stone case, then called out, "Come in."

Gabriel appeared, a mug of beer in his hand. He had a waxed canvas satchel over one shoulder, and she realised he must do that to keep his hand free for the cane. That suggested he needed the cane more regularly than he'd implied. She didn't need him exaggerating his capabilities, especially if they were likely to have further visitors to the site without any warning.

She got up, ceding the desk chair to him, then leaned over to grab her case of stones before he got too close, tucking it on the bedside table. He smiled, briefly, and he must feel the same way about his, she realised, for all she wasn't sure what kinds of stones he carried in any specific detail.

"So. Beithir."

He leaned back, then shook his head slightly. "Moment."

Rathna waited, he was clearly trying to figure out how to say something difficult. Rushing him seemed unlikely to improve things, so she rearranged herself slightly. Sitting on a bed was fundamentally undignified and awkward, even if it seemed necessary.

"Downstairs, they asked about you. And me." Gabriel shook his head. "Pardon, that wasn't clear. They asked if I were here about the door, and if I was with you. I said you were senior. I didn't explain precisely our positions - mentioning I'm a Penelope might not go over well here, the nearest local Guard is up near Fort William."

Rathna leaned forward and peering at him. "Is that often a problem you have?" She was now, frankly, rather intrigued. She'd thought that the Guard certainly were not always welcome everywhere, but no one particularly feared them.

Gabriel shrugged, a little twitch of his shoulder. "Often enough to plan for it." He considered. "I don't think smuggling is the issue here, but there might be a number of things they'd rather not have the long nose of the Guard noticing."

"Do you often run into smuggling, then?"

"Mostly, the Guard leaves smuggling alone unless it's harming people or causing real damage. Rare plants or animals, or ones that are dangerous to move. Every ten years or so, someone gets the idea to try and move ginsies and harvest their claws, or their teeth."

Rathna contemplated that. "People with a death wish, then."

"Oh, they're only lethal for about half the people. If you've survived a bite, it's no more dangerous than transporting adders." He wiggled his hand, but there was something in the movement that had a flicker of something potent. "But you have to pop the tooth or claw into whatever potion you're making within a minute or so of removing it. So, easier to bring the ginsy where you have your alchemical whatsits, than bring all your breakables into the deep woods."

She raised an eyebrow, since that last part came across very much as an idle young man. She was increasingly sure that was show, but what he was intending to show was becoming less and less clear. Why he was picking what he did. If he were picking. He was very confusing, and becoming more so, not less.

"We were supposed to be talking about venomous beithirs," she pointed out. "Do you have a good background in natural history, then?'"

"I admit, I've never been very fond of reptiles. I was horse-mad, early on, and I always took the side of the knight over the dragon." He shrugged slightly. "I know snakes have their place in the grand scheme of things, but they've always made me a bit uncomfortable. The idea of a large one, with venom in its tail, about which I know bugger all, that worries me."

He had now changed registers at least four times inside

six sentences. While part of her wanted to figure out how he'd done that, and why, that did not help the conversation. Or the fact he'd hit on something she had been thinking about from decidedly different angles. She watched him for a long moment, then in as neutral a tone as she could manage, she asked him, "Why do you assume snakes are a problem?"

Gabriel blinked at her, set the mug down without looking, securely on the edge of the desk. It was a decidedly uncomfortable sort of look. She could see something going on behind his eyes, like a hundred little shifts in energy, in connection, like a portal about to open, all humming power and potential. Then it flattened out immediately, so quickly that it almost convinced her she hadn't seen anything at all.

"Venom does get my attention." His voice was mild, now, yet another way of speaking, if she only had time to properly index them, each of their particular resonances, like half a dozen songs. Then he stretched out his hand. "The options, as I see it. One, there is a beithir, as described. Two, there is a legend of a beithir, but it actually is some other sort of creature of unknown description. Three, there used to be a beithir and they are now extinct and the legends remain. Four, we are having our legs pulled, possibly to keep us away from whatever is actually causing the problem."

She had to admit the logic there. "Five. Someone is using the legends deliberately for multiple reasons, including keeping us away."

He nodded. "A variation, but you're right, possibly with different consequences." He turned his hand palm up. "It seems a rather forbidding sort of place for anything of size to live."

Rathna contemplated, then she asked, "What do you think about dragons? Besides taking the side of the knight."

Gabriel leaned back, and he was at least giving her question due consideration. She appreciated that about him, even on the short acquaintance they had. It was quite rare, in her experience. Especially from men. "There are the custos dragons. I don't know much about them, of course, bar knowing they exist, and having seen one at a significant distance once."

Rathna nodded. "Not a banking family, then." Her voice stayed even. That was more than she knew for certain, for all she'd heard the tales.

"Not a banking family," he agreed. Which wasn't much help on what his background was. She supposed it was unlikely one of the direct line of the banking families would become a Penelope. And she knew perfectly well he'd gone to Schola, not to Dunwich, where most of the likely candidates from the trading and banking and shipping families ended up. She was also, by this point, fairly sure he was deliberately distracting her, and she had no idea whether to appreciate his deftness or be bloody annoyed at it.

"Dragons." She repeated it as firmly as she could manage.

"No one's seen one in the wild, as it were, for a good two hundred years. And they're scarcely the sort of thing you can hide under a pillow. I suppose it's possible there are some somewhere remote. Well, like this."

If one were going to hide a dragon in a lot of empty landscape, there certainly seemed to be landscape to spare here. And mountains, even. "They have to eat an awful lot, I gather. There are sheep here, but why would a village keep feeding one up, if it were wild?" She found herself thinking out loud, the way she would with Morah Avigail.

"Metal forging." He ticked things off on his fingers. "Use of the shed scales for something, crafting or magic. Some alchemical preparations, though honestly, most of them have better substitutions available. And there's plenty of old scale still around. You don't need much for any of the potions I know." Gabriel glanced over toward his room. "I did read a curious theoretical article six months ago, I can look at my notes tonight."

"You brought notebooks from six months ago with you?" He kept being annoyingly distracting. It was in the way he clearly set up his life, his mind, making assumptions about how to do things that seemed entirely ridiculous until she thought more about them. "How many notebooks are you carrying around?"

"Twenty. Well, duplicates. Wouldn't do to lose my only copy to a flood. There's quite a good shrinking charm, it came out two years ago? It requires specially prepared paper, but there's a place in Trellech that sells bound journals, quite reasonably, or the loose paper for you to have them bound."

It was the last sentence that convinced her they lived in entirely different worlds that happened to intersect here, in this remote inn. She let out a breath, because there were so many things there she couldn't begin to untangle. "Snakes. Not all places think they're horrible."

Again, he gave that little tilt of his head, and deliberately leaned back. "Oh?"

"India. Plenty of myths and tales about the naga. Both the..." She gestured with her hands, an ordinary physical snake. "The snake. And the powers that look like snakes." She'd never had good words for this, how to put the stories her mother had told, with their interlacing of Bengali words, a few Hindi phrases. And she'd certainly never explained it to a puzzling Englishman who kept listening to her rather than dismissing what she said.

He nodded again, that curious restfulness, like he was drinking in what she told him. "And they're not dangerous?"

Rathna snorted. "Anything with power can be dangerous and often is. You know better." It came out tartly, and she regretted it for a moment, until he grinned at her. It made her bold enough to go on. "They can grant favours, if you ask properly. Knowledge. Wealth. Fame."

"It's always intriguing to me what categories people put there. You notice, it's usually not happiness. Or well-being. Or even a good honest love." There was another one of those flashes, a wistfulness in his voice that was entirely fleeting.

"Curing disease, as well, which is rather more practical." Her mother had told her of the yearly festivals, making clay snakes to sit on the shoulders of clay goddesses, to be praised and feted and asked for blessings. And then about how you removed the snakes and used the clay that made them to cure illness, when you returned the goddess to the waters. She didn't know how to explain that to him, though, he'd surely think it was all superstition.

"Are they seen as inherently magical? Dragons, our dragons, are, I suppose."

Rathna considered. "Beneficent magic. Quite capable of making a point if crossed, but the stories often end well, when someone makes amends. They don't..." She searched for the right word. "They don't necessarily hold a grudge. And they're everywhere, the naga..." She gestured with her hands, to indicate the physical snakes. "Not like here. Even if they're poisonous."

There was a brief flinch again, something he clearly wasn't fully able to hide. She watched him, letting the silence settle. Two could play that game, and apparently were going to have to.

Gabe felt on very uneven ground, and he wasn't sure how they'd ended up there. Rathna didn't respond like other people did. She wasn't afraid to challenge him, and he found he liked that. Most of the time.

At the moment, he was hating it. He did not want to talk about the snake in his head, or what it had meant, or what he thought it meant, or any of that. There was, to be frank, a nine-month chunk, just after he turned eighteen, that he would be delighted to forget in its entirety. That was not an option, though, so he would have to muddle through. The immediate problem was what to say to Rathna.

"Do you believe in omens?" He hadn't meant to ask it that way, but it was how it came out. He would have to go with that. She looked him up and down, like she thought he might be teasing her, or assuming something. He shook his head slightly. "I mean. I had one."

That made her eyes widen slightly. "How do you know?"

Gabe let out a breath. "It's, I've never talked about it."

And he'd only just met her. "Even with my parents." He didn't even know if he wanted her to push or not.

When he looked up at her again, she was watching him. Uncomfortably like a snake, actually, almost unblinking, as if he were a problem she were intending to solve that had layer after layer of magical rites and rituals. The kind of challenge that took months or years to sort out. He was even less sure what to do with that.

He was utterly tempted just to flee, out into the dark, to go for a long walk until everything hurt too much to continue. That wasn't on, so he looked away again, suddenly ashamed that he'd ended up trapped in this place where everything he could say was wrong or terrifying. Both.

The silence stretched on and on. He heard her breathe, the inhale shockingly loud in the room. "You asked me about portals." It was not at all what he'd expected her to say. Though honestly, he wasn't sure if he'd expected her to pry, or her to ignore that sudden vulnerability, the swerve into the far too personal. This seemed like the latter, only there was something in her voice that connected them.

Gabe nodded cautiously, and dared a quick glance up. She was sitting on the bed, one leg tucked up, the other hanging off the end. She was watching him, but it was the sort of steady observation he knew from the other Penelopes. Someone solving something, not to be jarred until they were good and ready. He reached for his beer, because the cushioning seemed a very good idea right now. "I did." It seemed safe enough to say.

"Portals are a tear in space. You went to Schola, you know this, why they make us study maths and geometry, music and astronomy."

He nodded, following that much. "Laying out the world

in space and time, in varying combinations." That had been drilled into them early and often once he'd started school.

"Think of a portal like astronomy for spaces here, under the earth. And the parts just above the earth."

Gabe frowned, distracted by the implications of this. "You're saying they're not something built from the outside, the space here...." He gestured with his hands, the broad shape of a door, and then had to steady his beer. "But from below?"

Rathna grinned at him, suddenly visibly pleased. "Plenty of people don't make that jump." She gestured. "There are three main types that we make. As we talked about. Stone, plant, and water. What we don't usually mention is that there are others, we just can't make them."

Gabe tilted his head, thinking through that. "The Fatae, then, before the Pact."

"You have a very good memory." She was peering at him again, but it was a different sort of look, one he found less distressing, certainly. "Yes. Over the water. If you don't do stone."

"Are there other elements that could be used, do you think?" He gestured slightly. "Core materials?"

"There're theories about that. Plenty of them." She spread her hands. "But making a portal is time-consuming, expensive, and doesn't have a high success rate as it is. Keeping one running is easier, but, you said you had one near where you grew up. That's, what?" She was visibly calling up the details. "Not long after the Pact, it must be stone based. Stone is steady, but inflexible. Water is more flexible, but needs regular attention. Trees are flexible, but even if they're grown from yews, they don't necessarily last as long as one would like. There are several portals that probably won't last another decade or two."

That presented a particular challenge. "And I suppose you can't just replace them."

She shook her head. "We'll have to find another location. Nearby, we hope, but it's not simple. Looking at the notes, well. Would you put a portal part way up a mountain in the back of beyond? If you'd had a better choice?"

"I'd assumed that was to have somewhere remote enough it wouldn't be obvious to the quarry folk. But there's more than that."

Rathna nodded. "Here, that would be the type of stones, how they're placed and layered. Mountains are tricky because they're more prone to change, or having been changed, but this one was last active a very long time ago, I gather. They'd not have put a portal here twenty years ago."

That was a pleasant distraction. "Why not?"

"A geologist - non-magical, but quite good - figured out that the whole area, the basin, had been a volcano. He sorted out what kinds of rocks were here, and why. Without that, without being able to tell what's where, a portal is much trickier. And needs significant upkeep."

"Only this one needs a bit more than the usual."

"That is the problem. I can see why they didn't go for a tree, here. But I wonder why they didn't go for water, there's certainly plenty nearby, there must be some underground as well."

"Is there anything else in your notes, what they told you? What you can see that I have no idea about?" He leaned forward a little, relieved they'd moved off the difficult topics. He still didn't know how he'd let that slip happen. Usually he was far more careful.

Rathna looked up at him, considering. "There might be rather a lot of that. We don't know each other's skills well yet."

Gabe snorted. "Fair. Permit me to be more precise. What you can sort out about why they put the portal there, in particular. Were there other sites considered, were there difficulties in the initial - um. Construction's the wrong word."

"We say seeding or growth." Rathna said it absently, as if something in his questions had caught her attention again. "Depending on how likely the audience is to snicker."

Gabe smiled a little at that. He felt she was, at least, not putting him firmly in the audience certain to make rude comments. That was perhaps a little progress. He settled himself a bit more comfortably, took a sip of beer, and waited as patiently as he could. It left him looking around, taking in the room.

She was tidy, in the way of people who'd never had space they felt was truly theirs. It was quite different, he'd found, to the tidiness of someone who naturally wanted everything in its place like Aunt Witt and Lucy. All of her personal items were tucked back, where they would take the least space. Her bags were in the corner, her clothes in the wardrobe, he suspected, her case of working stones on the bedside table. He didn't move anywhere near them; he knew far better than that.

Her ankle boots, where she'd tucked them under the bed, were not expensive, but solidly made. They'd probably been resoled at least once, by the few marks he could see on the uppers. Sensible, practical, and reasonably comfortable, though. She wasn't making do with something that didn't fit.

She had a couple of books on the bedside table, as well as the folio of papers she was currently reading through. The books had bookmarks, the sign of someone who was entirely careful with books. No personal items, no photographs or shrine objects or whatever it was she preferred. Not that he'd brought much himself, but he had a few small things and he always set up his shrine to the lares, at the very least.

"Right. His handwriting is awful." Rathna looked up and cleared her throat. "There's no good explanation about why it's there, other than that the measurements he took indicated that would be the best location. But the measurements he listed in his earlier report, any of the other possible locations might have been better. Certainly, potentially easier to get to."

"Where were the other sites?"

"Down in the valley where this road meets the river. That's rather more public. Given that, I can see an argument not to choose it. A bit further along the loch, um, Archtriochtan. I'm sure I'm getting that wrong. Or they were looking at a site on Loch Leven, the main one, further east from the quarries.

"Nothing up on the mountain with the beithir story?" Gabe considered that, rather wanting a map, then giving in and asking. "Is there a map, or should I go grab one?"

She held out a piece of paper, with the locations marked in a rough pencil. "Nothing on that mountain. And nothing here about why they chose halfway up a mountain."

"The man who, your colleague, was he the one who'd make the final decision, or would others have to approve it, or consult or whatever the thing is? And would he normally have kept notes?"

Rathna shook her head. "Randolf Warrington was his name. He'd make the final decision. We used to work in at least pairs, often trios, but these days, we're too few. Especially for something remote, up here where someone would be working on it for two, three months, at least." She tapped her finger on the folio in her lap. "I would have expected better notes, honestly. It's as if he left out half of it, and not the half I'd expect."

"What would you expect?"

"Oh, it's normal to have a lot of failures, finding the proper spot. He left all of that in and left out the part about what made the place he chose particularly good. It makes an odd shape, what he said."

Gabe shook his head. "Would it help to go to the other spots and see what they're like? I mean, if we can't fix this portal, wouldn't the logical thing be to try one of them?"

Rathna frowned. "It's disrupted things, being here. Repairing it would be best. But... that's not too far to ride tomorrow morning, is it? For the horses?"

"Not at all too far for the horses. It might be more than you want to do, but ..." He shrugged "Your choice."

Rathna glanced up at him, considered. "If we take a reasonable break for lunch. I should manage. Sitting down somewhere that's not moving."

Gabe sketched a bow. "I'll see about our packed lunches, then." He stretched. "It'll be a long day tomorrow. See you at seven again?"

She nodded. "Seven." She was still thinking over something. Gabe, for his part, wanted a good look at his own notes, the ones he'd be hard-pressed to explain to just about anyone. He stood, claimed his mug back, and said, "Good night."

The expedition the next day was lengthy, though the weather was, Rathna had to admit, very obliging. She could see small bushes beginning to flower and smell the scent of heather in the air. They spotted any number of birds and small mammals. Seeing the world from horseback, faster than she could walk, and from a height, had some appeals.

At least until she had to get off. They had started with the site up on Loch Leven, which meant going down through the village and further east. By the time they'd gone through, women were out sweeping the steps, seeing to the morning chores. Gabriel rode comfortably, nodding at them as if he'd done this thousands of times.

It made Rathna consider him. That gesture, touching his cap, or that little precise nod he gave, should have come from someone else. Someone with much more of a rigid idea about class and place in society than he seemed to have. He'd treated her like an equal from the start, for one. But she'd also seen him in the bar. He didn't pretend he wasn't English, wasn't posh, wasn't a young man, emphasis on the young. But he somehow made it mostly not matter. He didn't hold it over anyone.

When they got to the first of the considered sites, he swung off his pony. Immediately, he came to offer her a steady arm, which she rather needed by that point. Her legs had stiffened up. They left the ponies tethered safely and walked out to a point on the edge of the loch. The site itself was a little exposed to the road, perhaps. But the road didn't seem too busy, and one of a number of illusion or keep-away charms might have served well enough. It would certainly have been easier to bring through a cartload of materials than the site Randolf Warrington had chosen.

Rathna took her time with the measurements. Again, working through each piece, systematically and diligently. He did something, as well. She wasn't certain entirely what, other than that it involved his own set of working stones. He was also using some sort of device to peer at the location that had been the focal point. They fit like eyeglasses, only with several lenses that swung into place or out of the way, like a jeweller's loupe duplicated a dozen times.

Once she realised she was drawing out her own measurements so she wouldn't have to get back on the pony again quite yet, she stretched. "Not quite ready to go yet." She'd try actually saying so, and see what he did with that. "Can I ask what that is?"

Gabriel looked up with a grin. "We all have our tricks, right? You've a wider range of stones than I usually carry, I've noticed. If you'd be willing to talk through them some night." When she didn't give an answer one way or the other, he let it drop. "They're different lenses. Some let you see shimmers of energy, some let you see things up close, some further away. Would you like to try?"

"On the site?"

"Oh, I was thinking something simple to start. Ah. Here. This should be good." He gestured for her to join him, looking out over the loch, undoing the catches on the gadget, before he handed it to her. "Don't touch the lenses, they take an annoyingly long time to clean, and we want them later today. But any of the metal's fine. Here's the strap. Close your right eye for right now."

He waited for her to put it on, not offering to do it for her, and in fact taking half a step back. Once she had it in place, the weight both somehow reassuring and a tad unpleasant, all at once, he said, "The lens that's on, right now. It lets you see at a distance. Take a look up there, close your left eye and open your right."

She looked up and then startled. It was as if a bird - a raptor, possibly - were flying right toward her. She opened her other eye, and realised it was quite far away, well out over the water.

Gabriel grinned at her. She could see him bouncing on the balls of his feet for a moment. "That's a peregrine falcon, isn't he gorgeous?"

Rathna had to admit it - he - was. She wasn't too sure about this being out in the countryside, she'd never been inclined to it. She liked her nice sturdy roof that kept out the rain and the wind and the chill, suitable for books.

But there was something about the freedom of the bird that was compelling, the way it swung and swooped. She didn't say yes or no, just a little thoughtful "Huh. That's clever." Gabriel beamed at her, for just a moment, all that charm and pleasure aimed right at her, before he seemed to dampen it down deliberately.

"Do you want to look at anything else here? If not, we should probably get on, if we want to look at the other two sites. And maybe the one that was chosen, depending on the time."

Rathna nodded. "We should get on. Can you give me a leg up?" Last time, she'd found a rock, but she found herself willing to see what he did with the offer. There was another flash of that smile again, before he showed her how that worked. He bent, she put her knee in his cupped hands. On his count, she pushed off the ground, he helped her lift, and she was somehow up on top of Verity and not falling off the other side.

By the time she'd settled herself, he had reclaimed Livet, and was mounted. "Ta." She felt thanks were in order, somehow.

"A pleasure, and you're learning fast." Again, she had the distinct feeling that was exactly what he meant. There were plenty of men who'd have taken advantage to get closer than they'd needed to, or assumed one thing gave permission for another. He had been utterly professional, using a skill he had to help with what she was still learning. It was bafflingly novel.

Perhaps he didn't fancy women at all. She'd heard a little gossip that that was often true of the men who became Penelopes. That would at least make sense of the data she had available.

The other two visits went much the same as the first. The sites were, in significant ways, better than the chosen site. The one in the river valley was again a bit close to non-magical buildings and travel, but not so much so it would cause a significant problem. The third site was more remote, but still down in the valley, by a smaller loch. When they finished their measurements there, she found a smooth flat rock to sit on, and then peered at him.

"I don't see why he chose the side of a steep mountain.

It's not in his notes. It's not anything in the sites themselves, unless something has dramatically changed in a few years."

Gabriel shook his head. "I'm not finding anything out of place either." His eyes went to something behind her, further down the side of the loch. She worried, for a moment, it was something dangerous, but then he shook his head minutely. "Turn around slowly, there's a deer behind you. About twenty or thirty feet."

A deer didn't seem entirely impressive to her, but she trusted he had a reason, and turned around slowly, pivoting on the stone, keeping her notes in her lap. Behind her was, indeed, a deer, a buck, she thought the name was. It had antlers, at least, and it was really rather large. Not quite as tall as the ponies, but rather closer than she'd expected.

"Is that, is that..." Rathna didn't even know how to finish that sentence. Dangerous? Normal? Expected? Magical?

Gabriel's voice was low, awed and delighted. "That is a red deer buck, in the prime of his life. See the antlers? My, he's beautiful."

"Is he dangerous? Is there a reason he's here?"

She caught how Gabriel shrugged, very slightly. "I suspect he's hungry. There's likely more nearby, maybe further down the loch. We could go, let them have their supper in peace."

Rathna was still caught by it. Not just the buck himself, though that was an impressive sight. The afternoon light made his coat shine almost copper, and the antlers were broad and impressive. But there was something about how Gabriel was taking it, like it was a glorious surprise of a gift, something he'd hoped for and never asked for. That, itself, was almost contagious. They didn't move, either of them, for a few more minutes, until the deer wandered a bit further away. Rathna quietly packed up her book and notes, while Gabriel led the horses on foot further down the road.

"You - you know a lot about wildlife, don't you?" It was a more personal question, she realised that, but today had brought home that he had skills he hadn't mentioned. Possibly he didn't even realise how unusual that was in her experience.

"Leg up again?" he asked. "Or there's a rock, there, might do."

"If it's not a bother?" She left it as a question, but felt rather pleased when he bent down again. It went much more smoothly, now that she knew what to expect, and he was still settling into his own saddle when she was ready to go.

Gabriel was quiet for a few steps, setting the horses back toward the inn. "I grew up in Kent, with plenty of land around. My father took me out, regularly, and taught me about everything that lived there. Badgers, bats, hares and rabbits, stoats and weasels, hedgehogs, all sorts of birds, and plenty of trees and plants. No deer, though, not near us. We had a couple of really excellent herons, though. And falcons."

Rathna suspected there was more to it than that, the way Gabriel acted. And she noticed he wasn't at all specific about what kind of land, if it were an estate, or a magical village, or something else. She didn't press, though. "I'm London born and bred. A different sort of wildlife."

It made Gabriel grin. "Still have birds, though I admit, you probably have a lot more signs of rodents, on the average." He tilted his head. "Did you know the Greeks kept weasels instead of cats to keep the rodent population down? Cats hadn't domesticated us properly yet, not there."

"Oh, you're a cat person, are you?"

There was a flicker of something quickly hidden again. "Not at the moment, not when I was in apprentice digs. But I'd like to be again. Not that I have anything against a nice hound. But that's more space and time than I'm likely to have for a good while." Gabriel spread out one of his hands, holding the reins of his mare easily with the other one. "So, thinking about a cat."

"And if you get called off on a longer investigation, like this?"

"That's part of what I'm figuring out still. Soon, though. I miss having one around."

"Morah Avigail had a cat until recently. Named Book." She missed Book. And she was sure Morah Avigail missed her more.

"I'm sorry. That must be hard. For you, too?"

Rathna nodded slightly. "For me, too. Though Book was very much her cat, and just tolerated me."

"The one I grew up with was a grey, named Glaucus. He was always trying to get at Mama's ink." That conversation carried them most of the way back to the inn, the various small stories. Rathna found she rather enjoyed it.

Gabriel had honestly enjoyed much of their day. The riding had been pleasant, the weather lovely, and the scenery outstanding. He could see why the people here loved the area so fiercely, and perhaps why a portal was put here, not nearer Fort William. It would make a stunning location for visitors who wanted a bit of - well, a lot of - epic and dramatic mountains and valleys to roam.

He was pleased Rathna seemed to be relaxing a little, too. Something had shifted for her, but he couldn't begin to figure out what. She didn't have the reactions he expected, not to him, not to anything. When they got back to the inn, he let her go off, taking his time with the horses.

Five minutes later, she was back again. "Can we go back out? Somewhere? Do you mind?" He'd got Verity untacked and was working on grooming her.

Gabriel blinked at her. "Out?" He wasn't at all sure what she meant.

"I got some sandwiches, for tea. Some bottles of beer. Can we?"

There was a note of urgency in her voice, like she needed to be anywhere but here. "How long for?" He'd need to make some further plans if she wanted to be out after dark.

Rathna chewed on her lip. Decidedly upset about something, then, the way she was showing it. "Until dark? Nearly dark?"

"All right." Gabriel kept his voice even, like he would with a nervous witness in a case, or a skittish horse. "Let me just saddle the mares up again. How about we go a bit further up the road, the other way? There's supposed to be an overlook up there. Or a bothy."

The new term distracted her. "Bothy?" Then she blinked. "On the horses?"

"A hut, used by shepherds and other folk like that. It's usually got a roof and walls and some water nearby, but not much else in the way of comforts. Probably a good view, though, we're not short on those. And the mares will be fine." He turned to get Verity ready, leading her out a bare minute or two later. "Here you go, let me get Livet."

Once they were on the dirt road again, going west this time and further up, she was silent for a good ten minutes. They rode slowly but steadily, the horses at a walk. Finally, Rathna said, "Thank you. For - for this."

"You're the one new to the saddle." Gabriel was, frankly, enjoying the riding. Livet had a nice gait. She wasn't mean-spirited, just wanted to know what he would expect of her. And Verity was a nicely built and amiable mare of good sense. They were riding in spectacular scenery, the weather was smiling on them. It wasn't exactly solving the puzzle of the portal, but he also believed that you needed time for ideas to come together.

"You must think me queer." Her voice had a tight note in it.

Gabriel shrugged. "I'm sure you have your reasons. Whatever you need a reason for." He added, after a moment. "If the road stays this good, we can stay out until close to dark, and sunset's not until..." He waved a hand at the horizon. "About eight."

"Oh. Yes. I keep forgetting." It was light far into the evening this far north, and then that sort of hazy twilight. She fell silent again, and Gabe didn't press her.

The road turned into more of a track, but it was clearly tended, there weren't holes or pits. After about a mile from the inn, a good quarter hour, they came around a curve between the mountains. He halted Livet with an easy shift of his hips and legs, and shaded his eyes with his hand. "There's a bothy there. Mile and a half from the inn. Is that far enough for you?"

Rathna chewed on her lip again, but then nodded. "Well out of sight is what I wanted."

"We'll have that. And maybe a bit of a space for a bonfire, going into the twilight."

She glanced over at him, startled, and he had another one of those moments of realising they were working along very different views of the world. Instead of pressing, he waved a hand, and told Livet to walk on.

Twenty minutes later, they had found the bothy. It was not in the best repair, but they didn't intend to sleep there, so that was fine. He'd put a halter on both mares, and let them graze, with the saddles over a fence post, and water from the bothy's bucket and a nearby spring, rather than summoning it. By the time he'd done all that, she'd unfolded the blanket from the saddlebags, and set out the various wrapped packages of food, tied up in different bits of cloth.

Rathna had sat down, one leg pulled up under her, leaning her head in her hand, curled up and looking miserable.

Gabe was not sure what to do with this at all. Asking if he could help was the obvious thing, the thing he wanted to do. But she had not told him why she needed to get away, and he refused to pry. Or to give into his desires to pry. Instead, he took a breath, let it out, and took his place on the other half of the blanket, keeping well away from any sense of crowding her. Then he reached for one of the beer bottles and opened it. There were four, which was about right for all evening and a ride back in the twilight.

"Beer?"

Rathna looked up, and there was a haunted look to her eyes. That made him certain something had terrified her. She nodded and reached blindly for the beer. He leaned to put it securely into her hand, then withdrew. He opened his, with a second slight click and hiss of the bottle. He took a swallow, then another, before setting it down on his other side.

It was a grand view, down into the valley, with Beinn a' Bheithir, the mountain with the particular story, off to the northwest. When the silence continued well past five minutes, he rummaged in his jacket pocket, and drew out his notebook and pencil, turning the book sideways and beginning to sketch.

It took her at least half an hour to notice. That was enough time for him to have sketched the outline of the two peaks, making them more or less properly detailed, and some of the surrounding landscape. He had stopped, trying to decide how to crosshatch the shading, when Rathna finally spoke, "Why aren't you asking me?"

"I said I wouldn't." He kept his voice calm and even.

She made an incomprehensible noise, somewhere

between a snort and a whimper, but he didn't turn around to look at her. It would startle her, he'd done more than enough with animals who were hurting or terrified to know that. And she was perfectly able to tell him, or tell him to ask, or whatever else she wanted, once she figured out what that was. Sooner than he'd expected, she cleared her throat.

"You're a very strange man."

Gabe permitted himself one little shrug of his shoulder. "Most people don't notice."

As he'd suspected, that was enough to entice her forward a bit. She had a drink from the bottle, he could hear how the beer moved, then she inched closer. "What are you drawing?"

"The mountain. That one, there, that's where the beithir was." He pointed with the end of the pencil. She leaned around to peer at the sketch, and he turned the book to make it easier to see.

"You're quite good." Rathna sounded startled. "To do that in a few minutes."

Gabe couldn't quite restrain his comment on that. "More than just a few. I was taking my time, especially if we'll be here a while."

"Are all Penelopes good at sketching like that?" Excellent. Now he'd got her mind engaged again. That was promising. Most promising. Also likely much easier for her. And whatever else this conversation turned into - he was still laying bets with himself about the options there - he would like to ease things, if she'd let him.

"Most of us can sketch the scene of an investigation well enough to be going with. Aunt Mason made sure I could do better than that." He permitted himself another shrug since the first one had worked out well. "I like being good at things I do. It seems simpler than being bad at them, in the long run."

Gabe could tell she had no idea what to make of that. People often didn't. He wasn't motivated by money, or property, or social status. He'd had all of those from birth, by a fluke of luck that had, admittedly, been very kind to him, as well as materially generous. None of that was about what he did, or how he did it. He had choices about that, and he chose to be excellent.

Rathna took a breath, the kind of cautious inhale that suggested she was working around to something. "When I went into the inn, Gormlaith said someone had delivered a letter for me. From Morah Avigail."

Gabe considered his options, navigating between the Scylla of his mother's etiquette lessons and the Chaybdis of Rathna's insistence on her privacy. "I hope everything is all right with her?" Phrased carefully.

"Oh." Rathna breathed out. Again, he'd said something that wasn't what she expected. Honestly, though, this time it was an entirely reasonable sentence, the sort said by reasonably kind and caring people everywhere. "She is doing well, thank you."

Gabe nodded and waited to see if she'd say anything about why the letter was upsetting. He didn't have long to wait, thankfully, because she continued promptly. "There was someone who came around there, looking for me. By name."

"And not someone you know, obviously, or would know of."

Rathna shook his head. "Morah Avigail was fairly sure he wasn't magical. Certainly not schooled here, she couldn't feel the touch of the Pact, and she usually can."

Gabe raised an eyebrow. That made Mistress Avigail

Levy really rather notably sensitive to those particular currents of magic. Quite likely part of the talent that had made her a skilled portal keeper herself, now he thought about it. "Huh." He considered. "Did she get his name, or any other details?"

There was a long hesitation, and then Ratha untucked the letter from her pocket, and handed it to him. Her hand shook, the paper wavering. Gabe nodded and closed his notebook, letting it fall in his lap as he stuck the pencil behind his ear. He took the letter, gently, unfolding the single page, being careful not to jar the seal. He could feel the slight buzz of the magic there.

Mistress Levy's handwriting was neat and precise, the kind that was easy on the eye, while still having a fair bit of character. He couldn't help a bit of analysis. A woman in her eighties or maybe nineties trained at Schola. There was a particular curl to her lower-case A that was drilled into students at the time, to avoid confusion with the O. The letter was only a few sentences, centred on the page, the letters small, controlled, but with a certain amount of spread in the width, that suggested an expansive emotion.

The text was perhaps less revealing. He scanned it, then looked up. "A recent arrival from India, in his early twenties, who gave his name as Vivek, no family name, but from Calcutta."

Rathna nodded. "It means, um. Wisdom, I believe. Maybe discretion."

"And this says he was a medical student, looking to find you, but unwilling to explain why."

Rathna nodded again. "You - you know the Guard. Is, is that normal? Would he, would he hurt Morah Avigail?"

Gabe made himself take a breath, considering the issue from all sides.

Rathna waited, not sure what she wanted Gabriel to say. She felt entirely unsettled, not only the letter, that desperate rush to be away from people. There was no way Vivek could have made it to Scotland, even if he knew where she was. Surely he didn't. But she'd felt like she had back at school, early on, when she had no idea what she was doing, or even what was possible. When people apparently did miracles, without so much as blinking.

Gabriel was watching her, carefully. Then he nodded. "Have a bit more beer. It's a cushion, it will help. Also, it has vitamins."

There was a dry amusement in his tone that she realised was him teasing her. Gently, but teasing. She blinked at him, owlishly, and then took a sip of the beer. And another. When she'd had the third, she gestured at him with the neck of the bottle. "Yes?"

"So, there are two pieces here. What he could find out from our people. And what he could find out from the non-magical folks."

She noticed he avoided any of the phrases she'd heard so often in the magical community. Incapable, mostly, that was considered surprisingly polite. The ungifted. The others, or the rest. Instead, he went for the pragmatic phrase. Rathna nodded, cautiously.

"May I ask you some questions now? So that I can tell you what information he might be able to find, potentially?" Gabriel's voice was even and careful. Much like he used with the mares when they were skittish. Firm, clear about what he wanted to do, but not at all fierce.

Rathna took another breath, another sip of beer for good measure, and then nodded. "You may."

"You mentioned that you were orphaned at eight. May I ask a bit more about your parents? Right now, especially the kind of thing that might be in official records, if you'd rather avoid talking about more personal things."

She sucked in a breath, more sharply, but she could see where he was going with this, and if she wanted his help, anyone's help, she'd have to share something. She looked away, across, over to the mountains.

"My mother was an ayah. She was from Calcutta, in Bengal. She worked for a family there, from when she was eighteen. When she was twenty-two, they returned to England, and she came with them on the voyage. They, they abandoned her. She had no ticket home. No support. And she never saw the little ones again. They were eight and six and four, she'd cared for him since he was born." Her voice got soft at the end. "She never talked about it, other than remembering them, in her offerings, her prayers. The children."

Rathna expected him to make apologies, or to say it must have been a mistake, and she wasn't sure which would be worse. Instead, he was strange, again. When she looked at him, he was watching her. Then, gently, he said, "That must have been horrible. For her, and for them. The children. I'm sorry."

There was something there that made it clear, he understood. She wasn't sure how. Perhaps he'd had a nanny. Then he went on, just as carefully. "She stayed in England, then? And your father?"

She let out a long breath. Perhaps she could get through this without losing every scrap of her self-control. "Ma," She gave it the longer a, the way she'd always said it. "She stayed in London. She got work here and there. She learned English better. She tutored other ayahs who had been abandoned. They had a house, run-down, but a dozen of them together, and she met Baba. He had been a lascar."

"Sailor or servant?" He knew the word was used for both, then.

"A sailor for years. Then he stayed on as a servant, someone coming back. But when he met Ma, he found work at the docks. Steady, they could marry. A year later, they had me. Just me." She looked out over the mountains again. "When I was six, he went away, never came back. A special voyage, they wanted steady men. He could make enough to, to..."

She stopped, completely unsure how to explain the difference between knowing that the money would run out before the end of the month, and being fairly sure it wouldn't. How even at the age of six, she'd known that was a life-changing thing. "It would have been much better." It sounded feeble to her ears, as it must to him.

Gabriel nodded. "And you love him." Again, strangeness. Love, not loved. Which was true. She had adored him, and she still woke up in the morning, loving him and missing him, even if he'd have had no idea what she had become.

"We managed. Ma worked for a family. They had a daughter my age, I played with her. But Ma got sick, she died, all in a rush, a fever. The... Mrs Cappleby kept me, she didn't have to. Just decided she'd feed me and clothe me and let me keep playing with Alice. But two years later, her husband got a posting to India, a big promotion, and they couldn't bring me there. She looked at the orphanages, she found one that was, they tried not to be awful."

Again, Rathna had no idea how to explain that. That trying not to be awful wasn't the same as managing it. That she knew how much worse it could have been. How she mostly had enough food, and mostly had a warm enough blanket, and there weren't many rats or mice or leaks in the roof. How she got to go to school, but no one had time for her, it was just the ordinary lessons and whatever books she could cadge.

"And then Mistress Levy met you, the second year at Schola, and I assume you didn't go back to the orphanage?"

Rathna shook her head. There was one last piece, something she'd never actually told anyone directly. People had guessed, she knew that, and the teachers at Schola had known, if they'd bothered to look at her files. But telling someone was different.

"Ma and Baba, they didn't have magic." Saying it, it felt like it reverberated in her, a gong being rung fit to shake her apart. Instead of just looking at the mountains, she had to close her eyes, screw them shut, so she didn't burst into tears.

Gabriel didn't say anything for a long time, and she had no idea why. She heard a little rustling of something. His voice was even, now treating her as a skittish horse for certain. "Open your hand?"

She did, though she could feel how her fingers were trembling. He put something in it, small and flat, not at all heavy. She thought for a moment it might be a stone, but when she peeked out, opening her eyes for a second, it was a square of chocolate. Excellent chocolate. He'd produced it from somewhere. She knew it wasn't in with their packed food. Daring a glance at him, she found him leaning back, so careful not to crowd her. She gave up trying to make sense of it, and ate the chocolate.

It was only when she was done, the sweet and the bitter mingling beautifully, that she could look at him again. He waved a hand. "Excellent magical remedy. I always keep some on hand. There are others, of course, but not nearly so tasty." Then, as if it were the most normal thing in the world, he continued. "You've taken to magic like a fish to water, then. That's - that's very impressive."

Rathna blinked at him. "Impressive?"

It was his turn to shrug. "Not many people become Portal Keepers, you must know that. It's a rare knack. Certainly rarer than what I do by a long shot, in terms of magical ability. I use charms and all sorts of other things, of course, but most of them are fairly rote. More about being clever than having strong magic." And clearly, he was going to be clever whether or not he was using magic. "You, well, I don't know a lot about how you do your work, but it's clear it's a deep river, understanding things, how the portals go."

She hadn't thought about it that way, the different ways the magic might be for people. It wasn't something people talked about near her, they never had. Before she could bog down in that line of thought, which would certainly keep her up at night for a while, puzzling through it, Gabriel cleared his throat. "Right. That gives me some ideas on the records side. Which is one of the things I do, besides magic. You have come to the right place for a spot of help."

He had that cheerful teasing note in his voice again, and she managed to smile back at him, rather shakily. He went on more gently. "Your birth should have been recorded. Do you know if your mother wrote to people back in India?"

"Oh, yes. She had two sisters. The younger one, especially, they wrote regularly."

"So your aunts would have known about you. No mother can resist writing about her baby, I'm sure." Something in how he said it made her look up at him. He wasn't wistful, that wasn't it at all. Instead, it was a sort of rigorous logic that wasn't sterile, wasn't cold. It was about tracing a line of warmth and light, paying attention to what mattered, how people talked about what they loved. "And - your father, that's trickier. It would depend on the details. But your mother, her death would have probably been recorded. A little tricky, I'm assuming she wasn't ever Christian, so no parish records."

"No, of course not, but she was on the civil register. And I remember people coming by to ask, sometime. A census."

"Right, so Vivek could have found your birth records, your mother's death record. And then if he were very stubborn, perhaps your entry into the orphanage. Or perhaps your - it would have been marked as apprenticeship - to Mistress Levy, even young as you were. I think I'd have to check the rules."

Ratha frowned. "But how would he know the name?"

"I'm - pardon. May I ask where your last name comes from?"

Oh. That. She looked off over the peaks again. "Our

people, they didn't use last names, not the way you do. They're clan, family, group, based on profession. When Ma and Baba married, they were encouraged to pick something easier for the register, and Ma's family, some of them, were gem cutters. That's where I think I get some of my magic from, the stonetouch."

"Huh." She had, apparently, just given him something new to chase, an idea, because he got a sudden gleam to his eye. "So, if he was looking for you as Rathna Stone, he must have known that's what they picked. It's, well, it's theoretically possible to look for you without that, with just the first name. But unless he knew exactly where and when you were born, which register you'd be in, that would be a terribly long search. Finding the orphanage must have been even more so."

Rathna wasn't sure what to say, other than asking, "So he might have found it from paperwork?"

"Possibly. But he must have been very diligent. That suggests someone who wants to find you. And he's a bit younger than you are. Not an older relative."

She shook her head. "Morah Avigail would have said, if he were older. I wonder why he didn't introduce himself better, though."

"Do you live on a warded street? I'm assuming not."

Rathna shook her head again. "No. Not far from the Spitalfields portal and the warded streets, but two blocks off. Her family's all in and out there, they intermarry. The Pact works a bit differently for her kin, I think. I've never asked. It seemed rude. And the Silence doesn't, I mean, it hasn't punished her for talking about it. Doing the family rituals, the celebrations, there are parts with magic in them. That spark, the..." She wriggled her fingers. "The tingle. But the rites work for everyone, the way they need to. It's about the community, not the magic."

By this time, she looked out, and the light was beginning to fade. Gabriel stretched. "Well. All right. There seems to be no imminent threat here, not to you, not to the Silence, not to Mistress Levy. If you'd like, I could write to P - people I know. Double check."

"I, I'd like that." She brushed off her skirts. "We should head back, shouldn't we?"

"Probably, yes."

"Thank you." She couldn't look at him while she said it, but she could and should say it. "For taking me seriously. Listening."

"A pleasure. That's an interesting puzzle you've got there. I'm glad you're letting me help." He seemed like he was about to say something else, then changed his mind. "Sandwiches first, and then we'll head back?"

They didn't talk, either of them, while they ate, just looked out over the mountains and the starkly cut valleys.

SIXTEEN

MONDAY, AT THE INN

The next morning, both of them were quiet. Gabriel waited for Rathna to decide what to say. And she was entirely quiet. Not withdrawn, he felt, not upset she'd told him, but not wanting to talk about it again. Other than the basic pleasantries, and the necessary communication about setting up for the morning, he left her alone.

By the time they stopped for lunch, however, he felt that had gone on long enough. "First, I left a letter to go off to the office, this morning, and an enclosure for someone who can find out a bit more."

Rathna looked up, startled. "But someone might, you didn't write it down, did you?" It was a sudden burst of fear, and it made Gabriel very sorry he'd said it that way.

"I used all the Guard precautions. I'm very good at them. Only two people can open it."

"Two." Rathna's voice was flat now. "May I ask who?" She had settled back in all her dignity. Which made answering a little tricky.

"One of the senior Penelopes. And to my mother. She has a knack with that kind of question, figuring out who might have what information, how to ask about it. Together, they're quite fierce."

Rathna didn't know what to say to that, then finally she tilted her head. "Do you have a father?" It was a flat and blunt question.

"Yes, but he's in the Guard. If I wrote to him, it would be all official. Mama might or might not tell him, I left it up to her discretion. I suspect it will depend on if she needs him to help."

"Help?" Again, the flatness.

"Mama is very good at talking people round, but Papa's more impressively fierce in the ways people recognise. Sometimes you want one, sometimes you want the other. Together?" He gestured with his hands. "Well. Terrifying to be on the wrong end of."

There was a long silence, then Rathna said, her voice crystal clear. "Last night, we didn't talk about your people." She said it the way one of his mother's official social circles would have, wanting the lists of names, threading back through the Gold Book, of the begats and begots.

They hadn't. And Gabe had been rather hoping she wouldn't notice for a while yet. He didn't want to lie to her, not at all, she deserved better than that, for one thing. But he wasn't sure he wanted to tell her the full and detailed truth just yet. A lot of people got very odd when he did, and when they knew the official side of him. He took a breath. "Papa is in the Guard, a Captain. We have a house in Kent, and a townhouse in Trellech. Papa stays there a fair bit, when he has to work late." Technically two townhouses, but only after Grandmother eventually died. "I've a sister, Charlotte, she's two years younger."

"Apprenticed somewhere?" Rathna unbent just slightly. Clearly, she didn't know enough about the Guard to pick up on a few cues. That was good.

"Not formally, no. Everyone expects her to get married soon. She helps Mama with some charitable projects. And she reads a lot. And draws and paints." The proper ladylike pursuits, even if Charlotte was inclined to turn hers to writing children's stories and illustrating them.

Their parents didn't know about that particular aspiration, but she'd told Gabriel, shown him some drafts, and he'd thought they were very finely done. She was a much better artist than he was, for all he could do a good sketch. "She has a suitor, likely to propose by the end of the year. He's still apprenticing, of course."

That got a nod. "Aunts? Uncles? When I - last night, it sounded like you understood aunts."

"I don't have any of my own, not by blood. Mama had a younger brother, but he died in South Africa, when I was little. Papa was an only child. But I have some adopted aunts and uncles. Aunt Mason, that's the senior Penelope I wrote to."

Rathna raised her eyebrow. "That's an odd name."

"Well, technically, Aunt Elizabeth, but everyone calls her Mason. So." He shrugged. "Uncle Magni, Uncle Gil. I mentioned him before. Uncle Gil's a specialist in architectural warding, he's the one who had me reading a lot of the related things, before I even got to the Penelopes."

That made her furrow her brow. "Gil - not Gilbert Oxley?"

Gabriel looked up, sharply. "The same. I hope that's not a problem?" It was a very small world sometimes, and he hoped he hadn't just put his foot in it.

"Oh, no. But he's written some very interesting articles,

but he almost never goes to academic meetings. When he does, he's always with people. I mean, is there a chance you might arrange, I don't know, if that's not a problem?"

Gabe blinked for a moment. He hadn't quite expected that. Uncle Gil was very well known in his particular field, of course, but it wasn't like one tripped over architectural warding specialists all that often. Even Gabe didn't, and he went looking for them. "I'd be glad to." Then he added. "Look, actually, something from Aunt Mason got me thinking, when I was reading notes last night."

Rathna tilted her head, looking uncertain. "Yes?" As if whatever it was wouldn't be that relevant.

"Can you tell me about what's going on, the ground around here? Beyond what we looked at yesterday. You said it was a very extinct volcano, a caldera, if I have the term right."

"The basin that formed it, yes. And then there were glaciers, that's where all the..." She moved her hand, indicating the sharp cuts of the mountains and valleys. "They cut through the landscape."

Gabe nodded. "All right." he said. "And the volcano was before that?"

"Well before. Well, the most recent ones." She stretched out her hand. "I have some maps, a few copied articles." She looked out, back down over the loch. "Why do you ask?"

"I'm wondering what else is underneath us. How it would be different here, rather than down in the valley. Because that's the thing those three other points have in common, they're all near enough sea level."

It made Rathna suck in a breath and make the sort of face that strongly suggested she was doing six kinds of maths in her head. Gabe left her to it without interruption. No sense in jogging her elbow, as it were. Instead, he set about putting out their lunches. Chicken sandwiches, this time, with chutney, nice and sturdy.

More than five minutes passed, long enough that Gabe was getting rather hungry, before she shook her head. "That's a good idea. Let's eat, have another look around. I'm trying to remember something."

Gabe silently passed her a flask of tea with her sandwich, and set to eating his own, downing it quickly. He had to admit that the mountains were good for his appetite. Once they were both done, he packed things up while she got out various of her tools.

"Let's walk a grid. Look for anything that seems not like the ground around it." That seemed a fairly broad instruction to Gabe's way of thinking, but he stood, found his cane, and began to walk across and back, looking at his feet.

Half way through, when they were near the portal stones themselves, he stopped. It wasn't very different, but there was something here. "Rathna?"

She turned. "Something?"

"I'm honestly not sure."

She marked her place by dropping her shawl on the ground, and came over. Then she knelt down, and said, "Do you have your, the thing with the lenses?"

He had his satchel on, and he took it out, then out of the protective case. "Here." He handed it over to her carefully, and backed up, so as not to block the light. She put it on, and he was relieved to see that even with her excitement about whatever she'd found, she was careful with it. Then she arranged the lenses, and peered, angling her neck awkwardly to avoid shadows.

"Hah!" It was jubilant. "If I cared about academic honours, I could get a paper out of that."

It was an odd way to put it, but Gabe had to smile before his curiosity got the best of him. "What is it?"

"That, Gabriel Edgarton, is a fossil. I'm not sure what kind of fossil, I can only see a bit of it. But a fossil."

Gabe blinked at it. He knew the theory of fossils, of course, but they weren't a thing he'd had cause to study, yet. That was apparently about to change rapidly. Before he could say anything, however, there was a deep rumbling from further up the hillside.

It sounded like a thunderstorm rolling in, but the sky was bright blue. Out of the corner of his eye, Gabe saw both horses throw their heads up wildly, and swore under his breath. Without a further word to her, he went to them, doing his best to settle them.

The noise had eased off, but they were still bristling, snorting, their nostrils flaring, all the signs of something truly dangerous, much more so than a wandering sheep. Rathna followed him down after a minute, and said, "Do you know what that was?"

Gabe shook his head. "No. But I'm thinking we should go back to the inn and talk about the next steps, not here." He looked up the mountain. He couldn't see anything dangerous, but that didn't mean anything. Things were generally somewhat less dangerous if you could see them coming.

Rathna looked where he did. "I'll pack up." A better division of labour. "You don't think it was finding the..." She gestured silently.

"I'm not sure." His mind felt itchy, like there was something he wasn't putting together correctly. He'd have to get back and settled and see if he could sort it out. Even if that took a while. He wondered if this was what Geordie had been warning them away from, or if there were more concerns up here than they'd realised. For right now, he busied himself petting the mares. Long steady pats on the neck and shoulders, the kind that relaxed them, reassured them that someone was looking out for them.

SEVENTEEN

By the time Rathna had washed up and changed, Gabriel's door was closed, and she suspected he was downstairs. It was past five, but it was a weeknight, so she thought it wouldn't be too busy yet. No one had been outright awful to her, at least. Rather, they left her thoroughly alone, other than the obvious gossiping. That was fine, she could deal with murmuring. She had for most of her life. The orphanage, Schola, the more polite mutters of the other Portal Keepers until she proved herself competent.

There was a crowd over at the bar, and some sort of darts game in progress. Or at least she assumed it was darts. She couldn't see either the board or what they were throwing at it. She did manage to catch Gormlaith's attention, and got a nod that promised beer and supper. She took out her book, one of the novels she'd brought with her, and tried to settle down. The noise on the portal site had unnerved her, more than a bit.

It would be one thing if they knew what was causing it, but they didn't. Rathna knew about rocks, and geology, and portals, and a number of other things that weren't terribly relevant at the moment, like hidden rivers in London, and the implications of ritual architectural spaces on the flows of magic and energy. She did not, however, know much about what made that kind of sound, or what you did about it.

And she did not know as much as she'd like about fossils. She knew they shouldn't attempt to move the one they'd found, but she didn't have materials to identify it. At least not clearly. She desperately wanted access to a proper library, but that would require someone trekking back to Fort William, and at least back to Glasgow to a portal, if not further.

She had wanted to take the train up, because of the worries about some of the things in her testing case. She could go, or Gabriel could go, but she didn't much want to be out on that hillside by herself, even assuming she could manage Verity on her own. And Gabriel didn't have her skills. Though he might, she supposed, discover something else useful.

That of course, raised the question of what she had with her that might be more useful in identifying whatever it was there. She assumed it was a dinosaur or something equivalent, and not dragon bones, or beithir bones, or something of the kind. If beithir had bones that might fossilise. Or had been around at a point when they might. Dragons had, she knew that, though not many.

The darts game got more heated, she could hear the voices getting louder. Something shifted from the burble of more or less good-natured teasing to something that set her back on edge, immediately. It was nastier, sharper. If she'd been back home, she'd have expected a footie brawl about to spill out into the street. She glanced around, but the men had shifted, a solid wall of backs, and if Gabriel were with them, she couldn't see him.

One voice lifted above the rest. "You're proper cam, then. We'll not play with you."

There was a roar of sound, ten or twenty voices together, rolling over each other, like a thunderstorm crashing and destroying everything in its path. Rathna glanced at the door, to make sure she could get away, trying to judge how quickly she needed to do that. By the time she looked back, there was a sound of something slamming down onto the solidity of the bar, and Eoin Macdonald was bellowing. "Haud yer wheest!" He did it three times, then again and again, and by the fifth time, the roar had quieted to a disgruntled grumble. Whatever the words meant, they worked.

He nodded at someone. "Ye'd best be away." To the others, he said, "Rest of you bloody well settle. Jock, come back Monday." The grumbling got louder, but less angry, as if he'd made the call they wanted him to make.

Gabriel emerged from the crowd, turning his shoulder sideways to slide through the barest gap between the larger men. He headed straight for the stairs, and Rathna followed him. At the top, he paused for an instant, glanced at her, and jerked his head towards his own room. She followed, hoping that someone would remember they hadn't eaten and produce a tray.

By the time she got to his room, Gabriel was sprawled on his bed, as if he'd flung himself bodily on his back, his feet hanging off the edge. She eased the door closed, frowned at it, and then gave up trying to add additional charms for privacy. She suspected whatever she did would do badly with whatever he'd already set. She could feel the faint charge of magic under her fingers.

When she turned back, he said, eyes closed, "Pardon. I played that badly." He sounded utterly disconnected from the world, as if he were discussing some move of chess or bohort or pavo, something that didn't touch him at all.

Rathna looked around, cautiously. The room was on one hand much like hers, more or less a mirror image, but his desk had a dozen books piled on it, as well as a small stack of maps, unevenly folded. He'd apparently brought a portable coatrack with him, because his cloak was hung over it, and she could see several other things peeking through the folds of cloth.

"Are you all right?" It wasn't the right question, not really, but it was the one she had, the one that was polite.

Gabriel pushed himself up on one elbow, then sat up. It was as if he were gathering himself up again, tucking whatever was wrong away. "I expected something more or less like that. I didn't handle it well." He gestured. "Have a seat, I suppose?"

She chose the desk chair, tucking her feet under it, not sure how much space to take up. The space, for all it was an inn room, felt distinctly his, a sense of his presence in a way he didn't actually exude most of the time. As if he'd made a miniature castle here, somehow. Feeling slightly less at sea, she tried again. "What happened?"

"I was playing darts. And doing well enough. Then they took offence, and..." He looked away. "I don't know if you caught that. Called me bent."

Rathna frowned, and then looked at him, up and down. She knew what Morah Avigail's people thought about that sort of thing, and she knew what the laws were about it. But she'd had her suspicions about her house-master at Schola. Not that she'd ever shared them with anyone. He'd been kind to her.

She peered at Gabe for long enough, without saying anything, that he said, "Go ahead and ask." As if he expected her to.

Given that instruction, she couldn't resist. "Are you?"

Gabriel shrugged. "I haven't found it relevant enough to figure out, honestly. I'll need to marry sometime, family reasons." His voice was a curious mix of flatness and humour, as if he'd said something along these lines often enough to begin to find it quietly hilarious. She had even less idea what to do with that than the words themselves.

"But people assume." She didn't make it a question. That much was obvious on first meeting him, even without the events of a few minutes ago.

"People assume all sorts of things. That I'm bent. That I'm weak. That I'm easy pickings." He wriggled a hand. "I don't play bohort or pavo. What I said is true enough, I'm not competitive like that. But I also hate the talk, around the playing. The puffing yourself up, boasting, needing to be bigger than everyone else."

Rathna considered him. "I've been thinking you have a very clear sense of who you are, actually. Not that you share it, exactly." She hurried to add that. "But it's like you know everything around you." She gestured at the door. "Even if that's building yourself a castle."

He caught her meaning quickly, and it won her a momentary smile. "If we get a quiet evening, glad to talk you through the warding methods. Variations based on Woodworth, Hereward, Blake, Fixton, Drumgoole, Asch, and Fredericks." He reeled off the names fluently, like he wanted her to ask about it.

Rathna blinked at that. "Blake and Asch? Goodness, how did you ever reconcile them?" She then glanced at the door. "Not tonight, though. We should sort some things out. Should I go see if I can summon a tray?" She didn't want to go down into that room again, not tonight, but clearly if someone were going to do it, it would need to be her.

Gabriel considered. "I've some supplies in my case. Nothing terribly exciting, but enough to manage til morning. And enough to share."

"You seem to have packed a number of things not on my list." Rathna gestured with one hand at the cloak and whatever it was hanging on.

"Better to be prepared. And as I said, good at various charms helpful in packing."

"We should definitely discuss, if you're willing. Sometime." Then, cautiously, she asked, "Were you afraid downstairs?" It was nagging at her.

Gabriel shook his head. "Not exactly. People can do all sorts of unpredictable things. I didn't think they'd swing at me, not in a way I couldn't duck. They were awfully drunk, this early." His tone was analytical, back to that sense of distance. "But I'd rather not go back down, and I don't want to ask you to go."

It was at that moment there was a knock on the door, three distinct raps. They looked at each other, and Gabriel called out, "Who is it?"

"Gormlaith sent me up. Open up, dearie."

That was not a phrase one expected to hear after a near brawl. Gabriel flung himself off the bed, in a rolling motion that Rathna couldn't make sense out of. One moment he'd been sitting, the next he was at the door, light on his feet, opening it cautiously.

On the other side was an older woman, well into her seventies, with grey hair in a bun, a shawl around her shoulders. "Gormlaith said you'd be wanting a bit of the tales about the beithir. Gather you're better not downstairs. Come along to mine, down the valley. Supper and stories."

It was utterly incongruous. Rathna couldn't help think of all the fairy tales and border ballads she'd ever heard, how strangers offering gifts were not what they seemed. On the other hand, the promise of supper and information, both, appealed, rather a lot.

Gabriel glanced at her, and she gave him a tiny nod.

"Where are we going? How far? And pardon, mistress, your name? I'm Gabriel Edgarton, this is Mistress Rathna Stone." Rathna noticed immediately that she got a title and he didn't.

"I'd be Sorcha Macdonald. I've a cottage, down in the valley. A mile walk."

That would be an annoying slog back, but they'd done worse, clambering around. Gabriel nodded. "That's most kind." He made a slight bow at Rathna. "If you wanted to grab whatever notebook you want, I'll lock up here."

Sorcha cackled, apparently to herself, and went out to the landing to peer down the stairs. She had a cane, Rathna could see, though she leaned on it more heavily than Gabriel did. She went past, to her own room, gathering up her notebook, and her stones, wanting them with her, before she locked the door and set her own warding going. Gabriel was a moment behind her. There was no time to talk through this, they simply had to trust it would work out.

Gabe found himself, thirty minutes later, sat down at a table in a cottage. It was, he thought, a traditional crofter's cottage. There was one room with the hearth and a small stove, a large kitchen table, a few chairs at one end. The other half, he suspected, was her bedroom. If there had been children, they'd either have slept in the front room, or perhaps up in a loft in the rafters. He glanced around and saw a few photographs, but no sign of anyone else living here. No husband living, then.

There were, however, a wide range of herbs hanging from the rafters, drying. Looking around at them, he was fairly sure this was a woman who did more than a fair bit of her own magic. Green magic, the kind that relied on herbs and plants and the harvest of her own hands to guide the magic she had in her blood. The room smelled wonderful. There was mint, heather, and other sharp and herbal smells that made everything feel refreshing and soothing all at once.

They had followed Sorcha down the road, going at her pace, which was thankfully about the speed Gabe was comfortable at, on a dirt road with some uncertain footing. It was still light out, it would be for ages yet, but he was hoping they didn't have to do the whole walk back in the dark. She had bustled about, making tea, stirring soup, and generally being hospitable.

Now, each of them had a steaming bowl in front of them, and a loaf of thick flat bread on the table along with butter and jam. It was capped off with a steaming mug of tea. "Scotch broth." Sorcha said with a nod, when Rathna peered at it cautiously. "Mutton, barley, vegetables."

Rathna smiled at her, relaxing. "It smells wonderful. I didn't realise how hungry I was."

Gabe took a spoonful, then looked up. "Delicious, Sorcha, thank you. Much appreciated, beyond that."

That got him a cheerful cackle. She set to her own bowl for a few bites, before she glanced from one to the other. "So, Gormlaith was telling me you're interested in the old stories." She gestured toward the mountain in question. "Grew up here, this cottage. Lived in the lea of it all my life, except for my schooling."

Gabe blinked for a moment, and she added, as if she'd been waiting to drop that piece of information. "Alethorpe. Local healer, me, near enough. At least to keep going on with until someone else could get here. I was midwife to Gormlaith's mum, and Eoin's, and most of the younger folk round here." For values of younger that stretched into their forties, if not fifties, then.

Gabe nodded slightly at her. "How far around?"

"This whole side of the loch, dearie, up to Kinlochleven."

Gabe thought about that, the distance. "How many magical folk, then?"

It made her laugh hard enough she had to stop eating.

"Oh, lad, we've more flexible lines than most. We keep the Pact, the Silence. But plenty round here with a touch of magic in their blood, enough for second sight or spotting a magical hart, or what have you. Plenty who'll gladly take my salves and teas, and if they work a bit better than the herbs should, no one thinks too much on it."

It made him grimace, thinking through the implications, but Rathna picked up. "So, plenty of people know about the stories, of the beithir?" She paused, just a beat. "That's not just people having us on?" Gabe was impressed. She managed just the right sort of tone, just a little cautious, but friendly.

Sorcha laughed again. She was a woman who liked a laugh. "Oh, quite real. It was, anyway. There're legends every few feet, here. D'you know about the massacre, when?"

Gabe shook his head. "Only the barest mention."

That got a more sombre nod. "Back in 1692, after the rising. You ken the rising?"

He nodded. "The Jacobite rising." He tilted his head, trying to remember. Scottish history wasn't particularly favoured in any of his education, but he'd picked up a bit here and there. "James the Second went into exile, just before that. And there was fighting, and some complicated set of agreements and oaths."

"We'd be calling him James the Seventh, lad, but that's fair enough. The Maclain of Glencoe was supposed to swear the oath, went off, told he was supposed to swear it somewhere else. All to make for trouble, the way I see it. They sent troops out, plenty of whom had reasons not to like our folk. Cattle raids, other raids, all that." She waved away what Gabe knew had been several centuries of skirmishes, at the least, with a flip of her fingers. "And the troops came, and one day, ordered to kill everyone in Glencoe. Men, women, children, babes in arms."

Rathna hadn't heard this before, apparently, because she sucked in a breath, "Here?"

"Up and down the glen. Near enough here. But some of the men, they had a decent heart in them, and they turned up late. There's tales about a few passing on a warning, as much as they could, so people could go to the hills. But thirty-eight souls killed, crofts burned, all their things taken." She shook her head. "That's the first tale, that explains it here."

Gabe nodded slowly at that. "Not the last, though."

Sorcha snorted. "Well, not the first, either. The beithir's before that, probably. Gormlaith said she'd told you that, more or less. The mountain, and the cart."

Rathna nodded. "That much, yes. Do you think they're still around?"

"I've not seen them, but I've not seen plenty of things that are real enough. Could be a private sort of wyrm." She shrugged. "But if so, maybe that door shook things up. I know we're needing one, I was one who said we do, after the Scourge. It's a terrible long trip, to get supplies here, someone to help, if there's a great illness."

Gabe had been chewing on something. "It seems an awfully small village, beside the quarry. To put a portal here, not in so many other places."

Sorcha turned her head, peering at him, rather like a raven might. "True, true." She shrugged. "We've our own lord, built a grand house nearby, trees to be harvested, the quarry. And men like that, they have their powers and their comforts."

Gabe gestured with one hand, in the approximate direction. "Strathcona, isn't it?" He added to Rathna. "Scottish, but spent a lot of time in Canada. Not magical that I've ever heard, and I think I would have." He waved his hand at Sorcha. "That would explain a rail line, but not a portal, no?"

Sorcha shrugged. "Powerful men, who can tell what they take a fancy to."

Gabe couldn't argue with that and sensibly didn't. Instead, he said, "Any other places we should know about? Ossian's cave, I've heard about that, but not been up, not yet."

"Plenty of smaller tales." She then glanced over and asked Rathna. "Do you know why the portal's there, then?"

Rathna made a frustrated sound, blowing her hair out of her face. "No. The notes are not much help. Do you have an idea? Did you help, with the sites?"

"Ah, the like of him wouldn't listen to the like of me. Old enough to think he knew it all."

It made Rathna smile. "I didn't know him well, but I gather he was a stubborn old man, especially his later years. Though what he was stubborn about, that varied."

Sorcha pushed back from the table, going to fuss with something on the stove. Gabe lifted his hand, silently, spotting this as a chance for her to think, and instead said, "This is a wonderful meal, Sorcha, much appreciated. The bread is wonderful."

"I suppose you don't get bannock, then, where you're from."

Gabe shook his head, and Rathna picked up. "I've heard about it, but never had a chance to try." That sort of talk carried them through until Sorcha returned to the table, rather visibly having girded herself for one last bit of information.

"There's one more thing. Not a legend, something else." Her voice was cautious.

Rathna spoke before Gabe could. "We don't tell people where we got information. Either of us. They might guess, I suppose, but - we won't tell."

Sorcha looked from one to the other, then nodded once, as if making a decision. "Well, then." She gestured. "Man came, a year or two before the portal. I could sort out the date if I looked at my records, I suppose." Her voice trailed off. "Thought a lot of some mineral, there. Something unusual. First found here."

Rathna frowned at that, and Gabe caught it. Not something she knew. He picked up the conversation. "Not a thing they mine, though? From the quarries?"

"Magic, no. That's slate, the quarries. Not the best quality, mind, but plenty of it, they don't mind the waste." She shook her head. "Seems awful to me, digging down like that, but no one's asking me, and it keeps plenty with food on the table and a roof over their head."

Gabe nodded. "So something else. Thank you. That gives us something new to look for." He then coughed and added. "I told Gormlaith we'd gladly pay for information, and you've been rather helpful. I'd be very pleased to make sure you could restock your tea."

The last sentence shifted her from dubiousness to a smile. "Ah, observant, you are, lad. I am a tad low, true." She shrugged slightly. "People pay for my work, I suppose this isn't too different. Not more than you'd give someone else, though, and I'll be asking for the gossip.'"

"No more than anyone else." He rummaged in his pocket, pulling out the coins. He slid them across the table, and she gathered them up, nimbly enough. "I suppose we should get back. An early start tomorrow, and I'd rather walk in the light."

She looked him up and down, and said, "That leg of yours, not an easy injury." It wasn't a question. Gabe rocked a little with it, the way she went right for the point where it would move him. Near enough physically.

"No, ma'am." It came out instinctively, but she'd been kind, and she was certainly due respect for half a dozen reasons. "I muddle along."

That got him another sharp look before she shook her head. "Finish up, and I'll wrap up a bannock or two for ye. Go along then."

Ten minutes later, they had made their final goodbyes, and were back up the hill. When they got to the inn, thankfully, no one was lingering in the entry hall, and they could slip upstairs without further comment.

NINETEEN

TUESDAY, BY THE PORTAL

The next day, they climbed up to the portal again, in silence. Neither of them had said much over breakfast, and Rathna wasn't sure what to make of that.

The site was undisturbed, at least visibly. The fossil was where they'd left it. Rathna sat down on the ground near it, pulling out her notebook and doing her best to make a sketch, before she looked up. "Can you sketch that? Precisely? With measurements?"

"If you give me the measurements, sure." He tilted his head. "You think there's something in that?"

"Possibly. What I want is a good geological library. But that would mean someone going back to Trellech. Possibly London, the Natural History Museum. But I don't have good connections there. I'd have to go through the Portal Keeper's Guild."

There was a longer silence than she'd expected, and when she looked down, Gabriel had his head down. If she hadn't known better, she'd have thought he was avoiding her. Before she could say anything, he glanced up. "I would be glad to go. Use my connections. You'd have to be clear what you were looking for, but I can take notes, or do duplication charms, if I get a chance."

She considered him. "Even in the museum? I mean. Do you know how to deal with non-magical folk?"

He shrugged for a moment, a twitch of the shoulder. "My oaths to the Silence work like anyone else's." There was something quite odd in his tone, but Rathna didn't press him. "And I'm well trained in libraries. Mostly, one makes an appointment with the relevant librarian, and flings oneself on their expertise."

Rathna had to admit that Gabriel was charming, that his presentation would likely go over well enough in London, and that he could be most engagingly curious. "Well, and if you go, you can, what, ride up to Fort William?"

"Ride to Fort William, train to Glasgow, portal from there. I'd rather not do a same-day trip, mind, that's a long haul, and I'd be coming back in the dark. Can you manage if I'm gone for a night? Or would you rather come with?"

Part of her wanted to retreat to something she understood, but both of them going was a waste. And she wasn't at all sure how to negotiate going somewhere with him, either. "How about I arrange with Gormlaith for trays in my room. I can spend some time writing up all the notes and going through what I brought with me. Tidying up the loose ends."

Gabriel looked up, and there was a sudden smile, as if he'd been a bit worried she'd insist on coming up to the portal by herself. Or perhaps coming with him. "That would do nicely. And I can make notes on the train."

"Do you - I mean, you must have rooms in Trellech."

"I mentioned my parents have a townhouse, I have my own set of rooms there. I'll work around to my own flat sometime, but it's convenient, and I can grab a sandwich when I'm working late, which is rather often."

Rathna considered. It rather implied staff, as well as the room, but she wasn't sure how to ask. "Will your parents be there? I mean, you were asking your mother about, about. Vivek." She hadn't been able to stop thinking about him, the implications of him.

Gabriel shrugged. "I can go hunt them down, if I need to. If Mama's not in Trellech, she'll be at - in Kent." He paused. "Do you want me to take a letter to anyone else? Or drop it in Trellech, so it goes through quick?"

"Morah Avigail, if you would." She hesitated. She'd prefer to ask him to take it round, but adding Spitalfields to his list seemed rather out of the way.

He considered it, as if he were running a map in his head. "I should be able to take it to her, if the portal traffic isn't too bad. At the least, I can drop it at the Trellech portal. Write up as much as you'd like and let me know how to find her?"

She smiled at him, suddenly. Being cut off had felt awful, and she was, she admitted, still more than a little worried about Morah Avigail's health. That settled, she gestured. "So, what we want to do, ideally, is identify this fossil. Do you think you can manage to come off as an amateur geology sort, out here hiking, stumbled across something interesting?"

He considered that and then nodded. "If you tell me what the terminology is. Or lend me a book I can read on the train. I admit geology's not something that's come up often. I'll have to mention the lack."

"To your Aunt Mason?"

She was startled by his sudden grin. "Oh, yes. She'll be annoyed she left it out of my notes. No problem, I like tweaking her nose. Metaphorically." He gestured. "I'll be a bit at the sketching, to do it right, if you have something else you want to do."

Rathna stood, brushing off her skirts. "I'm curious about whatever that mineral was, they mentioned. My notes had a little about it, something called withamite, but I don't know much about it. That will be the other main line of questioning."

"Not common, then?"

"No, not common at all. I'll want to know the composition, and whatever properties it has that have been identified, where it's found, what it looks like."

The last one made him laugh again. "I suppose that would be a help, rather." He made a few more passes with his pencil. "So what else should I research, or ask about? I can set Mama to some of it, or one of the Penelopes, if we need someone to do more work on it."

Rathna shook her head. "I feel, on the whole, the brief was entirely inadequate. And I suppose they probably don't have a great deal of reliable folklore for the area in Trellech."

"It would probably be better not to rely on it." He seemed very amused. "I mean, maybe the Trellech Library. Or the Guard Library. But that would be a longer visit."

"Is the Guard Library any good?" She was curious, she'd never had a chance to see it.

He took a long time to answer, as if he were sorting through what to say. "I think it could be a lot better, but the current head librarian is close to retirement. He's the sort not inclined to change. And there is a lot of good material there, if you know how to find it."

She snorted. "And you do, I'm quite sure."

He grinned at her again, that flash of something like sunlight. "I have my ways. In this case, Aunt Mason and Aunt Witt and Doyle initiated me in the mysteries. It's got an entirely unique shelving system. And of course, the kind of things the Guard care about, and the kinds of things anyone else cares about, they aren't always the same."

"Plenty on, oh, catching criminals?" She said it lightly, but there was a sudden stiffness in his shoulders. "Something else?" She wasn't sure if she should apologise.

"The Guard does plenty besides arresting people. Warding, a fair bit of the infrastructure support, one way or another. Locks, bridges, the city walls. Not the portals, but the spaces about them, so they work well. Sorting things out."

She nodded, and then couldn't quite leave it alone. "A sore spot?"

Gabriel was quiet. She could hear the scratching on the paper. Just about the point where she was going to go away for a bit. He spoke again, his voice resolutely even. "Papa has a bit of an insistence about it. Though, admittedly, Papa is a bit of a romantic."

It seemed a very odd thing to say about one's father, not that Rathna was the right person to pass judgement on it. "I'm glad." She swallowed. "The police in London, the ones I've seen. It's all about safety and criminals, and keeping the wrong element from getting out of hand. I'm sorry if I misstated."

He looked up at her. "Accepted." There was a new note there, now, something that wasn't the civil kindness she'd come to expect from him. He wasn't upset, exactly, but it was as if her mis-stepping and apologising had changed something for him. Though, of course, it was hard to tell by a single word.

"Papa takes his Guard's oath very seriously. All his oaths. And I grew up around the Guard. Here and there, someone breaks their oaths, but not that often. Your London bobbies, they don't have quite the same origin."

That made her stop and think. "Not from the same source, then. They wouldn't be, I suppose."

"Papa has a long spiel he gives apprentices, when he's got one. All about the origins of the Guard, and about how thinking about it as a knightly order isn't too far wrong. Protecting the people who can't protect themselves. Sometimes that's non-magical folk from magic. Well, like the beithir. Sometimes it's criminals, yes. But a lot of their work is being available, when people need a hand. The brash folks, the ones who want to charge into something without figuring out what's going on, they don't last."

She had not thought of it that way at all. She was cautious around anyone with a uniform, she had been since the orphanage. They'd come to represent someone with power over her. Whether it was the staff at the orphanage, or the constables on the way to and from school, they hadn't wanted to spend time sorting anything out they didn't have to. They'd just made assumptions.

She'd had less trouble than the boys. People always assumed boys, especially with skin like hers or darker, were up to no good if they lingered near a shop. And with Morah Avigail's family, she'd heard far too many stories of soldiers in other places, mostly in Eastern Europe. About soldiers who'd used all their power to terrify and burn and kill.

Rathna didn't think she would ever be likely to meet Gabriel's father. Or his mother. But if he was an example of the kind of person who'd grown up around the Guard, maybe they were like he said. Or at least the ones he knew.

She then cleared her throat. "I'll go do all my measurements. Yell when you're ready for lunch, right?" That would give them both space for a couple of hours, likely. He was no more inclined to stop early than she was. Perhaps by then she could come up with some safer topic.

TWENTY

Gabriel ran his hand through his hair, wondering how to go about this. He had had a long day already, the train down to Glasgow then to Trellech for a quick stop to consult with Aunt Mason. As he'd expected, she hadn't had immediate solutions to any of their problems, but the promise of a beithir had her quite excited. There was apparently something interesting in both the venom and the bone structure.

She'd enthusiastically agreed to send along whatever notes she could round up in the next few days. The mail was reaching them reasonably promptly, at least. Of course, Aunt Mason had asked him about the portal keeper, and what he could share. For once, he found himself not inclined to talk. Gabriel knew he was an amiable conversationalist. He'd near enough been bred to be one, along with his magic and capacity to inherit the title in some hopefully far future day. But he wasn't sure he wanted to talk about Rathna. Not right now, anyway.

it wasn't that he couldn't. Most of what they talked

about was about the current case before them, and he'd be writing it up in his report, eventually. Not the details of the portals. There were, he was coming to feel, good reasons those weren't lightly shared. And not her personal business.

Even if he thought Aunt Mason might understand. She wasn't Indian; he knew that quite well. When he'd first met her, he'd wondered about where she came from. His mother had been clear that she was of Albion, and that was what mattered. Then, she'd sat him down with books about the Dutch East Indies Company, and a place called Indonesia. Or at least it was now.

When Aunt Mason's grandparents were there, people called it half a dozen things, but mostly the Malay Archipelago. That fact had got him on a long exploration of the way place names changed over time. It was followed promptly by who decided what places got called in the first place, and what an archipelago was, and why one might be interesting. He'd spent a good six weeks of bothering Cook to make things with different spices so he could learn properly what they tasted like. He had, he admitted now, been a small terror as a child.

Of course, he was quite sure he wasn't fooling Aunt Mason, but she hadn't pressed him further. He was sure she'd get him eventually. She always did. The sun rose, the sun set, Aunt Mason noticed things. He wasn't sure what she'd tease out from him, but there would be something. There always was. Perhaps by the time she put the effort in, he'd be able to figure out why he didn't want to talk about Rathna and be ready for it.

He'd had time to stop by his father's office for five minutes, but only five, before Papa was expected at a meeting. That was easier to manage. Papa was not nearly as observant as Aunt Mason, not unless he was duelling or focused on one of his current cases, but he noticed things. It just took longer. He'd handed over a letter for Mama as well as the one for Papa, and one for Charlotte.

He'd worked on them on the train, so they were entirely up to date about the things he talked about with his parents. Scenery, the stunning red deer, the legend of the beithir. He'd done a few sketches for Charlotte, of the deer and the glen, she'd like those. He hadn't mentioned his trouble in the pub, or much about Rathna, other than that she was pleasant to work with, and he was learning a fair bit.

They'd ask him more, but like Aunt Mason, they'd wait until a better time. Once he left the Guard Hall, he wished he had time to stop by and see Uncle Magni and Uncle Gil. But he didn't have time to trek out to their home, outside of Trellech, and they might well not be there anyway.

Uncle Magni had retired from the Guard, but from not from teaching duelling, and Uncle Gil often was researching in one library or collection or another. He did drop two letters to go to them in the post box outside the Guard Hall, and they'd get them tonight.

It was lunchtime by then, so he grabbed something, a meat pie, from the food stalls in Portal Square. Eating it, sitting on the bench, while he waited for the next portal to Southwark, he watched the portals, thinking about what Rathna had told him about the different types.

He wondered if they felt different, or if you felt the difference if you were going between two portals of the same type more, or different types more. Or if there were other qualities. There were all manner of things that couldn't go through a portal without disrupting their magic, and he wondered if anyone had ever tested the effect thoroughly. Perhaps the age of the portal mattered, it was possible there were generational changes or some such thing.

Finally, his slot came up. There was no convenient way to get to the Natural History Museum in London from any of the portals. Southwark meant he was less likely to run into various aristocratic scions who didn't understand that he had a schedule to keep and certainly didn't want to be flirted with.

His plan was to go from Southwark to the museum by bus. Then he'd do the research, hopefully get a list of books available for purchase, get them in Southwark. If he timed things right, he'd have time to call on Mistress Levy in Spitalfields before taking the portal there back to Glasgow. That way he could get a train back first thing in the morning.

Much of the plan went well enough. He'd had a reader's ticket at the British Museum reader's room since before he began his apprenticeship, all the Penelopes did. Though in his case it had been decidedly awkward until he was of age. He gathered the library staff thought he must be some sort of prodigy, to have a ticket signed by the Principal Librarian directly.

The Penelopes didn't need to consult non-magical sources terribly often, but some rare books were only available there. And sometimes you just needed a copy of a sixteenth century *sortes* book full of entirely ridiculous theories on divination for a single paragraph. At any rate, it made handling things at the Natural History Museum much easier.

It took him quite some time to copy out what he wanted, and to get the bibliography list from the librarian. He made it back to Southwark before the bookshops closed, and was able to pick up all of the most recommended titles. Two others would be sent along promptly to Aunt Mason, who could forward them as needed.

That meant that at half-six, he was standing outside Mistress Levy's home - and Rathna's - trying to decide how to handle this call. In the end, he knocked, smartly. There was a fair chance Mistress Levy was at supper, but at least he could deliver Rathna's note directly, and see if there was a message in reply.

The door was opened, cautiously, by a middle-aged woman. A small establishment, then, to have what he suspected was a single maid. She looked at him, entirely dubious.

"Good evening. I am Gabriel Edgarton, I am working with Mistress Stone at the moment. I have a letter for Mistress Levy from her, and I would be glad to take one back, if she wishes."

Whatever it was the maid was expecting, it was not that. She looked him up and down, then bobbed in something that was not quite a curtsey. "If you would come in and wait, sir." Her voice had an accent to it, something he wasn't overly familiar with, but with a Germanic roundness to the vowels, perhaps. He came in. A mirrored table stood to one side, a chair on the wall beside it. Both his knee and ankle were complaining a bit, all the walking today, and much of it on hard surfaces and uneven cobbles. But he suspected, if Mistress Levy were at home to a guest, she would appear out of nowhere.

He was not entirely wrong. The maid disappeared upstairs, and five minutes later, there was a creak on the staircase, and Mistress Levy came down. She was slow, stately, using a cane like his mother did, rather than the way

Gabe did. A cane for balance, for fatigue, for support, rather than one to prop up a particular injury.

Gabe stood, his weight as evenly balanced as he could arrange, his own cane along his left leg. He bowed, properly and formally, junior to senior, in the sort of precise etiquette that either pleased the elder generation, the ones who remembered Victoria in her youth, or at least amused them.

In this case it amused, and she waved her hand. "Come, come." She nodded toward one of the side rooms, what must be the parlour. She had the same rhythm to her voice. He did not know much about the Jewish community here, other than that there was one. And he had not been able to brush up beyond the few things Rathna had let slip.

He followed, letting her settle down in what was clearly her personal throne, a comfortable wing chair of a deep burgundy. Gabe waited a moment, then presented the sealed letter Rathna had given him, with a slight bow, before retreating to the facing settee that was clearly intended for a guest.

She looked him up and down. "Edgarton, I presume?"

Gabe nodded. "Penelope Gabriel Edgarton. I gather assumptions were made by the Ministry chap." He said it as dryly as he could and was rewarded with a flash of amusement. "Rathna was startled, when we met."

Mistress Levy nodded, and then passed her hand over the seal, and it gave way. "Beg pardon."

"Of course. Rathna is quite well. I apologise for bothering you in the evening, but she was hoping I might get the letter directly to you."

That got him an absent-minded nod, and Gabe settled in to observe the room as unobtrusively as he could. The room, Mistress Levy, and whatever else he might notice. There were photographs on the mantelpiece, various collections of a large family who looked very like Mistress Levy. Rathna was in a few of them, what looked like the past ten or fifteen years, at what might be weddings or some other similar celebration. The room was a little small, a little overly Victorian for his tastes, but well laid out, with bookshelves on any wall that could hold them.

There was a rustle of paper, and then she cleared her throat. "Do you go back tonight?"

"I was planning on going from here to Glasgow, but I could call first thing in the morning, if you'd like more time to write, Mistress."

There was a single nod. "It will take me some time. She has questions. I wake early, call any time after half six."

That was awfully early, but it would let him get to Glasgow in time for the morning train. "Of course, Mistress Levy. Right around then, I suspect."

She nodded. "And you have somewhere to stay?" It was a polite question, though he suddenly suspected that if he said no, there would be a guest bed made up.

"I've rooms in Trellech, I'll go back there." He could go home to Kent, proper home, where he'd grown up, but that would mean talking to his parents. In Trellech, he could get a late supper from Cook, curl up with a book, and enjoy a properly comfy bed in his own space with no questions asked.

Mistress Levy nodded "Half six. I will have some reference materials for her as well, if you can take them."

"Of course. I know she'll appreciate that. And I will as well."

That got him another flash of the smile, and then a little dismissive nod. "A pleasure to meet you, Master Edgarton." She gave him his other proper title, the one he'd earned.

He stood, and bowed once, the proper formal bow

again. "Likewise, Mistress Levy. It's been delightful to work with Rathna, and see how skilled she is." As long as one wasn't asking her to ride anywhere difficult, at least. Then he withdrew, for the last portal hop of the evening, and the hopes of a good sturdy supper.

Rathna had spent a day and a half cooped up in her room, and much of that half staring out the window. It was frustrating and annoying. She didn't know precisely when to expect Gabriel back, or when she should start worrying.

And she couldn't go downstairs. Even without the other concerns, Gormlaith had mentioned there had been a new man. He had said he was there to hike on to Fort William, but Gormlaith thought that wasn't the whole story. It might be something totally innocent, but Rathna figured an innkeeper's wife saw plenty of people come through.

He was a white man, Gormlaith had said. Or rather, she hadn't commented on the colour of his skin, just his ginger hair, and that he wasn't Scottish. That meant he wasn't Vivek, but it might be someone else who didn't intend anything good.

When the knock finally came, around two in the afternoon, she was lying on her bed, contemplating whether a nap would be worth trying. She startled, pushing herself to sit up, and tug the wisps that had escaped from her braid. "Come in?"

Gabriel put his head around the door, then came all the way in. "Sorry to be later than I hoped. Mistress Levy wanted to take the evening to write to you, so I went by first thing this morning."

"Very early, I'm guessing." She snorted. "She likes being up early." Then she blinked. "Wait, you met her?"

Gabriel nodded. "Briefly. She didn't ask me much." He came over and handed her the letter, promptly.

Rathna couldn't help but ask. "Did she seem all right?" The moment it was out of her mouth, she realised how personal a question it was. Not just about Morah Avigail, but about Gabriel, bringing him into her worries.

He settled down cautiously on the desk chair, perching. "You've been worried about her." He didn't put it as a question. "I went by around seven last night, and she came downstairs to see me. I introduced myself, handed over your letter, she read it briefly, and said she'd want longer to respond, could I come by in the morning. Only, you know, more expectation than request."

Rathna laughed at that, she couldn't help it, despite being startled Morah Avigail had come downstairs. "I know the precise tone, yes. And you said you could?"

"I did. She asked if I had somewhere to stay, actually. I went back to my rooms in Trellech, but would she have made up the spare bed for me? Or had Sarah do it, anyway?"

Rathna nodded. "She takes hospitality seriously. In her way."

Gabriel nodded and looked thoughtful. "I suspect she'd have a fascinating conversation with my mother about that, actually. Mama has very strong ideas about being hospitable. At any rate, I went back to Trellech, came back at half six, and made it to Glasgow for the early train in plenty of time."

She turned the letter over in her hands, and he stood, immediately. "I'll let you read it. I assume we're not going out to the site this afternoon? I have books, when you're ready."

Rathna nodded. "Let me read, first." Time enough to tell him about strange men downstairs later. He nodded once and left without comment.

Morah Avigail had written several pages, though her normally precise handwriting got a bit ragged by the third. The letter began by addressing the various questions about the portal, and Rathna's ideas for what to do next. And theories about the implications of the fossils, which was rather more help.

There were pages - she must have been up half the night - about the implications of the fossils and the volcanic caldera. Normally, you wouldn't get both in the same place. Morah Avigail had included sketches, but she had laid out the theory of a great inland sea, laying down the blanket of fossils, then a volcano forming afterwards.

The notes wondered whether that might be the reason for the location, that the portal was set where the rocks changed from volcanic to sedimentary, with those possible veins of withamite. Morah Avigail had gestured at half a dozen magical theories that might be proven or disproven by this, listing off the references and related portals. It was a tremendous feat of knowledge and expertise, especially given Rathna knew this was not a topic that came up often. However, there were no answers, just a long list of things Rathna should investigate properly.

More observation, ideally at different times of day and

night, some specific tests, a mention that she had handed that Penelope Edgarton a book that might be of use. The phrasing made her smile. But once the business was concluded, Morah Avigail noted that the young man had been suitably polite. If a bit inclined to linger on the family photos while waiting for her. Morah Avigail certainly hadn't missed a thing. There was nothing about Vivek, neither good nor bad, and Rathna had no idea what to make of that.

She read the letter through again, sitting at her desk, so she could take notes of the specific approaches to try. Then she went across to knock on Gabriel's door. He called out "Come in?" very promptly. He had a stack of books on the end of the bed, sorted roughly into piles. She blinked at them, distracted. "I didn't expect you to come back with books."

"I copied out sections from ones in the library and got them to tell me which ones I could probably buy. Then I went and bought them. There's two more they'll be sending along to Aunt Mason. She said she could sort out how to get them up here promptly."

The assumptions in those three sentences rocked her back. "You bought..."

"The Penelopes have a budget for that sort of thing. I'm fairly sure your lot must, too? But if you'd rather, we can put them through on my side, and they'll disappear into our collection of books. I'm not sure it's fair to call it a library, it's a bit slapdash and chaotic. Book piles?" He waved a hand.

"I, I suppose." She actually didn't really know how that worked. No one had ever sat her down and explained it. Perhaps she could figure out how to ask. Then she coughed. "There's someone downstairs in the inn Gormlaith didn't care for. I don't know if he's staying on." She then considered. "Which would mean up here. Well, that's not good."

"It is not a large inn, no." He frowned. "Are you - would you rather be somewhere else?"

Rathna took a breath, letting it out slowly. "There isn't anywhere else, though. Even if it were polite to ask Sorcha, she doesn't have room. We can't go into Glencoe village."

"No, and no." Gabriel nodded. "But I have a tent."

Rathna blinked at him, opening her mouth, closing it, and blinking some more. Finally, weakly, she said, "A tent?"

He nodded. "Quite a nice tent, actually."

Of course, if he were going to carry around a tent, it would be nice. She was sure of that. "Where would we put this tent?"

"Ah, now, that's a good question. I'm not sure either of us is fond of the idea of near the portal. Mind, Aunt Mason did help me get some sets of warding stones out of the quartermaster."

She vaguely knew what quartermasters did, and she supposed the Penelopes must have access to the Guard stores. Warding stones, that was a different conversation, and not one she was sure she was up for right now. "The question being whether they work on a beithir."

"Quite. And I'd rather experiment in the daylight, when we're awake and alert. We could take it to the flats, by the river. Or we could go along off to the bothy and have the tent for comfort..." He waved a hand. "I'd rather not sleep in the bothy, honestly, the tent smells nicer. But one of us could if you'd prefer a bit more privacy." He let his voice trail off, clearly sensitive to the fact she might not want to share with him.

Rathna hesitated at that, thinking. The fact he admitted he had no particular surety about his preferences, or even if he had them, was a point in his favour, if a notably perplexing one. Surely that was the sort of thing a person might know. And he'd conducted himself well so far. That was several dozen more points. She was quite certain he wouldn't do anything without her permission, even if he were inclined. And he didn't seem at all inclined.

"Let's see how it goes, if we've got options. Do you think one place is better than the other?"

"If you'd like options, the bothy. There is a divider in the tent, just fabric, but still...." His voice trailed off. "But if you don't care, I'd prefer the river."

"What do we need, then?"

"Food. To let Gormlaith or Eoin know where we're going. I suppose we should walk, rather than take the horses, unless someone could ride with us and bring them back."

Rathna was baffled. "How do we do that without going downstairs?"

Rather than answer, Gabriel got up and went to go peer out his window. The desk was in the way, so he leaned over, rather far. "I've got a rope, it should be fine." He spoke in a breezy tone that was either confidence or an utter disregard for his own well-being. Quite possibly both.

She looked from the window to him. "Wouldn't it, aren't there notice-me-not charms? Surely you know them."

"People can see through them. Especially if they're looking for you. Far safer to go out the window and knock on the kitchen door."

Rathna said dryly, "Your definitions of safer make me wonder, Gabriel."

He gave her another of those flashing grins. "I didn't break my ankle climbing. I'm quite good at it, I promise."

She could see she was not going to manage to convince

him. "All right. What should I pack? And what do you propose about how to get me down?"

"Oh, I'm thinking I let myself down, maybe our bags too. Then I'll go chat with Gormlaith and Eoin, get them to distract the uncertain visitor while you come down, and we can go from there."

She had to admit it was quite a sensible plan, other than the part about going out the window, but he seemed insistent on that, even positively gleeful. Rathna let out a breath. "Right. I suppose we need to move the desk? Do you want to clear your things?"

Gabriel shrugged. "Packing, then the desk and rope, and then we'll go from there. Warm things, it will get chilly at night, even with the charms. Light's no problem. Anything you might want for the site in the morning. Change of clothes." He rattled it off without judging her, not like she might forget something, more like he was ticking off things in his head. Given that she felt she'd have forgotten warm things, or a change of clothes, she considered that generous.

They reconvened twenty minutes later. His saddle bags were full, and he had an additional tubular bag that must be the tent. Though how he'd fit it in his trunk, she had no idea. It seemed quite long, though not very heavy. He had a coil of rope ready to go. "When everything's down, undo the rope, and I'll bring that with us. Do you trust the lock on your room, or do you want me to add something that bites a bit?"

Rathna contemplated for about a second. "Add whatever you like." She didn't know much about his protections, but he knew more than she did. He went across to her room, then stopped at the door. He did something with his hands that smelt for just a moment like the metallic taste just before a thunderstorm, and felt like the shudder that came with a roll of thunder. Then he dusted off his hands, did something to his own door, and added, "When you go down, pull the door closed behind you."

Moving the desk was easy, and he'd tidied everything off of it. Five minutes later, he had the rope attached, and he had unlatched the window and lowered their bags. Then he was slipping through the window with a wave. "See you downstairs." He was deceptively strong for his build, lowering himself slowly and steadily, down to the ground. Once he was down, he waved up at her, and she untied the rope, fumbling with it, before dropping it out the window.

Gabe thought the early evening had gone really rather well. He had climbed down from the window very deftly, and Eoin and Gormlaith had been very helpful. They'd sent one of the younger men who could use a bit of extra coin along with them, Coll. He'd had a pony cart, so they hadn't had to haul everything along to the river themselves. Gabe had paid him well, and Coll had made it clear he'd keep his mouth shut.

Then, it was all about setting up the tent and setting out the wards Aunt Mason had given him. The wards were simple enough, four square stones carved with symbols that matched each compass point.

The tent took a bit more effort, honestly. It was a comfortable two-person model, with space for a well-padded bedroll for each of them, a line of fabric down two-thirds of the centre for a bit of privacy. He found a suitable bit of flat ground. Rathna had been glad to do her share, helping him remove the rocks, then holding the tent in place as he arranged the poles. Magic helped, of course, they were designed to be obediently stable and sturdy.

Other charms and enchantments, woven into the fabric, made it fold up far smaller than one might think. As did the bedrolls, which were partly an ingenious series of layers of wool and cloth, and partly a charm that filled those internal channels with air.

Gormlaith had included a hamper, with plenty to keep them well fed until supper the next night, and said she'd see about someone to help them get back. It was a good plan. Even with the window.

Now, however, they had an evening to spend, and Gabe wasn't entirely sure where to start. They had ended up settled on a pair of flat rocks near the river, for a lack of anything better to do. It was not yet twilight, and the tent was well back from the road, by a little grove of trees that mostly hid it from view. He felt safe enough to focus on the river rather than watch for possible trouble.

The silence grew and grew before Rathna spoke. It wasn't anything he expected, but instead a question. "What is that?"

Gabe followed the line of her hand, pointing at a shape moving along the banks of the river, coming over toward them. It was a modest size, bigger than a house cat, smaller than a truly large dog. The way the ears were set, to the sides of the top of the head, that angle was a little different. He watched it come closer. The light was still good enough he could see the lines of stripes, a tabby effect of the fur, but somehow different than the few tabby cats he had known.

He rummaged in his cloak pocket, pulling out his field notebook, where he'd copied in the relevant material during his preparation for this trip. Flipping through the pages, he ran his finger down the lists, and then said. "Huh. They're not common, but that's a Scottish wildcat. It must be."

"A cat? Someone's pet?"

"Wildcat." Gabe couldn't help smiling. "We don't know a lot about them, but they were recognised as a species, oh, 1907. It's thought they're related to the Asian Wildcat, and the African." It looked, if anything, more like a tiger than a domestic cat, a stocky body, a large head. The tail, now he could see it, was unusually thick and fluffy.

Rathna leaned forward, peering at it. "It's not like a house cat, is it? Much bigger, for one thing."

She was quite right. Rather a lot bigger, near twice the size of an average house cat. "There's a rare treat, then. The deer, now this."

"You don't have a speciality in summoning wild animals, do you? Like the fairy tales?" Rathna's voice was a mix of curiosity and uncertainty, as if she didn't know what to do if he said yes.

"A strong interest, yes. The ability to call them to my hand, no. I'm actually rather partial to badgers, but not up close, ta." The cat came a bit closer, to within about twenty feet of them, then turned and went off, as if to stalk something in the taller grass.

She waved her hand, taking in the notebook, the cat, the spot down the river where they'd come close to the deer. "You just seem more like a naturalist than a Penelope, sometimes."

Gabe shrugged. "A lot of the Penelopes are interested in nature. Both so we can identify things when they come up in cases, and so we know where our reagents and materials come from, or should come from."

There was a pause, as if she were tracking something down in her memory. "That's why you were late. You went over to somewhere, Skye, for things." She felt as if she were trying to articulate a magical theorem in class. "So the location matters, sometimes, for you?"

"It depends, but yes. Things from smaller islands some-times matter. Locational charm components, some naviga-tional ones."

"Not a thing I know a lot about. My stones, yes, I know where those came from." She admitted more quietly, "Mostly not top spots, or they're not gem quality."

Gabe had assumed that, especially having seen Mistress Levy's home. Workmanlike, tended to, certainly well-kept, but gem-quality stones like the set he'd been given when he started his apprenticeship were an expensive thing.

He'd spent years building up a working collection that didn't lead to difficult conversations when he was collabo-rating with someone touchy about their materials. For most things, it didn't matter overmuch. But there were a few kinds of charms and ritual magics where the quality mattered very much indeed. Some of those could be lethal or at least rather dangerous if they went wrong.

He'd never managed to explain to his parents, who'd given him his set, why it could cause problems. Uncle Gil had advised him not to keep trying, it wouldn't change anything. Mind, Uncle Gil was the one who suggested the secondary set, and introduced him to an antique dealer in Trellech who'd helped him find most of those stones.

He shook his head, slightly, realising the gap in the conversation. "Does that matter for you?" Gabe didn't specify whether he meant the stones, or the reality of where they came from, largely because he was curious which way she'd take it.

There was another of those long pauses. It was clear from her body language, the way she played with a fold of her skirt, that she was thinking rather than offended. "I feel very young, with the other Portal Keepers. Some of them, they've had aunts or grandparents, or great-grandparents, doing the work, the stones getting passed down from person to person. Even Mistress Avigail got hers from someone else in the community. Not close family, but, kin, as they'd count it."

Gabe nodded, watching her more closely. "And you don't have that."

She shook her head, looking away from him to the river, but she kept talking. "I remember my mother, I was eight when she died. And I remember my father, though less well. Six to eight is a long time, in some ways. But I wasn't old enough to have them tell me most of the family stories. To pass things down. I know the childish things, not the grown-up ones." She hesitated, then asked, all in a rush, like she was afraid of what would happen if she waited. "What are your parents like? What is it like to know them now?"

"Ooof." He let out a grunt of a breath. "That's not an easy question. I love them. They love me. They've been -" His voice caught, remembering. "They've been generous, with their support. Not just things, though I suppose you've gathered we're posh." Not that he wanted to explain exactly how posh, not right now.

Rathna snorted. "The fact you can pull a coat rack, a tent, and who knows what else out of your trunk did give that away. And the wand. And if I got a good look at your working stones..." She let her voice trail off, pointedly.

"Some people are touchy about it. I - you deserve my best work, like I said. My best tools. Even if I didn't think you did, which I do, for the record, the work does, the portal, figuring this out. It's one thing to not give my all if it's a personal puzzle, but when it's an assignment. Portals matter for everyone."

She leaned back, looking at him as intently now as she'd

been watching the cat earlier. "I can't imagine you not giving your all, even for something personal."

Gabe spread his hands. "A lot of people find it rather annoying, actually." Plenty of people, including most people at school. The Penelopes, on the whole, were like him that way, it was one of the reasons he felt safe with them. Driven, even obsessive, finicky, perfectionist lot they all were, him included.

Rathna harrumphed. "Silly of them. Doing good work matters." Clearly, something she felt just as strongly about. "But you do things right, anyway." She didn't frame it as a question.

"Of course." He leaned back, watching her reaction.

She grinned once, and he liked how she was more relaxed with him. A bit despite herself. Then, more cautiously, she said, "What was your training like?"

It made him snort. "All sorts of things. A bit awkward at times. More than two-thirds of the Penelopes are women, and the two years ahead of mine, all the other apprentices were women. The War." He'd turned eighteen the summer before it ended.

"But you apprenticed, rather than...." Her voice trailed off uncertainly.

Gabe gestured. "The ankle. I broke it in March of 18, and - well. They probably wouldn't take me now, but they definitely wouldn't have for a year." He kept his tone light, because he still had no idea how to tell anyone about it. Even if he was fairly sure people in his life had guessed parts of it, that wasn't the same as talking about all of it.

She tilted her head again, peering at him once more, trying to sort him out. As she did, they both felt a sudden mist come up, rising from the river. "Come on." he said. "I can put a warming charm on the tent, we can settle in where it's more comfortable."

Rathna nodded, and they both stood. In the near distance, they could hear the rustle of something moving. The cat, some sort of rodent or hare, something else. He had no idea.

Once they were settled in the tent, Rathna had to admit it was surprisingly comfortable. Also, more than a little intimate, in a way she wasn't entirely sure she disliked. Gabriel gave her plenty of space, but they pulled the bedrolls forward, so they could sit facing each other.

He'd poured out tea from a flask, and added, with her permission, a slug of brandy. The result was warming, and remarkably refreshing, especially once he'd added the charm that made the tent feel cosy and snug, rather than exposed.

Gabriel was sitting with one leg stretched out - the bad one - having taken his boots off and tucked them to one side, replacing them with slippers. She had ducked back into her half of the tent to slip out of her jacket and pull one of the long lengths of woven wool shawl around her. Something in the change of location must have got to him, too, because when he spoke again, his voice was quieter, reflective. "I never really fit in, you know."

She blinked at him, confused. "You're - you're a man.

Magical family. Posh. Well-spoken. Clever. Why wouldn't you?" It didn't make sense to her.

"Clever's not actually always an advantage. And the posh is complicated." He looked away, rotating his ankle slowly, as if it were something he permitted himself only when alone. "I didn't go to tutoring school, though honestly, that was a good thing." His voice turned amused.

"Why not? I mean, I thought people usually did. I didn't, they just showed up when I turned twelve, and took me away to an office and made me do tests. And then the next September, off I was taken to Schola, with not a lot of explanation."

Gabriel frowned at that. "I thought they were supposed to explain. Though it might have been harder, with an orphanage, rather than your parents. It's permitted to tell parents where you're going, but the orphanage, maybe not." Then he shrugged. "I was a terror as a child. Wanting to know why, about everything."

"Seems to me, that works well for you now." Rathna was amused. "Did you climb out of windows, too?"

"Papa made it clear I was not to do so." Gabriel sounded quite offended. "So of course I didn't. Well, not until I got to Schola. I snuck out some nights."

"I'm fairly sure you weren't supposed to do it there either." Rathna pointed out.

"It was only the first floor. The first few times." They moved up floors in the houses as they got older. "Anyway. No tutoring house. So when I got to Schola, I knew people a little, but just the sort of being at the same parties, some-times. Not well."

"And you didn't make friends in your house?" She hesi-tated. "You said you were in Salmon House."

He nodded. "My parents were Fox. Everyone thought I

would be too." He shrugged. "But I'm not particularly deft with my hands, like people in Salmon are supposed to be. I admire people who are. I can do some things well enough, like the sketching, and I have perfectly readable handwriting. But making things, designing objects, talismans, that sort of thing, I'm not good at."

"You keep implying you're not very skilled. What's your standard, then?"

Gabriel drew himself up. "I have a perfectly accurate estimation of my own skill. But I can show you. Hah." If he'd been anyone else, he'd have stuck out his tongue at her, she rather thought. There was a moment of the impish boy on the cusp of adulthood in him.

He stood, and went back to his pack, bringing out a moderately sized book, about the size of a journal, but rather thicker. He carefully undid the catch and then came to offer it to her. "Be careful, all right?" He was audibly nervous. She almost couldn't reach for the book, as she realised that this was something important, critical. "Go on." Gabriel was more insistent. "You'll appreciate it."

She looked at it carefully in the charm light hanging above. It seemed, at first glance, the sort of commonplace book plenty of people kept, with quotations or sketches of plants, or other things they might want to reference. She didn't have one herself, but she knew plenty of people who did. The cover was a muted blue leather, a bit darker where oils from fingers had touched over time, but smooth, without any decoration.

Then she opened the cover. There was a gloriously decorated frontispiece, the sort of thing with leaves spreading and coiling across the page that would not have been out of place in an illuminated manuscript. There was gold leaf, and the pigments were almost glowing, reds and greens and blues. She knew, suddenly and instinctively, that they were properly made from crushed stones. She could feel the ancient power, even with her fingers just on the narrowest strip of the page.

Rathna almost handed the book right back. This was not magic meant for her. It was certainly not art meant for her. The vines had a curl to them that was free, in a way she didn't know illumination could be. It was balanced, elegant, gorgeous, but it flowed with life, not the mechanical perfection she'd seen. Beneath the curves, she could see the letters GAE, and there were little symbols tucked into the spaces between the vines and the letters. Books, peeking out, what she thought must be a particular small pony.

"Your middle name?" She asked it because she didn't know where to start.

"Anthony. My grandfather was Antonius." He was leaning forward, bouncing a little on his toes.

She gestured. "Sit, sit." Then, she added, "Next to me, if you want to show me things. I'm not sure I dare turn the page."

"Oh, it's charmed for preservation. It's a very practical book." Rathna thought it was smugness for a moment, then she realised the emotion rolling off him in waves was something else. Delight, pure unalloyed pleasure. Pride, even, though not, she thought, in himself. He sat down beside her, a few inches to the side, careful not to touch her. "Turn the page." He gestured, his fingers flicking out.

The next page was more mediaeval, a fancy initial letter, and some marginalia of animals and plants and a bracketing vine. She peered at the text. The words were the right shapes, the right length, but when she looked more closely, they were nonsense. It read 'Tdeq er tdn akkg kb cmaqenh wdk qerir ej tdn ikqjejc mrgejc wdy mjo cknr tk rhnnl mrgejc wdy.'

She ran her finger along it, not quite touching the page, and then looked at him. "Cypher. Letter substitution?"

His smile got bigger, and she hadn't known that was possible. "A simple one, easy enough to break, even without the code word." He leaned to indicate the words. "This is the book of Gabriel, who rises in the morning asking why and goes to sleep asking why. The repeated words make it simple."

"So why the code?"

He laughed. "There's more than one kind of cypher. And more than one trick in the book."

Rathna snorted. "There would be." She frowned. "Will you tell me the code word, or do I have to work it out myself?"

There was a pause where she was certain he was weighing the amusement of the second option. "Mason." Just the one word.

He'd mentioned that before. "Aunt Mason, you said." Rathna peered at the book in her hands. "Did she, did she make it? Or did she just do the text?"

Gabriel leaned back again, so he didn't block the light from above as much. "Keep going, and I think you'll figure it out."

Rathna did, turning slowly page by page. She could tell the text was mostly in code. Even the parts that seemed to be entirely sensible descriptions of plants, their habitats, and functions seemed like they had their own secrets. Other parts were descriptions of stones, with illustrations, or star charts, or something she thought might be about measuring the flow of water in a river.

There were illustrations of animals tucked into the

margins, delicately limned paintings of flowers, as if they were caught by the golden light of a setting sun. There were architectural sketches, different kinds of buildings and doorways. There was a section she suspected had to do with gods and goddesses outside her knowledge. And, glowing, a page that seemed to be about stained glass that was overlaid by a delicate film of translucent colour like a window.

Any one part of it might have been a solid journeywork for a painter or an artist who worked in books. The combination was a masterwork, even before considering the text and content. There were dozens of artistic styles, many of which she could barely name. Secretary hand, Gothic lettering, Greek letters, what she thought might be Phoenician, some Egyptian hieroglyphs, alchemical symbols, a set of squiggles that must mean something to someone.

The art was just as varied. It ran from something that evoked the earliest of the cave art with a raw ochre, to exquisitely detailed paintings that might have been a photograph. The bulk of it held to that mediaeval and Renaissance style, but even there, it was so varied that to believe it came from one hand beggared belief.

"Does your Aunt Mason ever actually sleep?" It wasn't what she'd meant to ask, but it made Gabriel arch back and roar with laughter.

"Yes, she does, I have been told. That is - that is the result of thirty years of practice, teaching herself how to do all the hands and the styles. And it's..." He cleared his throat. "That was my present, when I finished my apprenticeship. I had no idea. She'd been working on it since I was eight. All the things she's learned about looking at a case, all the hints and tricks. It makes sense to me, it's meant to be a memory palace, more than every detail written down."

Rathna had to trace down a faint memory of that. "The

idea that you have an image in your head, and that reminds you of the thing you need to know." She peered at the book. "Is that what the inside of your head is like, then?"

Gabriel shrugged. "Probably. As much as you could turn that into art." Then his voice got softer. "I haven't shown it to other people. I mean, not beside family."

That was a very new thing, then. "And you showed it to me?"

There was a shy little shrug, the first time she'd really seen any sense of vulnerability from him. "You, you understand." He waved a hand at the book. "You don't just understand, you appreciate, properly."

Not that she could read a word of it, though she supposed given time, she might work out some of the simpler codes. He was right, though; she did. "It's not just about you. It's about the wisdom, the collection, having it passed down, sharing it. She could have done that in dozens of ways, and she did those too. But this is, this is living. Breathing."

Gabriel bobbed his head. "That, yes. You think it's beautiful."

At that moment, she rather thought it wasn't just the book that was stunningly distracting. He had leaned forward again, earnest and attentive, entirely focused on her. The charm light made his blond hair glow, and the page was open to something with glorious reds and blues. She knew he wasn't interested in her, he'd made that clear, but for a moment, a very long and desperate moment, she wished he were.

"Gabriel. Gabriel. Wake up. I had an idea."

Gabe rubbed his face, blinking slowly. They had been up talking until it was dark, quite late. He had tucked his book back into the waxed canvas case that kept it safe somewhere in the midst, and stretched out on his bedroll, as Rathna had on hers. Somewhere, eventually, he'd drifted off.

He usually had a horrible time sleeping with other people nearby. The two years at Schola when he'd shared a dormitory room had been awful, even without anyone being particularly difficult about it. Having his own living space during his apprenticeship had been awkward in some ways. He knew he'd missed side conversations that mattered, that the women in his year had shared. But he'd had his own space, and that had won out. He hadn't expected to sleep well, but somehow he had.

"Gabriel, wake up." There was a note of amused frustration in her voice, then she nudged his shoulder. He rolled onto his back, then back onto his side, propping himself on one elbow. Woolgathering certainly wouldn't help.

"Yes?" He worked on getting his eyes to focus.

"I had an idea. Can we go up there? Right now? Really soon?"

Gabe let out a sigh, then nodded. "Sure. Um. We should pack up the tent. I suppose. Or we'll have to come back to do it."

"That will take time." She sounded like a toddler who wanted to do the thing right now. It reminded him of Del's son, back when he was old enough to talk, and not really old enough to do much else on his own.

"Are you up for going up yourself? I can pack up and follow you. It'd be twenty, thirty minutes."

She lit up. "That's a good idea. I can take my bag. And um, the hamper? So you can bring yours and the tent. Is that fair?"

"That's fine." He stretched a little. That would give him some time on his own to work the stiffness out of his ankle, too, which he'd honestly prefer. She disappeared into her half of the tent, and there was a rapid rustling of fabric. He took his time stretching, and considered how to go about all of this efficiently.

By the time he was ready to get dressed himself, she had reappeared, her hair in a braid looped and pinned into a bun, and her working tweeds on. "Right, do I leave you something for breakfast?"

"I'll eat when I get up there. Be careful, all right? We don't know about the beithir. Drop the things and run if you hear anything odd. Look, take the warding stones with you - one at each compass point, about thirty feet across, and you trigger them by touching them and saying "Watchful guard, protect me."

She nodded. "You won't be long." It was a certainty, not a question.

He shook his head. "Fifteen, twenty minutes behind you. Maybe a bit more, but you should be able to see me coming."

Rathna picked up her own saddle bags, putting them over one shoulder, the hamper in her other hand, and set off with a wave. Gabe got dressed, then finished packing up the bedrolls, compressing them back down into their flattened forms. He followed that with the tent, finally casting the charms that would shrink it to something more manageable in length and weight. His estimate was just about right, he'd be fifteen minutes behind her, twenty given his speed up hill. He'd need the walking stick, too. His ankle was twinging worse than usual.

By the time he got back up to the portal site, much of the early morning mist had burned off, and it was rather sunny. It was only about half-seven in the morning, not a time he preferred to be up if he had a choice. Rathna was working away, her bag and the hamper about fifteen feet away from the portal. He left his bags there, and rummaged in the hamper for something to eat, coming out with bread and cheese and a hard-boiled egg.

Taking his food to a rock near her, he settled down and watched. She was doing something with her stones, measuring something, but he couldn't figure out what it was. She kept going back and forth between three or four stones, from different positions, as if she were attempting to narrow something. When she glanced up, he waved one hand at her, but didn't interrupt.

After a good twenty minutes, she came to settle down on the broad rock beside him. Closer than she had before last night, as if it had made her more comfortable with him on a much more basic level. "So."

"So?" Gabe was amused, she was clearly about to burst with it.

"Did you figure out what the mineral was that they found here?"

Gabe nodded. "Withamite. Named for the man who found it in 1825. Um..." He rummaged for his notebook. "An epidote mineral, does that mean anything to you? And that it sometimes has fibres radiating through it, in a sort of cross pattern. Manganese rich, they think, but they're still sorting that out."

"Hah. I didn't ask you before, because I didn't want to prejudice myself." She looked delighted. All of a sudden, she reached out to take and squeeze his hand. Gabe wasn't at all sure what to do with that, what she meant by it, or what he should do.

He didn't want to let her go, particularly. There was something infectious about the light in her eyes, about the way she was so delighted by what she'd figured out. He was sure she'd just done something rather clever, and he'd appreciate it even more when she explained what.

In the meantime, she was still holding his hand. He squeezed back, and she wriggled into a more comfortable perch on the rock, not letting him go. It was rather as if she needed to keep herself from floating off into the clouds.

"When I did the initial tests, I had some odd results. The spinel kept reacting, rather strongly. And the peridot. And of course my igneous and metamorphic samples, but we're surrounded by both of those, that's ..." She wriggled her free hand. "That's not very useful. And then a bit of reaction from the limestone, but the fossils explain that enough."

"No." Gabe was following that far. "So it's more useful,

I agree, to look at what you didn't expect to see react. Were those the only two?"

"The garnet a bit. And I couldn't figure out what they had in common. While you were gone, though, I went through my notes and looked at the lists of what minerals have in common. I thought it might be something more like iron, or maybe aluminium. But this morning, I was, you know how it is when you're dreaming? And I woke up, sure it was the manganese."

Gabe considered that. It was a somewhat unscientific process. But not one he was going to complain about, at all, because that was how he did some of his best work. He got it from his father, that part, letting things come together, until all the pieces snapped into place, and he could do something about it. "No, I do that too." She might be nervous that he hadn't said anything, or that he disapproved of her process. "That's quite clever. And you were right. So what do we do about it?"

Rathna blinked at him, and then smiled broadly, still lit up. It was as if she'd half-expected him to say something quite different and had been unexpectedly pleased he hadn't done that. "That, now that's a question. I suppose we need all the books we haven't hauled out here."

Gabe nodded. "Unless there are more things you'd like to test, now that we know?" He waved a hand at the hillside. "Is there a way to find out if there's a, oh, a vein of the with-amite, or whatever, and where it goes?"

Rathna blinked at him several times, and then she leaned forward, suddenly, like the swoop of a falcon's dive, and kissed him on the cheek. "You're brilliant. Yes, yes, there is. Let me go see about that." She dropped his hand and sprang away from him, back to her container of stones.

He blinked after her, completely unsure what had just

happened. Oh, he understood that she had something to try. That part had been quite obvious. And that he'd said something sensible. Also obvious. For values of sensible that he suspected were going to involve climbing a craggy sort of mountain.

The kiss, though. He had no idea what to do with that. It didn't fit the previous experiences. Something had changed for her, even the most junior apprentice would see that. Something last night, or perhaps while he had been away. Though it seemed odd to have something change about her reactions to him when he wasn't even there. To have it change so much that she kissed him, even a really quite appropriate peck on the cheek, such as friends might share. That was startling. And he did not know what it meant. Which bothered him.

The more baffling part, though, was that it wasn't unpleasant. He had liked the way it felt, how she was beginning to trust him. She had been stiff and self-protective when they met, and with all the reason in the world. Certainly, she had unbent a bit, as they'd worked together, permitting a discussion, rather than shutting down any question he had.

He had liked that a great deal. She was intelligent, observant, resourceful. All virtues he appreciated. And it was just far more pleasant to have their work be an exchange, a partnership, than something formal and walled-off.

The kiss had not felt intrusive, brief as it was. He was cautious of people being too close. It was too likely they'd foil the cane, or lean on him wrong, or block his wand, and he hated that. This, though, it felt almost natural to have her there. It had felt like that last night, sitting next to her, watching her fingers turn the pages so carefully. He didn't know what he felt right now, and it was a new, demandingly interesting puzzle to work out.

He was still trying to decide what to do with that, and making no progress, when he saw someone come up from the grove of trees by the wood. "You the folks my nan had to supper? Sorcha Macdonald?"

Gabe waved an arm. It was as good a password as any. "We are, yes. What can we do for you?"

"More what I can do for ye. I'm Jamie Macdonald. Nan said you were curious about caves, up here. I can take ye in if you like."

Gabe looked over at Rathna. "Now?" he asked.

The man shrugged. "Good a time as any. I've a day free. Cows don't need me."

Rathna straightened up and then stretched. "I have more research to do, but that can wait. I think it would be good to sort out if the cave is relevant."

Gabe saw a ramble upwards in his immediate future. He wished he'd had a better chance to prepare, but he had his hiking boots, he had his good stick, he'd manage well enough. Gloves. "Do you have a light, or should we do a charm light?"

"Oh, I've lanterns. And some rope and all. Pony down there, and a cart, for when we're done."

Gabe let out a little sigh of relief that he hoped wasn't too obvious. If he only had to manage the cave, and not hauling everything back to the inn afterwards, or setting up camp again, that would be a lot easier. "Right. Cave it is. Let me get some things out of the packs. And we should probably eat something more and pack up something for lunch."

"Brought mine." Jamie was amused. "And some to share from Nan."

Rathna was not entirely sure what climbing up to the cave was going to involve, but it clearly required a fair bit of rope. Gabriel, for his part, had some idea what to expect. She, on the other hand, had a good knowledge of geology, but she had not generally been one of the ones clambering around on the less accessible bits.

So she settled on the rock, staying out of the way. Gabriel and Jamie discussed what to pack, and what not to pack, and what things they might need at the top. Jamie had apparently brought along two canvas bags that went on their backs, and one for himself.

There was food to be packed, of course, and steel flasks of tea. But also they wanted a first aid kit, and some smaller bits of rope and twine, lanterns, candles, even a bottle of extra lamp oil. She thought the last one a tad ridiculous. She knew both she and Gabriel could do a light charm handily.

"Rathna, can you pack up your stones? You might want to pack a wrap around them, for cushioning, in case you slip." Gabriel called out to her from where they were working. She nodded, and considered, then repacked the stones into the fabric roll one of Morah Avigail's daughters had made her for a present. When she had to pack things up small, it had its place, though she usually found it more trouble than it was worth to remember which stone was where.

That done, she tucked it into the pack she'd been handed and settled back on her rock, watching Gabriel. She wasn't entirely sure what she'd done, or more to the point, what he thought about it. Or what she thought about it.

She hadn't intended to touch him like that. Not to take his hand, certainly not to kiss him. He'd made it clear he wasn't inclined that way. But he also hadn't pulled away either time. She didn't think he'd even stiffened with discomfort, though he hadn't encouraged her, either.

There was no changing the past, so she would just have to avoid that in the future. Watching him, though, she tried to figure out what had changed for her. Part of it was him showing her that gorgeous book. Even more, what he'd said about it, how he'd understood. About having something shared with you, not because of birth, but because someone cared that you knew it. Cared that you carried that learning on.

She still didn't know much about his parents, other than the little he'd said. That he loved them, that was obvious. That they were still alive, to be loved in the way you loved living, breathing people, that was obvious too. But that he'd had that, and yet clearly needed and wanted the relation-ship he had with his Aunt Mason, that said something about him. Mind, Aunt Mason was baffling as well. Exceptionally talented, ferociously clever, and utterly baffling.

Gabriel himself seemed an endless supply of surprises. She had thought herself someone who didn't like surprises.

They had, in her life so far, been generally disruptive, even when they'd turned out well. Being told she was magical, and that she could not tell anyone at the orphanage, even hint at it. Being made to take an oath about it, with almost no preparation. Arriving at Schola with no idea what to expect. Morah Avigail. Living in a magical household.

Her apprenticeship she had had warning for, but not how some of the other Portal Keepers treated her. It wasn't her race, there, so much as it was her age, her lack of roots in the community. Anywhere. The Portal Keepers liked roots and foundations.

Gabriel, though, he had those roots, and he used them to launch himself. Out windows, in a literal sense, and now, into another unknown. He was almost fearless. Almost. The beithir had worried him, she could tell that. And the man in the inn. He wasn't foolish, just working on a very different scale of risk.

And he was lovely to watch. His hands were deft, tying things onto his pack, coiling rope, making a harness to test something that fit snugly around his hips. She liked how certain his movements were, even as he steadied himself to avoid undue strain on his bad ankle. He moved to put a foot up on the rock, then tightened the laces, before wrapping the whole in something like a long cloth bandage. Extra support, she supposed.

She had managed to stop staring at him by the time he was done. "Rathna, have you done much climbing?"

Rathna shook her head. "Not more than scrambling. Nothing this big. Or with ropes."

Jamie looked her up and down, then raised an eyebrow, silently, at Gabriel. Rathna did not like the implicit judgement there, but she couldn't really argue with it. And she knew better than to claim a competency she didn't have.

"Right. Getting up to right below the cave is not that difficult, I gather. A steady walk, until we get to, what was it, Ossian's Ladder. Which is near enough straight up."

Jamie just nodded at that.

"So Jamie will go up first, set a rope, and you and I will follow. If we need to, one of us can pull you up. You'll want gloves for that, leather if you have them."

She shook her head. "Just cotton."

Gabriel went rummaging in his bag, coming up with a second pair of leather gloves. Very well-made ones, the leather was supple and visibly soft. "Put those on?"

She did. Before she could think to tell him no, he cast a charm on them. It made them shrink on her hands, from the loose slip of his larger hands to her proper size. They fit snugly, like an intimate embrace, and she barely restrained herself from shivering. "Keep them. I suspect we'll want them again before we're done."

Rathna looked down at her hands, then back at him. He was already turning away, with a "Right, let's get on, shall we?" He grabbed his cane, extended to a full hiking stick size, and set off, to pick up the long slow slope angling up from the left side of the cliff face to the right. They had to go most of the way across the face of the mountain first, and that was a largely pleasant walk. Then they picked up the path that angled up. This was more work, but it wasn't much worse than hill-walking she'd done in other parts of Albion from time to time.

Gabriel set the pace, steadily, evenly. He was in good enough shape that he kept up a quiet conversation with Jamie. Rathna was far enough behind she couldn't quite hear what they were talking about. The area, maybe, or the wildlife, because Jamie would periodically stop, scan the landscape, and point at something.

About forty-five minutes in, they stopped for everyone to take a break, and Jamie passed around bannocks, which crumbled pleasantly in her mouth. The tea was bracingly strong, too, and quite restorative. No one said much at all while they rested. All of them were busy breathing and drinking tea. After ten minutes, Gabriel brushed his hands off, and said cheerfully, "Ready to go on?"

Rathna wasn't entirely sure she was, but she wasn't going to admit to that. Not with both of them being so fiercely ready to keep going. She nodded. "If you don't mind my pace."

"Oh, no, works well for me." There was something about this that was lighting him up, and Rathna tucked that away to chew on later. He set off again, humming now, and Rathna followed.

In half an hour, they were at the bottom of that so-called ladder, which was nothing remotely like a ladder at all. Rathna looked up and up. It was steep - not quite vertical, but near enough. There were plants and sort of rough bushes, growing in a way that made her think it would be much worse in a month when more had grown. Gabriel was eyeing it thoughtfully. "Jamie, setting the rope's a good idea. Do you know the best route?"

That got an amiable shrug. Jamie looped a broad coil of rope over his head and across his chest like a bandolier, took a pickaxe out of his bag, and then set off, using the axe to help anchor him here and there.

Gabriel looked up, leaning back. "He knows what he's doing." His voice was quiet, reassuring. He didn't look over at her, but that just meant he didn't catch her looking at him. Probably. Assuming he didn't notice things was probably not the sensible thing here.

"How do you know?" she asked.

"See how he's going up? He anchors his foot, then a hand, over and over. Making sure he's got something steady, three of the four points. And how he's got a hold of that bush, there? The roots won't be deep, not growing into the mountain, but they're better than loose rock."

"Most things would be better than loose rock, surely." She couldn't keep the amusement out of her voice. Or the edge of something she didn't want to admit might be fear.

Whatever he heard, he looked over at her. "He'll anchor a rope, and you and I can use that."

"How do we get the rope down? I - up is one thing, but climbing down would be awful."

"In this case, I know a handy bit of magic there. First things first." Then, still looking at her, he asked, "Are you worried?"

"About the climb? A bit. But I want to know about that cave. How big it is. What's in there. Stones, I hope, interesting stones. Not a beithir."

"Jamie knows other people who've come up. No one was stung. Eaten. There's apparently a little tin box with all the names."

Rathna blinked. "Some people have very strange amusements, were you aware?"

Gabriel laughed. "Oh, yes. This isn't entirely strange. Practical, if you live somewhere with so many mountains. Though I gather the first people to climb this one were in the 1860s."

Rathna contemplated that. "At least that anyone knows about."

"Fair, fair. Writing things down is a particular kind of claiming, but not the only one." He looked up again, watching Jamie continue to climb. "Ah, there, he's getting up."

It would be a fairly long wait, and Rathna found a rock, safely away from the edge of the path that plummeted down the side, to perch on. "Have you climbed? Like this?"

"Snowdonia, some. A few other places. Enough to know what I'm doing." She glanced at the ankle, she couldn't help it. "After the ankle, mostly. Since you're curious." He seemed more amused than resigned. "Going up like that's easier than rough ground, on average."

"Any advice, then?"

"You'll have the rope to steady you, and take your weight, we'll rig you up." It wasn't terribly helpful advice, but it would have to do for the moment. As they watched, Jamie got up to the top, and disappeared from view briefly before he waved from the entrance, and prepared to throw the rope down.

The climb up was not quite as difficult as Gabe had anticipated, but he had started out a tad pessimistic. Not that he'd said so to Rathna. Her part was in fact straightforward. He'd tied a workable harness around her, and Jamie had pulled her up, with Gabe anchoring the slack in the rope below. A useful technique. He'd been pleased to discover that Jamie had quite a bit of experience in the mountains.

Jamie had been quite certain there was no beithir lurking in the cave itself, which was why Gabe was willing to climb up, sight unseen. Well, how one saw into a cave a good twenty feet up was an excellent question, given that he was fairly sure none of the three of them were shape-shifters. He certainly wasn't. But Jamie said he'd been up, and that Gabe would understand. Which suggested something queer about the cave.

Once Rathna was safely up, however, it was his turn to climb. That turned out to be tricky. The two of them had slid in the rough mud and muck of the vegetation. Twice, when Gabe put his foot down, it slipped, then again. The third one made him angle his foot, jamming for leverage, doing his best not to panic. Panic never helped anything, even if it felt like a good idea at the time. He'd had that drilled into him by Uncle Magni and his father, from nearly as long as he could remember. Clear head, more choices.

This proverb did not help at all when he was doing his best not to dangle from a branch by one hand, ten feet up a rock face. Falling would be bad, but he didn't particularly want to look like a fool in front of Rathna. Or Jamie. But mostly Rathna. He wedged his other foot into a crack and rearranged his hand on the rope, to get a better grip. He tried to convince himself that it was that she needed to trust him. But perhaps, just a little, it was his sense of pride.

Normally, he was competent; he didn't need to be prideful about it. He did what he was good at, well, and consistently. Aunt Mason had pointed out that brilliance was an easily tarnished coin, people never remembered your brilliance too far down your road. Your consistency, though, your reliability, those are the things that made you shine over and over. They got you the best projects, the interesting ones, the ones no one else could solve.

She'd had a bad time of it, two years ago, a case that had frustrated and worried his father, kept him late at the office. He'd been firmly into his apprenticeship, working all hours, living in rooms in the apprentice hall. It had taken a bit to piece things together, since he was only seeing his parents once every week or two for supper. Rarely both at the same time. His mother had been worrying, he knew that, even before Aunt Mason got hurt.

It was only later that he'd found out what she'd been working on, the sort of puzzle that would have drawn her like a moth to the flame. She'd tried the logical, sensible thing of a ladder against a wall of a mysterious home, and been launched into the air. She'd broken her arm - thankfully, not her writing hand - and done something to her magic that made the world spin around her.

She'd been plagued both with a sense of persistent vertigo and - worse, she said - an odd song that played on and on, like no other music she'd ever heard, she said. That had only eased six weeks later at the end of July. He had been sent along as the sacrificial offering to her boredom, to keep her entertained, in any remnant of his free time. It had been by the universal agreement of every other Penelope and both his parents.

This was not getting him further up the cliff. And it was certainly not reliable to strand oneself in the middle of a cliff when your partner was waiting for you. If that was the word, and he rather thought it was.

Gabe grunted, stretching for the next foothold, bracing on his bad ankle so he could get leverage to step onto the good one. From there, he could see the next good footing, and the next. He made his way more steadily up the cliff now, and then Jamie's strong arm was there, giving him a haul up.

Rathna hadn't even noticed. She was deeply immersed in peering at the cave. He could not decide if he were aggravated she had not watched him climb, or whether he was glad she hadn't seen him flail. Since dithering about that wasn't any good at all, he stretched and said to Jamie, "Quite slick now, better to go down by abseil, or something close to it." Jamie grunted, and nodded, then turned away to see to the ropes.

Gabe stretched again since the climbing had done his

shoulders no favours, and then went to join Rathna. She glanced up at him and smiled. "No beithir."

"Jamie said I'd understand why he was sure." The cave was tall and narrow with enough space for two or three people to stand side by side at the entrance. It angled steeply up from the initial ledge, at forty degrees or a bit more. But it was, for all the height, not overly spacious.

Certainly not the lair of something reptilian, unless it were quite small. It also didn't have the right sort of smell. He didn't care for snakes, as he'd told Rathna. But he'd been close enough to the custos dragon in the bank to get a sense of the smell, and he'd been around lizards and such before. This was nothing like that. It was damp, chill, entirely shaded.

"What have you found?" He turned the topic to what they were here for.

"Stronger readings from the manganese stones, all of them. And pointing that way. I'd like to run the line to the back of the cave, see if I can isolate a vein of it. It might be quite small, just a thread, but that would be enough to carry magic, or align it, or something of the kind."

Gabe flicked his fingers. "You think that's what's going on?"

"You are the naturalist." Rathna's voice was amused. "Posit for me a magical creature, known to make its home here, where the feature we have been able to isolate is a particular mineral."

Gabe laughed. "I feel like I'm back in Trivium and discussing logical proofs."

Rathna turned to grin at him. "I hope I'm kinder than Mistress Parris." Who was known for being particularly strict about the amount of distraction she permitted.

"Right." Gabe took a breath. "Taking as a given that the beithir is real, for the moment."

"Given." Rathna turned back to examining the stones, and running through the precise checks she was using. She was using one of her stones hanging from a little cage, much like a pendulum, only aligned with a compass and metal grid.

"There is no beithir in here, so it must live somewhere else. It does not live in the village, or in the riverbed, or more people would have seen it. If we posit that it is attracted to something in this stone..." He thought through the implications. "Is there a chance someone is mining the stone? Or interfering with it somehow?"

He heard a sound from behind him, and turned to catch Jamie, hand coming down from his mouth, silhouetted against the light from the entrance. "Jamie?"

"Might be a thing in that. Would have to see a man." It was the sort of answer-non-answer that Gabe expected. They were strangers here, albeit strangers who were not wanting the beithir to make trouble.

"Right." Gabe took a deep breath and went on. "Do we know much about the properties of withamite? Or whatever else it is that's up here? In terms of disruption to the portal?"

Rathna paused in her gestures, though she didn't lower her hand. Gabe stepped forward, moving to take the grid and compass, holding them steady for her. She nodded at him and went on. "There might be something in that. I'd need the books you brought back. Research."

Gabe let out a long breath. "So. You get the readings you need. We go back down the mountain, Jamie distracts our uncomfortable guest, and we go about it from there."

"You make it sound so easy." Rathna's voice was relaxed, comfortable.

He couldn't bow without shaking the grid he was hold-ing, so he used his free hand to give a little wave, a gesture at the thing. His father would have done a mock-salute, but that was not a thing Gabe had earned, not in any of the roles he had in the world. "Take your time, do the thing properly."

Rathna smiled at him and turned back. She remained blissfully focused. He admired that about her, not like him with all of his distractions. Aunt Mason had said it could be a gift, the way his mother noticed things that seemed not to matter until they did. Gabe found it alternately essential and utterly frustrating, how his mind would go haring off. Now, he did his best to settle into the even steady breathing he'd been trained in, keeping his hands steady.

It took long enough to do the readings that his stomach was growling by the time Rathna was done. Jamie had hunted out the visitor's tin, and they all signed, careful to use the names that wouldn't cause confusion if read by non-magical folk. Rathna signed with a single initial R and her last name. Gabriel did the same with his.

They took a brief break for some sort of rough meal and then began the complex descent. He went first, so he could belay Rathna down. It was better than the climb up, but he could feel his ankle aching and complaining by the time he was perpendicular to the ground properly again. Rathna leaned into the rope like she'd been born to it, apparently entirely trusting that he had her safely. He did, of course, but he didn't know how she could relax into it like that with so little experience. It was like watching someone dive into the water and know it would let them slip in easily.

The hike back down the mountain was jarring. He often found downhills more difficult, the way it was harder to adjust for where the ground met his foot. By the time they were back at the pony and cart, he was well past ready for a ride back, and a good rest. And not up for conversation. A couple of times, Rathna opened her mouth, where they were facing each other. Then she'd close it again without saying anything, leaving him to stare off at the moving landscape in silence.

O nce they got back to the inn, Jamie went ahead to see whether it was safe for them to go up. A moment later, Gormlaith came out.

"That man's gone away, for a day or two at least. You come in, have a wash up, I'll make something filling for supper."

Rathna nodded, watching Gabriel. She thought he needed it rather more than she did, but she knew that pointing that out wouldn't do any good. Instead, she said, "May I come see about what the options are? Gabriel, why don't you go up first, and then I can take my time when you're done."

It wasn't the most subtle thing, and she saw immediately that he recognised it for what it was. But there was enough deniability to pass in front of the others. He shrugged. "As you wish, then." He slid out of the back of the cart with a grunt, and murmured to Jamie, who said, "I'll be bringing the bags up in a minute."

Rathna nodded. "If the doors are closed, just leave them outside, please."

The resulting details occupied them all for a good quarter hour or so, but by the time she came upstairs, she'd sorted out a hearty sort of plan for supper. Certainly Gabriel ate enough for it, even without all the clambering. She could hear the water running in the bathing room, and it was a good thirty minutes more before she heard a knock on her door. She'd left it slightly ajar for just that reason, and she called out, "Yes?" The door creaked as she turned around, and Gabriel looked in.

"All yours. Knock when you're ready to go down."

What she wanted to do was at least give him time to put his feet up, perhaps even have a nap, but again, things she couldn't suggest. "Mind if I take a bit?"

Again, she was certain he spotted what she was up to. He waved a hand. "Take your time. I've books." He turned abruptly, without saying anything further, leaving her to go along to the bathing room. He was courteous, at least, and he'd made sure the tub was well rinsed out from the grime she knew was thick about her own ankles. She rinsed out her clothes as well as she could, Gormlaith had said she'd make sure the laundry got dealt with promptly.

Which left Rathna to change into something more comfortable and knock on Gabriel's door. "Ready when you are."

She didn't hear anything, so she knocked again. Then, cautiously, she tried the door, and while the knob did not turn, she did not feel the strength of his wards. It was only then she saw a slip of paper that had fallen out of the door. It said "Downstairs," and the date, April 14th.

Rathna made her way into the pub downstairs and glanced around. Gabriel was not only downstairs, but he looked very much freshened up, if perhaps a little too bright-eyed and sharp. He was in conversation with a couple of men in the corner, men she'd seen there before, but they were treating him well enough. He caught her entrance and made a little gesture. She could only interpret it as some sort of indication he'd be along, eventually.

Gormlaith swept over. "Table, somewhere quiet? And rolls and butter to be starting with?"

Rathna couldn't help glancing over at where Gabriel was sitting. "I suppose." After his adventures with the darts, and the mysterious lurking man, and for that matter, the problem of Vivek, she wasn't sure what she thought about unknown people right now.

"Ah, he's had a talk or two with them before. Good steady men. Near enough close cousins, as we count it. They'll not be trouble, they know better. Beer with your bread?"

Rathna considered, then nodded. "Please. A pint of whatever you think would be good with the stew later." Gormlaith went off, humming to herself. Rathna was left with nothing to do but watch the people. She'd assumed she'd be talking to Gabriel. She hadn't brought a book down, and she didn't particularly want to climb upstairs again. She might be a bit better off than Gabriel was, but her legs were complaining, her shoulders as well.

After about twenty minutes, he exchanged hearty farewells with the men, and got slapped on the shoulder for his trouble, with a fair bit of laughter. He came over, where Rathna had demolished two-and-a-half rolls and most of her pint. As soon as he settled down, she could see he was a bit off kilter. Enough that she suspected some sort of potion.

"Good conversation?" It seemed a neutral enough place to start.

He nodded, then glanced over her shoulder as Gormlaith appeared with a tray. "Lamb stew, plenty to go round.

Here we are then, you be letting me know if you need anything else." Two large bowls, steaming, with a thick broth around chunks of meat, potatoes, carrots, and what she suspected were both turnips and parsnips. She let out a long breath. "I admit, climbing's hungry work."

"It's the thin air, they say." There was an undercurrent of bubbling almost-laughter running through his voice. He let her eat a few spoonfuls, perhaps because it let him do the same. "They kept an eye on our mysterious stranger, turns out. Quite useful, a bit of nosiness."

"Did they tell you, though, that's the question?" It came out a little sharper than she'd meant it to.

Gabriel's eyebrows went up, but he apparently took it more in the teasing mode than she'd meant it. "A fair bit. Not a local, not a Sassenach. They thought him likely from Edinburgh, from the accent."

"Is that a good thing or a bad thing?"

"A curious thing. City folk, not the most common up here, for all sorts of reasons. He said he was up here for a bit of climbing, but he didn't do most of the things climbers do, looking for supplies, maybe a guide."

"Is Jamie not the only one round these parts?"

Gabriel laughed rather loudly. "Oh, probably the best, but not the only." He shook his head, drank a good inch of his beer, and set the glass down. "Plenty of men'd made a bit extra, taking someone up. But the man, he gave his name as Jack Brown which is near enough John Smith as makes no difference, and is almost certainly a false name." He was spinning out his thoughts as he went. Rathna was alternately fascinated and horrified by this, and thinking it would be for the best if she could get him upstairs promptly.

"Did he give any hint what he was looking for?" She tried to get him back on the topic, at least.

"Something something mountains, something something unspecific, know it when he sees it."

Rathna snorted. "Which could be a flower or a bird or something. Or could be -" She frowned, her voice trailing off. "Do we think he might be after the withamite?"

"Or possibly a beithir scale, if beithirs have scales, which I realise now no one has actually ever said." He was definitely giddy and should not be further trusted in public. She finished up most of her stew, and said, "Come on, I want to get back to my books. Eat up. I need your help."

There was something in her tone that made him look at her, wide-eyed. Then he promptly said, "Of course." He set to finishing his stew with the sort of appetite only a man in his early twenties could entirely manage. Rathna shook her head, and went to talk to Gormlaith. They'd be back upstairs, let them know if anyone strange turned up again, please, and maybe something for an evening tidbit for later.

By the time she got back, Gabriel had finished his stew, and was pushing back from the table, looking more wobbly. She immediately offered her arm, with a "Mind giving me a hand? I'm not sure about the stairs." Again, it was a feeble attempt, but he didn't complain.

She took the right, of course, to leave the left for his cane, and together they managed to get upstairs without complete embarrassment. Though she was sure more than one person was snickering. She didn't care at the moment, as long as she could shepherd Gabriel into his own room. "You settle, I'll gather my books."

Two minutes later, she was on the foot of his bed, books piled next to her. He was stretched out, diagonally, feet pointed off away from her, He'd laced his hands under his head, eyes half-closed.

"Gabriel, what did you think of the stone measurements? I know you were paying attention."

He didn't say anything, and when she looked up, he was watching her. "Gabe."

She blinked. "Beg your pardon?" He was making even less sense every minute.

"Gabe. My friends call me Gabe. Not that I have many, but." He let out a long breath, the sort of thing that in a novel would be a beleaguered sigh. "Gabe." It sounded almost as if he were trying to convince himself of something.

Rathna swallowed. She wasn't sure what to make of this, what he meant by it. If he'd mean it in the morning. For now, though, she found herself nodding. "Gabe. All right." There seemed to be a dozen things she wanted to ask now, to say. Were they friends? What did he mean by friends? Why did he not have more friends? What did friendship with someone like him mean, anyway? She'd never really been sure what friendships meant to the magical folk, how they were the same and different.

Instead, he gave her one of those glowing, delighted smiles. "Gabe." It had all the smugness of a child who's done a thing they meant to do and had it turn out right. There was an innocent delight to it that was ridiculously charming. Or would be, if she weren't fairly certain that he'd done it for at least five reasons, only one of which she was spotting right now.

She shook her head. "The withamite, Gabe?"

"Oh. Withamite." He settled into it with a little wriggle that was mental as much as physical. "You were getting a fairly direct line back into the mountain, weren't you? Hiking up over the top's not a thing, that's a fairly steep climb, and the rocks are still slick with snow melt. But I'm wondering if somewhere back there, in the crevices. Crevasses? No, that's glaciers."

The hint of the fumble in the middle of his analysis also had a charm to it. Or would if she weren't decidedly worried about how much pain he must have been in to take something rather strong, by all the evidence before her. He went on with that same cheerful tone. "The question is, do we need to solve the problem of the beithir to solve the problem of the portal?"

That was an excellent question, and she encouraged him. "Go on, what are you thinking?"

"Well, the beithir may or may not exist, and if it exists, it may or may not lair on that particular mountain. It has a number to choose from, after all. And at least two lochs. Frankly, if I were going to lair somewhere, I'd probably pick a different mountain, that one seems rather sharp to lounge around on."

She snorted. "Gabe." She let the amusement show in her voice. She was rewarded by him opening his eyes, lifting his head, grinning at her, and then letting it fall back on the pillow with a thump.

"On the other hand, bright mistress..." She had no idea how to take that one, and therefore let it go without comment. "The portal is a relatively recent change. The withamite might well be relevant. Would the construction have been done assuming a fairly steady presence of the same mineral content in the underlying foundation, then?"

That made her suck in a breath. Because he had just managed, very smartly, to pull together a set of things even the Portal Keepers didn't talk about very much. The portals certainly had variance designed into them, but one of the ways the stone and water portals were vulnerable were if the underlying geology shifted. The tree portals were more fragile to the slow ageing of trees, but more flexible in other ways.

If that was what he did when more than a little affected by pain potions, she didn't want to think about what he was like with his full wits engaged and aimed at something specific.

"It would have. And you are quite right in your implication that changing the underlying matrix would affect the stability. I didn't see any sign of mining, though. Usually it would require a fair bit of material to be removed, or altered."

"Like a dam, in a river?"

He was bloody well too smart for his own good. She nodded. "Like a dam in a river." She frowned, tapping her fingers. "Wait. If we posit that Jack Brown is similar to a beaver, instead of taking things away, blocking it up. That might have the same ..." Not the same sort of effect, that was imprecise language. "The same magnitude of effect."

"Altering the flow, somehow. Perhaps taking some material away, a distance from the portal? But as you say, blocking a river?"

"Yes. I could do some more investigation of the relevant leys. It might take a bit of riding."

"Ah, riding, I'm at your service, dear lady." The further endearment rolled out of him freely. "Riding, I'm excellent at." It occurred to her that it didn't involve nearly as much weight-bearing on the ankle.

She shook her head. "I am going to take my books back to my desk, and my maps, and I will be busy with that for the evening. I don't think we need to go out terribly early. I'd rather wait for the mist to clear a bit. Say, leave at half-nine?"

That would give him time to sleep off whatever he'd

taken, and her plenty of time to enjoy a bed. Not that the bedroll had been uncomfortable, actually.

He waved a hand languidly, still lying down. "I'll think." He sounded cheerful enough about it. Whatever else he was, he seemed to be a reasonably cheerful sort of man through and through. He hadn't been nasty when he was in pain, and he hadn't turned mean on the potion - she could only presume a potion - or the beer.

Rathna nodded and then rummaged in the pile of books. "Reading that might help you. If you end up bored." It was an overall guide to minerals and their uses as materia. She suspected he knew a fair bit of it, anyway. "G'night."

With that, she managed to get herself back to her own room. She gave herself five minutes to ponder the ridiculousness of this man who climbed out windows and scrambled up cliffs. And who could then come out with a synthesis of magical theory she knew she'd only barely hinted at. Only five minutes, mind, because she had a lot of work to be getting on with.

By the next morning, Gabe felt rather more himself. His ankle still ached, but it was the dull ache he was used to, not the rather more demanding throb of last night. He'd been told, by three separate healers, that there was nothing actually wrong with the bones, not anymore, but that it would continue to hurt. Why it continued to hurt, however, they had insufficient answers for.

Gabe had smiled and nodded. When he'd got back home to Kent, he had taken his mare out. He'd ridden as far away from anyone as he could get, and then cursed for a good hour, until he'd gone hoarse. And then again, when he'd had a chance to recover. Then he'd come back, joined his parents for supper, and done his best not to let the pain stop him. Most of the time, it was a sort of predictably diffi-cult portion of a life that had a lot of good things in it.

Last night, he'd needed the potion. And frankly, he'd needed to lie down and keep his foot up and not move for a good solid chunk of time, with the cold wrap on. This morn-ing, his ankle was complaining more than he'd prefer, but not much more than usual. Getting his tall boots on had been annoying, but once they were on, the extra reinforcement was more than worth the fuss.

They got going easily enough, with a late breakfast, and then a pleasant ride out on a surprisingly sunny day. Rathna had become a good deal more confident on horseback, he'd noticed. She was riding more easily, at least at the steady walk they were doing. He'd suggested a large circuit, up past Loch Achtriochtan, and then coming back toward the village. She was doing well enough that she could follow his patter about the local wildlife. A hare, a pine marten, a golden eagle. He was really having a fabulous time spotting new animals this trip.

She let him keep it up for half an hour, before she was looking at him more closely, as if she were measuring him up.

He shrugged and let her win. She'd more than earned it, after all. "Pardon if I was a little silly last night. The potion - I don't usually talk to other people once I've taken it."

That made her tilt her head. Good, he'd disarmed her a bit. She hadn't nagged or fussed last night, which was gloriously pleasant, but he wasn't sure she'd be able to restrain herself in the light of day. It wasn't a failing he blamed anyone for, but most people had it.

Uncle Gil at least understood how the fussing was rather worse than the hurting. Cousin Del understood that fussing over things you couldn't fix was a waste of energy. And his mother understood the waste of energy part all too well. But on the whole, people tended to want to fuss, even when they weren't actually doing it.

Rathna wasn't doing any of that. Instead, she looked like she had a hundred questions. And rather like some of them might not be the ones he'd heard so many times before. She thought for a moment, as if weighing her options carefully. "You don't take it often." It wasn't a question at all, it was the same tone she used to lay out her observations.

"No. The steep downhill did me in. It just hurts, I'm not doing more damage." It seemed to matter to him, that she understood that. Usually he didn't care if people understood, he just cared that they let him get on with things.

"Pain is generally a sign you're damaging something." Again, not a question, just the steady statement. She was watching him more closely now, letting Verity walk along with Livet.

"In this case, it's a sign that the thing didn't heal right in the first place. It aches, it complains. Somewhat like a cranky relation, who's never satisfied. Papa's mother. The food is too hot, the food is too cold, the food is too spicy, the food is too bland, the sun is too sunny, the rain is too damp. Only mostly, my ankle complains about weather and angles."

He saw Rathna's eyes flick to the stirrups. She was riding to his left, so she could see perfectly well he was riding with his feet out of the stirrups. "Don't saddles have these things for a reason?"

That made him grin, broadly. "Oh, they do. But plenty of people have done amazing things on horseback without them. They're actually quite a modern invention, comparatively. At least in the west. Xenophon would have been so jealous." Her expression turned puzzled, and he added, "Great Greek general against the Persians, also wrote one of the earliest books we know on horsemanship. The Indians and Chinese had stirrups early, and the Byzantine empire. But they looked a bit different. We got these from Genghis Khan and the Great Horde. More or less."

"You were entirely horse mad as a young boy, weren't you? Like some girls are."

"You say that like I've grown out of it." He leaned over and patted Livet on the shoulder. "I like riding. I feel free. Especially these days. Anyway, stirrups help in some specific situations, leverage and bracing, but they're also sometimes limiting. And a lot of people find them less than comfortable for long rides, especially at a trot."

Rathna considered that. "Is it less bouncy without the stirrups?"

Gabe nodded. "You don't need your ankles and knees and hips to keep flexing properly, you can just go with the movement. The other way it's easier is if you stand in the stirrups, so you're out of the saddle, just balancing. Easier on the horse, that, but tiring if you do it too long, and rather hard on the thighs. Look, here we've got a bit of road. If you drop your stirrups, do you think you can stay on?"

She wriggled her feet free, leaning slightly, getting the feel of it. "Maybe. If I slide off, will you stop?"

"Always." It came out without him even thinking about it. "But you won't. You're getting quite a good seat, for how little time you've spent in the saddle. When this is over, you should have some proper lessons. I'd be glad to."

She was concentrating hard now, but she nodded. "How do I trot?"

Gabe pulled along next to her and clucked. "C'mon, Verity, c'mon, Livet. Trot on." He gave the command clearly, and the mares responded, picking up an amiable trot. He could see Rathna wobbling. "Just like the walk, but more bounce. Let Verity show you where she is and stay right on top of her. There we go. Take a breath. Good."

They made it a good fifty feet down the road, before Rathna managed to get a word out. "Enough!"

Gabe brought both mares back to a walk and patted Livet again. "Good girl." Then he brought them to a stop. No one else was coming. They could take a minute. They were enough past the loch now they should probably turn around soon, anyway. "Trotting's probably the hardest thing about riding, honestly."

"Going faster is easier?"

"Canter's much smoother to ride to, if the speed doesn't bother you. And jumping on a horse that likes it, well, that's like flying."

The expression on her face was delightful, the mix of puzzlement, curiosity, and a certain amount of bafflement at why anyone would do something so foolish. Which was also just about right. He was about to say something else, when he caught a flash of light out of the corner of his eye. He wheeled Livet in place, and said sharply, "Rathna. Is that the portal?"

It was a deep blue light from about the right place, though the actual portal was occluded by the hill. She twisted around, rather than try to turn Verity. "Yes. And there's something there." She pointed at a flickering gleam of light closer to them, on this side of the mountain's base, and he caught it. It was rather like a signal light or mirror, a brief flash on and off. And none too far away, either, perhaps only half a mile. On second thought, it didn't seem plausibly like a signal, the angles would be all wrong for that, but perhaps more like one place affecting the other.

There was no one nearby at all. He couldn't even send her for help. There was no one closer than Sorcha, not for certain. "I'm going. Come after me, more slowly, see if you can spot anyone who can help, or take a message to the inn."

"Gabe, what are you..."

"I know how to use my wand." He was gathering

himself, and Livet danced in place for a moment. Heavy-built pony that she was, she could tell when it was her time to shine. He needed to size up his best path, first. It was maybe half a mile from here to those flashing lights, and he didn't want her to come to harm. The road curved around, there was something of a path, cut by the deer, maybe, he'd take that. "Keep hold of Verity, she'll want to come with."

Then he was off, shifting his weight, feeling the mare beneath him gather her haunches. They launched off into a gallop, dust rising up behind them. He hoped Rathna could find someone, he didn't know what he was going to find. His first idea of a path, he had to turn aside from, then circle wider than he meant. He spared a look behind him, but he couldn't see Rathna any more, and he hoped she was all right, before he pulled his focus back to his single goal.

Gabe got the reins into his right hand, as he was urging Livet on. He hadn't bothered to pick up his stirrups, so he just kept on, feeling them bang against his boots. He had to dodge around a few larger scattered boulders, then finally, he was coming up along to where those flashes of light had come from. He slowed Livet down just a hair, preparing to launch himself out of his saddle as soon as he could figure out his target.

His father's training, Uncle Magni's training, echoed in his head. *Know what you're doing before you do it. Train your reactions, but don't rely on them. Be responsible with your power.* All the things they'd taught him, drilled into him, over and over, until they were in his bones, so deep he'd never forget them.

He had no idea who he'd find, or what. It could be a man, a woman, a magician, someone without magic, a beithir. He had no idea. If it was a person, a stunning spell would do nicely. But if he were attacked...

He let his mind run down the trees of choices, how each choice opened up new branches, and closed others off. Now he was twenty feet from a boulder, and the light was coming from right by it. Fifteen, twelve. Then, precisely at ten feet, he drove Livet into a halt, using his legs and his seat to cue her. Her legs came up under her, all the weight and momentum shifting. As soon as she'd stopped, he flung herself off her back.

Rathna sucked in a breath, as Gabe took off at what was clearly a full gallop. Verity wanted to go along. Horses were herd animals, after all. She managed to keep Verity standing still, long enough to see Gabe chasing along, and then she followed, going along the road where he cut across on a looping curve.

Seeing him riding full out, he had been telling the truth when he said he was an excellent rider. It was as if he were glued to Livet's back, like a centaur, no sign they were two different beings, with two different minds. Livet was going full out, exerting herself in a way that Rathna was even more surprised by.

He'd said to go for help, or find help. But she could see no one, no hint of movement that looked like a cart or a horse, anywhere along the road. Sorcha's cabin was the nearest she knew about, and that was nearly two miles up the road toward town.

Gabe was making a large loop, and she peered after him. She didn't trust herself to ride at speed, but she trusted herself to run. She slipped off Verity, tossing the stirrups over the saddle so they wouldn't bang. Then she pulled the reins over the mare's head and took off at a steady run on foot. Verity came easily enough, trotting along at her side in some bemusement.

Her method might be somewhat slower, but it was more direct. She could leap a small stream easily enough and coax the mare through it, where Gabe had circled around. As she started running again, she had a good view of him. He galloped up to where the flashes of light were coming from, intermittently in no obvious particular pattern, then pulled to a stop.

Before she could say or do anything, he flung himself forward, off the horse, at what seemed entirely the wrong angle. Instantly, he curled his arms over his head, bent, and did a somersault, coming up on his good foot with a little bounce. It seemed an exceedingly desperate way to dismount, but it worked.

She wouldn't have believed it if she hadn't seen it, mind. She was too far away to do anything, even call out, but she kept running, to get close enough she could at least see what was going on. Livet clearly was dubious about the whole affair, as she backed up warily, a good ten feet, before sidling over toward her stablemate. Rathna managed to grab her reins, at least.

Once she had the mares settled, steady enough she could focus on something else, she could see Gabe clearly. He was about twenty feet away, somewhat silhouetted by the sun. She could see another shape, someone else, back in the rocks, but she couldn't see if it was man or woman, or anything else specific.

"Come out." Gabe's voice was clear, like he'd practised shouting that kind of thing for hours.

There was a muffled reply, Rathna couldn't hear it.

Gabe could, and it didn't please him. His back stiffened, and he moved his feet, into something she was beginning to suspect was a thoroughly well-trained duelling stance. He had a wand; he knew how to use it. Duelling wasn't the only reason to have a wand, but it often implied it. She might not know all the formalities and etiquette, but she knew that much.

"Come out." Clearly, Gabe felt he had to give whoever was behind those stones another chance.

This time, there was no sound she could hear, just a blast of deep red light shooting out. Gabe shifted, one hand coming up like a conductor's would, holding an orchestra in place with the lightest shift of a finger. It was as if he were surrounded by a globe of glass, and the red light hit it, and then faded, as if the globe itself were transforming it. Rathna thought that was rather like some of the water portal techniques, the transmutation of it.

Then he was doing something, a curve of the wand, elegant and precise, and light shot out. The light from his wand was a golden yellow, like the highlights in his hair, steady and glowing. It was the sort of glow that infused everything around it, not quite honey, but something similar. She could hear a curse from his opponent, but nothing clear.

Gabe took a step closer, but another shockingly red burst came out, flying awfully near his head. It was enough to make him duck, then take a couple of broad steps to the right, repositioning himself.

He followed that up with three rapid sharp thrusts of light, these a deep blue darker than the light by the portal had been, the kind of night sky you fell into. Whatever he'd been hoping, it seemed to be keeping his opponent off balance, because the next shot from behind the rocks went decidedly wide. Gabe took another step to the right, another forward, "Come out, would you?" He sounded almost hopeful.

Whatever he hoped, it didn't happen. There was another flurry of spells, this time a sickly dim green, rather like pond scum had been smeared all over the magic. It made Rathna's head ache, in the precise way that a badly tuned portal did, when something was not right, and getting worse. She frowned, trying to figure out what was doing that. They were too far from the actual portal, she thought, blinking against the light.

Gabe continued holding his own, more or less. He was parrying those green slashes of light, or they were bouncing off that clear globe around him, a bit of both. But one of them drove him sideways, down onto his left knee. There was a moment where his head bowed. He had to catch his breath, perhaps.

In that moment, there was an explosion of movement, something taking flight from the rocks, soaring up overhead. She couldn't get a good look at it, the sun was at the worst angle. But it was a small bird. Not a raptor, she was fairly sure, the shape was wrong.

"Buggering damnation." Gabe's curse echoed around the rock walls. He let himself fall to a seated position, one knee pulled up to his chest. Rathna looked at the bird and back at the stones.

"Gabe?" She called out as clearly as she could. He was behaving like the duel was over, if not actually satisfyingly won.

He waved his free hand, the left, without the wand. "Come over, please." Then he rummaged in his pockets and took out a handkerchief, patting his face. She carefully took Verity's reins in her left hand, and Livet's in her right hand, walking between them. Then she thought, and went to Livet's side, reaching to find Gabe's walking stick still attached to his saddle bag. She brought it over, leaving the mares standing.

"Is it safe?" She offered the stick, then her other hand. He peered at both for a moment, then took her hand and let her pull him upright. He was still breathing hard, panting, as if the duel had been a great exertion.

"He's gone. Blast." Gabe wiped his face again, then unfurled his walking stick. He tested his left foot firmly on the ground, wriggling it, as if he had to start with that before he could think of anything else.

Rathna took a step back to give him space, getting a better look at the stones. There was a little inset nook, where water and time had worn away some of the stone, and a standing pillar or bit of rubble. "He was back there?"

"Behind the stone. I'll have a look in a minute."

"How." She looked over her shoulder, up into the sky. "How did he do that?"

"Shapeshifter. Blast. We'll have to hope none of the eagles want a mid-day snack. Some sort of small bird. A thrush, a robin, a wren. I didn't get a very good look."

"You were," Rathna pointed out evenly, "A little busy at the time."

Gabe's head snapped up, as if he'd been about to feel sorry for himself. "I lost him." His voice was flat.

"I am no expert on duelling. Certainly not the expert on the matter in this conversation. But you seemed to be holding your own until he changed the rules of gravity on you."

Gabe blinked at her, several times, then his face cracked into a smile. "Wise lady." He took in a breath, let it out.

"Could I ask you to grab the flask from my bag? Let me get myself sorted, and then we'll see if there's any evidence."

"Another place where you are far more expert than I." she agreed. She went to the saddlebags, rummaging until she found a flask. "Your working stones, too?"

"Please." He was looking at the stones, the sort of frowning eyes half-closed way she looked at stones. She tugged his stone case out of his bag. She patted Livet on the neck as soothingly as she could, and then came back over to him, leaving the horses to browse the scattered grass on the ground.

He took the case from her, letting out a small sigh of relief, tucking the wand into his sleeve without comment. "Can you do a light charm and hold it where I tell you?" Then he glanced over. "No one on the road?"

"No. And I didn't like the idea of trying for Sorcha's, even if she were there."

Gabe considered that, then nodded. "Fair enough. How'd you catch up so quickly?"

It made her laugh. "I got off the horse and ran. I'm fairly sure Verity would scold me if she could, that's not how this is supposed to work, but it seemed much more sensible than falling off."

Gabe grinned at her. "Well, aren't we a pair, then?"

"You are the one who - was that a somersault?" Rathna tried to sound arch and failed utterly.

It made him bow, a low bow, deliberately courtly. "I have a number of skills I may not have mentioned yet." Then he straightened up. "Actually, one more case, would you? Other saddlebag, the small black one. It's a proper evidence case."

Rathna went around to Livet's other side and

rummaged. The case was right at the top, a leather case tightly wrapped around something solid inside. "This?"

He nodded, and she brought it back, handing it to him. Gabe ran his fingers along the fastening, and it popped open. "Right. Can you hold this, don't touch anything inside, just the outside, here? And be ready to make a light?"

Rathna felt rather like a healer's assistant must. "Of course."

Gabe made his way to one side of the stone that was blocking their view. There was a fair bit of greenery back there, the same sort of moist green smell as up near the cave entrance. She stayed a step behind Gabe, letting him decide what to do. "Light, please. Up here, over my right shoulder. Don't touch anything, tell me if you accidentally do."

She concentrated, bringing her magic into her hand, murmuring the incantation they all learned, "Fiat lux," and then getting a clear glowing sphere. It tickled her hand slightly as she held it, but she moved, holding it over Gabe's shoulder.

He was focused entirely on the ground, moving slowly, indicating where he wanted the light. She found it exhausting to keep up with him, to slow herself to his pace, as he looked over every inch of ground.

Finally, two-thirds of the way through, a good hour into this process, she felt, he stopped. "Hold out the case for me, please." As he spoke, he was drawing something from a pocket in his vest, two thin silk gloves, from a delicate silk pouch. She stepped to the side, where he'd already searched, and held the case carefully out, her hands as steady as she could make them.

From the case, he took a pair of tweezers, a small glass bottle that had a pad of cloth in it, and a small bottle of clear liquid. He opened the bottle and took the cloth in the tweezers. Then he poured some of the liquid on the cloth, and bent down to a specific spot on one of the stones. Rathna could just see a darker spot, and when Gabe brushed it with the cloth, he brought it up. She could see a greenish-black there, moss, perhaps, but also a deep red stain, more prominent.

"Blood." He sounded tremendously satisfied. "That will do us some good."

It took him another forty-five minutes to search the tiny space to his satisfaction, and they found nothing else of note. She, for her part, could not entirely figure out why the man had been there, what this stone had to do with it.

"What do we do now?" Rathna was cautious once they were back outside.

"Gather up the ponies, ride back, send a package off to the Guard, and honestly, falling over in bed sounds wonderful." He looked drawn, now.

"You definitely get first go at the bath. I can see about trays in our rooms."

Gabe nodded. "I'd like to talk it through with you. When we've..." He swept his hand over himself. "Washed. Tidied."

"Of course." She suspected, the way he was, he'd need a hand up the stairs, and she didn't lay bets on him staying awake to talk. But he was a man of constant surprises, so who knew.

THIRTY

Gabe felt awful by the time they got back to the inn. Getting back on Livet had taken most of the rest of his energy and he still had a dozen things that needed doing. Riding back, Rathna kept looking at him. She didn't fuss, but she was watching, carefully.

It was reassuring that if he slid off into the mud, someone would notice right away. But he was stuck on the uncomfortable realisation that she deserved more honesty than he'd given her so far. At least she did now.

Instead of asking him anything, she stayed quiet, keeping an eye out. When they got to the inn, she said, firmly. "You go up. I'll get help with the horses. Wash up, I'll see about food." She hesitated. "I assume that was the questionable man?"

"Likely. He matched the description, including the voice. I'll tell Gormlaith, one of the Guard will be coming by." Gabe couldn't stop from sighing. "Rathna, thank you. And if I'm not flat on my face asleep, come in when there's food, all right?"

She raised an eyebrow but nodded. Gabe found himself

running on pure stubbornness and willpower, but twenty minutes later, he was in the bathtub. The bath was, unfortunately, not terribly restful. He kept feeling a little itchy, on the cusp of something, like he had when he was newly eighteen.

He was older now, and at least a bit wiser, and he wasn't going to go and do anything dramatic. At least he hoped not. On the other hand, it meant that lounging in the bath wasn't really on. He knocked on Rathna's door and called out "Bath's yours," before he went off to write his initial report, and the cover letter for the package.

It took him twenty minutes to dress in something adequately comfortable and wrap his ankle with the cooling wrap again. It didn't hurt as much as it probably should, which was worrisome. It took three times that - about three times as long as it should have - for him to write up his report.

He blessed the fact that not only did he have one of the quite new magical journals, but that all the more remote Guard posts had one. That meant he could write one letter, addressed to the nearest Guard at the same time as the officers back in Trellech who doled out duties. Everyone would get the same explanation of what had happened and what was needed next.

He got confirmation ten minutes later that someone would be by in the morning to collect it and get it back to Trellech. And that the wheels were in motion for the appropriate judicial approvals for a blood trace. That was all he could do for now, then. Before he could figure out his next step, there was a knock at his door. Rathna's voice called out, "Supper."

"Come in." He set his journal aside and pushed himself to sit up more than slouch. Rathna opened the door, bringing in a bed tray. Then she disappeared, coming back with a smaller tray she set on his desk, and a wooden bucket with a quartet of beer bottles. "Refreshment, as well. If you don't want beer, I can get something else?"

He answered the question she was not directly asking. "No potion, at least not yet. Beer's a fine idea, though. Um." He gestured. "Close the door, so we can talk, make yourself at home?"

She closed the door. "May I do the privacy charm?"

Gabe was relieved he didn't have to. "Go ahead. It shouldn't interfere with any of my warding. But don't touch that package, that's the evidence." He gestured to where it was sitting on top of his trunk. "I'll need to swear no one else has touched it but me when I hand it over."

"Silence oath? I don't know how that works, your evidence."

Gabe nodded. They all swore an oath to the Silence to keep magic secret, to keep them safe, from others who didn't have magic, so she knew that one. It pressed on them in different ways, if they tried to break it. Exceedingly convenient, at times, but also terrifying, in a way that spoke of primordial panic.

But she'd likely only made an oath on the Silence when she was twelve, and perhaps for the beginning and end of her apprenticeship. He made them fairly routinely. "Silence oath. We're talking about people's lives, with evidence. We have to not only be honest, but be proven honest."

That made her frown in thought, he'd distracted her. He pushed himself into a slightly more comfortable position, and considered his supper, as she opened and handed him one of the bottles. A hearty stew, two rolls and butter, and what looked like a bit of toffee pudding. That would do quite nicely. She waited until he took a spoonful. "You didn't say you duelled."

That made him cough. "No. The wand does perhaps imply it."

Rathna just raised her eyebrow, and Gabe knew, everything coming together, that he'd be telling her all of it. It was like something clicked into place, unyielding, the same sort of omen-clad certainty he'd had four years ago.

"There's a lot I didn't tell you." Gabe swallowed. "Shall I now, then?"

She met his glance steadily. He was sure she must be uncertain what was coming, but she was fiercely determined to hear it. "Yes. Please."

"There are several parts." He couldn't sort out how many right now. "First. My parents." Gabe watched her. "I have told you the truth, as far as it went, but not the whole truth. My parents are Lord Richard and Lady Alysoun Edgarton, of Kent. Papa is also an officer of the Guard, like I said, and a magistrate. He oversees several divisions of the Guard who handle specific kinds of problems, unusual cases. Aunt Mason works with him regularly."

Watching her face was the sort of thing that in any other moment would have been fascinating. It was exactly the kind of thing he'd enjoy teasing out and puzzling through with other Penelopes for days. Now, though, he was on tenterhooks, hanging, waiting to see what she made of it. Of what that made him, in her eyes.

She didn't react, not deliberately. Her face went from focused attention to bafflement to a rapid sorting through what he'd told her before, and how this fit. When her face settled, there was a sort of distant pleasantness. "And that makes you what, then?"

"Papa's heir. Though we all hope, very much, not for a

long time to come. His father lived to his nineties, and Papa's not yet fifty. Mostly, that's duties to the land. The family estate is Veritas, in Kent, the portal I mentioned. Beautiful countryside, a small village nearby."

Rathna blinked. "And you're a Penelope."

"I am excellent at being a Penelope, it turns out. And very happy being one." He could hear his voice getting defensive. So many people had questioned that decision, all along.

"But you don't need to work."

Gabe considered. "I do not need to work for the money. I take a salary, it would be worse for the people who need one if I didn't. But I give most of it to good causes." He flicked his fingers, setting his spoon down. "The Trellech Library roof fund. The Temple of Healing. Veterans homes. Also bookshops."

Then he took another breath and let it out. "I work because there is a thing I can do, that helps people. That brings justice, understanding. Betterness." He fumbled there, he'd never really explained it to anyone. His parents understood. Aunt Mason had her sometimes ridiculous desire to know how everything worked, underneath. The other Penelopes had their own reasons for being driven.

Rathna nodded, frowning, that same distance still there. "And they arranged your apprenticeship?"

Gabe flushed. "Not really. I mean, I've known Aunt Mason since I was seven. And other Penelopes. By the time I was halfway through Schola, everyone but Papa was clear where I was going to end up. I think he hoped I'd go to the Guard, honestly."

That made her glance at his ankle, and he nodded slightly. "The ankle settled it." He let out a breath. "So. The ankle."

The word caught her attention, sharply; she leaned forward. She wasn't dissembling with him, or if she were trying to, she needed a lot more practice. "Yes?" It was almost a breath, so soft he barely caught the word.

Gabe closed his eyes. He wanted desperately to watch her reactions, and he wasn't sure he could bear to. Then he took a long breath and let it out. "I turned eighteen on March 4th of 1918. They were starting to call men at eighteen, then, they were desperate. I'd have until I left Schola in early June, but that was it." Then, it came out in a rush. "I've never told my parents most of this. Or anyone else."

That made her raise both eyebrows. "You have your reasons." She left it at that. She didn't ask him to tell her, or why he was on the edge of telling her. Or any of the things any of his inquisitive family and adoptive relations might have done.

"May I tell you?" It slipped out that way before he could stop it.

"Please." Then she considered and gestured at the bed. "May I?" That was promising, that she didn't want to be further away. He nodded, and she moved to set the bed tray down on the floor beside the bed. She sat down about halfway down the length, facing him, one leg tucked under her and the other hanging off the edge.

"Two weeks later, I was home from Schola for the equinox break. Mama and Papa had been in Trellech for the night, some party or event. I had a - it wasn't quite a nightmare. That's not the right word. Nightmares aren't real, they're our fears, our worries. This was real. This was seeing what would happen. Not just seeing it, but feeling it."

Now he couldn't look at her. He closed his eyes, one

hand in his lap, the other tucked under a fold of the blanket where she wouldn't see him clutching at it.

"A true dream, then. A prophetic one. Your omen." Rathna's voice was careful. Again, she didn't ask him to go on, just made space for it.

"Parts of it - I have a sort of cousin, my parents helped him, he's not blood related.. I call him Del, his last name's Delwyn." Gabe took a breath. "He's a Lord, inherited the title before he was twenty, when I was six, seven. He went to fight, he was hurt, his head. He's... he's home, and he's alive. But it, he doesn't think the same way. He can't. He can't do the things on the family farms he used to. He can't read, not much. Someone's got to keep an eye on him." Which for Gabe had always felt like the bitterest blow. Del was happy enough, but he was different, in ways that kept hurting and aching.

There was a silence, as if she'd nodded, then realised he still had his eyes closed. "There are men like that, near us. It's hard. For everyone. Better when they're kind, still, and not everyone is. But there's this gap, there's no bridging it. What was. What is now."

Gabe nodded, fervently. "Part of it was dreaming. I was too close to the fighting, I don't know how or why. Del wasn't supposed to be, either. But there was a moment where I knew I'd - I'd died. Felt it. Woke up screaming."

His hand was clenched in the sheets now, enough his wrist and arm were beginning to shake with the strain. "Later that morning, I went out riding. I've always loved it." Always had, always did, always would. It was one of the certainties of his life. He managed to open his eyes for an instant. Rathna was sitting there, leaning forward, attentive.

Now, if he could put what happened next into words.

Rathna didn't know what to do or say. There was a delicate, fragile balance here. First, learning the reality of who he was, what he was. Gabe was right, he hadn't lied to her, but he'd laid a path for her to follow along that wasn't the truth.

She had wanted to ask him why, why he hid that. But then he'd gone on. Gone on with telling her something he hadn't told anyone else, not the parents who obviously loved him, who he just as obviously loved right back. Not the other people he'd mentioned, who he also loved and respected and trusted. He hadn't told any of them, and he was telling her.

She didn't know what was right here, other than holding that trust as gently as she could. "I'm listening."

Gabe had closed his eyes again. She could see his hand clenching at the sheet, the way the muscles were bunching, but she didn't call attention to it. She didn't want to disrupt the balancing act he was doing, or trying to do.

"You asked about snakes." His voice was almost a whisper. "I went out riding. And my horse, she shied. Not like her. There was this instant, where there was no time, and all the time in the world. And I flashed back to the dream, and it was like a tremendous adder was looming, fangs out. And in its mouth, there was my death. Soon. Pointless. Utterly worthless. Not doing anything for anyone. Mud and blood and screams and nothing." He shuddered, his shoulders shaking silently, his hand still clenched, but the rest of him didn't move.

Before she could figure out what to say or do, he went on. "I could stand dying if it did some good. Or at least might. This, this wasn't that. And I knew it. Knew the day, knew the hour. Knew what it would feel like." He swallowed hard, like he was on the edge of nausea.

Rathna wanted to shift closer to him, but she didn't want to upset him. Instead, carefully, she reached out her hand and rested it on his right knee, the one closer to her. It was absurdly intimate to touch him like that, but he let out a little sigh, a shudder that didn't look so desperately in pain. Then he took a deeper breath and let it out.

"I knew," His voice caught. "I knew I had a choice. If I stayed on Invicta, I'd die. By the end of July. If I let myself fall..." His voice trailed off for a moment. "I'd hurt. I'd change. But I'd be alive in a year. And I was selfish enough to, to fall."

That caught her attention, immediately. To be that young, that alone, in that moment, and to think the choice to live was selfish. She waited to see if he'd go on. When he didn't, she cleared her throat. "I'm glad you did. That you're here."

It shook him, she could see that immediately. He carefully unclenched his fingers, as if he'd hurt them, then opened his eyes, looking at her searchingly. She stayed right where she was, hand on his knee, looking at him as evenly as she could. "You don't think I'm selfish?"

Rathna shook his head. "You are ridiculously clever, Gabe, and thoughtful and observant. You're kind. You're considerate. I dare say you'll make an excellent Lord some day. I haven't known you long, but I see you thinking about what things are like for me. What will put other people at ease. How you go well out of your way to do that. Not just when it will benefit you. Plenty of people do it then, that's easy. You do it when it's not easy. When no one will notice if you don't. You do it like breathing." It came out of her in a rush, and she realised it was all true.

She didn't know what to make of some of it, her mind was still catching up, and her heart. If he was to be a Lord, she knew she had to squash down whatever infatuation it was. That was harder and harder, when he'd let her see something so intimate. It was like looking at the veins of magic in a portal, the glow and the hum, at the most delicate stage of creation.

Then something occurred to her. "That explains how you broke your ankle. But surely..." She wasn't entirely sure how to ask this. "Didn't you have access to healers?"

He let out a puff of breath. "Many of them had gone to the War. Or the rehabilitation hospitals. All sorts of places that needed them. And there are..." He hesitated. "This is going to sound like I'm mad. Out of my mind."

Rathna gestured, a little circle of her hand, encouraging. "What is?"

"That moment, where I chose? It was like the Silence oath. That kind of weight, consequence. Not just about one thing, about everything. It was like, it was like one of the old magics. Where you go to the Fatae, and you come out, and it's been decades. Or the promises you make, they bind you in ways you hadn't seen. I felt it all tighten, and then I chose, and there was, there was a cost."

He waved a hand at his ankle. "It wasn't an awful break. It should have healed fine. And I can bear weight on it, that's not the problem. It's that it hurts. I always know it's there, I can't ever forget. That it's the cost of my life."

Rathna didn't know what to say. She had a feeling, that song of magic she heard in the background, that that wasn't quite it. But she couldn't argue with him, not without a much better sense of things. "How is it right now?"

He shrugged. "It hurts. Less than it probably should, actually. The wrap keeps it cold, which helps. I'll take a potion when I go to bed. Two days running isn't the best idea, but..." Another little shrug, as if that were just how things were.

"You should eat a bit more, then. If you can. If you're going to add a potion." She glanced at the tray. He nodded, and she got off the bed to settle it in front of him again. It gave more space between them, but she shifted to settle down closer to the foot of the bed.

She waited until he'd had a good ten bites, and half of the roll. "Why did you tell me?"

Gabe looked startled. He set the roll down, carefully. "It felt wrong not to. Papa is an amazing duellist. He has been since he apprenticed. That's what Uncle Magni teaches. He was in the guard, twice twenty years man, now he tutors. He taught me, too."

He took a careful bite of the bread, chewing and swallowing, like he was giving himself more space. "I'm good, solidly good, but Papa's brilliant. Things come together for him, he says, when he duels. All the little threads. Like you, and the portals. And me, and the things I do. But if you have that gift, Papa's very clear, you have to honour it. Or it goes away."

Rathna nodded slowly. That part was entirely logical and sensible. Very much what she expected. "Why haven't you told your parents? Or... anyone. It's clear you have other people who'd listen."

There was that little half shrug again. "My father is made of honour and loyalty and service to magic." He said it like it was simple fact, water was wet, the sun rose in the east. "And Mama is... Mama is a bit more complicated, but she's clear-sighted. She understands layers. I could maybe tell her, but I couldn't expect her not to tell him. Do you see?" Then he grimaced. "I'm sorry."

She waved a hand. It didn't explain why he hadn't told other people, but she could see enough of it. "I - I remember my parents. They weren't like that, but I understand, enough, I think."

That got her a shy little smile. "I'd like you to meet them sometime. Mama would have lots of questions for you. And Uncle Gil, of course."

It got her to look at him. "What would they make of me, then? I mean." She gestured at herself. Decidedly not from that sort of family. "I mean, not even magical blood. Never mind the rest of it."

Gabe blinked at her, then looked at her, as if he were considering an entirely new map of observations. He was silent for a good minute before he shrugged. "If we wrap this up reasonably promptly, which seems a bit more likely than it did this morning, they're having a costume party soon. We could go, you could get a good look at them without anyone prying too much."

She was sure it was a generous offer, but she couldn't for the life of her see how he'd make it work. Instead, she said,

"Eat your stew." She reached for her own plate again, and at least set him an example.

They ate in silence for a good few more minutes until he was working on the pudding. Then she blinked. "Wait. You think we're going to have this sorted sooner than later?"

Gabe grinned at her, broad and delighted. She felt rather stupid now, but he made that all right, like it was a great gift to share his idea with her. "If our mysterious bird man was doing something to block the flow, we have an idea where now. What happens if we remove that dam?"

It rocked her back, the implications. Not just that he'd made them, when she hadn't. Not just that he was probably right. But that he'd apparently done that while exhausted, hurt, and telling her his greatest secret.

Before she could stop herself, she found herself saying, "But what happens then." She didn't exactly want to spend more time in this inn than she actually had to. She missed London, and she worried about Morah Avigail, and she wanted more of her books. But surely they'd wrap things up, and he'd disappear into the Guard Hall, or Kent, or wherever it was he spent his time.

He tilted his head. "I hope you're my friend, now, Rathna." It was suddenly cautious. "I'm not very good at having friends. But I hope you are."

That was another thing she had been trying to sort out. "Why don't you have friends, Gabe? You're charming, thoughtful, clever. Funny. Easy to talk to. I'm not good at friends, but I'm none of those things, except the clever and maybe the thoughtful."

It made him smile, but it was the sort of faint smile that had pain under it. "I was good friends with two boys from the village. They died, early in the War. Six weeks apart. And at school..." He shrugged. "I knew what I wanted, very early. I wasn't a swot, a brown nose, not exactly. I didn't care about the marks, though I did well on that count, because why not. But I wasn't up for fooling around when there were things to learn. I always had more I wanted to know. Not like the Owls, in the books, though a book's a fine thing. Not like anyone, really."

"That song, the one I hear. You had that. Early. A lot of people don't. A lot of people never do, I guess."

He gave another of those shrugs. "I don't know how to be friends with someone my own age, someone who's just as skilled at what she does at I am at what I do. But I think we've made a start, haven't we? I mean, if you're willing?"

She wasn't at all sure what she was getting herself into, but she knew, all of her knew, that she wanted to find out.

G abe woke the next morning to a sharp knock on his door. "Guard's here."

He must have fallen asleep as he was while they were talking, sometime after he'd finally taken his potion. The tray and the beer were gone. He could feel someone else's wards on the door, Rathna's. But he was still in dressing gown and slippers, on top of the bed, but under a blanket. That was a tad embarrassing. That wasn't Rathna at the door, either. Eoin.

"I'll be five minutes. No, better make it ten. Breakfast, after?"

"More like lunch." Eoin laughed. "But we'll feed you. I'll be telling him you'll be down."

Gabe glanced at the side table, fumbling for the pocket watch. More like lunch was right, it was nearly eleven. That meant the Guard had probably come from Glasgow this morning. A courier, likely. He stretched carefully, hearing one of his shoulders pop, then he rotated his ankle cautiously. Nothing hurt too badly, the dangerous sorts of pain. It hurt, just less than it might have, given the last two days.

Next, he looked quickly at his journal. Nothing new, other than saying that a Guard was on the way that morning, and the judicial approvals were expected by the time the sample got back. That was unusually speedy. It made him wonder who had a particular interest in the results. No names on the courier, but nothing unexpected to deal with.

That done, he could slip out of his pyjamas and dressing gown quickly, and into trousers, shirt, and vest. Entirely presentable. He ran a comb through his hair, ducked down the hall to the loo, and then washed his face, trying to get the sleep out of his eyes.

In eight minutes, he was on his way downstairs, cane in his left hand, and the evidence case in the bag over his right shoulder. He looked into the main pub room, and a man in Guard uniform, in his mid-forties, was sitting there. Not someone Gabe knew well, but yes, one of the couriers. Someone must have sent him out specially.

Gormlaith was behind the bar and gestured with her elbow. "We've fish and chips, or sandwiches, for lunch. Mistress Stone's out by the stable."

"Thank you. Let me pass things along and then see if she wants lunch. If I could get a cup of tea, though?"

"Oh, sure, tea." Gormlaith went off for the hot water, and Gabe came across to the table by the window. "Guard - Orland, isn't it?" The name hit him at the last minute.

The man ducked his chin. "Wasn't sure you'd remember me." He nodded. "They sent me up this morning. Awful far way out you are." He reached to the chair beside him. "And Penelope Mason insisted I bring this up to you." He handed over a parcel wrapped in brown paper, the two books he was expecting, and a letter tucked in the outer string addressed to Rathna.

"Ta for bringing that along." Gabe grinned. "As to the far from everything, that's what we're here to see about. Making it easier to get here." He nodded. "How much did they tell you?" That was the way to do it, since Gabe wasn't sure what he was permitted to pass along.

Guard Orland snorted. "You had a duel with a man turned into a bird, have a sample of blood for testing, Judge Mackenzie is ready to sign the permissions. Can you do an expanded report before I get back? So..." He hesitated, doing the count in his head. "Hour and a half to Fort William, three to Glasgow. Judge said she'd be around until six."

Gabe did some rapid calculations of his own. "One of the Healing Temple garden parties tonight, isn't it? Anything in particular to be specific about, do you know?"

Orland shrugged. "You know the sort of thing she likes, I gather. What makes this the thing that will help your goal." There was a little note of a question there.

"I'll manage something. Need to talk to a couple of people first about what the next steps look like. I know Her Honour prefers that, too. Very big on next steps, she is."

"You know her, then?"

That made Gabe grin. "She knows my parents, she's known me since I was in short trousers. It does give me an advantage these days, because I know what she wants to see the first time. On the other hand, she knows just what to expect from me, and won't ever let me get away with slacking. Two-edged sword, that."

Orland chuckled, a bit ruefully. "Think you could get them to make up a package of sandwiches or somewhat for me? I didn't fancy the look of the options in Fort William."

"Sure. Let's hand my evidence over properly, and then we'll see about the food." Gabe took a deep breath, and Orland did the same, extending his right hand as Gabe put his out. They clasped wrist to wrist, so that Gabe's palm was over Orland's pulse, and the other way round.

"By the magic in my blood and my oaths as a Penelope, I, Gabriel Anthony Edgarton, swear, O Silence, that this evidence has been touched by no one else. I swear that it has been properly prepared and sealed to the pursuit of justice in a case of needful public good. I give it over to this man, Guard Orland, to pursue that justice." The words were the standard ones, but at the end, he could feel the clutch of the Silence around him. For him, it was as it had been since the day of his ankle. That cold fear not of death - death would be over - but of losing his abilities to think clearly, to move, to do all the things he loved. He shuddered with it once, not bothering to hide it.

Orland picked up smoothly enough, though he wasn't eager for the oath. No one ever was. "I, Guard Horatio Orland, swear, O Silence, by the magic in my blood, that this evidence has been properly handed to me. I swear I will protect it with all my strength until it is properly handed over to another for the pursuit of justice." He swallowed hard, his hand clenched for a moment, and then relaxed, and he nodded.

Gabe let his hand go, and they both took a breath, the automatic settling of people who took these oaths, and felt their weight, over and over again. "There. That's done. Let me see about some food for you. Anything you don't eat."

"Not haggis, this trip. Near anything else."

That made Gabe snort, and he went off to talk to Gormlaith through the kitchen door, coming back out. "She'll have something for you in five minutes. Anything else, or?"

Orland waved him off. "No, I'm fine. You have things to be doing, I'm sure."

Gabe did. He wanted to see what Rathna was up to and let her know about that letter. He tucked the package into his satchel and made his way out the front door. He turned toward the stable, but frowned when he saw someone riding in circles in the dirt packed courtyard.

Jamie was perched on the mounting block. As Gabe got closer, he saw that Rathna was learning how to post to the trot, figuring out how to rise up and down. When she saw him, she carefully settled Verity back into a walk, and aimed directly for him, cutting across the circles she'd been making.

"You didn't say there was a way to not be jostled all the time." She was laughing, teasing him. Perhaps he hadn't been an utter fool last night after all.

"We were a trifle busy. And posting is a bit of an advanced art." Gabe nodded at Jamie. "Jamie giving you some tips, then?"

"Mostly he got me started and kept an eye on me. You still owe me a lesson, though." Then she looked him up and down. "You've talked to the Guard, then?"

"I have. And I think you and I should talk to Gormlaith and Eoin - and Jamie and his Nan, if we can - about the next steps. I'll need to write up a more detailed report before Orland gets back to Trellech with the evidence." Then he added. "Oh, and there's a letter for you. From Mistress Levy, I'm assuming." He made as if to get it out.

Rathna shook her head at the movement. "I can wait a minute or three for it. So I should go untack and meet you inside?"

Gabe smiled at that. "Yeah. Though I can give you a hand?" Rathna swung off, more smoothly than she'd been doing, and picked up the reins to lead Verity back. Gabe called out, "Jamie, is your Nan free? Handy?"

"Could be. She's down the hill. Should I be getting her, then?"

Gabe nodded. "I'd like her sense of the community. Yours too, please. I'll see about a space with Gormlaith, and some food and drink, by the time you're back." Jamie nodded, gave an amiable wave, and swung himself off the mounting block, making a beeline for the road.

They untacked and groomed Verity in silence for a couple of minutes, before Rathna said, a bit cautiously. "I hope it was all right to let you sleep."

Gabe nodded. "I'm sorry, I must have fallen asleep on you? Abysmal company."

That made her laugh. "You had good cause. And you're normally such an interesting conversationalist. I took some more notes. Do you have a plan, then? If you want to talk to the people you're rounding up?"

"Not just them, but I think they'll know how to do what I want, which is a community meeting. Tell me if I've got the theory right, before we go in. There are magical energy flows, and the portal was designed to tap into a set of them, fairly directly. You don't need to tell me how or where they go, if you'd rather not."

"I think you've earned yourself a look at the maps, and I can show you on the ground, sometime. But not a thing to share the details of, no."

He smiled at that. "So, the next step is to see about undoing whatever it is our mysterious bird man did. But I'm thinking it can't be too complicated to undo, because they'd have noticed a whole host of new folks poking around. Geordie would have, anyway. He spotted us right quick."

"Huh." Rathna paused in her grooming, leaning against

Verity. Gabe found the image really rather appealing. Her hair had come out of the braid down her back in wisps, framing her face. She was pleasantly flushed from the ride, and she'd entirely lost the stiffness she'd had when they met. Not just that they knew each other now, had tested out what that meant, but that she was more at home in her body somehow.

Also, it just proved his point that riding was excellent for people, and the world would be better if more people did that more of the time. "No, I agree. So we get them together, figure out how to ask the larger community, and then... do that?"

"Exactly." He gestured. "Figuring out how to undo the dam, that might be a trick, but I'm hoping you can figure it out. I have some ideas, but I have no idea if they'll work with a portal. We can test things. At least get a sense of the options, and what other skills are needed, right?"

She ducked under Verity's neck, going around to the other side. "You're thinking about all the possible options, aren't you? How each one changes things."

"Papa does it with duelling. Mama does it with looking at things. I do it with doing things. Seeing the patterns." He shrugged. "That's why I want to go into warding, as a specialty. It's all that sort of patterns."

"And," Rathna said, "You're on familial terms with one of the current experts in the field."

Gabe laughed. "That's a benefit, certainly." He patted Verity on the shoulder. "She all set on your side? Seen to the hooves?"

"Did them before I rode, let me do them again. Jamie explained that." Gabe stood back while she carefully ran her hand down each leg. Verity was well-behaved and not inclined to jerk her foot out of the way or kick. That done,

Rathna smiled. "I'm learning rather a lot more than I expected. But this is good. I like getting better at the riding."

Gabe offered his right arm to her. "An escort, then, in to lunch? I'm famished. And we have a lot of plotting to do."

"Thank you, kind sir." Her voice had a teasing note to it, the same relaxation she'd had leaning back against Verity, and he liked that very much indeed.

THIRTY-THREE

When Rathna came back from the bathroom, she could hear people gathering downstairs. They were about thirty minutes out from the meeting to discuss what to do next. That afternoon, the four they'd talked to - Gormlaith and Eoin, Sorcha and Jamie - had agreed that letting people hear what the options were would go a long way. Not that people wouldn't argue and be stubborn, but there was a good chance they'd see what the next steps should be much more clearly.

They'd also sorted through who should say things, and what should be said. Most of that was for Rathna to do. Gabe had made it clear, every one of his actions, the way he deferred to her, that she was the expert. Oh, he'd certainly added his comments. She appreciated that, she'd never run a meeting like this, or even been at many of them. When the Portal Keepers met, she was by far one of the most junior, and her place had been to listen. This would be different.

Now, however, she had to figure out what to wear, something she had never been good at. She laid the dresses she'd packed out, frowning at them. The burgundy one she'd worn on the train had been cleaned, but it was decidedly dull, as it was designed to be. There was a blue one, but it was nearly navy, and also rather dull. She could wear a skirt and blouse. There was a creamy white dropped waist blouse, and a deep green skirt, to go under it. She was standing there, wrapped in her dressing gown still, when there was a knock on her door. She pulled the gown around her, and said, "Who is it?"

"Gabe. I had an idea."

She sighed, but nodded. "Come in." When he opened the door, she saw he was infuriatingly, already dressed and looking particularly sharp, given he was wearing country tweeds. They were obviously well worn in, but they fit him precisely. The shades of brown in the tweed brought out highlights in his hair like the little glints of mica in rock. He had a deep green tie on and matching pocket square that somehow managed to anchor everything together brilliantly. There was something subtle of the same colour as cufflinks, peeping out from his jacket at the wrists.

He took in the clothing on the bed in one glance. "Ah. Sorting out what to wear. I'm sorry, women have it so much harder."

Rathna shook her head, frowning at the options and not liking any of them. "I'm not sure what would be best."

"You want to present yourself as the expert you are and be taken seriously." He said that as if it were the most obvious thing.

She, frankly, would be glad to settle for not being insulted to her face or laughed out of the room, but his goal did rather presume those didn't happen. "And how do you suggest I do that? Not having your trunk on hand."

That made him laugh. "Moment." He disappeared back across the hallway before she could stop him or say anything. He reappeared less than two minutes later, with several pieces of cloth draped across his arm.

The top piece was a muted yellow, not quite mustard, a colour she would never have expected him to have around. He laid one item on each of her outfits, rather like a fairy godmother giving gifts. The yellow turned out to be a shawl of soft wool, set on top of the burgundy dress. The navy dress got something in a beautiful cream, with some sort of embroidery along the edge. The blouse and skirt got a broad rectangular shawl of a deeper green and blue. It brought out the green of the skirt in a way she had entirely not expected. She blinked at it, and then at him, baffled.

"In matters of clothing, I am Mama's child, through and through. Thankfully. Papa doesn't know what to do if he can't wear a uniform. I got those in Skye, as presents, no reason you can't borrow one of them for the night." He waved a hand. "I'll let you try them on. The cream blouse and green skirt is probably the most professionally polished. But I think you might like the burgundy and yellow rather a lot, and it would look particularly fine on you." She just blinked at him. He grinned at her and withdrew. "You've twenty minutes."

Fifteen minutes later, she had not managed to take off the burgundy and yellow. It was entirely unlike what people here wore, what white people wore, but Gabe had been right, it looked splendid on her. It made her wonder who on earth he was buying a shawl that insistently yellow for. It wasn't his mother, not if she looked anything like him.

She had put her hair up, in a coiled braid pinned into a bun low on the back of her head. She was peering in her hand mirror one more time, when he knocked again. She stood up, feeling that he'd want to inspect the results.

She had swapped out the locket she usually wore for

her guild token. It was a small gold disc, stamped on one side with the symbols of her proession. The lemniscate on the other side was filled with an aquamarine for her Schola house, and a shimmering labradorite on the other for the portal energies. It shouldn't match, but somehow the colours gleamed. The flash of the labradorite brought the aqua and the gold, the burgundy and the yellow into union.

He opened the door and immediately beamed. "I was right!" Again, he sounded like he was getting the chance at a delightful gift, his ebullience flowing over. "Come on, shining mistress of magics. It's our time to make an entrance." He escorted her downstairs by his presence, rather than an arm through hers. Walking into the pub's main room before him was one of the most terrifying things she'd done, even given the scope of her past few days. But she took a breath and walked in, her head high.

There were perhaps thirty or forty people there, a good proportion of the local magical community. Some she recognised from her time at the inn, other faces she was sure she hadn't seen before. Perhaps two-thirds men, but a fair number of women, and a few small children.

"Good evening, everyone." She spoke as clearly as she knew how, and at least the music lessons back at Schola had set her up well for that. "Thank you for coming, for your time. We need your help and we want to know what you think would be best." She gestured at herself and at Gabe. He'd taken up a place behind her to her right, not quite leaning on the bar, but the next thing to it. "I am Mistress Rathna Stone, one of the Portal Keepers."

Rathna glanced at Gabe, who picked up readily. "And I am Gabriel Edgarton, an analyst with the Guard. A Penelope, if you know the term." Then he settled back again, giving her the stage.

"As I think you all know, gossip being what it is..." That much she understood, how a community passed the news. Spitalfields had taught her that very well indeed. "A few years ago, there was a portal established, so that you would not be so isolated in times of need. So that we could get needed supplies, healers, treatments here. Only, the portal stopped working. We think we know some of what's going on, but we need your knowledge of how things are, how things should be, here."

There was a low hum from the people there, but no one attempted to stop her, or heckle her, so she went on. "Our investigation suggests that someone, perhaps several some-ones, has somehow blocked the flow of the energies that fuel the portal. The portal isn't dangerous, but it won't work unless we can fix that."

"People, lass?" Someone called out from the back. "Not something?"

"We've been told about the beithir." Rathna kept her voice even. "And it may, indeed, be relevant. But we think the problem is this alteration by people. Deliberately." She glanced over at Eoin, who brought out a large map pinned on a bit of board.

"Here is the portal." She indicated it on the map. "And here's the loch, of course." Which they'd all know. "Yester-day, we came upon someone doing something here." She indicated the final spot. "Looking through what we know so far, we think that must be one of the key points for the alter-ation. But before we explore further, we needed to hear from you. What you know about the land, that spot, anything unusual you might have seen or heard or felt in the last few months. Crops behaving oddly, or plants, or cows or sheep."

There was another round of low-voiced conversation, longer and louder this time.

"What will you be doing, then?" That was an older woman. "Will we be having more people up here fussing at things? Sassenachs?" English, she knew that meant.

"Our goal is to fix the portal. If we can't do that, we'll have to report back to Trellech, to the Ministry, and they'll decide what to do about it. But if we can fix it, we'd like to." She added. "It would be a help for trade, too. Cattle. Sheep. Plenty of folks in Trellech wouldn't mind another source for butter, or heather honey, or all sorts of handwork. Besides the whiskey you're doing well with, of course."

She'd floated that idea in their discussion that afternoon. Gormlaith had immediately lit up, talking about the various cottage trades people took up, and how getting things to market had always been difficult and unwieldy. Rathna had been thinking about the markets near her, the ones that had all sorts of different things for sale. There was another murmur, but the questioner sat down looking thoughtful.

Another stood and said, "And you think you know how to fix things? You're a bit of a thing, and both of you young, he's barely grown." That was a gesture at Gabe. "And you're not proper from Albion, even, are you?"

Rathna had been sure that would happen. And she was also certain Gabe would insist on stepping in and had resigned herself to the fact she'd have to manage his reaction as well as her own. She felt herself stiffen before she forced herself to breathe. This was a particular kind of attuning herself with the flow of what was happening, working by feel. Finding the thread of the magic she heard, and trusting it would see her through. Tensing up wouldn't help that at all.

To her surprise, Gabe didn't make a move. As far as she could tell, he didn't even open his mouth. The pause meant she looked gathered, together, unflustered, when she spoke again. "I won't deny being London born and bred, sir. Or being on the younger side of forty. But I got top marks at Schola, and I know my work, sure as you do yours." She reached to touch the guild token. It gave her a place to leap from, though, and see if she could, perhaps, fly.

No one had explained so many things about how the magical world worked, when they had dropped her into it. They assumed she knew, like fish knew the water, or birds knew the air. Rathna had had to work it out, bit by bit, on her own, figuring out the safest ways to react, what it was permitted to ask about. She wondered, all of a sudden, if that were part of the problem here. No one had explained.

Rathna took a breath. "Let me tell you a bit about how portals work. What they do, how they connect places so far away, but safely enough a babe in arms will laugh, going through it. It's an old magic, an ancient one. We learned it from the Fatae, at the time of the Pact. We make spaces, of stone or wood or shaped with water, that hold the magic, make arches and passages out of it. Each of those spaces is unique, beautifully unique. I don't know all the magics of yours, not yet. She's sleeping, you see, I haven't been able to have a proper chat with her. But I want to. She's made of such sturdy stone, and there's a carpet of fossils all around her. Not so many portals have that. Nor such beautiful mountains, rising up and framing her, nor such a glorious view."

She let her very real appreciation of the land they stood on flow out of her, did her best to let them hear it. "I want to hear what she sounds like, properly. I want very much to give you all more choices. Not to make you live like city folk, or even town folk. But Gormlaith and Eoin, Sorcha and Jamie, they've been generous and kind to us. Others of you, too. I think it would be a fine thing if you could put a bit more by for the lean times. If you'd be able to send your children to learn new skills and come back home after. Get news proper fast, or extra hands if there's a flood or avalanche."

She took the briefest pause before forging ahead. "You're all proper independent, and I appreciate that. My family at home's like that, doing for themselves, not wanting interference from outside the community. But I want you to have the choice. Not have it taken from you by someone out for their own gain."

That set off a much louder round of conversation. No one was exactly yelling, certainly no one was yelling at her. But it was as if there were twenty or thirty conversations going on. She took a breath, took the mug Gormlaith handed her with an approving nod, and waited for them to settle down so she could explain what the next steps were.

The next morning, Gabe was late to breakfast. He'd fallen asleep as soon as they were done with the aftermath of the meeting. It was entirely embarrassing. Things had gone well, though. Rathna had hit precisely the right note. Better still, she'd been able to do it in a way that spoke to the people of Glencoe far more effectively than Gabe could have. He was everything they resisted. She was a surprise, and she'd used that well.

Now, however, he was late. He finished brushing his hair and ran his hand over vest and trousers to make sure everything was fastened. He had his wand tucked in the holster, and his full kit was set up, ready to be tucked into the saddlebag. He snagged his walking stick and made his way downstairs. Rathna was in a corner table, chatting to someone, who stood as Gabe came over.

"Pardon. Hope I didn't keep you?"

She shook his head. "I was getting a bit more of the lore. It seems to be about evenly divided if there's a beithir or not, and if there is, whether it's a problem. Which isn't much help to us but at least balanced? It makes me wonder what the beithir thinks of having the local magic disrupted, though."

Gabe snorted. "Frankly, I don't care so much about the beithir as long as I don't have to make a run for the loch. Running is not my strong point. But that's sensible, isn't it. Not liking its local habitat messed with." He seemed to consider that entirely logical on the creature's part.

It made her grin, and then food appeared in front of him. He glanced up, nodding at Gormlaith. "Were you just waiting on me?"

"I'm all packed and ready, yes. And arranged our lunch. Enough if we're out there for tea." She expected it to be a long day then. She might well be right, though this had the sort of feel of a puzzle on the edge of being solved.

"Right, then." He set himself to eating as quickly as reasonable, and within a quarter of an hour, they were in the stable, working on the horses. Rathna did her fair share of grooming, while Gabe got the tack ready and onto the mares. Then they set out. It was a clear day, warming up a bit with a crystal-blue sky.

Gabe aimed directly at the spot where he'd fought the duel. "Let me have a look first, in case anything's been moved." It hadn't. That would be too easy, really.

When he came back around the other side of the standing stone, Rathna was sitting on a blanket, her eyes closed. She had her hands held out with the palms down, a few inches above the ground, and her eyes closed. Gabe stopped, not wanting to interrupt whatever she was doing.

It was a good ten minutes later when she opened her eyes, shook out her hands, and stretched. "Oh. Sorry. Come sit?"

"I won't disrupt anything?" He was cautious.

"No. Nothing of note on your end?"

He shook his head. "I feel an itch of something, but I don't see anything obvious. I could try some disillusionment work, but only if it won't interfere with what you're doing."

That made her tilt her head. "You took music. Tenor. This would be easier if you were a bass, but you can hold a pitch steady, can't you?"

"Certainly?" He certainly knew about various musical techniques for resonance and magic, but they weren't something the Penelopes routinely used, since they rarely worked in consistent pairings outside of apprenticeship. "What am I doing?"

"Let me sort out the pitch, and you hold the drone, I'll wander and see if we can find what's blocked."

"When you put it that way, it seems quite simple, considering." Gabe stretched slightly, considering the best position for this. If they were going to be at it for a while, he didn't really want to be standing. But sitting on the ground was not the best position for singing, either. "Breathing's all right?"

"Oh, fine. Just keep matching the pitch." She seemed quite certain about this, and she was certainly the expert in figuring out what was going on with the flow and with the portal. She considered, stood up, and took out a small metal tuning fork from her pocket, before striking it on the standing stone. It set up a D, right in the middle of Gabe's range. "That, please."

He hummed for a moment, feeling the note in his body, as much as hearing it in his ear. Then he took a breath and opened his mouth, focusing on keeping the sound even and clear. It was an entirely different sort of singing than chamber music, certainly quite different than opera. It echoed off the stone.

Rathna let him get himself steady, and then he heard

her pick up the fifth, clear and perfect, the Pythagorean tuning, of course. There was space there, between the notes, the space that made temples and castle walls, the kinds of notes that anchored the strongest warding.

Her voice was more than just pleasant, it had a resonance that suggested she was in chest voice, nearer the bottom of her range than he was. He'd guessed as much from her speaking voice. She kept up the resonance easily, taking the same small breaths he did, the kind that tapered and picked up the sound again.

Once she was settled into the tone, she began moving around, walking steadily. He could hear the slight bobble here and there, as she took a step, or navigated some of the looser rocks on the ground. He did his best just to focus on keeping the drone up for her. Once she'd done a full circuit around the back of the rock, she came back, and now she did something he'd never heard before, not quite like that.

It had its roots in mediaeval chant, he thought, at the very cusp of polyphony. Where he held the drone, her voice moved and shifted. It didn't have a tune, not as the modern ear would recognise it.

Instead it was something ancient, something that came with smells and colours and a quality of light none of them knew anymore. From the time of the Pact, or before, certainly. It was pleasing to the ear, but it was something more than that. Enchanting, in the truest sense of the word. He had to work not to get distracted, to do his part in this music and be the anchor that let her voice fly.

It wasn't just her voice, though. He could hear something shifting. Feel it. It was like the faint vibration of a cat's purr. He closed his eyes to focus on his other senses. Then she hit a particular pattern of notes, and he heard a sourness. Not in her voice, but something behind her, something in the resonance of the stone. Rathna took a breath and then did something about that. He could hear the determination in her voice. The pitch became even more clear, like she was wielding a wand of her own.

He had a moment of utter distraction, then, about what she might do with a wand. He wanted, all of him, desperately, to give her one, to see what it opened up in her magic. Whether it made her confident, made her eyes glow with certainty. What kind of wood would suit, or the shape, whether it would be the patterns he knew, or something else, that suited her particular background.

Still, he kept singing, taking a breath here and there, trying to find the places where she didn't need that support as acutely. He was terrifically glad that she was the one figuring out how this went. He wanted to say it was like a healer and a scalpel, only it wasn't. It was gentler than that. Like water against stone, slowly easing away everything she didn't need.

Finally, as his voice began to get creaky, she brought the music to a steady end. Whatever the issue was, it wasn't resolved, not exactly. But he could hear, in the silence, how something had shifted in the magic, in the flows of the energy. She walked back to him, brushing her hands together, as if she'd been running the magic through her hands, as well as through her voice. If she'd touched anything, he hadn't noticed. But he had to admit that when his eyes had been open, he'd been looking at her face, not what else she might be doing.

He looked up, suddenly shy, and not at all sure what to say. Because something had shifted for him, too, and wanting something he didn't know how to name properly. She came over, entirely at ease, and folded herself down onto the blanket beside him, reaching for a bottle of lemonade. "Thank you. Not many people keep as steady."

Rathna's comment, her offering a topic, felt like the best gift he'd ever been given. Better than his wand, better than his working stones, better even than Invicta. He took a breath, rummaging for a bottle of lemonade for himself, before he turned back to her. "More of your guild secrets?"

"Mmhmm." She sounded entirely content. "They protect themselves. It's not something easily learned."

That made him laugh. "No. Entirely not. Layers of musical theory I can only gesture vaguely at. Can I ask, is it music for all of you, or other modes as well?"

"All of us can do music, it's the easiest one to use together. Morah Avigail feels things. A faint vibration."

"I had a moment thinking it was like feeling a cat purr. Subtle, but undeniable."

Rathna tilted her head, considering that. "Or a horse, underneath you. How you know if they're content, or nervous."

"The quality of the movement, not just the movement itself. I see. Or feel, rather."

Rathna tipped her lemonade in his direction. "So, there is a block, it's right around this spot, but I don't know why it's blocked. You said you could try some disillusionment."

Gabe contemplated that. "Anywhere in particular?"

She gestured vaguely at the space. "Behind the stone, somewhere in there."

The disillusionment charms were finicky, they took training; they were tiring, but they weren't particularly difficult. The trick was that the charms relied on people not wanting to see things. Breaking them meant having to want to see them rather a lot, and not be fooled by the false cover. He finished his lemonade. "More singing after?"

"Likely, yes, though if we figure out what's blocking it, perhaps less."

That was promising. He brushed his hands off and leaned over to snag his working case out of his saddlebag. He opened the fastenings, running his fingers over the protective thin quartz layer that kept each stone in place. He stopped at the long compartment on the far right, opening it and drawing out the rectangular clear sunstone. It was about the size of his palm, if a bit narrower. He touched his fingers to it, the sign of respect for his tools he'd had drilled into him. Then he stood, leaving the cane behind. He'd need both hands for this.

Rathna had been watching him, but she got up, following him a few feet behind. He gestured. "Just don't block the light, anywhere else is fine." He went back behind the single standing rock, into the half-circle space, and began by doing the obvious thing, looking around. He didn't honestly expect to find anything he hadn't found on his thorough search, but sometimes the light struck at a different angle, or some shadow fell out of place.

He heard Doyle's voice in his head. Lucy, as he was now permitted to call her, his apprentice mistress. She had been merciless in drilling him at this kind of deliberate precision. His intuition was a fine tool, she'd said over and over again, but that wasn't enough. He had to be precise, steady, look at everything. No shortcuts. So, he took a breath, and centred himself in the habits she'd taught him until he did them instinctively in his sleep.

Still nothing. He inhaled one more time, concentrating to feel the magic gathering, the way it raised the tiny hairs on his hands, like the moment before a lightning strike. This was the part that was so delicate, calling the power and focusing it precisely. He let the magic begin to spill into his right hand, as he raised the stone in his left, peering through it. Vikings had used these to navigate, and some clever sort had worked out how to use them to see clearly in a different way, before the Pact.

As he looked through the stone, he gathered his thoughts like he had his magic, focusing on clear sight, on not being fooled. On seeing what was truly there. It took a moment, as if the world went fuzzy with the effort, the gleam of the stone around him turning muted and shaded. Then, there was a pop, like diving down in the lake at home, and there was a gap there, back into a crevice. Big enough for a broad-shouldered man to walk inside comfortably enough, certainly enough space for the two of them.

Rathna heard the illusion break, a second before she saw it. It was like a string snapping on some instrument, a sudden release of tension. Or, she realised, as if there had been a faint tremulo of strings that had stopped abruptly. Then there was space in front of her, broad enough to walk comfortably, back off into the rock. It curved, and she suddenly expected it was following the seam of some vein of mineral or ore.

Gabe let his hand fall to his side, the clear stone he'd been using still cupped in his hand. "Well. That's something. Do we go in?"

"Do we think anyone's there?"

Gabe cocked his head. "Moment." He went back around to his case, coming back with a small bag of something, stones, perhaps, and the cane. He then found a flat spot on one of the stones, and laid out eight small quartz points on it. Then he drew his wand, tapping precisely in the centre with a murmured word. Two of the points, where he was standing and where she was, lit up. Nothing else did.

He nudged one of the stones with the tip of his wand, experimentally, and it stayed dim. "Just us. Shall we?"

"You think we should." Rathna wanted to, very much, but the idea of walking into a strange space suddenly unnerved her.

"I can go first. And I think it might be quite informative." Gabe rearranged things, settling his stones into a vest pocket, making it bulge, getting his cane in the left hand, his wand in his right.

She couldn't argue with that at all, and nodded at him, then let him go first. The tunnel was surprisingly comfortably sized, she'd been in full-blown mining tunnels in coal mines in Wales that were not as spacious. She wondered why, if they'd used magic to hollow it out, or if they'd hit on a natural lava tube, where the core had eroded away. Or perhaps this was an ancient cave made for some other purpose that had been used by whoever their mysterious bird man was. She couldn't see tool marks on the stone, but that didn't necessarily mean much. She wasn't able to look terribly closely.

It turned, as she'd thought, angling off to the right after about eight feet, into the depths of the mountain. As they stood in the arch of the entry, Gabe made a light without asking her, and then went forward. After a moment's reflection, she did the same. If he ended up having to fight, to use his wand, he might need the extra light.

The tunnel went on, about ten feet from the curve, maybe fifteen. It was disorienting, once she was away from the entrance, figuring out how far things were. It felt like time was shifting, too, not just space. They went slowly but steadily, foot by foot. The floor of the tunnel was even, and quite smooth, with a few loose stones. Gabe kept going steadily, barely glancing back at her, focused intently on the way ahead. She thought him rather like a hunting hound must be, the way there was nothing in the world for him but investigating this strange new space.

Then he came to a space that opened up a bit. Whatever the tunnel had been, this had been altered by human hands. The cave itself, but there was a raw, broken seam along one side, where someone had hacked in with a pickaxe. Two were lying on the ground, and she winced to see tools treated badly. One seemed like it had been dropped next to the worksite, and she wondered if Gabe had interrupted the mysterious man earlier, in the middle of more mining. There was, however, no one there, and no sign of anyone being there recently. It smelled a little stale and musty. Gabe circled the space, perhaps fifteen feet across, taking his light with him, and Rathna moved toward that scar in the rock.

She could see that the tunnel stopped, leaving a mostly round room, fifteen feet across, about ten high. There were a few bedrolls on the other side, a few crates serving as something like a table, an old beaten up trunk for a chest. Gabe came up beside her without searching them. "I'd like a look at that, but the rock, first."

She risked reaching out to touch it. There was a shiver under her fingers, and now she had to figure out how to put it into words. "Mining is an unnatural act. A human act, exerting ourselves on the rock. It's not like farming, where there's a cycle, where there are limits, natural limits, most of the time. Or growing a tree. It's fast, often, very fast, compared to the rock forming. Out of time, out of sync with the way the rock wants to be. Can you feel it?" She wondered if she wanted him to.

Gabe reached out cautiously, touching just above where

her hand was. First his finger tips, delicately brushing, then he pressed his palm flat. "Like an upset beehive."

Rathna nodded. "It sounds sharp, to me. Angry. Edged." She frowned. "More than most mining." She took a step or two closer, looking more closely at the vein that had been opened up. She could see olive-green crystals in a bed of deep pink, and patches of a darker crystal that shimmered between the colour of antique gold and green in the light. She inhaled, bracing herself and opening to what she might find, both at the same time.

There was a shock, sharp and sudden, and for a moment she utterly lost track of where she was and what she was doing. When she came back to herself, her charm light had gone completely out, and she could feel a sturdy weight behind her. It took her perhaps far too long to realise she was leaning back against Gabe's chest, that he had a hand under hers, making sure she didn't drop her stones.

Rathna let out a breath and felt it catch in her chest. She tried again, breathing in, then out, more steadily. Only then did Gabe speak. "You all right there?"

"Not sure." Her voice came out a bare whisper, and she tried a deeper breath again. This time it worked, and after she did that once more, she managed to shift her hand, settle the stones into her other hand, and wriggle her fingers. "What happened?"

"You touched the exposed mineral here. That's mineral, right? The withamite?" She nodded faintly, feeling a sort of distant sense of nausea that was beginning to settle. He went on. "And then you went rigid, stiff. A bit like lightning, only..." His breath went out in a rush. "I was worried. Really worried."

"Like me, watching you duel." It came out of her mouth

before she could stop it, and she managed to turn a little. He looked horribly abashed.

"I do know what I'm doing with that. Is this... " He gestured at the stone. "Expected? Normal?"

"No." She was certain about. "There's something odd here, wrongly odd. But I think I know how to fix it, if we can keep them from coming back here."

"If this is the spot that's the problem, we should be able to get a Guard down to camp. Pay folks from the village to keep watch until then. And we should have the blood trace, sooner than later."

Rathna nodded slowly. "I'd like to try something. It might solve the problem, it might not, I don't know. I honestly don't know what to expect."

"In your considered opinion, is it the best choice?" Gabe took a step back, letting her turn to face him, which she did.

She glanced over her shoulder at the rock. "I do. This is, I suspect it's what a healer feels like, if they can't treat someone. It's, it's pulling on me."

Gabe nodded. "What can I do to help, then? Bring you a crate to sit on?"

She shook her head. "They might have evidence." He was clearly willing to ignore that if she needed it, but there was no need. "If, if you'd stand behind me? In case? I'll be singing again."

"Of course. Would it be easier sitting down?" He was audibly thinking through the options.

Rathna eyed the level of the mining. "Standing. I need to be able to touch it." She looked at the wall, finding the right place. "Take the stones, here. And stand behind me. Do what you think you need to if I can't tell you what to do." Her voice came out clear and crisp.

"This is yours to decide." He was quieter, but steady.

She could feel him behind her, just as sturdy, as she concentrated on the edges, the sharp feeling. "Singing?"

"If you could match that D again. I don't suppose you can do the octave down?"

She heard him hum for a moment, then pick up a pitch, a little flat, before he cleared his voice, and the next one was nice and steady. And without the tuning fork. That made a nice foundation for it. She hummed to herself, an octave and a fifth above, finding the pitch, settling into it, then she nodded. She felt him take a breath as she did, and then they were both louder, the sound resonating in the chamber, bouncing off the walls, coming back to her. She'd been told about the effect, now she had to hope she could use it properly.

Just holding the pitch wasn't the magic, it was the movement, the way the notes made new shapes out of the energy of the rocks. Once she was sure the space was stable, she took a breath, and reached out her hands again, both of them this time, to better balance the energy. She'd hoped but hadn't been sure that it would help. There was a jolt to her body, but this time, she kept singing, leaning into it. There was something there, pulling her along, closer.

Suddenly, she realised what so many of the warnings in her training had been about. She'd been told over and over again how easy it could be to get lost in the channels. How she'd know if she might be in that situation, as it would be obvious. She'd always worked with settled portals before, where the channels were well worn over decades or centuries. Morah Avigail and the others had been right, there was nothing like it. It had a compelling thrum to it, something that made her feel fully alive, tapping into something deep and ancient and made of pure magic.

Rathna let her voice go where it felt right. There wasn't

a prescribed method for this. She had to trust that her training had taught her what she needed to know. First there was the shift up and down, feeling out the fifths, then the fourths. Then it was time to begin working her way through the patterns she'd practised painstakingly, repeating them back to Morah Avigail from memory. Then it was like swimming in a river, figuring out how to align herself with the currents, not fight them. There was nothing but the music and how it filled her.

It was working, too. She could feel something, deep beneath her fingers, shift. It wasn't anything so ridiculous as the rocks moving. More as if something within them were realigning, like smoothing out hair ribbons or laces after they'd been used, uncoiling all the kinks and folds.

But it took time. Rathna knew she'd slipped into the slowest time they touched, the rocks, who were so old that centuries were near enough nothing to them. The damage that had been done here was a fleeting spark. The quarry, a few miles away, was an older, deeper one, but a sort of old ache, no longer argued with. She just took her time, knowing what she wanted was to ease the constrictions, make everything smooth.

Then it was time - perhaps past time - to pull herself away from that seductive ease and flow. She pulled one hand off, carefully, and then she couldn't quite bring herself to move the other. There was something comforting about it, restful. Beautiful. Decidedly beautiful. Then she felt a hand on her wrist. Not pulling, not pushing, not reaching down to touch the rock. This was steady fingers curled around her wrist, giving her a reason to remember what living was in a human body, not a mineral one.

Gabe was not at all sure what to make of what Rathna was doing. It was a kind of magic he didn't even have words for, never mind properly informed opinions about. He'd gathered from their conversations so far - and from the fact that no one, but no one, really talked about the portal magics - that they held mysteries. This, though, was something else.

She hadn't even seemed upset that she'd near fainted. Or perhaps she had, he'd just caught her fast enough her knees locked instead of giving out. The way she'd leaned against him, though. They were going to have to talk about that. He didn't even know where to start. His upbringing had prepared him for mothers throwing their unmarried daughters at him. Not for a growing something he couldn't label properly for a colleague who was as gifted and magically skilled as she was intelligent.

He'd wanted something like his parents, hoped against hope that he might find it. That sense of trust and laughter and matched wits. Here Rathna was, trusting him like

Mama trusted Papa. No, more like Papa trusted Mama. All he could do was hold steady, and wonder at it.

He thought she'd been doing well, he hadn't wanted to interfere, but then the feel of things shifted, the hum changed. Not the sound, but the feeling. He shifted his hand, careful not to touch the stone, not to force her to move, but just to support her, remind her of her body. He knew all the theory, how it was easy to fall into the magic and never come out, though he'd only had a few scattered temptations like that himself.

She shivered as she leaned back against his chest, and he held as still and steady as he could. Then she pulled her hand back, slowly. It was as if she wasn't sure about his touch, but didn't want to let it go either. She almost turned more, but then paused, taking the kind of deep steadying breath he knew was about finding her skin again, what was her and what wasn't. He didn't step back, didn't disrupt the balance, holding as still and quiet as he could. It was like watching Papa after a duel he'd fully thrown himself into. He'd seen that only twice, but he'd also seen what Mama did after, how she let Papa come back to himself.

Finally, she turned around. The brown of her eyes had a golden glow, a bit like the colour of the crystals. Then she nudged him slightly, two fingers to indicate what she wanted. He took a step back silently, giving her space.

"Is it - how is it?" He wanted to ask so many questions, but those five words were all he could manage in the moment.

"Better, I think. Much better. But we'll need to make sure they don't alter it again. And I'll need to see to the portal itself, once she's settled. A day or two, probably. It's hard to tell how long."

A day or two. He sucked in a breath. "Until then?"

"Reports. Making sure no one gets in here. Figuring out who did."

Gabe snorted. "That's mostly for the Guard, not for us."

"You can't tell me you're not curious. I can tell, Gabriel Edgarton, that you are." Her voice was amused and arch, and she glanced away from him, over his shoulder, to the pile of bedrolls and the scattered crates.

"If you're going to use my name like that, the full thing is much more impressive." He tried to tease her back, but it felt a bit unnatural.

"Gabriel Anthony Edgarton." Now she was smiling. "What do you think we should be doing, then?"

She brought her chin up. All of a sudden, he understood what people perhaps saw in kissing. Or being close. Or wanting any of that sort of thing at all. Before he could stop himself, something else came burbling out. Despite all his training in keeping his impulsive curiosity under control, everything Lucy had tried her best to drill into him, "I'm wondering what it would be like to kiss you. To be honest."

Rathna blinked at him several times. She wasn't upset, he could figure that much out. But he wasn't sure what else was going on, in her head, behind her eyes. Then she nudged him again, two fingers in the centre of his chest. "Explain yourself."

He spread his hands. "You did ask." It came out sounding far more uncertain than he wanted. "That's what I was thinking."

"Last we talked about anything remotely related to kissing, you said you hadn't found it relevant to figure out."

Gabe coughed, and then went on, as carefully as he could manage. "I am beginning to see how it might be personally relevant, and not just a thing other people do."

It made her snort. She was amused. That was good.

Certainly better than upset. "I am not yours to experiment with, Gabe. So we're clear." She gestured. "Are you sure it's not just that I'm handy? Or that there's rather a lot of magic right here at the moment?"

He took another step back, cautiously, trying to gather his whirling thoughts and feelings. "My parents wondered if I might prefer men. We know people who do." Not that he'd say who, not yet, anyway. Other people's secrets were not his to be telling. "Aunt Mason told them I knew my obligations well enough, I'd sort out the puzzle in front of me in my own time." He waited the appropriate beat. "Also, as she pointed out, I might be gay."

As he'd hoped, that got an actual laugh out of Rathna. "And you've never actually been interested in anyone." This was what he sounded like, when he was working out the parameters of a puzzle.

"A few academic sorts of crushes? Seeing the kind of person I'd be wanting, if they were the right age, in totally different circumstances." Both Uncle Gil and Uncle Magni at different, equally embarrassing times, before he'd realised it was far more about what he found intriguingly attractive in general than them in specific. Creative intelligence, a devoted loyalty, relentless deep affection for the other. "You know how some people have, what's the word, a pash for a teacher? I never quite had that, not the way people seemed to mean it? But I could see the shape of it."

"Men or women?" She was definitely gathering data now.

"Honestly? Both." Gabe spread his hands. "Cleverness seems to matter more than anything else. A particular kind of cleverness."

"Why me?" Now her voice had gone a bit more flat,

pressed together by nerves. "I'm nothing you ought to be wanting to kiss. Or anything else."

"You are brilliant." Gabe understood, intellectually, how she must have been diminished. At the orphanage, at school. In all the ways people of status and power chipped away at the people who didn't have any or enough. He'd never been on the wrong side of it, but he'd certainly been around for it, and sometimes when he couldn't do much to help. "And you're - I keep thinking you're beautiful. The last few days. The meeting, you were gorgeous."

"Only because you'd lent me... who on earth was that for, anyway? The shawl. It's - the colour's not a thing most people would wear."

He grinned. "Aunt Mason." He watched her, and added, "Her skin's a bit lighter than yours, but the same sort of tone. Malaysian and Dutch, that side of her family."

That rocked her back on her heels. The implications of it, he could see her sorting through this. "And your parents like her? Trust her?"

"Papa thinks she's brilliant. When she got hurt a couple of years ago, he was beside himself. Fussed over making sure she had everything she could possibly need, harangued the healers as only he in his tripartite role could do. She's doing fine now, but it was a bit touchy for a month or two. Family."

"And your mother doesn't mind?"

"Mama thinks she's brilliant, too. They plot together. Mama comes up with ideas, and Aunt Mason figures out how to make them happen."

Rathna shook her head. "You have a very strange family, Gabe. But if you brought me home, they'd... you can't have anything to do with someone like me. Even casually. Romantically, I mean."

"I don't know about ever after. Yet." He swallowed. "I mean. For all sorts of reasons. You asked me what I was thinking. I'd like to kiss you. I am very sure of that. Probably not just the once, either. I think maybe neither of us has enough information about what happens later. Who knows, we might hate kissing, which would mean it wasn't a puzzle to be solved at all."

Rathna cocked her head, watching him silently, as if she were listening to him as intently as she listened to rock. Then she took a step closer, and took his hand in hers, lacing her fingers through his. It was a bold move, and a delicate one, and for a long moment, she didn't do anything else. She just stood there, her eyes half closed, intent on something so private he couldn't begin to guess what she was thinking.

Then, all of a sudden, she tugged him closer. Her free hand went around his back, pressing against his shoulder blade. She tilted her head at the last moment so their noses didn't collide, and then they were kissing. It was nothing like what he'd thought. Books rather skimmed over the details, he realised. But she was right there, against him, warm and so very insistently present.

He felt clumsy, like he knew nothing, and he hated that feeling. It made him shiver. Instead of pushing him away, she tightened her grip on his shoulder, angling him slightly. Even better, she was showing him what to do. Not just the physical. He was perhaps a quick enough study there, but what it meant. Why one might want to.

And oh, Gabe wanted to. He wanted a lot more of this, all of a sudden. He wanted to kiss her, and figure out the other things you did with someone, when you liked them and wanted them. He wanted to learn all the things that were in the pillow books he'd heard about, and the erotic French postcards. Many of them weren't right, he knew that, but he wanted to learn what was, what two people could get up to together. He and Rathna, specifically.

He felt her tongue against his, the way they were so close there wasn't anything but her in his world, how it drowned everything else out. Finally, though, she pulled back to take a breath, though she didn't move her hand, or encourage him to move his. His right hand was now around her waist, even dropping to her hip, as if he'd wanted to keep pulling her closer and closer.

"We do seem to have a puzzle to solve." She tried to make it light, but her voice cracked in the middle. He immediately moved his right hand up to cup her cheek, and he realised she was crying. Silently, but her skin was damp with it, a tear forming by her eye.

"You think you can't, with me." It came out of him in a rush. "That I'll - make you be secret."

"You're going to be a Lord. Posh. Expectations. Social commitments. Your family must go back and back and back."

"They do. And I care about the land, the obligations to it." He let out his breath in a puff. "Veritas is gorgeous. Besides being home. I want to show it to you, the ducks and the herons and the falcons. And the mirabiles, if we can find them, deep in the woods. I want to take you riding, and swimming in the pond, and show you the secrets of the house, every single one of them."

He inhaled again, thinking about all the things he wanted now. Needed. "I want you to get to know Mama and Papa, and Uncle Gil and Aunt Mason and Uncle Magni, and Aunt Witt and all. And Lucy. And I want to, I want to do what you think is right. About respecting all

Mistress Levy's done for you, how she cares about you. Whatever you think is right there."

There was a lot more there, too, and it came out in a rush, but he hoped it proved how much in earnest he was.

She swallowed. "A puzzle." She sounded so cautious.

"Our puzzle." He was clear about that. They would sort it out together, something that the people who loved them would be glad for. Everyone else could go hang.

Two days later, Rathna finally had a chance to catch her breath. They had been caught up in a flurry of activity, once Gabe reported the cave and what they'd found through his journal. She was exceedingly envious of his journal, mind. She'd have given quite a lot to be able to write to Morah Avigail and get a reply back as promptly as possible.

She felt like she saw Gabe constantly and yet had no time to talk to him. His initial message had summoned help promptly enough she half-suspected someone had been lurking, waiting to be called.

Gabe had insisted on a thorough search of the cave. That had produced a new case of evidence to be turned over. Several hairs from the bedding, for example, a few books that had smudges of fingerprints here or there. They had all been bustled off to Trellech for further investigation, while other Guards looked out to see if the people responsible showed any sign of coming back.

Gabe himself had been out riding through the area, looking for anything else out of the ordinary. She had thought about going with him, he'd left space where she might have asked. But in the end, she had stayed, wanting to keep reassuring the rock that everything was sorting out, going up to the portal, and feeling it slowly beginning to wake.

She'd worried, in there, that the fossils made a difference. She'd spent the first night reading, until three in the morning, finally finding references that suggested how the fossils might change the portal. How they should have been taken into consideration from the start, certainly Someone, probably her, was going to need to write a treatise on it. Eventually.

Her notes gave her enough to try something new, laying out a pattern of alignments, drawing on everything she'd learned about the reversals of the poles, how the precession of stars played with where north was, a dozen different facts and skills she'd learned as an apprentice. She laid out a painstaking alignment of local stones, small chips of withamite from the cave, and sang her heart out.

It wasn't until today that it had finally worked, and Rathna had spent the afternoon there, feeling the hum in her head and beneath her hands, hearing the portal restored. She thought she understood why Warrington had put the door here, and why he hadn't written it down. It would have made him sound entirely batty, no one would have taken him seriously.

It wasn't just the withamite, though that was certainly part of it. But the fossils, she thought, made something like a carpet of grass, drawing magic in a far different way. It made her wonder about the portals on the Devon and Dorset coasts.

Once she was certain it was behaving as it should, allowing for that carpeting effect, she ran all the proper tests, the ones that would ensure it could be used safely. Then, and only then, did she ask for a volunteer to go through the portal. One of the Guards stepped up for it, nervous but willing, an older woman, one of the regular couriers.

She went through, and two minutes later, stepped back out of the portal, spinning and bowing to the applause of her fellows. "Works smooth as silk," she'd said to Rathna. "Thank you, Mistress. I wasn't much looking forward to the cart and train show."

So when Rathna turned up at the inn at suppertime, she was feeling most pleased with herself, but suddenly at the end of her own particular usefulness. She wasn't sure if she should be planning to go home to Morah Avigail, or if she might be needed for something else.

Gabe's door was shut, but she knew both mares were in the stable, and she hadn't seen Gabe downstairs when she came in, so she knocked, carefully.

"Who is it?"

"Rathna." A moment later, he was opening the door, beaming at her.

"Come in! Have you eaten? There's food, is the portal, how's the portal?" It was his exuberant, cheerful self. Then he asked, suddenly more shy, "May I kiss you again?"

She blinked at him. "We've barely talked for days." she pointed out. "And you were gone when I got up, the last two."

"We have both been busy. But we are here now, and I didn't want you to think...." His voice trailed off. "Please?"

He was so much in earnest about it. Rathna waved a hand at him, and he retreated, giving her space to come inside and close the door behind her. He was wearing shirt-sleeves and trousers, with suspenders over his shoulders, giving him a rather university student sort of look, especially since he had ink stains on both hands. And both cuffs.

"What have you been doing to yourself? You've ink everywhere."

He shrugged. "There are potions for that. Doing the drawings that go with my reports, but I'm done now." Then he peered at her. "Are you upset? With me?" He was puzzling again. Both in the sense of being puzzling, and in the sense that she was sure he was trying to puzzle her out.

"Sit, Gabe. So I can - I don't know." No one had ever explained how this was supposed to go. Oh, she'd had the practical lectures from Matron at school, who'd seen to such things. And she'd done her share of listening to people talk about it. But she didn't know how this worked, when it was her and a man in a room, trying to figure things out, together.

Gabe sat promptly on the bed, tucking one bare foot up under his other leg. She shrugged out of her jacket and sat down next to him. "A sandwich would be grand later. The portal's working perfectly, one of the Guards, the older woman? She tested it. All good and smooth as can be." Then she glanced around. "I've done everything I was sent for, so I came back."

"I've reports to finish, but..." He waved his hand. "No sign of a beithir?"

That made Rathna think about it. "I don't know. I kept feeling like there was something else there. Besides whichever Guard was with me to hand me things. But I didn't hear anything, even when I got the portal flowing properly again."

"It could just be a story." Gabe was thoughtful. "I'd think so, except for that noise, whatever it was."

"No one here seems terribly bothered by it, I admit."

She shook her head. "I think it's there. I hope it's happy. As long as it doesn't want to sting me - or you. We're in its home, or at least its territory." Then she hesitated. "I think maybe the portal not working, the mining...." Her voice trailed off.

"Yes?" Gabe made the word encouraging, reaching to take her hand and curl his fingers through hers.

"I think that upset it. If it's a magic beast, maybe it's like a burr. Or a thorn in its paw? Foot? I don't know the proper word. And now we've fixed it."

Gabe nodded. "Maybe. I suppose Sorcha might write and tell us if anything comes up. We could ask her."

"Maybe it's happy now, and it will just take an occasional sheep or deer or something. Whatever beithirs eat." Rathna shook her head. "That's not entirely ours to solve, is it?"

"Scope of the work, and all that. No. Though I might suggest one of the others with an interest in natural history come up here for a walking vacation sometime. Later this summer, maybe. She's got a good sense of secretive fauna. And she'd like the deer."

"Not Lucy?" She'd caught the name before.

"Lucy Doyle was my apprentice mistress." There was something new in his voice. It wasn't how Rathna talked about Morah Avigail - or even more so, how she thought about her in her own head. But it was rather more like that than she'd expected. It was warm, and deeply fond, and respectful, all at once.

"You said I should meet her." It was a tad less overwhelming to think about that, than about his family.

"You should!" Gabe was gleaming again, delighted at the prospect. "May I kiss you?"

Rathna thought they should talk about this, but on the

other hand, she had to agree she'd been thinking about kissing him rather a lot. Often at the most tediously annoying times, when she knew full well he was at least a mile in the wrong direction from anything she needed to do. She shifted closer to him on the bed. "You may."

This time, they were unhurried. And he had picked things up remarkably quickly, angling himself comfortably to get an arm around her waist, letting her lean and be supported. When he pulled back, he was grinning again. "Will you come to Veritas?"

Utterly irrepressible. And so optimistic. She knew what was going to happen. The road she was going down was likely to break her heart somewhere along the way. The world was too big, and too sharp-edged, and too determined to keep her and people like her down and unhappy. But she hadn't realised until just now that that would break his heart as well.

She should do the right thing, and retreat to her own room, and back to London, never to see him again. Think of this as a brief fling, to be dreamed about to her deathbed.

Gabe reached for her hand, took it, and squeezed it. "You're thinking this can't possibly work, we should stop now."

She nodded. "I was. How do you do that? You're awfully sharp."

"Mama. And, well. It is the obvious part of the problem, isn't it? You needn't think I'm ignoring it solely for the momentary pleasure of kissing you. Though that is indeed pleasant, and I'd like to do that some more in a bit. And whatever else you might feel inclined to." She opened her mouth, and he shook his head. "I know you want to argue. So let's talk this out."

"You have obligations, Gabe, even if I'm not at all sure what all of them are. I know you have them."

"My actual obligations are to produce a heir. The usual sort of way is to marry someone willing to have a baby with me. Well, more than one is considered sensible, just in case. Two is the traditional agreement for people who want as little to do with each other as they can get away with."

"That does not seem to apply to whatever we might agree to." Rathna felt compelled to point that out. "Though - I hadn't ever, I mean." She couldn't even finish that sentence. This entire conversation was ridiculous.

"That is merely the usual sort of way. If you decide you would rather not go through the - I gather complexity is a good word - of pregnancy. And all the fuss of not being able to take a portal, or possibly work on one, well, that would be understandable. Adoption is a possibility. There are enough distant cousins not in anyone's line of succession who might do, and keep it in the bloodline, but that's not the only option."

"What does that mean for you? I mean, I'm sure people will disapprove."

"There are people in such elevated social circles who disapprove of which of the generally acceptable flowers one puts on the table at specific meals. I mean, I have an appreciation for attention to detail, if rather drilled into me by Aunt Witt and Lucy. Mostly Lucy, honestly. But that's absurd. They will always find things to disapprove of, and picking an obvious thing... Well, actually, that might be rather a lot of fun, so long as we didn't care about getting invited to their parties. Which we don't. They're tedious and boring and the food is generally awful."

Rathna blinked at him several times. "What do you - um, potentially we - care about, then?"

"I care about the land. Which is why I want you to come see Veritas. I don't think you can make up your mind properly without seeing it. It's the land I care about, and the land magics. I mean, I think it would be a thing to have my own children. I know Mama and Papa would dote, and really, they're very good at doting, they got a lot of practice in with me. But the land's the thing."

Rathna let out a long sigh. "So. What does that involve?" She was becoming resigned to the fact that Gabe would roll along into situations she'd never, ever dreamed of. Asking her permission all the way.

"Seasonal offerings. May, summer solstice, Lammastide, and equinox. And there's a few others, not agricultural. We have to make our bow at the hodening at winter solstice. But I'm not explaining the hodening now, we haven't nearly enough room here."

She blinked at him. "Did you just start speaking a different language?"

Gabe laughed. "I can explain all of it. But there are offerings, to the land, to the people. About taking care of them both, having care for them? It doesn't go into modern English very well sometimes, it's not at all a modern concept. But you know your literature, surely? The king is the land, and the land is the king. We're just responsible to a fragment of it, not the whole thing. I think being a king before the Pact must have been really rather exhausting."

Rathna thought it sounded decidedly odd, but Gabe was clearly completely in earnest, like he got about horses, being a Penelope, and climbing out windows. "And if I - if we were together." She didn't even know how to describe that. Saying she might be his lady seemed very forward, as well as an utterly bizarre statement to find herself saying. "What would I be expected to do?"

"You are a woman of exceptional and professional talents. Of course you should keep using them just as much as you like. Mama goes to the village regularly, she brings food and salves and things, to people who are sick. But you needn't do that. Unless you wanted to. We'd still want someone to see to it. But also, that isn't mine - or yours - to worry about until I'm Lord, not the Heir. Or something. As I said, we hope that will be ages and ages from now. Being as I'm very fond of Papa. And Mama."

Gabe was watching so carefully. Rathna hadn't run, that was something. A great deal, actually. But she certainly wasn't sure of anything, including him. She didn't move for a long moment, then she said, "It's a fantasy, Gabe. That you could ever bring me home. That I could - have any part there."

"I have thought about it." He kept his voice low and easy. Because he had, and he had a plan, if she were willing. He knew there were things he hadn't anticipated yet. Every plan had those. But he thought she hadn't quite seen the whole picture yet, it being an entirely new landscape to her. "May I tell you?"

She nodded, a small movement, and he shifted to take her hand, curling his fingers around it. "The thing about my life is that what I want, they can't take away from me. Not unless I commit some horrible crime. Loving you, making a life with you, plenty of people will disapprove. But they can't do much about it."

Rathna opened her mouth, then stopped, before trying a better question. "What do you mean?"

"I am my father's Heir, properly sworn. Nothing changes that, unless we go through a really quite tedious process to disinherit me. No, wait, we'll come back to my parents." He held up his other hand. "He won't. If he did, he'd be doing it for the good of the land, which I'm not inclined to argue with. But he won't." Gabe was utterly certain of that, down to the centre of his bones. "Being with you won't change that. That's one part of my life."

She nodded, apparently willing to wait on the topic of his father. Good.

"We might well have a harder time than most if we needed to rent a flat somewhere. But we do not need to do that. I could buy a townhouse if we had to. That's not money from Papa, it's money from Mama's side of the family, and it's fully mine as of finishing my apprenticeship. I'd rather not touch it, it's invested in useful ways, helping other people. But I could. Or, you know, we could always find a place somewhere there are other people like us." He picked his words deliberately here, reminding her that this would be a joint decision, whatever it was. That they were in this together.

"I'll grant you the fact that people with even more of a difference make a home together. Though I'm not sure you'd like the places they have to go to do it, sometimes."

Gabe nodded. "I'm sure I wouldn't." He let out a breath. "I am a duly oathsworn Penelope. My fellows won't care, they certainly have a varied set of personal lives. Honesty, I would likely fit in better. There's a fair few who aren't sure of me because of the title, and also because Papa's a Guard. Division of approaches, you see, and most of the Guard can be a tad rigid at times."

It made her laugh, as he had hoped it would. "Rigid is not a word I would apply to you, no, Gabe."

"You should have seen me before Lucy got her hands on me. Metaphorically speaking. She's very disciplined." He waved his free hand. "You, of course, are an exceptionally talented and highly trained professional woman, with a set of skills decidedly more rare than the top rank of Healers." He saw, immediately, that not only had she not thought of herself that way, no one had ever spelled that out to her.

He went on. "We rely on you, each and every person in the magical communities of Albion, for our safety, our food, our pleasure, our correspondence and bills. Daily. Hourly, in some cases. And there's what, two dozen of you able to work right now?"

Rathna nodded. "And six more who can do some work, but can't travel or be away from home." Her voice had a distracted tone. Now she was thinking as fast as he was talking, he expected. Excellent.

"You would have to murder someone, have to do something that got you thrown in gaol for a decade or more before they'd recule you." Gabe shrugged. "Being known as my beloved certainly doesn't qualify. It might be a scandal, but it's a known sort of scandal."

Her chin snapped up at the 'beloved', and she blinked at him, several times.

"If we do this thing, we do it for love and care, and wanting to be with each other. My parents set me a high standard, for who I marry, who I braid my life with. I think it's why none of the previous offers appealed at all." Then, gently, Gabe lifted his hand to touch her cheek. "I rather suspect your parents set you the same kind of high standard. You're no more willing to settle for less than the best than I am."

Rathna didn't try to say anything this time, but she nodded, then leaned into his fingers for a moment. He went on. "Society can go hang. I don't go to most of the parties, they're tedious and diminishing, and many of the people are really rather awful. Either we'll start getting invited to the more bohemian set, and have a lot of fun, or we'll find some other way to amuse ourselves. I don't really think that's a problem."

It made her snort, perhaps despite herself. When he didn't continue, she gestured. "Your parents. They matter, Gabe. You know they do."

He nodded. "They do. I suspect Mama will be startled, and Papa will be shocked. For a minute or two. And then they'll get over it. Especially if they already know you are thoughtful and clever and know all sorts of things they don't know. So you should come to the costume ball and make an excellent impression. And you can see if you want to keep me once you've seen me in my native habitat."

"I don't have anything to wear." Rathna protested, looking at him. "I don't even know what you wear for that."

"Oh, that's no problem. Aunt Mason has something you can borrow. The theme's Animal, Vegetable, or Mineral. She's got an outfit she can tint to be any mineral you'd like to be. Mama and Papa have seen it before, they'll know where you got it, but it covers all of you. A robe, long gloves that go well up the arm, a mask and some tinting powder for your face. All quite safe. One can either be very easy to guess, or very complicated, whichever you prefer."

"And what will you be going as?"

He shrugged. "I have a few options. I could do one of the red deer, actually. I've an antler headdress and mask, don't ask, it was relevant for a case. Some people get up to really rather odd ritual activities sometimes. We made one to figure out how the mask worked."

That made Rathna glance away, back toward where the portal was. "Could I do the withamite, do you think?"

Gabe threw back his head and laughed. "You'll have to help get the colours right. The suggestion of the crystal shapes. But yes, we can do that."

She smiled, then it faded. "But Gabe, I don't know what to do. How can I just walk in there? And that's no way to meet your parents, they'll be busy, surely."

"That is why you will stay over. And in the morning, I can show you the grounds, and then we can have a nice brunch. Mama always sleeps in after a party."

"Gabe." Rathna sounded uncertain, still, so he pulled out his final trump.

"Uncle Gil will be there. On Sunday, for brunch, I mean. A couple of the other people I care about. Just family, though."

Rathna reached out and poked him with two fingers again, making her point. "Gabriel Anthony Edgarton, you are a downright dirty cheat."

He laughed, and let the movement push him backwards, let himself fall back on the bed.

She snatched up the pillow from beside him and buffeted him with it. "You have this all planned out." Whap. "How long have you been thinking about this?" Whap. "You're not even arguing!"

Gabe grinned up at her. "Consciously? Three days or so. A bit before that. Since the tent, I think. I was quite sure you were gorgeous the day after the duel, when you were grooming Verity."

She thwapped him one more time on the chest and then shoved the pillow up toward the headboard again, as he pushed himself up on one elbow. "I'm not going to win this argument, am I? You've penned me in."

Gabe shook his head. "I want you to come and see for yourself. Veritas. Mama and Papa. Uncle Gil and Aunt Mason and Uncle Magni and the others. My sister, who has her own opinions. If you decide you can't, after you've seen it, then... then I'll be sad. Very. But I'll let you go. It's just that I want you to make up your mind based on the real thing, not your fears about it."

Rathna let out a puff of breath, and then she moved, settling down on her side, facing him. "There's never been enough, in my life." Her voice got very quiet. "And here you come, offering me everything."

Gabe shifted, reaching to take her hand. "You could have more than you realise. Without me. I know Mistress Levy's part of the community where you are, and that matters. I'm the last person to argue about heritage mattering. How it shapes us. But you could have requested quite a lot of things, when you came up here. A tent. A sizable working trunk."

He hesitated, before pointing out something more delicate. "The Ministry wouldn't buy you a complete set of working stones all at once. But you could replace a stone or two a year, with the funding they'll give you if you know how to ask. You have a rare skill, one they are going to continue to need for decades and decades to come. You have more leverage than you think."

Rathna couldn't make sense of that, tightening her hand. "But Morah Avigail...." Her voice trailed off.

"Mistress Levy has her community customs. Which include giving to the poor, taking in the orphan, and not being extravagant with money. There's good reason for that. I don't know the history, the reasons, the community, nearly as well as you do, of course. But I know that much. Having things makes people jealous, and that's dangerous. I know that part all too well. She needs to be safe, and she needed to keep you safe, once she had you. Being quiet, not making waves."

Rathna closed her eyes, thinking hard, it was written all over her face. She didn't move her hand for a good minute, before she opened her eyes and frowned. "And I could do more to help her."

"Whatever else happens," Gabe said, as clearly as he could, "I would be delighted to show you how to roust the best sort of healer for her out of the Healing Temple. They can't always help, but it's worth a try. I know people - and you will soon - who would be delighted to take that challenge on." Uncle Gil among them. Probably out in front, honestly.

Rathna let out a long breath, it came out mostly as a sigh. "So. How do we sort out my costume? And when is this party, and what do we do until then?"

"The party is this Saturday. I suggest we have a pleasant time tonight, pack our things, and go back through the portal tomorrow morning. We can leave the Guard to wrap things up and perhaps even catch our mystery bird man. I'll have reports to make, and you must too. Aunt Mason said she'd be glad to have us to tea tomorrow, for the costume fitting. And honestly, if Aunt Mason likes you, Mama and Papa will come right round."

"You are not making it any easier to face tomorrow, Gabe."

He grinned at her. "Yes, but you know you want to meet her. And I don't get to go over to her house all that often anymore. Always a good time, she's got some amazing things she's made."

Rathna considered. "And you said - she's Malaysian."

"Her mother's side. And Dutch and English." He

added, "She lives with another woman, Aunt Rosemary. She's a midwife. They don't - I mean, I know they each have their own bedroom, their own space." He blushed, because how he'd figured that out didn't bear discussing. "But you'll like her too, if she's not on call."

Rathna had to think about what to say that wouldn't be an insult. "That's not a thing people talk about much."

Gabe shook his head. "For some of the same reasons Mistress Levy's careful. Things can be dangerous. And not just the fast dangers, as Uncle Magni says, but the slow ones. The things that undermine everything around you." He gestured. "Quicksand, or a sinkhole, isn't that the word?"

Rathna closed her eyes again. "I'll come. Tomorrow, and the party. But you will tell me exactly what to expect, as much as you can." She hesitated, then added. "Almost no one explains properly. They just expected me to pick up, and I'm always sure I',m missing something. Morah Avigail explained. You have. But you ..." She looked up at him. "Promise me you'll keep explaining?"

"Always. See, that's why you want me, out of all the people you might choose. It's usually hard to get me to shut up, explaining things." He drew her hand to his lips, kissing the back. "Right now, before we pack, though. A bit more..." He didn't quite know how to ask for exactly what he wanted, which was to be with her, against her, exploring, for as long as he could. Learning more things he didn't yet know and wanted desperately to learn.

Rathna felt entirely overwhelmed. Gabe had arranged to spirit her into the house without meeting anyone late that afternoon. She had been shown to a lovely guest room decorated in soothing shades of blue-green with a bathing room all her own.

One of the maids had come to check she had everything she needed, even offered to arrange her hair. Rathna had refused. She was used to Sarah, of course. She and Morah Avigail couldn't work the hours they often did and see to all the cleaning and the cooking and being home for the butcher to call. But having someone help her dress or do her hair, that was entirely baffling.

She had, however, asked for help fastening up her outfit. The base level was more or less ordinary, though it had an overdress that covered her to the elbows, in folds of flowing fabric. There were long sleeves on the underdress that came down to points that covered much of her hands. There was even a charmed powder to cover her exposed skin, and tint it to match the dress everywhere it touched.

There had been a flurry of activity once she'd gotten

home. Working on her report, of course, seeing how faded Morah Avigail looked. Worrying when Sarah mentioned, privately, that Vivek had been seen in the neighbourhood, though he hadn't approached the household again. There was not enough time for any of it, especially given that she'd had to sort out this costume.

Elizabeth Mason had turned out to be a little shorter than Rathna, a flurry of energy and activity. She had bustled Rathna into the outfit and done a few charms to adjust the fit. Then, there had been far more charms, one after another, to turn it the colours Rathna wanted, matching them to a set of colour swatches Mason pulled from seemingly nowhere.

Rathna had quickly settled on something that had that odd pinkish-gold shade of the withamite. It was laid out with the vein running through a base of darker olive green stone, from her right shoulder down to her left hip. It was not a colour she'd seen outside some of the Indian community, but she thought it suited her very well. And she certainly stood out.

The end result was fascinating, however. As she set the mask in place, and finished the last touches of powder on her face, she thought it rather flattering, even against her skin. Then, as she covered the last patches, the effect was complete, and it would be hard to tell much about her beyond her dark hair. Just as she finished, there was a knock on her door, and a voice. "It's Gabe."

When she opened the door, the mask and antlers were quite impressive, and he'd used some sort of odd charm to create soft fur along his neck and shoulders. She ran a finger along it, tentatively, and he arched up into it. "Are you ready, bright mistress?"

"You keep calling me that." She then took a breath and nodded. "As ready as I'll get."

He offered his arm - no cane tonight, she supposed it would be too quickly identifying. "You are a breath of bright light, and you are mistress of your arts. I'll stop if you want me to."

Rathna shook her head. "Not on my account. I'll just be baffled about it. That is quite common with you." Then she took a breath and let it out. Gabe had kept his word, as she knew he would. He'd explained to her who the guest list included. He didn't know all of it, but the sorts of people.

One of the reasons for the costume party was so his parents could indulge themselves and invite people who would not normally move in their more formal social circles. His Uncle Gil, and his Uncle Magni, who were partners in more than one way. That had startled her, but Gabe had been direct and earnest about that.

He'd even explained where people would be, that his mother and Uncle Gil tended to sit, and would find some-where they could collect people easily, and enjoy the party. That had been another shock, realising that Gabe's Uncle Gil used a cane as well. He'd lost one leg just below the knee fighting in the Sudan decades ago now, apparently. It explained why he didn't go to public events terribly often.

They came down the back stairs and Gabe led her around the side of the house. That way, they could make a proper entrance, without anyone guessing they must have come from the family or guest spaces. The house was lit up by charms, outside and in, festive chains of paper lanterns tucked above the windows, and the foyer was busy with people. Gabe kept her close, smiling and bowing without saying much. She followed along, trying not to cling to him.

This was more people than she'd seen together at a

social gathering approximately ever. Certainly she'd been in big crowds in London plenty of times, and at various other events, but this was a party and there must be hundreds of people there. Well, at least two hundred.

They poured into the foyer of the house, then spread out to either side, into two long rooms. "Ballroom's at the left, facing out onto the lawns. The food is to the right. Various places to sit and talk or stand and talk, all through. We can escape to the library when you want a break, but that's family and close friends only, Papa's very particular about the warding."

That made her smile, knowing that there was an escape. She kept looking around, being caught by the costumes and the designs. They were on the more fanciful, abstract side here. Gabe's was rather more literal than most. However, the antlers were set so that he wasn't in too much danger of causing harm to anyone, or of getting caught in a door or a chandelier. They were proportionately fairly small antlers, now she got a good look at them, narrower than his shoulders.

He guided her deftly through the long dining room to the right, gathering up particular treats with cries of delight, and pressing certain things on her, and not others. He then leaned closer. "Fortify ourselves first, then we'll go see about Mama and Papa and whoever else is handy."

She looked around as he guided her into a quieter room, with nooks for talking. Some sort of morning room, she assumed, decorated in deeper blue and cream, that made her feel a bit like she was standing in a fountain. "How are you going to introduce me?"

"I'd thought as simply my guest. I didn't make it clear I was bringing you, the person I was working with in Scotland. Aunt Mason knows, of course, but she might not actually have told Mama anything useful yet. It will mean dodging a few questions, but we can just tell them to wait for tomorrow."

"And you want to play it this way..." She stopped as someone went past her, in a flurry of brilliant orange and black of a butterfly. Then someone after her who seemed to be a jackal, from the shape of the face, but not quite, not with ears like that.

"Set animal." Gabe said in her ear. "Sort of but not actually a jackal, highly disputed but associated with the Egyptian god of that name."

Someone else went off after them, with an oddly long-jawed mask and stripes down the back, in a particular pattern, that stirred memories of some news story. Gabe was peering at it, trying to place it, and she suggested, uncertainly, "Thylacine?" It seemed an awkward costume to try and eat in, but Gabe was managing well enough through a panel in the underside of the mask's muzzle.

"You see the game? Mama didn't host costume parties until I was about twelve. She swore she wasn't going to host a costume party until she was sure people would rise to the theme. Now, though, she likes them. It lets Mama and Papa invite all their friends who aren't in the expected social circles. This theme gives plenty of scope, but also it's rather beautiful. See him, there?" He pointed across the room, more a gesture than pointing. "Some kind of bright ocean fish. I'm afraid I'm not very good at fish that don't live in English ponds."

It made Rathna laugh. "Well, I'm glad there are things you don't actually know. What's she, do you think?" Really quite voluptuous, not at all the current fashionable figure, but the woman was laughing, her head thrown back in a shimmer of iridescent blue feathers.

"Twilight nightjar. They live in the New Forest, mostly. Gorgeous colours, though, that's exceedingly fine work." He then nodded at someone who seemed to be some sort of plant. "That's silphium, I think. Extinct now, we don't actually know what it looked like. But that black stalk, and the yellow flowers, see, up along the shoulders? And those little inset hearts, I read an article that suggested those were the shape of the fruit." It was rather abstract, but visually striking, as if painted and embroidered on a deep green tabard over a long tube of a black dress.

"That's what one of the contraceptive charms is based on, I remember being taught that. When the plant went extinct." She nodded. "So we do our best to guess?"

"Mmhmm. There are cards in the entry. We fill out a card that says what we were, and who we were. And then we fill out cards to identify other people. After the party Mama goes through them, and whoever came up with the best costume that no one guessed wins. You're definitely in the running. It takes her a while, though, since some people write very odd descriptions."

Rathna frowned. "Why do it that way?"

Gabe laughed. "Test of observation for the Guard and Penelopes here, and a useful training device for everyone they teach. Papa takes the cards in and demonstrates how five people will describe the same costume about eight different ways."

Rathna snorted, then was caught by someone coming through. "Is that a jack-o'-lantern?" Another costume that seemed rather awkward to wear, circular as the turnip was. Very traditional.

Gabe tsked. "A tad out of season, but I admit it's nicely made. And the lighting charms, from inside, that's a new approach to getting a proper flicker." Then he stretched.

"All right. Shall we go make our bows? And then I can show you a good time, let you do your share of observing." He drew back from her for a moment, his eyes disconcerting behind the mask. "I want to let you take your time at what you see, without being pressed. That's why no name. That's for tomorrow, right?"

Rathna saw the point of the plan. She nodded, just once. "That's how we'll do it." Immediately, he had pivoted, offering his arm again. The other guests parted in front of him. It was as if he'd suddenly put on a cloak or a sign declaring he had a purpose and lived here, and they should let him through.

The way involved two hallways, two more large rooms, near the size of the entire ground floor of Morah Avigail's house. She had the sense, once more, of him being like a hunting hound, with that fixed goal, out ahead of him. Even more so when he took an abrupt left turn, into a smaller room. It looked down the entire length of the house, across the ballroom, through to the foyer, and down into the dining room.

A woman was seated in a chair, dressed in something that was glowing and shifting. On someone else it might have been garish or too demanding, but the glowing lights simply shifted in a dance. "Mama's a dance of mirabiles." Gabe explained. The near-mythical creatures of the deep quiet woods, rarely seen. "Aunt Mason knew someone who could do the charmwork. Very new technique."

Beside her chair stood a man who was glowing, like a candle, with that warm light, with a mask of a bird's head and beak. "And Papa's a Babian bird, out of the Arthurian tales. They give off light. Mama said the wings are very impressive when they're fully unfurled."

To their right sat another man, clearly costumed as a

mouse. He was like something out of the pantomime she'd been taken to see as a special treat for the orphanage when she was ten. More elegant than that, this was a scholarly sort of tidy mouse, but still a mouse. The man made a slight gesture with his hand, some sort of specific sign. A moment later a broad-shouldered man, his size enhanced by a lion's mane and mask, came over to join the group. Rathna could see there were silver strands among the gold that was his hair, not the mane that went with the costume.

Gabe brought them both up close enough to speak easily and quietly, then swept down in a bow, clearly entirely aware of where his antlers were at all times. As he straightened, she made a little bob. She could tell he was being ridiculous on purpose, not because it was actually required.

"Mama, Papa. My colleague, whose name shall remain a mystery until tomorrow."

His father inclined his head, showing off a beaked mask as the light shifted around him. "You are most welcome, and you clearly tolerate our son's foibles well."

His mother smiled at that. She wore only a half mask that shimmered around her eyes. "And you are beautifully dressed. I recognise the maker, of course, but I gather you are some particular stone?"

Rathna spread her hands. "My lady, telling you would be depriving you of the fun of your own game. I've gathered from Gabe that you don't often get a puzzle that challenges you."

She saw, an instant too late, all four of them react to her use of Gabe's nickname. Not a thing his colleagues generally did, of course. It was too late to do anything but forge ahead. Gabe, for his part, had the little bounce to him that indicated he was delighted with the world. If he was fine with it, well, they'd manage.

His mother laughed, though. "You're quite right. I'll look forward to finding out the answer and delighted we'll get more chance to talk when there isn't the press of - rather a lot of people. Gabe, darling, you should make sure to say hello to your sister if you can spot her. And of course, anything you need, my dear," That was to Rathna, directly, "You have only to ask. Brunch at eleven."

Someone else was coming over, and the postures of all four shifted again. The lion-masked man quietly said something, and wandered off again, and an older woman came over, clearly wishing to talk with Gabe's parents. He took the cue, waved a hand in something that was nothing like a salute except in the broadest possible strokes, and encouraged Rathna away back toward the foyer.

"Mama, Papa, everyone, good morning." They were settled in the morning room, with the French doors to the side terrace open. The weather outside was glorious, showing off the estate to perfection. Gabe held the door open for Rathna, then offered her his arm, cane in his left hand as usual. They had both been up and about an hour ago, long enough to walk down to the lake and back by the stables so she could meet Invicta properly.

"This is Mistress Rathna Stone, of the Portal Keepers Guild. Rathna, my parents, Lord Richard and Lady Alysoun Edgarton. You've met Aunt Mason. And this is Uncle Magni - Captain Torham, to most people, retired from the Guard. And Uncle Gil, Master Gilbert Oxley. Down at the end is my sister, Charlotte."

He could feel Rathna's hand tighten on his forearm. He glanced at her, just once, before shifting his hand, the little twist that would permit her to hold it instead. She slid her hand down to grab his, and when he looked back at his assembled family, his father was standing up, and Uncle Magni.

"Please, do be welcome." There was a silence, and Gabe found it delightful, seeing his father somewhat wrong-footed. He was sure his father was trying to figure out how to handle names, and this was an unusual situation. They were decidedly en famille, but he had not made it clear to them what role Rathna might have.

His mother cut in smoothly. "You did call him Gabe last night, so I am assuming your work together has gone particularly well, on a personal level?"

Gabe laughed at that and then grinned at Rathna. "See, I told you."

She let out a breath, and then managed a smile, though he could tell she was still a bit overwhelmed. More than a bit. She then nodded. "Thank you for a lovely party last night. I had a much better time than I thought I might. And for your hospitality, of course. The house and grounds are stunning, even knowing how much Gabe loves them."

Gabe nodded. Then, taking in his assembled family, he picked up where his mother had left off. "Rathna and I are still sorting out exactly what we're doing next. But I feel I am making an excellent start on resolving the puzzle of whether I might like to settle down with someone." He was watching Aunt Mason particularly, who got a delighted gleam in her eye.

There was a moment of absolute silence, before his father laughed and shook his head. "You are constantly yourself, Gabe. Come on, get your food. I did have something to talk to you about, if you don't mind, Rathna. And please, we are informal in this setting, to at least a moderate degree."

Gabe gestured at the chafing dishes out on the sideboard. "We're quite informal about the meal - serve yourself, whatever you'd like, and I made sure there are things you prefer." And options besides the sausage and bacon he knew would be on the menu. He leaned over to add, "First names, or Lord Richard or Lady Alysoun for Mama and Papa. Or whatever you're comfortable with that's more formal, if you'd rather."

That took a few minutes, long enough for people to gather themselves and start talking quietly again. Gabe heard Aunt Mason claiming a forfeit from his father and mother. About him, he knew that, but she'd more than earned it. When they got back to the table, she tipped her glass at him in salute, but didn't say anything.

His parents kept the conversation to the party to give Rathna a chance to eat. As she finished her plate, his father cleared his throat. "Do you have another assignment yet?"

Gabe shook his head. "We're still discussing. Several things." He and Rathna had talked, cautiously, about what the future might hold. They had a possible connection to her cousin, now, the information had come through just as they came back from Scotland. If that went well, maybe there'd be a trip for her. Or him, as well.

"Council Member FitzAlan had a word with me this week."

Gabe's head came up sharply. "What about, sir?"

The cautious formality made his father grin for a moment. "What additional responsibilities you might be willing to consider, now you're fully established. There's a Council seat likely to come open within the year. He wondered if you'd be up to the challenge."

Gabe went ramrod straight. "Sir, with all due respect, bloody well not."

Beside him, Rathna blinked at him. His mother said,

"Forfeit, dear. Though Gabe, darling, I think we might all enjoy hearing your reasoning." Her voice was mild enough, but Uncle Gil was barely repressing laughter.

Gabe sighed and nodded. "Of course, Mama." He then turned to Rathna, wanting to make sure she had a proper explanation. "You're familiar with the Council, of course."

"Their portals, yes." Rathna said. "Including the one to their keep. But as individuals to talk to? No."

Gabe ignored his father's clear desire to go on. "They're - well, they're what would have been a King's or Queen's Council, once upon a time. Now the same purpose, but no royalty, see? There are a series of challenges, for membership, as seats come open. No one knows what they are, not in truth. They're not physical exactly. People who aren't physically strong or agile have made it through. It's something else. Or at least, there's a way through that's something else."

"Wits and magic, as much as... physical ability, then?" He could see Rathna's mind whirling along. "And what can they do?"

"Directly? They advise. There's a reason the Guard, the Judges, the Magistrates, are all separate, and bound to the Silence, not to the Council. But they anchor some of the land magics - for England, for Wales, for Scotland. Some other duties of that kind, that aren't local. There are rumours they anchor some of the warding at Schola and the other schools, though I'm honestly not sure how far to trust that. Uncle Gil and I keep going round and round about it, the sources are awfully contradictory." He restrained himself from the explanation of that. Or they'd be here until teatime, at least. "But where there's advice, there can be quite a lot of influence, one way and another."

Rathna nodded once. "Thank you, that gives me enough

to be going on with." She didn't ask him, but Gabe could hear it, wanting to know why he'd been so vehement.

That was what his mother asked him to explain, so he turned to the head of the table as he shifted to take Rathna's hand. "Mama, Papa." Then he grinned. "Assembled elders." That made Uncle Magni snort. "First, I didn't serve. That matters, and it will for decades."

His father almost said something, then didn't. It was the first time he'd been that blunt about it, and his mother was watching him closely now. "There are mysteries I don't know, painful and necessary ones, that you know, sir, and that Uncle Gil knows. And a great many other people. And I don't."

There was no argument to that. How could there be, since he was completely right? He gave them a moment, then barrelled on. "Second, I can think of at least half a dozen people who could do it better. I do not build alliances like they do. And I don't want to learn." It came out in a rush, and he took a deep breath. Again, there was no argument, though he could hear all of them waiting to pounce on the discussion.

"Third." Here, he glanced at Rathna. "In our conversations so far, Rathna has quite reasonably pointed out that a number of people might have some difficulty with our relationship, for any number of reasons. I noted out that there was nothing anyone could take away from me. If, sir, you decided to disinherit me on that account, you'd be doing it for the good of the land, and I wouldn't complain. Though, of course, I'd rather you didn't. But I have my work, a proper vocation. I have people I care for, and more than I'd thought to. I have plenty of fiscal support for whatever my whims might wish to indulge."

His father shook his head. "You are my heir, have no

worries about that. Though I admit this is - I gather your aunt told you about our conversation, where she laid even odds we'd be having this conversation about another man."

Gabe shrugged slightly. "She did, yes." Then he went on. "But I know perfectly well I could not place someone I care for in the position to be chipped away at. Being Council involves a great number of social events. Even if the Council Members themselves were civil. Even if they were friendly - and that's not bloody likely."

Bloody was unfortunately the entirely proper adjective. Lady Fortier had a nasty temper and quite a few biases, for one thing. "Even if they were fine, the social events wouldn't be. And I'd hate them, as well as putting Rathna through that. So, no. Tell Council Member FitzAlan it is a flattering suggestion, but I must decline for reasons that will likely become obvious in due course."

He felt Rathna squeeze his hand. His father had listened, intently, with his entire focus. Then he nodded, just once. "You've always known your own mind, Gabe." Then, carefully. "That does raise some further topics of discussion. I hate to pull you away now, but..."

At that, Uncle Gil broke in, as Gabe had hoped he would, having primed that with a note on Friday. "I gather Mistress Stone is quite interested - professionally speaking - in the warding of the house, and how it is placed in the landscape. I might perhaps take her on that sort of tour?" He grinned. "I'm sure Gabe's shown you the stables and the lake, but there's rather a lot more to see."

Rathna looked startled, and then she peered at Gabe, who spread his free hand out. "You were being really quite agreeable about the last night. As you have pointed out, I am a downright dirty cheat. But I keep my promises."

Despite herself, she grinned back at him. "You do."

Then, before she could be scared away from it, she leaned over and kissed him on the cheek. Brief, decorous, but decidedly public. "When it's convenient, Master Oxley?"

"Oh, do call me Gil, if you'd like. I suspect we're going to have rather a lot to talk about. I'm afraid I can't share embarrassing stories about Gabe as a toddler. I didn't meet him until he was seven. But I am sure I can dredge up quite a few about his schooling."

Gabe had known that was coming. It was inevitable. Rathna stood, making a slight nod to his parents. "I hope we'll have a chance to talk more later, but of course I understand you've questions for Gabe. If you have some for me, I'd be glad to talk when..." Her voice trailed off.

His mother beamed at her. "Ah, there, that's sensible. I'd be pleased to get to know more about you. We shouldn't be terribly long, and I promise, he won't want to flee immediately off to the portal. Besides, Gabe, Nanny wants to see you, if you'll pop round before you go."

Gabe nodded, and said, "I did expect this. And it's entirely fair, really. Given that we completely sprung things on them." Then he grinned. "Nanny makes the best biscuits. And you should meet her, Rathna, you absolutely should."

Rathna nodded, looking a bit overwhelmed again. Then Uncle Gil was getting the door. His father stood. "The library for us, I think. Bring along your tea, if you'd like. The rest of you, make free, etcetera, etcetera."

Uncle Magni and Aunt Mason looked like they were going to pick up one of their unending discussions where they'd left off. It was usually some detail of duelling equipment, or how terrain affected the casting of various charms. It kept them both cheerfully arguing, whatever specifics they were wrangling over. His sister waved a hand. "Tell me the good parts later, someone. I've a book to read."

Gabe stuck his tongue out at her - some things were eternal. Then he waited for his parents to go ahead into the library, bringing up the rear.

Rathna checked once more that Morah Avigail was settled comfortably in her chair in the parlour and had everything she needed. Her mentor waved a hand. "You fuss, Rathna. He will be along, I am sure."

Just then, there was the knock at the door. Rathna had to hold herself back from getting it. It had been nearly a fortnight - a very busy fortnight - since she had last seen Gabe. He had been called out on a case just after arranging half a dozen things as if they were as simple as breathing. Sarah brushed past her and opened the door, then came to the parlour entrance. "Master Gabriel Edgarton, Mistress Levy."

Morah Avigail did not stand up, but inclined her head. "Do come in, please."

He was carrying a bouquet of really rather fine flowers. There were golden yellow tulips, tucked among ferns and ivy for greenery, dotted below with smaller flowers, star-shaped yellow, bursts of tiny white, and even bluebells. Rathna was sure it meant something, but she had no idea what. He bowed, quite formally, and said, "Mistress Levy, a pleasure to see you again. These are for you."

Morah Avigail inclined her own head, peering first at the flowers, touching the tulips before looking up at Gabe, who just grinned. Then she snorted and said, "Sarah, please put these in water, and bring them out, when you've a moment. And you, young man. Say a proper hello to Rathna and sit down. You're rather tall to look up at."

Gabe turned to her now, and there was a gleam in his eye. "I have something slightly different, if you will permit the gift, Rathna." He slipped his hand into a vest pocket and drew out a small jewellery box. She blinked, they were entirely too new to each other to permit her to accept something like personal jewellery. He saw that moment and added. "Open it. I believe you'll find it entirely proper."

She had a suspicion then what she was going to find. Once she opened the box, she blinked. Inside was a pendant in a beautiful art deco style, a long rectangle of withamite, set as a carefully cut stone in silver framing. The stone itself likely hadn't been terribly expensive, but she was quite sure the skill required for the setting was a different matter. It was Gabe splitting the difference, just as he always did.

She peered at it and immediately reached to undo her master's medallion. Gabe was grinning at her, holding the case until she was ready. "I've a cuff, if you'd prefer that for the medallion." he offered. "I do that, usually."

Rathna shook her head. "You seem to think of everything. Thank you, Gabe, this is lovely. And reasonably proper." That made him grin more. She ventured a kiss on his cheek, before he took a step back to settle on the couch and she sat beside him.

Morah Avigail looked amused, at least, but made an

attempt at sternness when she spoke. "Do you have something you wish to say to me, young man, regarding your intentions?"

Gabe straightened his shoulders, reaching for Rathna's hand really rather daringly. "Mistress Levy, Rathna has been so kind as to favour me not only with her attention and the delight of her company, but with her professional excellence. I would like very much to move toward a more permanent sort of opportunity in both regards." He paused for a bare instant. "She is, of course, a grown woman, who needs no permission to spend her time as she wishes. But you are very dear to her, and I wish to ask for your blessing."

Morah Avigail's eyebrows had gone up at that, and then she considered, without directly answering him. "How did a Healer turn up on my doorstep near a fortnight ago?"

Gabe spread out his free hand. "A little favour from a chosen uncle of mine. I do hope the healer was of some help?"

"Yes, she was. I've a nutritive potion to take, and some other suggestions. She is calling round tomorrow, to check on my progress. Who is paying for that, then?" Very direct, Rathna realised.

Gabe said, his words clipped and precise, "I explained to Rathna that there are so few of you portal keepers. You could ask for much more in the way of support than you or she have. I understand why money would be a different matter, but in this case, I had a word with the proper office at the Temple of Healing. The Ministry is covering whatever costs are required."

"The Healer said there was a mikvah at the Temple I could use. For healing. I did not believe there was one properly set up there, but she assures me it is, and is arranging for me to make sure it meets my standards."

Rathna was watching Gabe's face closely. He clearly knew the word. "There are healing baths, sacred baths, all through the lowest level. But I understand the mikvah is a separate building, to ensure it meets with all the requirements - and can be seen by all concerned to meet those requirements."

She had not expected him to understand that thread and articulate it so cleanly. So much of Jewish law was not just doing the thing properly, but making it clear it was done properly, with no chance for confusion or an inaccurate perception. Of course, Morah Avigail would want to examine the pipes and the situation herself. She had not, however, expected Gabe to arrange for that.

Morah Avigail nodded. "And you have been busy elsewhere since then? Rathna was rather nervous, despite your letters." Worrying about a number of things, Rathna had to admit, like whether Vivek might pop up, or some other nameless lurking fear.

"Ah, about that." Gabe looked down. "Besides the family obligations for the first of May, I was called away on a case, and could not explain in person. However, if you will permit the indulgence, I would be delighted to see to acquiring journals for both you and Rathna. So that you may keep in touch with me and make sure I am doing as I ought. And of course, so Rathna and I may keep in touch no matter where our work takes us."

There was a long silence, drawn out, as Morah Avigail considered it. On the one hand, it would be desperately handy. The journals were still quite expensive, to have two presented was a generous offer. On the other hand, it was a very large gift, and Morah Avigail might decide far too much at this stage.

Morah Avigail did not say any of the things Rathna

expected. Instead, she said, "You have a particular reason for the journals. Explain yourself, young man."

Gabe nodded. "Various contacts in the Guard. Well, mostly my mother, actually. They have tracked down more information about the young man who called on you some weeks ago. He is a cousin of Rathna's, a medical student. We've been able to determine that he has an excellent reputation. But he is well known among his fellow students for his - well, they said 'rather obsessive' desire to track down a relative. Here in London, or who might be in London."

Rathna squeezed Gabe's hand, and he squeezed back. "Me?" She wasn't sure what to do with that.

"I have his address now - he had to fill out a form at several of the places he requested information. I would be delighted to arrange a meeting. If it goes well, perhaps we might look at -" He hesitated. "There are some logistical challenges, but it would be quite possible for you to go to India, to meet the rest of your family, if you decided you wish to."

The idea overwhelmed her. She wanted to; she wanted to understand her family, the kind of casual knowledge of aunts and uncles and cousins and family connections other people had. To know the family stories. Learn to cook some of the foods, perhaps. Something. But the idea of going by herself, that was far too much. Then she looked at Gabe, who was looking down, suddenly shy.

"I couldn't take that much time from work." Or Morah Avigail.

Gabe let out a breath. "In my line of work, we call that a sabbatical, or a working trip. Not much you could do about the time on the ocean, but it's considered an excellent chance to acquire books and documents about how things are done in other places. You could make portal connections across most of the Empire, if you had to, with ferries and trains to close the gaps, if you had to come back quickly. But it would be rather unpleasant, so a ship would be easier, going and coming."

That made her stop and consider. "Could - could you come?" Her voice broke on the last word.

Gabe lit up like a sunrise. "Logistics, but I suspect we could arrange something." Morah Avigail opened her mouth, and he went on, "With appropriate chaperonage, and such, of course."

She snorted at him. "I care about the appearance and not the fact here. For the record. Though we do not permit male guests over the age of thirteen in this house overnight outside of emergencies or necessary business."

Gabe nodded. "Of course, Mistress Levy. I quite understand." Then, impish, he added, "And it's not as if we don't have some other options, when that might be relevant."

Morah Avigail looked far more vibrant than Rathna had seen her for months. Her eyes were glowing, and she was laughing now. "I believe you may call me something less formal, if you wish."

Gabe considered for a moment. "Mistress, perhaps Aunt Avigail? I have other aunts I greatly respect. Who I suspect you would enjoy meeting, too."

"Arrange it, when I am further recovered." She inclined her head. "And is there other news, of what you did in Scotland? Rathna mentioned one of your notes said you would tell her when you could."

Gabe nodded. "Pardon that, but it's part of my training, not to write things down outside the formal reports until the case is settled. The blood allowed us to trace our shapeshifter - he's a thrush, it turns out. There were three men, mining the withamite, to powder and use to enhance a potion, mostly quackery, they were selling. But the withamite apparently holds magical energy particularly well, or enhances it. There are ongoing tests, some of the Penelopes are doing, and ...” He hesitated. “Whatever else, I’ve made sure you’ll get a copy of the report.”

Rathna caught that slight hesitation, and smiled. “I do hope you’ll be delivering it yourself, mind. And explaining it.” She tilted her head. “Perhaps a supper out, with the people involved, that I could come to?”

Gabe lit up at that, gloriously. “Of course, bright lady.”

It was so easy to bring that light to him, at least for her. “Sorcha wrote. She didn’t say much, but she did say the beithir had settled. I don’t know if she means an actual beithir, or a metaphorical sense of the mountains.”

“Sorcha has seemed less inclined to metaphor than many people I know.” Gabe pointed out. “Perhaps the former, then.” With that, he glanced over to Morah Avigail, to see how she was taking this.

Morah Avigail was delighted, she’d been watching their interplay with growing pleasure. Now, she flicked her fingers. “Go take your young man on a walk, Rathna. I’m sure you have quite a lot to discuss.”

Gabe stood and offered another of those little bows. “And you wish to think about what I’ve offered, of course. I do intend to treat Rathna every bit as well as she will permit.”

“Hmph.” Then she waved her hand, and Rathna stood up. She guided them out the front door, and said, “Where are we walking? Wait, no. First, explain the flowers.”

Gabe grinned at that. “Language of flowers. Very Victorian. From what you’ve said, I suspected it would amuse M... Aunt Avigail.” Hearing him say that with fondness made her melt.

"And what did they say that you're not telling me?"

Gabe spread his hands. "Nothing you don't know. Fern for fascination and magic. Sweet Alyssum, those are the little white ones, for worth beyond beauty. Bluebells for constancy. Lesser Celandine for joys to come. Charlotte helped me work it out, she's very good at that sort of thing."

"And the tulips and the ivy?"

"The ivy is for fidelity and marriage." Then he flushed, ducking his chin. "And the yellow tulip is hopeless love. That seemed important to get in there. To lead with."

Rathna inhaled sharply, and then slipped her hand through his. They were out on a public street, she shouldn't kiss him soundly, no matter how much she wanted to. Because he was irrepressibly himself. Because Morah Avigail approved of that. Because he loved her, and he said so and kept learning more ways to say it. She just squeezed for a long moment, before she found her words. "Where are we walking to? For the moment?"

"Would it be a bother to take me through the market? I'm actually looking for some spices for Aunt Mason. She asked if I'd keep an eye out." He was beaming at her now. "And I'll work on having somewhere private, soon as we can."

Of course he would be. She could set that aside for the moment. "Work or pleasure? The spices, I mean."

"Pleasure, in this case, so not urgent, but she's low on -" He tugged his little notebook out of his vest pocket. "Well, several things. Spice merchant? They're pleasant to smell and look at."

"And won't cause a lot of commotion, me with you." Rathna took a breath. "Did you mean it, about India?"

"I did. I wouldn't tease you about that. I don't know what - what the arrangements would be like. But from the cautious asking around I did, I think you could certainly get a break. You've worked, week in and week out, barring an occasional holiday, for what, a decade and a half now, including your apprenticeship?"

She nodded. "It just seems, it's something I wanted, to know the family. And it's not a trip I could make often, so you coming would make sense. Besides the fact..." She took a breath, then managed to say it out loud. "I want you there. With me. I know it will be all right if you're there."

Gabe stopped tugging her so she looked at him. "Rathna, you are brilliant and creative and gloriously stubborn. You could do this on your own, I am sure of it. However..." And now he was teasing. "I want to be right there with you. Seeing you figuring it out. India, and wherever else you decide you want to go."

Rathna took a breath. "You really are very compelling, Gabe. You know that. Someone has to keep you out of trouble." She swallowed. "But thank you. For the healer, and the journals, and figuring out my - cousin. And everything."

"My goal is to teach you how to reach for the things you can have. Leading by example. You'll catch on in no time, I'm sure."

She laughed and took his hand, tugging him off toward the market. "Come on. I do know where to find a treat you'll like."

"Gabe," Rathna reached out and touched his face. "Talk to me." It was not quite an order or a command, though she was certainly within her rights in this case. He was being difficult, and he knew it, and yet he couldn't stop.

He swallowed, then managed to look up to meet her eyes. "Pardon." They were up in his sitting room - also known as his personal library - after a pleasant supper together. The dishes were set outside for one of the staff to whisk away. No one was going to disturb them. He knew she expected there to be something else, now, for them to be progressing toward the bedroom. Only that kept not happening.

"One word is not talking, Gabriel Anthony Edgarton." She tilted her head, watching him closely, and then she shifted. She put her hand on his chest, just above his heart, resting flat. She cocked her head, the same way she did when she listed to a portal stone, eyes half-closed, concentrating. As if there was nothing in the world but him.

Which only made him feel worse.

"Talk to me, you. Please." It was the 'please' that got him. "What's going on in that brilliant head of yours?"

Gabe took a breath and let it out. "I know we should, I mean, you've made it clear you're interested in…" His eyes flicked down. It wasn't that he wasn't interested. His body made that rather clear, at regular intervals. He'd never really needed to learn the ways men dealt with that, and he found it terribly vulnerable now.

"I am, yes. When you're ready." Rathna shifted her hand to cup his cheek. "And you're not sure you are." She was, as always, precise in her language. He was in that queer liminal space, standing in the portal, not sure where solid ground was, or how he could get back to it. It was like that moment on Invicta, knowing that what happened next would change everything.

He closed his eyes. Quietly, he managed to say, "I'm going to be bad at it. I'm not used to being bad at things."

There was dead silence. Rathna didn't move, she didn't speak; she didn't even breathe. Then she slid her hand down to take his. Down his cheek, down his chest, grabbing his hand. "Your bedroom is through there?"

There were only two relevant doors, and either would eventually lead to the bedroom. He nodded, not opening his eyes. She tugged at him, first one hand, then taking his other, tugging him along like a tow boat took a great liner. He felt uncertain, leaden.

She'd apparently chosen the correct door the first time, because she brought him to the edge of the bed, then nudged him. "Shoes off. The rest of your clothes, if you can manage that. If you're willing."

Gabe screwed his eyes closed. It was tearing him apart, wanting something he had almost no practice wanting. He'd been ignoring all of this, cordially and amiably, for at least a decade. It wasn't just not knowing what to do. It was all the ways he knew he could mess things up horribly.

His father had never been explicit about it, but he had been clear since he was twelve that his parents still looked forward to their time alone together. And not just because they wanted to continue some great debate about duelling theory or discuss some detail of one of his father's cases.

Uncle Gil and Uncle Magni had been more practically minded, at least in terms of making sure he got his hands on the useful sort of books. But of course neither of them had any experience with women, and Gabe thought that made rather a difference. If he'd fallen in love with a man, it would have been vastly simpler, he suspected, they would just have given him advice.

All of that was entirely academic, anyway. Being here, with an actual person, with her own preferences and desires, he didn't know how to do that. He'd worked well with Lucy as an apprentice, because he respected expertise. But here and now, he wasn't sure what to do. And he wasn't sure Rathna knew what to do either.

Then he took a breath, and let it out, then another one. This wasn't going to go away. Not unless Rathna went away, and he didn't want that. She was clever, and observant, and she knew all sorts of things he didn't. Yet. And she saw things differently, heard the magic, felt it, in ways he hadn't realised people had language for.

They'd spent time together every day this week. Every time she left to go home, or off to work, he wanted more time with her. He kept turning over his shoulder to ask her something, or talk through an idea. He liked how she leaned against him, hand on his shoulder, to peer at a book, or how she moved when she was in her element, brisk and decisive.

Slowly, he reached to undo the top button of his shirt,

letting it slip through the fabric. Then the next, and the next. When he came to his trousers, he swallowed hard, and undid those as well, feeling the fabric slide down to the floor. He still couldn't look at her, not until she said, her voice much softer, "Gabe, love. We'll do this together."

That made his eyes snap open. Rathna had settled onto the bed, and she was looking at him, steadily. She wore a plain white silk shift, if that was the right word. It had a square neck and went down to mid-thigh. There was a pile of her clothing on the floor near his. She caught his look. "Later." Again, she was clear. "This is new to me, too."

He blinked at her, distracted now. He hadn't thought to ask, but he'd assumed she'd - well. She'd been much more experienced in what they'd done so far. Kissing and touching, and leaning and being together, without having a particular goal beyond pleasure.

"No one I liked enough to be that close to. I do like you, Gabe. We will figure this puzzle out together. I have read some books and heard some things. I've even been thoroughly drilled on the contraceptive and hygiene charms. You have read some books, I'm fairly sure. If not before you met me, by the time you introduced me to your parents."

Gabe blushed, then smiled. "Rather a lot of books. Though I think they left out many of the essential parts."

Rathna raised an eyebrow. "And what do you think is essential, then? Come here, come on." She scooted over in the bed, then shifted to tug down the covers. "This bed is enormous, Gabe, what do you do when you're all by yourself?"

He blinked at her. "Have space to sleep that's not covered by books?" That, now, that utterly broke any tension between them, as Rathna threw back her head and laughed.

"Of course. Well. No books in bed tonight. Come here, we'll start with what we know we like."

That, at least, went well enough. Once he was in the bed, under the covers, he ventured enough to unbutton and wriggle out of his underthings. The feeling of the sheets against his skin was entirely novel, enough to keep his mind from racing. Taking a breath, he settled his arm around her, feeling the silky fabric of her shift, and then the warmth underneath.

Pressed close against him, she couldn't fail to notice how he was rising to attention despite his nerves. Once she was satisfied with the position, she settled into reminding him what they knew. The kissing, he felt much more confident about that now. It was also easier lying down, somehow, the angles were easier. He could line up his body, his mouth, in new ways, and he could get both hands around her.

Then, it was easier for his hands to begin to shift, exploring the curves beneath the cloth. She arched into it, rather like a cat, or a dog, rolling around, revelling in the attention. He could give her that, all of that, there was nothing he wanted more than to focus on making her arch and hearing those little noises she was making now. They were a song of pleasure, one even he couldn't fail to identify.

After minutes - hours, he had no idea - he pulled back to peer at her. The light through the windows was fading. She moved more onto her back. "You should - feel." It came out shyly. He thought she might be blushing. She took his hand, bringing it down between her legs, where he felt dampness. That made him blink again, startled.

"I thought I needed..."

"I haven't done anything with someone else, Gabe, but

some people make their own pleasure." She was definitely blushing now, he could hear it.

"Oh." Then, to hide his own feelings, he shifted to kiss her again, beginning to explore with his fingers, how things fit together. Once or twice, he had to yank his mind back from going at it like a case, figuring out how the magic responded to this or that. Though, now that he'd done that, instinctively, she rather seemed to like it. Particularly so when he tried something gently, then more confidently, as he figured out where his hand might shift, what happened with different touches.

She was fully on her back, her hair coming loose, pooling on the pillow. She lay with her legs spread, one knee half bent, so she could rock her hips against his touch. She was utterly gorgeous now, entirely present in a way he wasn't sure she'd ever been with anyone else, at least since her mother's death. He wanted to give her that, over and over again, a time when there was simply joy and pleasure and love and beauty.

Then she opened her eyes and held out her hand. "With me, Gabe, love. Will you?" There were so many things she might have said in that moment that would have turned him shy and uncertain again. But doing this with her, a thing they were figuring out together, that made it so much better. She didn't expect him to know. She just expected him to be able to learn.

And learning, well, learning he was excellent at.

Gabe pushed himself up on his hands, settling his hips between her legs. It felt strange, a position he wasn't at all familiar with, but then she smiled at him. "Might need your hand, to - the right place." Rathna's voice was gentle.

He nodded and moved to adjust himself. It felt like he was in the wrong place for a moment, like all the angles were off, but then he felt her heat, felt a small dip. His hips moved, almost before he could stop them, and he pressed into a warm hot tightness unlike anything else.

Rathna arched, and he almost slipped out, distracted by the way her breasts lifted the shift. Then the angles changed again, just slightly, and he found himself slipping further in. An inch, then two, then he found it was almost like riding at a canter. The sway, the movement, the rock of the hips. He tried that for one stroke, then two, and then he found himself fully sheathed inside her, and there was nothing like it in all the world.

Rathna was watching him, her eyes wide open, like it was the best present she'd ever been given. She'd got one of her hands on his thigh, the other on his hip, just touching lightly, but then she brought one of her legs around his other hip. "Oh, yes. More of that." It had a purr he'd never heard from her.

It was provocative, amazing, delightful, and he could not have held still for anything on earth. He pulled out - almost too far, catching himself in the nick of time. He slid in, trying to find the rhythm, the angle. It kept changing, she kept moving. All that pleasure was wonderful, but no two strokes were the same. It made him catch his breath, and he knew he was, must be, doing things that weren't as pleasurable as they could be.

Then, all thought fled, because she was rocking with him. She didn't care, apparently, that this wasn't polished and easy. That he was clumsy at it, that he hadn't got the knack of rising to the trot yet. Moments later, he was beyond worrying about anything at all. He was caught up in the movement and the sensations, and the fact he was learning more every stroke about how to make this better.

It was the sort of challenge that might take a man a lifetime to learn, and oh, that was the best sort of puzzle.

The end, when it came, was far too sudden, too much of a rush. He found himself thrusting harder and harder, short sharp movements. They made her shudder around him. Then there was nothing but exploding inside her, the surge of pleasure and need all tangled up together.

He came back to himself propped on one elbow, much closer to her breasts than he'd expected to be, breathing hard. She was panting beneath him, and wriggling her hand down between her legs as he slipped out of her to touch herself. Before he could find words to ask, she shuddered beneath him, with a deep groan, before finally relaxing.

Not at all sure what to say, he shifted beside her, curling an arm across her stomach when she finally settled. She nuzzled at his ear. "When you're recovered, I'll show you how to do that to me." Her voice turned amused, as she added, "It might take a bit of practice. If you're agreeable."

He let out a snort, breathing in the smell of her hair and her skin. "Very diligent at practising, me." Then, he relaxed as well, letting himself drift with nothing but her warmth and her closeness, and how she'd made him tackle his fear of that particular fence.

Rathna stretched out, running a hand along Gabe's shoulder.

Her conversations with her cousin Vivek had gone quite well once they both more or less decided to set aside the oddities of what she couldn't talk about. Magic, but honestly, also Gabe's entire existence in her life. Vivek had apparently accepted the explanation that she was a particular kind of bluestocking. Or if he hadn't, he had been polite enough not to call out the issues in the story to their faces.

She'd had tea with him twice, after that first meeting, drinking in how he told her about their extended family, aunts and uncles and little children. How they'd all wondered what had happened to Rathna, and her mother, how he'd promised to try and find them when he got the chance to come to London. He'd be an amazing doctor, she was sure of that.

That had still not prepared her for today, which had been surprisingly long and baffling, even by her current standards for such things. Gabe had swept her up in the morning, picking her up from Morah Avigail's, and whisked her off to Hackney. Vivek had met them there, then knocked on the door of an ordinary sort of house. The Ayah's Home.

Vivek had immediately begun translating, explaining that this man - Gabe - was making arrangements to travel to India sometime soon. That he would like to pay the way home of some of the women, if they wished. They had been dubious, as any sensible woman would be.

The woman who ran the home had explained Gabe's bona fides. Rathna wasn't clear how his status translated into the non-magical world, but the word "Lord" featured several times, and worked the same general effect it often did. People were consistent in liking a title, apparently. Or at least accepting that Lords had eccentricities not worth trying to figure out.

It had probably also helped that she'd been there. Vivek had explained she would be going back to meet long-lost family. That she would need someone to act as a maid on the journey. No difficult work, but the show of the thing. And that she'd appreciate someone who could coach her in Bengali, now, and on the journey.

Rathna had not thought to ask for such a thing, but she agreed it was an exceedingly sensible proposal. She managed the bits she still remembered, smiling and beaming. She added that she looked forward to seeing her aunties, letting Vivek explain she had been born here and never met them. At that, the ayahs had drawn her into their parlour, explaining things in a gloriously chaotic mix of English, Bengali, and Hindi. Vivek and Gabe had withdrawn without her noticing.

Of course, Gabe was waiting outside when they were done, some two hours later. He had offered her his arm, and escorted her proudly back to his rooms in Trellech, where they had had a delightful time in bed. He was getting diligently experimental about the process now, and she was certain he spent his nights alone studying up on what he wanted to try next. Not that she had the slightest complaints, since he was careful to observe what she actually liked rather than whatever the books thought she should prefer.

He roused a little, when her fingers moved again, a muzzy, "Mmm, hey." Gabe was delightful in almost any mood, between his cheerfulness and his insatiable desire for all the knowledge. But she was beginning to think she loved him best like this, when he was relaxed and vulnerable in bed. When he didn't need to do anything or be anything at all, except right there.

"You are impossible, Gabe. But very kind." Her voice cracked a little at the end.

He shrugged slightly, and she could see him gathering his wits before he spoke again. "It was a problem money can solve. I have money. And we do need someone to make the proper show on the journey. And a way to talk to people when we get there, though Vivek said you've another cousin who can serve as translator."

"Still. You are utterly impossible. I can't think of another man who'd go at the problem that way."

That made him grin. "Well. I am unique. Probably a good thing, too."

That gave her an opening she'd been wondering about. "I was talking to Vivek. Not this time. Last week. And then I asked, today, about something."

He was a bit more wary now, and Rathna found herself running her hand along his arm, soothingly. She went on. "You dreamed of a snake. A great black snake."

Gave nodded, very cautious now, and he'd gone entirely still under her hand. There was, however, no way to go but forward. This was something he needed to understand. She had been almost sure after talking to Vivek, but now she was certain.

"Did you ever consider that you were given a tremendous gift, Gabe? When you chose to fall?"

He stared at her. It was so much like a snake might that she had to stop herself commenting on it.

"Among, among my people." That was the first time she'd claimed it that openly. "I told you, that the naga can give blessings. What if this, you, were one of them?" She could hear it now, the threads of music, the way he told the story, the way things were, and how they didn't match. How they needed to come into harmony, properly.

Gabe swallowed hard, once, then again. He closed his eyes, screwing them closed for a moment, as if he desperately wanted to hide. She didn't change what she was doing, just waited until his breath settled. "Let me talk out my reasoning, all right?"

He nodded, tentatively, and then shifted his hand, as if wanting hers. She moved, twining her fingers in his, feeling him hold tightly, as if she had become a lifeline.

Rathna took a breath and went on. "You, all you English, you all have assumptions about the Silence and the Pact, and what they mean. And I know some of that is actually written down with facts, but rather a lot of it isn't."

It was not what he'd expected at all, and he blinked at her, relaxing a bit. Good. The more his mind was engaged on the problem, the easier this would be. She was feeling her way through it, very much like establishing the flow for a water portal, how the magic went smoothly one way, and not another.

"And I know," she went on. "That there's more than one way to tell a history. And more than one form of magic. I know the Pact is a contract, an agreement. But I'm wondering if the Silence isn't something more. At least now."

Again, he blinked. She squeezed his hand. "Bear with me a minute. You've been in Spitalfields. You've felt the eruv magics, even if you don't have a name for them."

Gabe shook his head. "Don't know the name." His voice was uneven, but he was talking. That was excellent too.

"It's a Jewish concept. It's a space that allows the most observant to carry things on Shabbat. It makes a public space more like a home, that way. It has to be ritually enclosed, to a specific standard. That is physical, but among those with magic, it is also, logically, a form of warding, and used that way as well. It cannot do everything, it is not a wall, you see? But it can provide warning of danger, or it can... Morah Avigail's rabbi says it encourages a community to know each other."

That had indeed distracted him, and Gabe shifted a bit more onto his side, peering at her. "All right. Show me where it is, next time we're there?"

She waved her hand. "Quite a walk around the whole thing, but I'll let you step from one side of it to the other all you like." She took a breath and went on. "I am wondering if the Silence is like that, now. Maybe it wasn't at first, but what if it has a sense of itself, now? A sense of what it protects."

The expression on his face was one she was going to treasure for the rest of her life, most likely. It took a great deal to bring him to a complete stop and a re-examination of everything he'd assumed. She could see him almost reject it outright before his mind and his integrity caught up with him, and he started thinking it through, piece by piece. She let him do it without distraction, settling down quietly, letting her eyes close. She was quite sure she'd know when he was done.

It took him rather a while. More than five minutes. Perhaps fifteen. She honestly might have drifted off in there. Then his hand squeezed hers. "Tell me what you think it means. The snake."

Rathna shook her head, stretching a little. "You tell me. Better that way." For him, not that she quite dared to spell it out.

"If," She heard him swallow hard. "If what you posit is correct, if the Silence has some sort of desire, some sort of ability to act, however indirectly." Another swallow. "Which I am fairly sure no one has actually suggested in the extant literature."

"Gabe, love. Academic research later. Theory now. For one thing, we're not dressed for research."

That made him snort and relax again. "Then you think that the Silence took some action to protect me. But why me?"

She shrugged. "There, we wander into philosophy or metaphysics. I'm not sure. It's not just that you're heir to your father. I - plenty of other heirs went to fight, and plenty died. I looked it up."

Gabe nodded and ducked his chin. "There was a law, eventually. That both Lord and Heir couldn't be on active duty at the same time. Or if the Heir wasn't of age. Papa helped with War work, he didn't go over there. He's never talked about that, not to me. If he did to Mama, she's never let on."

Rathna said, gently. "Maybe to your Uncle Gil. Who served in the Army, hadn't he?"

"The Sudan, both of them, about ten years apart, though. Fifteen." Gabe shook his head, as if shaking a fly away. "But I'm nothing that special."

Rathna extracted her hand, and reached to tap his nose once, gently, which shook him out of whatever mood he'd been about to pick up. Something maudlin. "You said earlier, you're unique. You see things others don't. Or rather, you cut your way through problems. And very tidily, without throwing your power and influence around. Seems to me, a sensible sort of land magic might want more of that around rather than less."

There was a long silence, long enough she began to wonder if she'd pushed him too far. Then, almost inaudibly, he said, "And my ankle?"

"I don't know, honestly." She let out a long breath. "But I'm wondering if, well, magic, the energy to make it happen, has to come from somewhere. You've only an ordinary sort of mill pond near there, you showed me the map. No major river, no waterfalls. Certainly no volcanic chamber bubbling away, below the surface. Where would the energy come from? And you've said yourself, it's painful, it aches, but you can walk on it. It healed properly, except for that. The viper came for you, they come for the ones who die young. Something held it back, but that had a cost."

Now he closed his eyes, thinking so hard he couldn't do anything else. She waited and waited and waited.

Minutes later, he said, carefully, "What do I do differently, if you're right?"

That she had an answer to, thanks to the excellent ladies at the Ayah's Home. "In July, there is a festival, Naga Panchami, giving thanks to the naga for their blessings. I think - we were thinking to go to India. Can we make it happen that quickly?"

He nodded, still distracted, thinking through a dozen things. "We could. With a bit of help."

"We go, and we..." She curled her hand around his shoulder, as reassuringly as she could. "Learn how to say thank you properly. There. And maybe we figure out a way to say it here, too. At Veritas, I mean."

Gabe made a small incoherent noise, deep in his throat, and she answered the question with what she'd asked about that afternoon. "There's fasting. And offerings, of milk and sweets, lamps and flowers. And there are prayers, things to say, but that's what we can learn. The women today, they thought it would be a fine thing, for an English man to understand snakes. Properly."

There was another of those long pauses. "Well. Suppose we'd better set up language lessons for us both. And I'll see about when we can get tickets."

"In the morning." Seeing as it was late evening on a Sunday.

"In the morning." He moved his hand, as if to dim the light charms, but just before he did, he said, "Thank you. For seeing what I thought impossible."

That made her glow. It made her feel that this, now, was truly a partnership. Together, they were going to be amazing. And worth the blessing of the naga.

Gabe was settled in a chair, looking out an enormous window to the open ocean, when he heard the door from Rathna's bedroom open again. He stood immediately.

"All settled then?" She ducked her head, and he came to take her hands, then kiss her. "We should be setting out shortly. All your things stowed?"

"You act as if you do this every year, Gabe, and I know you haven't! How can you be so calm?"

He grinned at her, then wrapped his arms around her waist, swinging her around in an impulsive twirl of joy. "I know, isn't it wonderful? New magics to investigate, you get to explore portals in other places, India and all the places we stop along the way. And we'll get lots of lovely research and reading time in, while we're at sea." Then he grinned. "And other amusements, I'm sure."

She snorted and settled an arm around his waist, peering at the water. "It's all a grand adventure to you." He knew that tone in her voice. She was thinking through things.

"Some of it more serious, of course. But the ship, that's a kind of thing I know how to handle."

Gabe could feel her shiver once. "You're sure? There are other people here. And non-magical people."

He nodded. "Let's talk about that, then. I've got more information." He nudged her to come sit down on the rather ornately padded sofa. "Neha's gone to see to her cabin?"

Rathna nodded. "I told her to settle in, she could do the rest of the unpacking later." Neha was one of the ayahs, who spoke both excellent English and Bengali. She'd been tutoring them both, several hours a day, and she had a sharp sense of humour that delighted Gabe once she'd dared it with him. By the time they arrived, they would by no means be fluent. But her long-sleeping Bengali was coming back to her more quickly than she'd feared, Gabe was managing well enough. They would be able to be polite, at the very least.

"And the magic here." Their suite was in the row of cabins reserved by the owners for magical folk, like them. Most of the charmwork was not at all obvious, and Gabe had been impressed at how subtle it was. Substantial supplies of hot water, all the salt filtered out. Larger beds. Tables with charms that would prevent objects sliding around. And, he had been firmly promised, cooling charms that would make what was usually a hot and miserable journey at the height of summer quite pleasant.

"You know, I think... I think she might be magical. Not the way we'd define it? But the way she would. The more she's talked about the customs, the rituals. And they don't have the Silence, there. I mean, the people who go through British schools do. But that's only a tiny number." Rathna was puzzling it out as she settled against him.

Gabe curled his arm around more securely. "And that's

the trick, isn't it? The Silence oaths mean we can't quite ask. I suppose we can see if there's an opening. Asking what people believe about that. There are certainly stories - we could say someone told us one at a meal - about the magicians, snake charmers, all that. Wondering what's accurate, and what's put on for show."

Rathna let out a breath. "Oh, could we? I couldn't think of how to find an opening that wasn't awkward. But you're right, that's a thing we could hear about. Especially..." Her voice broke off again. This time, Gabe was sure why.

"I had a chat with Hugh Pelagius. Brother to the owner, he does this trip regularly. He's arranged for us to have seats with a table of academics, which should do nicely for our purposes. A historian - Republican Rome, I gather, nothing likely to pose a particular challenge for us. A specialist in mediaeval Italian literature. I admit I find Petrarch a bit baffling, but perhaps I'll learn something. A pair of chemists, who should at least be educational for me. No geologists, you can reign there, and I shall pass myself off as gentleman dabbler. No use of the title, just the sort who's been travelling for my education and who is going further abroad now."

He was, in fact, quite pleased at how that had turned out. He had no desire to sit with the sort of people who'd make much of the fact his father was a lord. Even if they couldn't quite place either his father or Gabe in the usual social scene. It was fortunate that the aristocracy had a reputation for eccentricity.

However, certain kinds of women, and their mothers, looked on anyone with a title as extremely promising, eccentrics or no. Gabe did not want to spend the entire trip being chased by them. Or glared at, though that was somewhat preferable.

"You pass yourself off as a gentleman dabbler because you are, Gabe."

"That is what makes it a perfect cover." He leaned over and kissed her. "And we can make it clear we are hoping to be betrothed, must visit your extended family for their blessing, and so on. Gives both of us a more than adequate excuse to retreat as needed."

"You're sure that's all right?"

"Absolutely. Expected, even. And Hugh promised he'd let us know if anyone looked like making trouble and take care of it. They take their hospitality quite seriously around here."

Rathna frowned, wriggling a little more into his arm. Gabe approved of that. "A magical family owns the ship, you said."

She'd been caught up in sorting out a wardrobe that would hold up not only to the trip, but offer some options once she got there. Not all of her clothing for that, though. Neha had said the best thing to do would be to buy Rathna several saris when they arrived. She'd assured them both it could be done quickly, for daily wear, and perhaps a few more decorative ones for special occasions. Both she and Vivek had made it clear that Rathna's aunties would insist on helping with that, and would know all the best options. Gabe made himself stop woolgathering, then nodded.

"There are several shipping companies owned by magical families. It's cheaper and safer, of course, to do some things with magic. This ship, for example, still uses coal, but they can use less because the boilers are more efficient. But of course, there's not enough trade to make it worth running an entire ship with solely magical passengers, not most of the time. They can manage a trans-Atlantic crossing fairly regularly, but to India only once or twice a year."

"And we do have a deadline." Rathna then looked up.

That was still sensitive, a thing he was thinking through, but he kissed her temple. "We're going. I'll sort out what I need to ask about it by the time we get there."

She nodded again, settling back against him. "And you don't mind that I'm making it difficult for you?"

Gabe snorted. "Rathna, beloved. If anyone is difficult in our gallivanting around on this ship, it will not be you, I'm sure of that. And I have everything I need right here, if we have to keep to our cabin. Plenty of space, lots of books, the food should be excellent, and we have each other. Those are the important things."

Rathna let out a breath. "And I can get home to Morah Avigail if I have to, quickly. Except when we're actually at sea." She shook her head. "The healer has been really helpful, she's doing so much better. I'm not worried about it, now, not like I was."

Gabe nodded. "And as you point out, what I need to do requires going to India."

"I could scarcely ask all my aunties and cousins to come to me, too. We both need to go. For our own reasons."

That made him smile. "But together. Though if you need me to go away for a bit, you tell me. I can go muck about pretending I know something about polo and cricket at the local watering hole or whatever."

"You'd have to deal with serving officers. And War veterans."

"And people with all sorts of awful biases, expecting that I agree with them, which is rather worse." Gabe shook his head. "No, if you asked me to go away, I'd go find a naturalist, probably, see about a trip into the jungle or up a mountain or something."

"Do you actually know anything about polo? Or cricket?" Rathna shifted again, peering at him, but now relaxed and amused.

"For that sort of thing, one mostly just has to smile, nod, and pick what seems a reasonable opinion expressed by someone else and stick to it. I suspect it's easier in India, because we won't have possibly seen the same matches." He tilted his head. "I'm fairly sure they're both called matches. But no, I did spend some time reading up. And I have notes. It's just all the language lessons have knocked it out of my head."

"And all the other arrangements. All this..." She waved a hand, taking in the two-bedroom suite, and the en suite bath.

"I have money. This is a problem money solves. Did Neha say the other ayahs were settling in?"

"They were delighted. And they're in three cabins, the six of them, so they can enjoy themselves. That was kind, not making them go four to a cabin."

"Money." Gabe repeated. "It was the easiest way to make it come out even and not have them have to deal with other people being difficult at them." He added, grinning, "Charlotte helped. We both had gifts from Grandmother to spend. She would dearly hate to know that's how we spent them."

Gabe was entirely sure that when his grandmother found out about Rathna, she would do her best to disown him. That had very little actual effect, however. As he'd told Rathna before, the things he actually cared about, other people couldn't take away, or wouldn't. His father made the proper show of distant respect, as a son should, but Gabe rather thought he'd appreciate the excuse to stop inviting Grandmother to the necessary family celebrations.

Rathna shook her head. "We're going nearly across the world to see family I've never met, and you're not worried about your grandmother?"

"Grandmother," Gabe pointed out, "has had decades to do as she wishes. If she changes, wonderful. If not, well. We had warning. Your relatives, however, are a delightful and glorious unknown. And also, if they don't treat you well, we will be making our lives halfway around the world from them."

Rathna snorted. "I am not sure what to do with you, Gabe." Just at that moment, there was the lurch of the liner beginning to move, a shudder through the whole ship.

Gabe tightened his arm around her again. "Enjoy me. Permit me to enjoy your infinite pleasures. And see, here we are, on a grand adventure, together."

She settled against him. "Together."

If you enjoyed *The Fossil Door* and would like to read more of this series, please sign up for my mailing list to get all the latest news and fun extras. Your reviews (on whatever review site you use) are much appreciated, too!

Read on for more historical details about this book and an excerpt from *Eclipse*, the next book in the series.

AUTHOR'S NOTES

Welcome to the author's notes for *The Fossil Door*. I started writing it in May of 2020, when we were still locked down, and it was a joy and a delight to spend a lot of time looking at completely gorgeous photos of the Scottish highlands, Highland Ponies, and various wildlife. As well as deeply enjoying both Gabe and Rathna, and their adventures together.

As always, my thanks to Kiya Nicoll, my excellent editor, and to my early readers. (Any remaining flaws are entirely mine, but they all helped make this book better.)

Before I get into the historical notes, a word about Gabe. He is the son and eldest child of Lord Richard and Lady Alysoun Edgarton, who I've come to adore over the course of multiple books. *Pastiche*, set mostly in 1906, is about the early years of their arranged marriage. After that, Richard is mentioned briefly in *Outcrossing* (at the end of the book). He is a significant secondary character in *Wards of the Roses*. Alysoun appears briefly at the end of the book, and they both have a part to play in the events at the end of *On The Bias*.

Originally, I hadn't planned for the hero of this book to be their son. Then I needed a name that might be heard as feminine, out of context, and I looked at this small kid I'd named Gabriel, adjusted his birth year slightly (*Pastiche* was still in the editing stage) and here we are.

I love Gabe for his curiosity, for his refusal to abuse the privilege he was born with, and his insistence on trying to put his gifts to good use. Most of all, I love him because he is so very much the product of his family, those he's had since birth, and those who have become chosen family since.

Which brings us to the beginning of this book. **Spitalfields, in East London** has long been a home to immigrant communities a bit unsure of their welcome. Originally home to Huguenot weavers, then to weavers from other places, it had declined into slums and tenements by the mid-1800s. An influx of Jewish refugees, mostly from Eastern Europe settled in. These days, there's a sizeable Bangladeshi community. By the 1920s, the Jewish community had established customs, communities, and spaces. The magical community of the area is rightfully proud that one of the three London portals is there, brought in to aid the silk trade originally. (We'll come back to the eruv.)

The approach of the Jewish community to magic (and the Pact) comes out of some lengthy conversations with friends. Namely, that magic is not the defining feature of the community, what matters are the ties of family, religion, and choices about your actions. (For all some rituals could include it easily, if magical acts like lighting a candle were on offer)

The **Portal Keepers** are, as you've gathered, an elite group of magical folk, who are responsible for a key piece of Albion's infrastructure. Only it's a bit more complicated than maintaining bridges and roads (a complicated enough problem), since the portals are to some extent living, breathing, vibrant magic with a mind of its own.

Being able to make portals was part of the original agreement of the Pact, in 1484, and since then, portals have been established around Great Britain. More recently, there have been a few established across water, such as the one on the Isles of Scilly, in *In The Cards*.

The portals present several complications, however. First, as noted, the ability to tend them is quite rare, far more rare than the ability to become skilled at significant healing magic or some of the other complex magical needs of the community. Second, rapid transportation (even if it's between known points) presents a number of practical challenges, if there is an outbreak of rebellion, contagious illness, a theft, a murder, or some other immediate need. The fact Albion has portals is what led to the creation of the Guard in the early 1500s, long before any country had what we'd consider a police force.

There are, as noted, portals in other countries, but where and how they were developed varies a great deal. In general, they do not do well crossing water - certainly not deep or stormy water - on a regular basis. Naturally, who gets a portal is also a politically charged question.

We've seen the **Penelopes** before. They're another thing that Albion figured out was needed. Albion has all sorts of known magics, things people learn in school or apprenticeship, that work pretty much as expected. However, in any society you're going to have people either experimenting (not always successfully) or using what they know to hurt other people.

The Penelopes are Albion's answer to both forensic science and to figuring out how to undo whatever dangerous magic someone has come up with this week. Highly skilled, the sort of people who absorb every bit of information in case it might be useful in ten years, they have their own particular ways of doing things.

While officially on the Ministry payroll as something like Analyst or Senior Analyst, everyone who works with them calls them Penelopes, after Penelope, wife of Odysseus. She used her wits to keep unwanted suitors at bay, unweaving the work of her loom every night to avoid an implied deadline, while juggling half a dozen other critical needs in her household.

As Gabe notes, many of the Penelopes are female, certainly many of the best of them. While Albion is much more open to both men and women in many professions (especially those that require stronger magical ability), the Penelopes decidedly skew toward women. Thus, people assuming an unnamed Penelope will be a woman, and why Gabe frankly expects that to happen much of the time.

Highland Ponies are a breed of pony much known for their sturdiness and sure-footedness. They're often used to carry loads of materials around the Highlands, though these days, mostly for pleasure riding. I was a serious horseback rider in my teens, and Livet is based in personality (if not in colour or breed) on my beloved Dorothy, who was round like a barrel, 14.2 hands tall, and terrified of sheep, but otherwise a seriously clever sort of pony.

Glencoe is of course a real place, and to the best of my ability, the landscape and general layout is as described. (Except for Gormlaith and Eoin's inn, of course, and the portal itself.) If you've not had a chance to see that landscape, many people have posted gorgeous photographs online. Ossian's Cave is a real cave, narrow and difficult to reach, as described. For many years, including in the 1920s, there was indeed a battered tin with the names of everyone who had climbed up there. The climbing techniques are also accurate to the period, though many of the technical climbing tools used now did not yet exist, or only in a very rudimentary form.

The geology of Glencoe is fascinating and complicated. It's a massive caldera of an ancient supervolcano, and it's actually the place on the planet where people figured out what a caldera collapse looked like. It's particularly interesting because sedimentary rocks (largely limestone) were laid down between volcanic cycles and in those bands of rock you do find fossilised plants. (This is also what led to the shale quarries, closer to the loch.)

Withamite is an actual mineral, named for its discoverer, Henry Witham, who identified it in 1825. As Rathna identifies, it has a high manganese content, and comes in shades of pinkish-red and some greenish-yellow.

The **wildlife** other than the beithir are as described. Red deer are quite large and impressive. And Scottish wildcats are deeply endangered, but large, stocky, and very furry. (My editor's eldest has been fascinated by them for some time, and I knew I had to let one appear somewhere in here.)

Beithirs are a dragon-like beast of Scottish folklore (I did not make anything up about them, other than the fact there might or might not be one lurking in the mountains around Glencoe in the 1920s.) They were most commonly supposed to be active during summer lightning strikes, which must be spectacular in the mountains of the Highlands.

When it comes to **Rathna's background,** there's a lot of difficult history. I've done my best to keep to documented stories. Rathna's family background is as described, from stone cutting families settled near Calcutta (now Mumbai) at the time.

It was not uncommon for ayahs - Indian women, employed as nursemaids by Europeans in India - to be abandoned in London. British families (mostly returning from colonial posts) would bring the ayah back with them, and then leave her in London, without enough money for a ticket to get back home, or a way to support themselves.

There was a home established to help give them somewhere to live until they could find a new position or a way home, and there was a system in place to help make sure they got home - but usually after a stay of some weeks or months. (Some records say about 100 ayahs a year stayed at the home.) Gabe's generous gesture at the end of the book is a little out of the ordinary, but not completely unheard of, at least for someone inclined toward philanthropy in that direction.

Of course, some of the women brought to England stayed. There were a sizeable number of men from India who had taken positions as servants or sailors (the word **lascar** is used for both during this period). While the Southeast Asian community was not as large in London in the early 1900s as it is now, it was certainly present and growing.

A couple of my early readers wanted a little more about Rathna being sent to the orphanage than she was willing to share in the text. Her mother had become nursemaid to a British couple, in the Civil Service. After her death, they continued to have Rathna live with them. But when Rathna was around ten, the husband was offered. a posting in India. Not knowing where Rathna's family were, or how to reach them, and knowing it would be impossible to bring her to India as anything other than a servant, a decent orphanage was the best option available.

It was not a great option. **Orphanages** of the period were underfunded, often heavily institutional, with strict rules, little in the way of individual care, and the bare minimum of education. As Rathna says, hers was a bit better than some, but that didn't mean it was a pleasant place to live. The fact she had magic - enough to get her into Schola, despite little understanding of what was going on - completely changed the arc of her life in ways she's still sorting through.

I loved having a glimpse, however briefly in passing, at two of the **great libraries of London** at this point in time. What is now the British Library was then in the great central court of the British Museum (I got to see it there, once, when I was young, before it moved to its current location in the late 90s.) Access to the library was free, but getting a reader's ticket involved an application process - especially if you were under 18. Gabe, being himself, has had a reader's ticket since he was 16. The Natural History Museum also has its own library, as well as amazing collections, and is the natural place for someone to start some research about a particular mineral.

Aunt Mason is my second favourite Penelope (my favourite would be Gabe, but it's close). I'm glad to answer a question here about why Richard Edgarton was so touchy about Kate and Giles not using a ladder in *Wards of the Roses*. Mason's love of creating illuminated manuscripts, both entirely her own creation and copying existing works, comes up in *Pastiche*. It was delightful to get to describe a little of what she might produce when given absolutely free rein. (If you are reading this and have some relevant skills, get in touch, I'd love to discuss a commission or two. I know enough about the art form to know what Mason is doing, and not enough to create it myself.)

Mason's background is as described in the book - a Malaysian grandmother and Dutch grandfather, whose daughter married an English man. There will be more coming about Mason's work as a Penelope and education in a future novella. Mason and Witt are, by the 20s, two of the senior Penelopes, dear friends, and utter opposites in how they work.

If you're familiar with the idea of an Order Muppet versus Chaos Muppet as a form of describing characters (and people), Mason and Gabe are both Chaos Muppets, and Witt, and Lucy Doyle (Witt's former apprentice, and Gabe's apprentice mistress) are both very much Order Muppets.

Speaking of Gabe, it became clear the more I wrote this book that he likely has what we'd now call **ADHD.** He truly was all over the place as a kid, never quite on the same timeline as other kids his age, and with very little patience for doing the thing he was supposed to be doing if it were boring. As an adult, he's got reasonably good coping mechanisms, so long as you let him climb out a window or throw himself off a horse or tackle a complicated problem on a regular basis. Possibly two of the three at the same time.

His **ankle injury** having healed but continuing to cause pain is rather common. About twenty to thirty people with similar injuries have long-term effects or pain. It's quite possible Rathna's right about some of the reasons for it, on a magical level, of course.

Cousin Del is indeed the younger Lord Delwyn who is referenced at the end of *Pastiche.* It's clear from Gabe's comments that the Edgartons took him under their wing as, effectively, a fostered cousin, making sure he could establish himself, marry, and settle down. The head injury in the War, however, has changed some things for him.

The costume party costumes are described in the text - all real historical things except for the mirabiles. (The history of silphium is fascinating and horrifying at the same time.) The Babian bird does show up in some Arthurian legends. The one invention is my own, the mirabiles, seen briefly in *Outcrossing*, they appear as a darting and dancing cloud of light, rather like larger fireflies with better choreography. They are only rarely seen, even in the magical communities protected lands. Gil and Magni are enjoying themselves dressed as the fable of the mouse removing a thorn from the lion's paw.

One thread of this series of books is the implications of what the War did to Albion's institutions, and **the Council** is one of those institutions (there will be more about this in two upcoming books in the series.) Gabe is quite accurate in his analysis here (though like all people who are not actually on the Council, there are pieces of it he doesn't know or understand.) And as he points out, the fact he didn't serve in the Great War will affect his social interactions for the rest of his life.

(I may or may not work around to writing a book about his actions in World War II, when he will be in his forties and at the height of his magical ability.)

A particular challenge of my books is that they are so tightly wound up in the perspectives of people who have grown up and been educated in Albion, and the ways that has shaped them. While many people believe that how Albion does things is the way magic works, that's not actually true. It's just that that's how it works for Albion. The end of the book brought a delightful chance to point out some other ways to look at things.

An **eruv** is an ancient Jewish approach to dealing with prohibitions against carrying objects in public and semi-public spaces during Shabbat (sunset on Friday to sunset on Saturay.) The eruv is a way of creating a continuous line connecting outdoor spaces, making them effectively part of private space, like a series of interconnected courtyards. This allows people to do things like carry keys or other minor household objects, carry children outside, or bring food to neighbours. They need to be carefully maintained, since it is essential that there is an unbroken line that encompasses the eruv (usually wire).

Spitalfields did not historically have an eruv (they currently exist in about 200 communities around the world). But honestly, they really should have, so they get one here. The more mystical approach, the idea that it gathers people into a larger community, is not just my own thought - and of course, a culture familiar with magical warding (as Albion is) also has ways of thinking about something like an eruv.

Likewise, Rathna realising that her approach to some things - snakes, for a particular example - might offer a way out of the ways Gabe's assumptions have tangled him up. The **Naga Panchami** festival is widely celebrated across India, with prayers, fasting, offerings, and festivities. Because the Hindu calendar is lunar, the precise date shifts a little between July and August. In 1922 it was July 28th. (So their departure in mid-June gives them time for the 3-4 week voyage, and a week or two to get to know Rathna's family.)

Finally, as Rathna and Gabe discuss in the epilogue, **not everywhere is bound by the Pact**. The Pact and the Silence, the underlying magical constructs of Albion since 1484, bind the people who've made it. Where it exists outside Albion (the United States, Canada, the various colonies and territories of the British Empire) are a result of colonisation and imperial assumptions - not necessarily the underlying reality on the ground. Various countries elsewhere (incluing continental Europe, never mind Asia and Africa) have their own takes.

One of these days, I'll figure out a book that can talk more about this from a useful angle.

Thank you so much for joining me in Scotland. Read on for an excerpt of *Eclipse*, set at Schola in 1924 and 1925.

"Come in, come in, pardon the unpacking in progress."

Thesan took a breath, hoping her nerves weren't too noticeable. This was new, and new was always a challenge. She wasn't at all sure why she was here.

Certainly, she was on good terms with other professors. But all of them were busy. Of course, there were their teaching and other duties, keeping track of three hundred and fifty students. More than that, all of them had their own personal projects and research that filled whatever available moments they had.

She and Rosemary were insistent on time for tea most weeks, to talk over the students in Horse House, so Thesan could lend a hand. Thesan also looked forward to the more irregular times she got to sit down with Raphaela in the infirmary and talk books, or to putter around in Helena's workroom, talking about how different materia soaked up magic. Last year, she'd somehow ended up adding in weekly trips down the pub in the village with Isembard, both of them doing some of their marking. That had been unexpectedly enjoyable.

But she'd never been in another staff member's rooms, except for Rosemary's. It had always been in their offices. Certainly, no one had shown interest in traipsing up six flights of stairs in the keep to her spaces. She'd never been included like that, and she wasn't sure she should be now.

This was not helping at all. Thesan ducked her chin, and smiled. "Thank you." Then, because there was no way around it, she asked, "What do you prefer to be called, when the students aren't around?"

Isembard came in behind her, carrying a small wooden crate filled with bottles. He seemed utterly at ease here. Of course, she gathered he'd known Alexander Landry for years. Decades. A family friend. His rooms were at the other end of the hallway, she knew that much, so he must be familiar with the layout.

But Professor Landry, whatever he wanted to be called, was not only a new colleague taking over the Ritual classes at Schola for the time being, but a member of the Council. She knew he'd been outside of Albion for some years, but not much more than that.

Wherever he'd been, he apparently had a lot of books even by professorial standards - a trunk full of them stood half-open across the room, and there were teetering stacks of others by the bookshelves, waiting to be put away. That, she could approve of, entirely. The rest of the furniture she recognised as dredged up from the attics, well-worn but still comfortable.

He waved a hand at her, genially. "In private, Alexander, please. We needn't stand on formality. You may hear my intimates call me all manner of other things. As we may also with Izzy, here."

Thesan, for her part, saw Isembard's shoulder twitch as

he set the case down. She suspected all of a sudden that he tolerated that particular nickname. When he spoke, though, it was with easy amiability. "The beer's the local, and not bad, there's brandy in there if you'd rather. Anything else, we'll have to order. I didn't make it back until yesterday either."

"Trouble with one of yours?"

Isembard snorted, grabbing a bottle of beer, popping it with an effortless charm, and settling onto the sofa. "Claudio's never a bother." Which meant that Orion had been. Then he gestured with the beer. "It's rather a thing, seeing the ceremony from the staff dais."

"They look so blasted young, don't they? Entirely children." Alexander was chuckling now. "Though the fifth years look almost human."

Thesan swallowed once. "I'm Thesan, except with my family." She was already two steps behind in this conversation, and they hadn't even made it through proper introductions yet. Then she blinked as Alexander handed her a bottle of beer. He'd somehow taken and smoothly opened one without her noticing. She was in entirely over her head already, honestly.

Isembard waited for Alexander to get settled, which gave Thesan a chance to get a better look at him. He was wearing formal robes, of course, the long academic gown with the hood and the various expansive decorations signalling those magics he claimed mastery in. He must be a good generation older than she and Isembard were. Mid-fifties, at least and she thought perhaps more like sixty. His hair had that distinguished salt and pepper effect at the temples against dark hair and tan skin.

She simply wore her Astronomy Guild master's medallion around her neck, the weight of it comfortably reassuring. After a moment she set the bottle down long enough to shrug out of the academic gown and her own hood, folding the length of black silk into a rough bundle for now and tucking it into her lap. It made her feel very young, giving up that bit of protective colouration but there was no point hiding it. In truth, she was still young for this job, and had been since she started seven years ago.

Isembard tipped his bottle at her and stood up from the chair he'd claimed long enough to do the same, before he sat, long legs sprawling out. He'd clearly had an active summer. She knew perfectly well he spent plenty of time in the salle, but he must have spent even more time outside than she had.

He'd gotten enough sun to tan, but more than that, he had a sense of relaxation to him she hadn't seen often before. A bit like a dozy great cat, where quick action was possible if needed, but perhaps not just this moment.

"Thesan explained things to me last year, and it was the best explanation anyone managed. I thought you deserved the same. Consider it a housewarming gift of sorts."

Alexander laughed, heartily. "Having tested them all yourself, then?" He then offered a smile to Thesan. "I appreciate any help I can get, quite honestly. I've hardly had time to get my bearings. We sorted out the teaching last minute, I'm still seeing what texts I can get my hands on, I barely remember how the class schedule works, and I'm only certain of finding the ritual classroom because they haven't moved it since my own years here." He circled his fingers. "You do realise that how they decide on the houses is one of the Greater Mysteries? No one ever talks about it. Outside, one presumes, the staff."

Thesan inhaled, and then paused. He was a member of

the Council, there must be oaths and binding magics and all sorts of things she could scarcely name, never mind understand. But Schola had her own mysteries, he was right about that. It wasn't her job to protect them, exactly. Schola, Thesan was entirely sure, could and would protect herself. But it certainly was not her place to share them foolishly.

"There's a reason for that." She looked him up and down, and then risked it, hoping her voice would stay even. "Promise not to tell it to anyone who's not a teacher here." She didn't put conditions on it, didn't ask him to swear on his magic, or by the Silence, or whatever else he considered relevant.

Alexander had just settled into the other easy chair, but he suddenly moved to the front of the seat, leaning forward and peering at her. It was decidedly disconcerting, but she dug her feet in, and held her ground.

She clung to remembering what Mistress Eridana had taught her, and her Professor, about how to deal with these times. When people with power came up against something she cared about. All she could do was wait. Silence was awkward, Mistress Eridana had drilled into her, but you could let the other person sit with the awkwardness.

When Alexander spoke again, his voice was quite different. Still comfortably at ease, still charming, but there was a new note in it she couldn't begin to name. Voices were not so easily charted as stars, unfortunately. "What promise would you prefer?"

Thesan turned her hand palm up. "Something you care about." Now that she'd said it once, it was easier to say it again. She then deliberately leaned back, remembering all the little tricks she'd learned so painstakingly. She caught the glance from Alexander to Isembard, and Isembard's shrug. He wasn't stepping in, wasn't arguing with her. That was something she hadn't been sure of.

There was a long silence, nearly a minute. Long enough for her to deliberately take another sip of beer, and then to meet Alexander's eyes again. When he spoke, he said precisely and evenly, "I have sworn certain things already in my life, on my blood, on my magic, on the magics that bind us all. I swear I will not share the secrets and mysteries of Schola unless required by those oaths, except with another who is entitled to them, who has the right and responsibility of knowing."

She could feel a spark of the magic. It wasn't like the Silence oath, it was something else, but it had the same intensity to it. Some small part of her was amused by the way he'd answered, but he was the new Ritual professor. If anyone had formal oath language at his beck and call, it should be him.

Isembard managed not to say anything for ten seconds, then he nodded. "That's a fine oath."

Thesan had to agree. "Thank you. For taking it seriously." Then she gestured with her own bottle. "What do you know from your own time here? Let's start with that."

That broke the sense of density in the room. Alexander nodded once at her, then settled back in his chair, crossing one ankle over the other knee. "I was in Fox, that must be obvious." He flicked his fingers at Isembard. "What, thirty years before this one here." Isembard lifted his bottle - about half empty already - and nodded. "First year, we arrived a week before the others, and they took us down to little cottages at the edge of the island. Seven or eight to a cottage. Not quite camping out, but rustic. Much more rustic for some of us than others, I'm sure."

Thesan nodded. "The cottages are used for other things

from time to time through the year, of course. But they're kept up for that week, particularly." She'd start there, something simple.

Alexander considered. "It was a good while ago, the details are a trifle faded. But I remember they gave us all manner of things to do. Tasks, games, a bohort puzzle every day. Nothing complex, of course. I'd learned some magic from my mother, a few things from my tutor, but others hadn't had any experience at all, doing magic for themselves."

"There's always a mix." Thesan settled back, and then ventured tucking one leg under the other, brushing her skirts out. "And that's deliberate, as I'm sure you realise. Now, if you hadn't then."

Something in it made Alexander laugh. "We are not born with all the wisdom of the Council, you realise. I was a more observant child than many, but that isn't saying much. I wasn't a young hellion like this one, though."

Isembard took it in good humour. "What I remember is being very good at some things - the bohort, they set us a flag puzzle - and awful at others." His voice had a rolling purr to it, easy and amused. "What was yours like, Thesan?"

She shrugged a shoulder. "I'm the middle child of seven. My older siblings all made it here - first in our direct line of the family." She paused, trying to figure out how to go on.

"Ah, but I was also the first of mine." Alexander chuckled at her expression. "You thought I'm like Izzy here, and his brother, the family here since the Conquest?"

She had, actually, but she had no idea how to ask even though he'd brought it up. In the end, she nodded once.

Alexander took pity on her and explained. "My father was French, my mother Egyptian. They met there, and left. That's some dire family history, and we have other topics for the evening a plenty." He said it so lightly Thesan wasn't sure how to take it, how to calibrate what 'dire' meant to someone like him.

He continued, more comfortably. "My father died before I turned one, and my older brother settled us here, thanks to a connection to some of the old families like the Fortiers. Not enough to get me into a tutoring house my mother approved of, but enough to coach me for the exams."

That was a topic Thesan didn't want to get into tonight, and she forged on. "So, five days of that, and then bundling everyone off to formal baths, and to change into proper uniforms, and getting their trunks taken to the right places without them." This year, she'd supervised that for Horse. It had all gone smoothly, but she hated the idea of getting it wrong, having some student not find their things where they expected.

"And then the ritual tonight." Isembard broke in, easily. "Sending each of them to the proper table. Making a show of it."

"Oh, that's a ritual I want to analyse. Do you know how old that is, Thesan?"

She did, actually. "The 1100s. Pre-Pact, certainly, though there are some later additions. I've got the text, as amended over the years. It attunes them to the house wards, but it also creates a, I suppose the best word is a passage. To connect them to the spirit of the house."

Isembard said, cheerfully, "She's got theories about this place. The Keep, especially."

Alexander leaned forward. "Not your usual thing, I'd have thought?"

"I spend rather a lot of time in the Keep. More than most people other than the infirmary staff." Her rooms were tucked up at the top of the Keep's tall tower, right below the Astronomy platform. At least so she wouldn't have to stagger across open ground in the middle of the winter every night after teaching. "Besides, there are some interesting stories, especially if you dig for them."

www.ingramcontent.com/pod-product-compliance
Lightning Source LLC
Chambersburg PA
CBHW032042050726
47590CB00001B/90